STRICTLY BUSINESS...

MARIAH ANKENMAN

JENNIFER SNOW

MILLS & BOON

All rights reserved including the right of reproduction in whole or in part in any form. This edition is published by arrangement with Harlequin Enterprises ULC.

This is a work of fiction. Names, characters, places, locations and incidents are purely fictional and bear no relationship to any real life individuals, living or dead, or to any actual places, business establishments, locations, events or incidents. Any resemblance is entirely coincidental.

Without limiting the exclusive rights of any author, contributor or the publisher of this publication, any unauthorised use of this publication to train generative artificial intelligence (AI) technologies is expressly prohibited. HarperCollins also exercise their rights under Article 4(3) of the Digital Single Market Directive 2019/790 and expressly reserve this publication from the text and data mining exception.

® and TM are trademarks owned and used by the trademark owner and/or its licensee. Trademarks marked with ® are registered with the United Kingdom Patent Office and/or the Office for Harmonisation in the Internal Market and in other countries.

First published in Great Britain 2026
by Mills & Boon, an imprint of HarperCollins*Publishers* Ltd,
1 London Bridge Street, London, SE1 9GF

www.harpercollins.co.uk

HarperCollins*Publishers*, Macken House, 39/40 Mayor Street Upper, Dublin 1, D01 C9W8, Ireland

Strictly Business... © 2026 Harlequin Enterprises ULC

Backstage Night with the Billionaire © 2026 Mariah Ankenman

Serving Up Off-Limits Love © 2026 Jennifer Snow

ISBN: 978-0-263-41940-5

04/26

This book contains FSC™ certified paper and other controlled sources to ensure responsible forest management.

For more information visit www.harpercollins.co.uk/green.

Printed and Bound in the UK using 100% Renewable Electricity at CPI Group (UK) Ltd, Croydon, CR0 4YY

Bestselling author **Mariah Ankenman** lives in the beautiful Rocky Mountains with her two rambunctious children and loving spouse, who is her own personal spell checker when her dyslexia gets the best of her. Mariah loves to lose herself in a world of words. Her favourite thing about writing is when she can make someone's day a little brighter with one of her books. To learn more about Mariah and her books, visit her website mariahankenman.com, follow her on social media, or sign up for her newsletter.

Jennifer Snow is a *USA TODAY* bestselling author and screenwriter of over forty novels and thirty screenplays. She writes romantic comedies and thrillers for Harlequin, Grand Central, Entangled, Penguin Random House and Thomas & Mercer, and her books have won awards such as the Booksellers' Best Award and have been translated into many foreign languages, as well as optioned for film. Her produced credits include *14 Love Letters* (Hallmark), *Christmas Lucky Charm* (UPTV), *Mistletoe & Molly* (UPTV). She had eight TV MOWs that aired on various networks in 2023, including *Christmas in Maple Hills*, *Sworn Justice* and *Christmas at the Amish Bakery*. More information can be found on her website at jennifersnowauthor.com.

Also by Mariah Ankenman

Accidentally Dating the Enemy
Cinderella's Bargain with the Billionaire

Serving Up Off-Limits Love
is **Jennifer Snow**'s debut title
for Mills and Boon Love Always.

Look out for more books from Jennifer Snow.
Coming soon!

Discover more at millsandboon.co.uk.

BACKSTAGE NIGHT WITH THE BILLIONAIRE

MARIAH ANKENMAN

MILLS & BOON

To aerials. Here's to dancing in the sky and only breaking one bone…so far.

CHAPTER ONE

Waking up to a drip of nasty roof water wasn't the best way to greet the day, but thanks to the leak in her ceiling today, that was exactly how Piper Pitts woke up.

"Ew!" she exclaimed, tossing her covers off and jumping up from the cot currently serving as her bed. "Oh, come on! It's not even seven a.m.!"

Life was really taking a cue from her last name these days. Every time she thought she'd hit the bottom, something came along to prove her wrong. She glared up at the ceiling where a small, discolored spot was slowly dripping brownish droplets of water. What were the odds that the roof would leak in the exact spot where she laid her head to rest?

"The way my life is going, a hundred percent," she grumbled into the small storage room she'd turned into a makeshift bedroom.

Grabbing the cot, she pulled it away from the dripping water. She'd need to grab a bucket from the basement to catch the water until she could figure out how to fix the leak. Not like she could count on her landlord to fix it. This leak would be item number sixty-seven on her repair list. The repair list she'd been sending him for months, that he kept saying he'd "get around to" but never did. Donald was useless. The only time he ever responded to her was if she asked for a rent extension. And then it was with a resounding "no."

"Jerk," she muttered.

Picking up the empty plastic bowl she'd eaten her takeout dinner salad from last night, she placed it under the leak.

"There." She smiled, nodding approvingly at her own quick thinking. "This will work until I can grab a bucket. Then all I have to do is look up a roof patching tutorial online and it will be smooth sailing."

For this problem at least. The other sixty-six issues were… less easy to fix. She rented the whole theater—complete with rehearsal spaces—and all of it was falling apart. Loose floorboards here, broken toilets there, and several other issues her landlord should be fixing but wasn't. Another person might hire legal help to force Donald to fulfil his obligations. But Piper was underwater in the funds department right now.

Plus, there was the small issue of her living at the theater in secret. If Donald discovered she was living here…he'd have means to break her lease and kick her out. There went her aerial studio and all the amazing artists who rented out the theater for their performances.

She could not let that happen. It had taken years of saving, a successful crowdfunding campaign and a loan she'd be paying off until she died for her to secure the deposit to rent this place in the first place, and to buy all the equipment she needed. Who knew how long it would take her to repeat that process if she had to find another place? Years probably, and by then she'd have lost all her students.

Besides, living here was only temporary.

"Extenuating circumstances." She sighed, remembering how her ex had lied to her, cleaned out their joint bank account and disappeared into the night four months ago. Leaving her with a lease she couldn't pay, which had resulted in her getting kicked out of her apartment. "And here I am."

She stared at the leak, wondering when exactly her life had gotten so complicated.

The life of an artist is a sad and poor one, Piper. I'm not paying for some silly circus school. You'll get a sensible accounting degree like I did or you're on your own.

Her father's words rang in her memory, the sharp sting of his conditional love still hurting even ten years later.

"Stop moping, Piper," she said to herself. "Put on your big girl panties. There's a lot of work to do and if you want to succeed you can only count on yourself."

Affirmation in place, she quickly dressed. As she grabbed a hairbrush to tackle her bed head, a noise from downstairs made her freeze. No one should be in the theater right now. There were no classes today and no performances scheduled until next month. Her heart raced in her chest as she listened, hoping it was just her imagination.

The distinct sound of shoes walking across the stage floor had her hopes dashed and her fear skyrocketing.

Eyes searching her room, she looked for her cell to call the police. She spied it on the floor next to her planner, cursing when she saw the black screen and realized she forgot to plug it in last night.

"Dammit, Piper!"

She moved to the door and carefully cracked it open. Maybe one of her students had gotten their days mixed up and thought there was class today? No. She'd locked the doors last night. How would they have gotten in?

She glanced down to see a tall white man with dark hair standing in the middle of the stage. His back was to her so she couldn't see his face, but he was wearing slacks and a flannel shirt. Was she being robbed by a lumberjack?

Quietly stepping out of her room, she tiptoed down the small set of stairs that led from the upper storage room to the back of the stage. As she moved, she spied a bat from the children's production that had been performed here over the summer. She grabbed the makeshift weapon in her hands and gripped it tight. The red plastic child's toy wasn't the best option against a burglar, but it was all she had.

As the man kept his back to her, she silently crept up behind him. He was tall, at least a foot taller than her, but she was strong from her aerial training. Lifting the bat high above her head, she brought it down on his back with as much force as possible as she screamed, "Get out of my theater!"

The man let out a startled yelp and turned.

Fear paused for a split second as Piper took in her intruder's face. Holy handsome, Batman!

Her jaw dropped open as the most beautifully piercing blue eyes she'd ever seen stared back at her with confusion and shock. Said eyes glanced at the bat and back to her. One hand reached up to rub the shoulder she'd hit as he opened his mouth and a deep, rich voice emerged.

"Did you just hit me with a Wiffle Ball bat?"

Her eyes darted to the bat and back to him. "Yes."

"Why?"

She scoffed. He broke into her place and had the audacity to question her defense tactics?

"Why are you in my theater?" she countered. "There's nothing here to steal. Haven't you heard the term *starving artist*? We got nothing, Jack."

"Kellen."

She frowned. "Huh?"

"My name. It's Kellen. Not Jack. But my friends call me Kell."

Weirdest. Robber. Ever.

"Okay… Kellen. I'll ask again. Why are you in my theater?" She lifted the bat again, preparing to strike once more.

"Woah." He raised his hands in surrender. "Put the bat down, ma'am. I'm not here to steal anything, I promise you. I'm here to do repairs."

She frowned, lowering the bat…slightly. "Repairs?"

He nodded. "Mr. Donald Noll hired me to complete repairs at the Star-Crossed Theater. This is the place, correct?"

Her brain started firing, catching up as his words sunk in. Donald had finally hired someone to fix all the issues she'd been complaining about. *Or so he says...*

She lifted the bat again, grip tightening. "Prove it."

"Excuse me?"

"Prove that my landlord hired you to do repairs. Because I've been asking for months and not a single contractor has reached out. Then suddenly here you are in the wee hours of the morning, somehow in my theater which was locked, claiming to be the repairman."

A small smile ticked up the corner of his mouth. A mouth she refused to think of as sexy…even if it was.

"I apologize for scaring you," he said, lifting a clipboard. "Here is the paperwork Mr. Noll sent me. He also gave me a key to the place, which is how I got in. He told me no one would be here this morning. Otherwise, I would have announced my presence."

Right. Of course Donald thought no one would be here. He didn't know Piper was squatting.

"I, um, came in to do some…repairs. Since Mr. Noll refuses to fix anything around here." There. That sounded like a reasonable explanation. Not that she needed to explain herself to this man. But just in case he relayed this interaction to Donald, she wanted her ducks in a row. After all, he might say he was here to fix things, but she wouldn't put it past Donald to send some creep to spy on her. Catch her doing something against her lease so he could kick her out.

Something like squatting…

Her defenses rose. She needed to play this smart. No trusting this guy, no matter how unfairly attractive he was.

"That refusal has come to an end," Kellen said, still holding out the clipboard.

Keeping her guard up, she held the bat in one hand while reaching out for the clipboard. He didn't appear to be dangerous. Honestly, he looked like a guy who would have a TV show called *The Handsome Handyman*. Nothing about him seemed threatening. He didn't even have a toolbox, which was kind of suspicious, considering he claimed to be a contractor.

She glanced down at the clipboard to see some paperwork. It looked like a work order of some kind. Donald's name and signature was on there, along with jargon relating to building repairs. A sigh of relief filled her as she finally felt safe enough to lower the bat. Donald indeed hired him.

He could still be a spy, a voice whispered in the back of her mind. Relieved that he wasn't a robber, but suspicion still swirling in her brain, she nodded.

"It's about freaking time," she said, handing the clipboard back.

Kell took it with a puzzled expression. "You said these repairs have been needed for months?"

She nodded. "Some for months, some for weeks. They keep piling up."

Kell glanced at the paperwork. "It is a rather long list."

"Wouldn't have been this long if he would have fixed stuff as it broke. When I told him about it."

A small chuckle left his lips. "Yes, well, as you said, *starving artist* is a common phrase but so is *scummy landlord*." He winked. "Don't tell him I said that."

She chuckled along with him, anxiety easing. "I won't. If you promise not to tell anyone about the…" She lifted the bat.

He graced her with a smile that had her heart skipping several beats. Good grief, this man was handsome.

"My lips are sealed." He rolled his shoulders. "Though my back might be sore for a few days."

Guilt sneaking in, she took a step forward. "Shoot, I'm

sorry. Did I hurt you? I really thought you were trying to rob me or…" She let her words trail off, not revealing the bleaker thoughts that had crept into her mind when she saw a strange man standing on the darkened stage.

His jovial smile slipped. True remorse and concern filled his eyes as he stared at her.

"I would never fault anyone for defending themselves. I truly apologize for scaring you. I swear I had no idea anyone would be here. Mr. Noll said the place would be empty and I would have free rein to do whatever I needed."

She snorted. "Sounds like something he would say. Why would he need to inform me, his tenant, about a repairman coming in? Leave it up to the boys."

Not only was Donald a scummy landlord, but he was also a sexist jerk.

"Would you like me to come back later?" Kell asked. "Is there a time that works better for you?"

He was asking her? That was a new one. The very, very few times Donald had sent someone in to fix things, the contractors never cared about her schedule. They could be in the middle of dress rehearsal, aerial silks hanging from the rafters and Joe Schmoe Blow would stomp all over her stage claiming he needed to get to the furnace room now. She wasn't used to consideration from people Donald hired.

Too good to be true! the voice screamed. *He's up to something.*

Tucking her suspicions away to examine later, she masked her emotions and put on her service-worker smile.

"Now works," she said. "Today is actually perfect. There are no classes, so the place is empty."

He smiled, making her heart race again. This was ridiculous. She was in the arts. Over the years in her career, she'd worked with some of the most beautiful people on the planet. Why was this guy making her heart pitter-patter like a schoolgirl with a crush? Must be the adrenaline from thinking he was here to hurt her. That was all. Leftover endorphins confused for attraction.

"Would you care to show me around?" Kell asked. "If you're not busy, that is. I have the list from Mr. Noll, but I have a feeling you can show me what's needed better than any list."

She sure could. In fact, she'd bet the last dollar she had a lot of the repairs needed weren't even on the list Donald gave him.

"I am happy to show you around, Kellen."

"Call me Kell, please. And you are?"

Sticking out her hand, she smiled. "Piper."

"It's nice to meet you, Piper."

He grasped her hand in his and shook. A spark of heat filled her palm at his touch, warming her entire body until her toes tingled. She quickly pulled her hand back, avoiding looking at him as she glanced at the bat still in her other hand.

"Not sure bashing you with a plastic bat is what most people would consider nice. I think most people would call it strange."

He shrugged. "It's a unique introduction. Can't argue with that. And what's wrong with being strange?"

A lot, according to every person who had ever bullied Piper for being the weird kid. Took until highschool and a yearlong waitlist to finally realize her "weirdness" was not a personality fault, but in fact autism. Not that her bullies had cared.

"Shall we?" he asked, indicating the back of the stage with his hand.

"Follow me," she said, turning, her cheeks heating as this man's gentlemanly charm once again set her off-kilter.

While her body heated like a coed on spring break, her mind reminded her that this man was sent from her enemy. He might say he was there to help, but she'd learned long ago that casual lying was common amongst most people. She couldn't let her guard down in case he was here as a spy for Donald. She'd been wrong about people too many times. Her best friend always said she was too trusting. Now more than ever was the time for caution. No matter how handsome Kell was, he could have nefarious intent. She had to discover if he was here for more than just building repairs, and if he was…she was in trouble.

CHAPTER TWO

Kell hadn't been hit with a Wiffle Ball bat since he was a kid. Then the attacker had usually been one of his brothers, Cash or Mal, not really an experience comparable to his meeting with the small, beautiful woman currently leading him across the empty stage. Kell felt terrible for scaring her. Damn Donald for not warning him someone might be in the theater. The guy had told Kell the place would be empty. He had also said the current tenant was a nightmarish nagging shrew.

Piper was as far from a nightmare as one could get.

The petite white woman couldn't be more than five feet tall, but she had the fierceness of a titan—and the strength, judging by the way Kell's shoulder still throbbed. His brothers' hits never hurt this much. Watching her walk ahead of him, he could see the muscles in her upper arms bared by the straps of the dark blue tank top she wore. Donald had said something about her being a dancer. Kell had known a few dancers over the years. Their workout routines were intense.

"We'll head to the basement first," Piper said, glancing at him over her shoulder. "That's where the big issues are."

He nodded. "Sounds like a plan."

She smiled, taking his breath away with the way her smile lit up the entire room. Not an easy feat, considering they were at the edge of the very large empty theater. Definitely not a shrew.

Piper was beautiful. Her pale skin was dusted with light brown freckles hidden among the vibrant multicolored flower tattoos cascading down both arms. Her dark brown hair was wavy and slightly tousled, like she'd just gotten out of bed.

He spied streaks of dark blue among the strands. Blue had always been his favorite color.

"Watch the second step. The board is loose and moves on you a bit." She pointed to the second stair of the steps leading down to the basement before carefully stepping on the right edge of it. He brought his clipboard up, making a note about the stairs on the paper. That issue had not been mentioned by Donald. Not surprising. A lot of landlords had no idea of all the issues in their properties that needed fixing.

Handyman work wasn't Kell's normal job. He and his brothers ran Thorson Realty, one of the most successful real estate agencies in the Denver Metro area and beyond. They catered to the wealthy, the elite. Snobs.

One might say Kell himself was in that category, but while he and his brothers did very well for themselves, they didn't exactly *enjoy* the trappings and pretentiousness of high society. Which was why they also headed up the Helping Homes division of the Thorson Foundation, a charity with many branches started by their late aunt and uncle and currently run by their cousin, Rory Thorson. Kell and his brothers repaired abandoned and foreclosed homes and donated them to those in need.

Along with his real estate license, Kell had licenses in nearly every area of contract work from electrical to plumbing to roofing. He was a jack-of-all-trades. In the housing market, that was.

"I think the electrics should be your first priority," Piper said as they reached the basement landing. She moved over to the far wall where the fuse box hung.

He made his way over to her, squinting in the darkness.

The only light came from a small high window on the opposite wall. The musty smell of dirt surrounded him. Standard basement smell. He breathed a sigh of relief at the lack of rotten eggs. Old buildings like this were notorious for gas leaks. He could fix a lot of things, but a gas leak called for the real professionals.

"Is there an overhead light we could turn on?"

Piper snorted. "Yeah, but it won't do much good considering it burned out weeks ago. Before you ask, it's not the bulb. I replaced the bulb, and it still doesn't work."

He turned to look at her in the dim light. "I'm assuming you told Mr. Noll about this?"

She rolled her dark brown eyes and let out a heavy sigh. "I did and he told me I must not know how to screw in a light bulb properly."

Wow, *jerk* was too nice a word for the guy. Kell couldn't say he had much cared for the man when he met him. Donald was rude, self-important, and never stopped talking. But a paycheck was a paycheck, and this one would be a gold mine for him and his brothers, which would mean extra funds for Helping Homes. He'd gladly take money from a tactless buffoon and use it to help those who deserved it.

Only…

"I swear the man thinks I don't have a brain cell because I have boobs." Her cheeks flushed a pretty pink as the words left her mouth. Her arms crossed over her chest. Clearing her throat, she ducked her head. "What I mean is, he's kind of a misogynist."

He nodded, doing his best to focus on grabbing the flashlight attached to his belt. He hid a smile as he pulled the tool free. Her tendency to speak what was on her mind without filtering it was refreshing and charming.

"Can't say I've known the man long, but based on our limited interactions I have to agree with you." He grinned over at her. "Again, don't tell him I said that."

She mimed zipping her lips and throwing away the key. He laughed, utterly delighted by this woman who only minutes ago had been bashing him with a plastic bat. She might call it strange, but he considered it an unforgettable introduction.

"Now," he said, focusing on the box in front of him. "Let's take a look and see what we've got."

He opened the metal fuse box, coughing slightly as a layer of dust kicked up with the movement. When was the last time Donald had someone down here to inspect things? The landlord was in for a rude awakening if he thought he could just slap a few coats of paint on this place and call it good. One look at the inside and Kell knew he was in for a hard job.

"How long have you been Mr. Noll's tenant?"

"I've been renting the theater for over three years now. It'll be four in six weeks, when the lease renewal happens."

He swallowed down a hefty dose of guilt.

This was the second time Piper had mentioned her lease renewal. The second time he'd had to hold his tongue. Because he knew something she clearly didn't. Something good old Donald must not have informed his tenant of. The reason Kell had been hired.

Yes, he was here to fix the place up thanks to his contractor licensing, but the main point of his contract with Donald Noll was to sell the place. Places like this were in high demand. Due to the historical nature of the building, it couldn't be torn down so they'd be looking for buyers who required a theater space. Not a huge market, but Kell already had a few leads from his high society acquaintances who were looking for unique spaces to host their galas and other functions.

Donald claimed he was tired of the hassle of being a landlord. What a joke. Judging by the state of this place, he'd bet the guy hadn't stepped one foot in it since renting it to Piper.

He clearly hadn't been keeping up with proper maintenance. A property like this, with its historical nature and location in the heart of the city, would fetch a large profit. Even in the current market. Kell was set to make a pretty penny from the repairs and even more from the sale. As much as it made his stomach sour to keep news of the impending sale from Piper, legally he couldn't say a word.

The thing about contracts was that they were there to protect both parties. In this case, his contract with Donald had specific language stating he was not to inform the current tenant of his plan to put the property on the market in six weeks. Piper's lease would expire, and she'd be out. Awful, but legally Donald wasn't doing anything wrong. Morally... that was an entirely different story.

Kell glanced over to Piper, guilt burning his chest as he swallowed down the terrible information he held. It wasn't like he knew this woman well, wasn't friends with her. He had no obligation to tell her her landlord was scum. Hell, she knew that. She didn't know he was planning on kicking her out, but unfortunately, Kell couldn't tell her.

If he did, he'd not only lose his contract, but it would open him up to a lawsuit; he could lose his licenses, and that could impact Helping Homes. He couldn't risk it.

"Has anyone come out in that time and done any repairs?" he asked, pushing his guilt down as he focused on the task at hand.

She frowned, face scrunching as she concentrated. "We had a plumber come out when the backstage bathroom toilets backed up. That was about a year ago. I can't remember anyone else coming for anything recently."

He swallowed down the rising rage. "No one? Not an HVAC tech or electrician?"

Many appliances required yearly maintenance. As the landlord, Donald was responsible to see to these things.

Piper shook her head. "Donald always told me he had someone come out to check things when I wasn't here, but I don't believe him."

Looking at the state of this fuse box, Kell didn't either.

"Well, I can't tell you exactly why the basement light isn't working, but I can assure you it's not because of your light bulb replacing skills. Which I'm sure are top-notch."

She laughed. "Oh yes, I'm the best light bulb replacer in the whole metro area. Ask anyone. I've won awards."

He chuckled along with her, charmed by her peculiar sense of humor.

He made a note on his clipboard, flashing his light around the basement when he finished. "You were right. Electrics will take top priority. Anything else down here need fixing?"

She leaned forward, glancing at his clipboard with a concerned expression. "How many things did Donald say needed fixing?"

"I have thirteen items to be fixed on my list."

"Ha!" Piper threw her head back and let out a sardonic bark of laughter. "Maybe it would have been thirteen two years ago. I swear that man just sends my emails to spam."

Unease crept into his gut. "How many emails have you sent?"

"About the repairs needed?" Her eyebrows rose as she lifted her hands and silently counted off on her fingers. "Over fifty."

Fifty! His blood boiled again at Donald's negligence.

"But some of those fixes were easy enough for me to do and some new things have popped up." She sighed. "I'm sorry to say this job is gonna be bigger than you planned for."

He was coming to realize that. In more ways than one. He took a quick breath to center himself and shove his true emotions about this situation deep down inside. Pasting on his friendly client smile, he shrugged. "I'm always up for a challenge."

She smiled back, a genuine one that nearly knocked him off his feet. Her smile warmed the cold, dank air around them, causing something in his chest to tighten.

"You, Kell, are my hero."

His smile dipped at her joy-filled words. Shame weighed heavy on his shoulders. Piper might think he was her hero, there to fix all her problems and leave her with a fully functional business space, but in reality, he was her executioner. Here to crush her dreams as he helped take away a space she clearly loved.

This was a nightmare.

CHAPTER THREE

FINALLY, IT WAS HAPPENING!

Piper took the first breath of relief in months. Kell was a literal angel. Donald might be a scumbag of the biggest degree, but her landlord had good taste in handymen. Kell was kind, competent and not too bad on the eyes either. She was so glad her first impression of him was wrong. She was also glad he didn't hold any ill will against her for smacking him with a plastic bat.

This could still be a scam, her inner thoughts warned. *Don't forget who he's working for.*

A dark cloud rained on her happy parade. Oh right, for a minute she'd been so excited about this place finally getting fixed she'd forgotten the possibility that Kell might be a spy for Donald. She'd been wrong about people before—just look at her jerk ex Larry.

Okay, so Kell might not be an angel. Maybe a devil in disguise? Whatever he was, she couldn't deny the fact that she needed him to fix up this place. If he was spying for Donald, all she had to do was make sure he didn't find anything to report back. She had to make sure he didn't find the secret room she was living in. That meant she needed to stay close to him while he was working here.

She glanced over at the way his forearm flexed as he wrote something on his clipboard, and her stomach did another somersault.

Sticking close to Kell wouldn't be a hardship. Remembering to keep her guard up would be.

"Any other basement issues?" Kell asked, marking something on his clipboard.

"There's a leak over in the far corner there."

She led him to the other side of the room where a small trickle of water was running down the wall onto the cement. The leak wasn't as bad as the one in her temporary bedroom, so she hadn't felt the need to address it yet. Now that Kell was here, she was going to mention every leak, flickering bulb and loose board in the theater. Hopefully he was being serious about being up for the challenge. Plus, the more work she gave him, the less he could be on the lookout for...other things.

Kell lifted his flashlight, pointing it up to the ceiling as he stared.

"Looks like the leak is coming from the floor above. Might even be above that. Do you have any other leaks anywhere?"

She huffed out a frustrated bark of laughter. "Only about a dozen."

Not counting the one in her secret bedroom.

Kell frowned. "Hmm, sounds like there may be roof issues if you have so many."

Exactly what she was thinking.

"A new roof is a big job, but if it's necessary I can call in my brothers."

"Brothers?" There were more of him? Were his brothers as helpful and as handsome as Kell? She shook her head. Not important. She'd promised herself after the humiliation of Larry leaving her high and dry, she'd be more practical when it came to love. She had to stop falling for every charming smile she saw. It only led to heartbreak.

Maybe what her best friend had always said was true: Maybe Piper's obsession with Disney movies as a child had warped her sense of what real relationships were supposed to be. But she wanted a love that inspired stories. One like her grandparents had. She swore she'd never seen two people more in love than Grandma and Grandpa. Sadly, chasing that dream had only led her to heartbreak. And what she needed to focus on right now was fixing up the theater, not scoring a date with a hottie handyman who might be a covert spy for her evil landlord. "Do they do contract work with you?"

He hesitated for a brief second before gracing her with a devastatingly charming smile. "Yeah. We have a company together. Most of the time we work separate contracts, but sometimes we work together on places."

"That's nice." She'd often wished for a sibling to play with, but sadly her parents divorced when she was ten and neither seemed interested in having any more kids. They'd barely been interested in her.

They moved on from the basement to the next floor where the dressing rooms and stage were. She took him through each of the five dressing rooms which, thankfully, needed nothing more than a few window frames repaired. The work needed in the backstage bathrooms would be a little more intensive. Three of the toilets didn't flush and nearly all the sinks dripped.

"Plumbing issues are common with old buildings like this," Kell said as he continued to make notes. "I don't think it'll need a full replumbing, but those sinks will need new faucets. I doubt Mr. Noll has ever replaced them."

She doubted her crummy landlord had ever replaced anything in this theater. Donald thought duct tape was an acceptable solution for any fix.

"How about the stage?" Kell asked, turning to her and motioning behind her.

She spun around, heart skipping a beat as she stared at her favorite place in the world. Making her way out of the bathroom, she moved backstage and sucked in a deep breath.

Years of lingering smells sparked a plethora of happy memories. The powdery smell of stage makeup, dank musk of costumes worn over and over again, the sweet floral scent of roses from the bouquets brought to performers to celebrate and just a hint of tangy, stinky body odor. Those stage lights could make an ice cube sweat.

"The stage is perfect," she said as she stepped onto the floor. It was the one part of the theater she insisted Donald keep up to date and running perfectly. After all, what good was a theater without a proper stage?

Kell stepped onto the stage, glancing around. He nodded, seeming to agree with her assessment. As his eyes moved upward, he frowned. "What's that?"

She looked up to see what he was pointing at. Her red fabric was looped around a pulley, attached to the beams just below the stage lights.

"That? Oh, that's my sling. I'm preparing for a show next month."

He glanced over at her with a confused expression. "Sling? What kind of show uses a sling?"

She grinned. "An aerial show."

"Ariel? Like the mermaid?"

A giggle escaped her. She couldn't help it. The man was adorable when confused. "No, though we have done mermaid-themed shows. Aerials as in silks, lyra, sling, trapeze, rope and a ton of other apparatuses."

He continued to frown. Clearly not understanding her explanation. A thought popped into her head. Why tell him when she could show him?

"Stay right here," she said, rushing off the stage to the pulley system. Quickly she lowered her sling and secured the rope.

"Stand right there and don't move," she instructed as she came on stage and grasped the red fabric in her hands.

Standing with one leg in front of the other, she turned on her back foot before lifting into the air and mounting the sling with a front balance. She heard a small gasp from Kell, but she ignored it, continuing to shift her body in the fabric until she had the sling around her back. She spun in the air, speed increasing as she pulled her body into a straight line. Swooping out her legs, she did a flare, bringing herself into a straddle.

Once she was there, muscle memory took over as she crocheted each leg into the fabric. Using her core strength, she lifted her body up and grabbed the fabric, pulling her chest through as she continued to spin.

"Wow!"

Kell's soft exclamation made her smile. She loved seeing people experience aerials for the first time. Not that she could accurately see him as she was currently spinning too fast to see anything. But the awe in his voice gave her a picture. Wanting to give him just a little more of a wow factor, she decided to do a small drop. Engaging her core muscles, she dropped her hands, letting go of the fabric and falling forward. She heard a loud curse as Kell started to rush forward, but she'd safely landed in a T shape with her arms out, the sling securely around her back under her arms.

"I told you to stay put," she said with a small laugh as she lowered herself to the floor, sliding out of the sling.

"Yeah, but you didn't say you were going to go all daredevil stuntwoman and scare the life out of me. I thought you were going to crash into the stage and crack your skull open."

She chuckled. "Trust me, that's one of the easiest and safest drops there is."

He raised his eyebrows. "That's safe?"

"If you know how to do it properly, yes." She placed a hand on his arm. "But it was sweet of you to be worried."

Something in his eyes heated at her words. Her hand

burned where she touched him. She quickly pulled her hand away, taking a small step back and glancing up at the sling. Good grief, the man was potent. She had to remember he was here to fix her theater, not date her.

"I've been doing aerials for thirteen years now. Started when I was fifteen and never broken a single bone. I promise it's safe if you do it properly."

That wasn't to say things couldn't go wrong. Even in the safest of environments with the proper training, accidents happened. While she'd never broken anything, she had had plenty of bruises, fabric burns and other small injuries over the years. Such was the life of a performer.

"It's like the Cirque du Soleil stuff then?"

She nodded. "Pretty much, but they tend to have more acts in their shows that we can't accommodate here."

No way would the Double Wheel of Destiny fit in this theater.

His gaze took in the theater, a curious expression on his face she couldn't decipher.

"Have you ever thought of finding a new place? One that could accommodate more…stuff. I'm sorry, I'm not sure what to call…" He waved a hand in the air at the hanging fabric.

She laughed softly. "We call them apparatuses, and no. I mostly focus on aerials, plus when I don't have an aerial show I rent the stage for stage plays and musicals. But I'm allowed to rent out the theater for performances," she rushed to say, in case he thought she was breaking her lease. Dang it! She'd forgotten the situation for a moment. She had to remember no matter how kind and handsome Kell was, she couldn't trust him.

He nodded, not giving any indication he was here as a spy for Donald. Until she knew for sure, she had to be careful. One slip and she could lose this place, her dream. She couldn't let that happen.

It had taken her years to get here. On her first day in aerial class as an anxious teenager who had only ever done community class gymnastics before, she'd known she'd found her calling. The very first spin in a hoop and she was hooked. She'd finally found a place she felt accepted, a place where she belonged. A place where her mind and body could be free to just exist without all the expectations of society. She knew, over her years of performing in traveling shows, that one day she wanted to provide that space for others. To teach aerials, put on her own shows, offer a welcoming place for those who needed it.

Which was why she had to make extra sure while giving Kell the tour that she skipped her secret bedroom. If Donald found *that* out, her butt would be kicked to the curb in a heartbeat.

"I've seen plenty of theater shows, but I've never been to an aerial show," he said, staring at the hanging fabric.

"Then I'll have to make sure you have a front-row seat at our next performance." Something inside her took flight at the thought of Kell sitting in the audience, watching her perform. Uh-oh, her romantic side was taking off again. Time to reel those thoughts in fast before she made a fool of herself again.

His bright blue gaze found hers, lighting up as his lips curved into a smile. "I'd love that. But maybe warn me how many death-defying drop things you're going to do so I don't overreact and rush up on stage to try and catch you."

A giggle escaped her lips. "You take the white knight thing seriously, don't you?"

He shrugged. "My brothers say I can be a bit overprotective."

Now that was something she wasn't used to. Her parents had taken a hands-off parenting style when she was a kid. She practically raised herself. She'd never had an overprotective partner. Most of the people she dated were other artists and performers. They knew she could handle herself and were generally too focused on their own stuff to worry about her. Except for Larry, but he wasn't overprotective. Larry was a loser who expected her to do all the housework, pay the bills and attend to his "needs" whenever he wanted. And then the jerk had the audacity to steal from her and run off.

Boy, could she pick 'em.

She wondered what it would be like to be with someone who worried about her well-being.

"Should we continue with the tour?" she asked.

He nodded. "Yes, we better continue. As…exciting as that demonstration was, I think we need to move on. If this place needs as much work as you say, it will take all day just to note everything down. I need to see every room in the place."

"You got it." She pasted on a smile, turning before he caught the lie in her eyes. She couldn't show him every room.

The storage room she'd turned into living quarters was at the end of a hall up a short staircase. She'd turned the entry to her room into one of those secret bookcase doors and stashed stage props on the shelves in case anyone got curious. They could easily avoid that. She hoped. White knight or devious spy, she couldn't risk Kell finding out about her living arrangements. It was her little secret.

CHAPTER FOUR

KELL STOOD OUTSIDE of the Star-Crossed Theater, unable to keep the huge grin from widening his lips. A steady thrum of eager anticipation sped up his heart. Today was the first official workday for this project. He always got a rush of excitement when he got to do repairs. Something about working with his hands, fixing things, bringing life back to the broken, always made him feel…complete.

Selling a six-million-dollar property was a rush in itself, but the high died out quickly. Staring at a home or building he helped restore, seeing the light in people's eyes as they finally got a forever home—that's what stayed with him. Warming him in the dark, lonely nights, giving him a purpose.

But today felt like more than that.

He stared up at the towering building. He couldn't wait to work on all the much-needed repairs, but that wasn't the only reason for this buzzing feeling low in his gut.

Piper.

Her name whispered in his mind, filling his chest with a warm sensation. The woman fascinated him. She was confident and beautiful and a bit odd. He couldn't put his finger on it, but there was something about her that drew him to her.

Bad idea, Kell.

He scowled as the thought popped into his head. A sigh left him, acknowledging the truth of it all. As intriguing as he found Piper, it would be a bad idea to do anything about it. For one, he didn't date. Kell was a casual-hookup-type guy. Relationships didn't work out for him. He'd learned long ago that love and happily-ever-afters were something other people got to have

Not him.

When a guy's ex found her soulmate immediately after breaking up with him—that was one thing. When it happened five times…that was a pattern. A pattern that told Kell he was destined to be nothing more than the stepping stone to other people's happy ending.

He refused to be stepped on any longer, which was why he'd sworn off dating. Couldn't get hurt if he didn't participate in the first place. Casual hookups were the safer bet.

He had no idea what type of dating Piper was into, but even if she was okay with his "no labels" policy, there was another reason he should not be entertaining romantic thoughts of her…

His phone rang, interrupting his musings. Pulling it from his pocket, he glanced at the screen with a scowl. And there it was. The reason he shouldn't pursue any type of hookup with Piper. Donald Noll's number flashed on his screen, reminding him of the second part of this job. The part Piper had no idea about. The part where he was basically betraying her by not telling her Donald was planning to sell the place right out from under her.

Swiping his thumb across the screen, he accepted the call and brought the phone to his ear.

"Mr. Noll," he said, affecting his cheery customer-service voice. "Did you receive my email?"

"What the hell, Thorson?"

That was a yes.

"There's at least twenty repairs on here that I did not stipulate," the angry voice hissed over the line.

Kell took a deep breath, counting to five. Over the years

he'd dealt with his fair share of PITA clients, but Donald Noll took the cake. Every phone call, the guy was angry over something.

"Yes, Mr. Noll, but you did hire me to do a full inspection on the building. I'm simply reporting the issues I found during my inspection."

Donald snorted. "Right, and how much will these additional *issues* cost me in repairs? I know how you contractors work."

Kell's teeth ground together as he did his best not to lay into the jerk. He could remind Donald that he hired Kell to sell this building because he was getting a two-for-one deal in repairs, but somehow, he knew that would go right over the guy's head.

"I understand it's more work than we initially thought, but the better condition the building is in when we list it, the higher price we can get for it."

A humming sound came over the line. "I suppose that's true."

Kell knew bringing it back around to money would work. He could always spot the greedy ones a mile away. Good for his business, but lately he was beginning to wonder if it was damaging to his soul. More and more he found himself wishing he could spend more time working on Helping Homes and less on selling high-price properties. But the truth of the matter was if he and his brothers didn't continue their high-end real estate business, their charity would suffer. They sunk a lot of their profits into their charity, so sucking up to people like Donald Noll would have to continue.

"How many of these fixes do we have to do to bump the price up?"

A cold shudder of unease slicked its way down his spine. This was his least favorite part of the job. Flippers always hiked up the price to places whenever they did some cheap cosmetic fixes. Donald wasn't a flipper, but it was clear the guy just wanted to slap a new coat of paint on the building, add another million to the price and call it good. Unfortunately for him, that wasn't going to work in this case.

"A lot of these fixes are necessary to even list the property," he replied, bracing himself for the reaction. He was answered by the expected string of angry curses.

"I thought you were the best real estate company in the Denver Metro area. What the hell are you talking about, Thorson? I hired you to make me money, not drive me into the poorhouse with repairs!"

Wow. Maybe Donald should audition for one of the plays the Star-Crossed hosted. The man was clearly dramatic enough.

"We can't list the property in the condition it's in," he replied in his most calming voice. "It won't pass inspection. You could list it 'as is' but that would drive the price down significantly. The type of buyers who will want this property don't want to put in a lot of repair work. They want a turnkey property."

He waited, listening to Donald grumble and mutter a few more choice curse words. After what felt like an eternity he spoke again.

"Fine, do what you have to do, but I want approval on any repair over a thousand."

He'd get approval on every repair no matter the cost. That was just smart business. He hadn't made it as far as he had in life by not getting things approved in writing.

"Of course. I'll start on the already-approved repairs and send you quotes before I start on the new issues I found."

"Good," Donald huffed. "Will any of this delay the listing?"

"It shouldn't. If anything big arises I can call my brothers in to help speed up the repairs. We should be able to put the listing on the market by the end of next month."

"Excellent. I want this place off my hands ASAP. As soon as that shrew's lease is up, I'm done with this albatross."

Kell clenched his jaw. It was bad business to tell your client to shove it where the sun doesn't shine, but the words were on the tip of his tongue. Piper was the furthest possible thing from a shrew. What kind of man called a woman a shrew anyway? A misogynist, that's what kind. Donald was that and more, but he was also Kell's client, so he held his tongue.

"Have you met her yet?" Donald asked.

"Ms. Pitts? Yes, I actually ran into her the other day when I came to do the inspection."

"Ha! Pitts. Perfect last name for that woman."

Kell's fist clenched as he held back his disgust at this man. His body vibrated with anger. What he wouldn't give to reach through the phone and punch the guy. But he couldn't. Good thing too, because that would probably void his contract and set him up for a lawsuit. Pity. Someone needed to teach Donald Noll some manners.

Needing to end this conversation before he did something stupid—like call his client a word his mother would ground him for, even as a fully grown adult—he rushed to speak.

"I'll send you an updated contract with the additional repairs to sign this evening. In the meantime, I'll get to work on the already-approved items."

Donald grunted out an agreement. But just as Kell was about to hang up, he spoke again.

"Thorson."

"Yes, Mr. Noll?"

"Remember to keep your lips zipped about the sale. I don't want Piper to catch wind of it and try and find a loophole to stay in the building. I wouldn't put it past a sneaky witch like her."

What was this guy's problem? Did his mother never hug him? From what Kell could tell, Piper was a sweet, caring person. Maybe Donald just had a stick up his butt because she expected him to actually do his job as a landlord and fix all the broken crap around the place. How awful that must be for him.

Regulating his voice the best he could, he gripped the phone tighter as he replied. "I really think it would be better if you informed your tenant you won't be renewing her lease. That way she can start looking for a new theater."

"I don't really give a rat's turd what you think, Thorson. You work for me, so keep your lips zipped or our contract is in breach, and I'll sue you for everything you're worth."

Which in addition to his vast wealth would also be his charity. Dammit! How had he gotten himself stuck between a rock and this jerkwad? Sucking in a deep, calming breath, he spoke between clenched teeth.

"Yes, Mr. Noll. I understand. I won't say a word."

"Good. Now get to work."

He could remind the guy that even though he was contracted to work for him, Donald was not his boss, but the line went dead as the jerk hung up. Slipping his phone back into his pocket he closed his eyes, counting to ten as he focused on his breathing. When he opened his eyes back up, he felt most of the rage melt away. It was still there, simmering in his gut. He feared it would remain until this hellscape of a job was over.

He made his way inside the building, heading past the front into the theater where he spied a sight that made his anger ease, and the warmth return to his chest. There she was. The reason not everything about this job was hell.

Piper stood on the stage adjusting a long dark purple sling. He knew what they were called now, thanks to her. There were six others set up on stage in various colors. They hung about six inches off the ground. Much lower than the one she had up the other day when she nearly gave him a heart attack with that drop thing she did.

He stood there and watched her for a moment. The joy on her face as she touched the fabric of the sling, flipping it so it lay perfectly for her students. Her care and attention to detail showed how much she loved her job, loved this theater. Rage started to rise in him again at Donald. How could the man think such awful things about Piper?

Not wanting to scare her again, he announced himself as he approached the stage.

"Hey there."

She glanced over at him, a warm smile lighting up her face. His breath caught in his chest at her beauty. What the hell was wrong with him? He barely knew her, and yet his heart was pounding in his chest from a simple smile. This was not good. He refused to fall down this rabbit hole again. No feelings. Just fun. That was his motto and he was sticking to it, no matter who life tossed in his path.

"Kell, it's so good to see you." Her cheeks flushed as the words left her lips. "I mean, it's good that you're here. Because you're fixing stuff, and we need stuff fixed and so that's why you're here and that's why it's good…yeah."

She turned, suddenly very interested in fussing with the sling in front of her. He dipped his head to hide a smile at her flustered attitude. This spark between them might be a bad idea, but damn if he didn't enjoy it just a little.

His happiness dimmed as he remembered what he was really doing here. The secret he was keeping from her. Bet she wouldn't smile so kindly at him if she knew he was about to sell this place out from under her. Guilt churned in his gut.

Dammit. He was no better than Donald.

CHAPTER FIVE

COULD SHE EVER be in the presence of this man and not embarrass herself?

Piper fussed with the perfectly hung sling, avoiding eye contact after her awkward overexplanation. Thankfully, Kell was a gentleman and didn't call attention to her rambling.

"Are you starting the repairs today?" she asked, still focused on the red fabric hanging in front of her.

"If that works for you."

His warm, deep voice sent a shiver of desire down her spine. She told her body to knock it off. She had a class in fifteen minutes. Her brain needed to be focused on instruction, not mooning over a hot guy. Maybe she just needed to hop back into the dating pool. It had been four months since Larry the Loser took off in the middle of the night with all her savings, leaving her with no way to pay the rent on their apartment. Which was why she'd been secretly crashing at the theater ever since.

Damn you, Larry!

A sigh escaped her. Larry's leaving hadn't hurt as much as his betrayal. If she was honest with herself, she might have jumped the gun on moving in with him. They'd only been dating a few months, and she let her romantic notions carry her away. Truth be told, after Larry left, she nursed a broken heart for three weeks. Shorter than her previous heartbreaks, but no less painful. Then one day she realized the stealing hurt more than the leaving. She'd simply let herself get swept up in the romance of a new relationship…again. She had to stop doing that.

"Works for me," she replied, finally turning to face him, pushing thoughts of jerk exes and money problems out of her mind. "I have a couple of classes today, but we're going to be on the stage so as long as we don't get in your way, it should be fine."

His brow furrowed, head tilting as he stared at her with a contemplative expression.

"As long as you don't get in my way? I think you've got that backward. I'm here to do repairs around your schedule. I'm the one that should worry about getting in the way."

She laughed off the comment. That might be the case, but years of masking and people-pleasing was a hard habit to break.

As a kid, she had found it easier to put everyone else's needs ahead of her own. She learned early on if she made a fuss, all that happened was punishment. Her parents hadn't been physically abusive, they never hit her or anything. But they also found her difficult and told her so on numerous occasions. They hated that she couldn't eat certain foods, were annoyed when she said clothes felt too tight or scratchy, got embarrassed when she cried at loud noises or bright lights.

When she finally got her autism diagnosis, she'd been fifteen and shuffling between her parents' houses. By then they'd basically washed their hands of her. The calls on birthdays and Christmas were their only communication these days, and that worked out fine for her. Still, it was hard for her not to bend over backward to make sure everyone around her was comfortable. Even if it meant she was on edge.

Kell walked up to the end of the stage, setting his tool bag down on the floor. He placed his elbows on the stage floor and leaned against the edge, staring up at her with a pleasant but serious expression.

"Where can I work today that won't be in your way?"

He was asking her? She wasn't used to that. Usually the people Donald hired—the few he had over the years—were rude and pushy. They didn't care that she had a business to run. Kell was different. Too different. Her instincts screamed. Maybe Donald hired Mr. White Knight here to throw her off her game. The possibility he was in league with her enemy was high. Too high for her to go all googly eyes over a few kind gestures and a sinfully sexy smile. She needed to keep her cards close to her chest.

And by cards, she meant her secret living arrangements. Time to throw him off the scent and away from her hidden bedroom.

"Um…" She filtered through the list of repairs he'd mentioned the other day on their tour, trying to sift through them all to make a decision. Pressure had her nerves rising. She wasn't used to being the one calling the shots. In her aerial studio, sure, but not in building repairs.

"Sorry." Kell held up a hand. "Let me make this easier on you. I was planning on working down in the basement on the electrical today. I will have to turn off the power for a while, which means no lights for a few hours. Is that okay?"

Relief filled her as he presented her with a clear plan. The yes-or-no answer was much simpler for her frazzled brain to process. And the basement was about as far away from her room as possible.

"Yes, that would be fine." She smiled, opening the sling and sinking down into it. The fabric swayed as she sat facing him, her feet rocking her back and forth along the stage floor. The soothing motion calmed her nerves. "With the windows, we'll get plenty of summer sun for light, so no overhead lights shouldn't be a problem."

He nodded with a smile. "Sounds like a plan then. How many classes do you have today?"

"Four," she said, pausing for a moment. A frown turned down her lips as a thought occurred to her. "But we do have rehearsal tonight at seven. The sun sets around nine, but the light will be much dimmer. We might need the overheads for the evening rehearsal."

"Not a problem." Kell reached down to grab his clipboard out of his tool bag. He scanned the paper on it before looking back up at her with a confident smile. "I should be done before five."

Right, because he had a job with normal hours. Nothing was normal when you were in the arts. Piper supposed he might have contractor emergencies that called him out at odd hours. Unless he didn't offer that service. Honestly, she had no idea. She didn't even know what his business was called. Wasn't like she was the one who hired him after all. He could be a guy Donald found at the grocery store that had a hammer and worked for cheap. Sounded like something her landlord would do.

A tiny voice in the back of her hear told her to search him out on the web, but she ignored it. Wasn't like she was going to date the guy. No need to vet him. Besides, she'd seen the invoice with Donald's signature. His work here was legit, no matter where Donald had found him.

And even if he was spying for Donald, Kell didn't seem like the shady contractor type of guy. She'd bet he had all the licensing and permits he needed…she hoped. As long as he made this place safe and whole again, she didn't care. Let Donald worry about the legality of everything. She was just happy things were finally getting fixed around here.

"I have two classes this morning and then two after lunch. The last one ends at four in the afternoon so we should still be good with no lights as far as all the classes go."

He inclined his head. "Then I'll make sure you have overheads before I leave."

She smiled, continuing to sway in the sling. "There's that white knight attitude again."

With a small chuckle, he gave her a dramatic bow, placing his hand over his heart. "My lady."

She giggled. The man was utterly charming.

"What classes do you have today?"

She looked out into the audience as she went over her classes in her mind. "This afternoon I have advanced lyra and rope."

"Lyra?" he asked, his face scrunching up in confusion.

"Hoop," she replied.

"Like a Hula-Hoop?"

A snort of laughter escaped her. "Um, no. If you rigged a Hula-Hoop, it would break the second you tried to mount it. Lyras, or hoops, are steel. A plastic Hula-Hoop could never support a person's weight."

"Steel?" His dark eyebrows rose as a soft whistle left his lips. "Sounds heavy."

She nodded. "They can be, especially if you have a solid one. The hollow ones are much lighter, but the solid ones maintain your spin better."

"Interesting," he said, gaze focused on her, eyes bright with curiosity. "Is the fabric a special material too?"

She grinned, his genuine interest prompting her to info dump in excitement.

"Yes. Aerial silks are generally made from nylon tricot, polyester tricot or polyester Lycra. Each fabric gives a slightly different stretch depending on what you need. But they're all highly durable and, when rigged correctly, can hold five thousand pounds."

His eyes widened. "Five thousand pounds?"

"Yup." She nodded. "You have to make sure you account for the drop force in aerials. A good aerial studio will make sure they can rig the weight of a car. I always tell people who are worried about weight that aerials is for every body type. Apparatuses can be adjusted for any ability. Aerials is for everyone."

She gave him a pointed look. He laughed, waving a hand in the air.

"Oh no. I saw that drop thing you did yesterday. You say aerials is for everyone, but I say I'm much happier with my feet on the ground."

"I'll get you up here one of these days," she teased.

He shook his head. "I guess you're doing the fabric classes this morning?"

He motioned to the sling she was sitting in. She nodded.

"Yes, I have a sensory sling class and then youth beginner sling after that."

"Sensory sling? What's that?"

She sucked in a sharp breath. He'd made her feel so comfortable, so at ease, she'd forgotten he was basically a stranger to her. She took a deep breath, preparing to explain and hoping he was the type of person who wouldn't be a judgmental jerk. She didn't think he would but…you never knew.

"It's a class for children with sensory needs. Kids who have autism, Sensory Processing Disorder, ADHD. The spinning and wrapping of aerial sling can help regulate their nervous system."

She watched his face as she explained, looking for signs of judgment. When she saw nothing but contemplation, she pressed on, revealing something she rarely did with people she didn't know well.

"It's actually how I found aerials." She paused, watching his face carefully. "My doctor suggested it after I got my autism diagnosis as a way to regulate and find a community of friends."

And, boy, had the doctor been right. Aerials had saved her during a time she felt her lowest.

Kell's thoughtful expression morphed into a warm smile. "Huh, wonder if I could get my brother Mal up in one of these things. He's on the spectrum too. Though he's not too big into community. More of a loner. Keeps to himself a lot."

She could understand that. There were plenty of times she got overstimulated and just wanted to be alone.

"But now I'm afraid you have more ammo to try and get me up into one of these things," Kell continued. "Though I can't see how spinning around and trying not to break my neck in a fall would help my ADHD."

He gave her a wink that made her heart practically beat out of her chest. Not only was he not judgmental about her neurodiversity, but he was also neurodivergent! No wonder they seemed to click so well.

Don't trust him, Piper! He's the enemy!

She scoffed at her inner voice. *Enemy* was a bit of a stretch, but her subconscious was right to remind her she didn't know this man well. Or what his true intentions might be. Tucking away that knowledge, she grinned.

"Mark my words, Kell," she said, pointing a finger at him. "Before you finish the repairs on this place, I will get you up into an apparatus."

He chuckled, waving off her promise. "Would you look at the time. I better get off to work. Lots of things to fix, wires and leaks and such."

He bent down and grabbed his bag, moving past the stage to the hallway leading down to the basement.

"You'd be surprised how fun it is," she called after him.

"Can't hear you," he playfully yelled back. "Too busy thinking about how my feet are safely on the ground."

She laughed as he disappeared. Relief filled her entire body. Normally she didn't tell people about her autism until she'd known them for a while. It wasn't that she was ashamed of being autistic. There was nothing wrong with being on the spectrum. But not everyone felt that way. She'd had dates break things off after finding out. Friends pull away. People treated her like she had some horrible disease instead of simply a difference in neurological pathways.

Happiness filled her as Kell not only accepted her reveal, but understood.

Loud shouts of tiny voices filled the air as the kids for her sensory class started to rush into the theater. She put thoughts of sweet, sexy handymen away, focusing on the class about to start. But maybe she'd check in with Kell after her morning classes. She had to make sure he wasn't seeing anything he wasn't supposed to. And if it happened to be lunchtime, maybe they could grab a bite together. After all, they both had to eat, didn't they?

CHAPTER SIX

Two and a half hours later, Piper waved goodbye to the students of her youth sling group. The morning classes had gone by without a hitch today. Thank goodness. Kids' classes tended to be a bit harried. Listening was a skill not all of them had perfected yet, which was to be expected. You had to have real patience to teach kids, and it took a special skill to teach the neurodivergent kiddos. Thankfully she knew what they needed because it was often the same thing she needed.

Understanding, patience, clear instructions and caring.

She just wished more people understood that.

The lights above the stage flickered for a moment before turning on full brightness. She squinted, averting her eyes as the stage filled with harsh artificial light.

"Guess that means he fixed them," she said, daisy-chaining the sling she'd just taken down. "One problem down."

A hundred more to go.

She gathered all the chained slings and placed them in their cubbies just off the stage. There were a few hours until her afternoon classes. Enough time to run out and grab lunch. She should check if Kell wanted lunch…and check in on him in general. There wasn't any evidence of her squatting in the basement, but she needed to be vigilant anytime the man was here. If that meant she had to spend more time in the presence of the sweet and sexy man, so be it.

With butterflies taking flight in her stomach, she made

her way down to the basement, hoping to find him still there. She did. He was crouched at the far end of the basement near the fuse box, placing tools and wires inside his bag.

"Got the lights fixed, I see," she said, chuckling softly at her own joke.

He glanced up at her, a smile curling his full lips. Holy cow! The man was unfairly handsome when he smiled. Her mind was going to all the naughty places it had no business going.

"Yup." He stood, brushing his hands off on his dark jeans. "Replaced some fuses, fixed some of the faulty wiring. You should be good to go now. As far as light anyhow."

Like she said, one of a hundred.

"That's good news, considering we have a show coming up and it'd be awfully hard to perform in the dark."

"What's the show?"

"It's an aerial performance of the most romantic story ever written, *Romeo and Juliet*."

He frowned. "*Romeo and Juliet* isn't a romance. Don't seven people die in that play?"

She waved away his denial. "Six actually, but that's not the point. It's a story of passion and how far a person is willing to go for true love."

"It's a cautionary tale about teenage hormones and impulsiveness."

Okay, then. It seemed like someone was a true-love doubter.

Kell uncuffed his flannel shirt, then rolled the sleeves up his arms before crossing them over his chest. She did not notice how muscled his forearms were. Not one bit. Her mind was still focused on how this man who was usually so positive and cheerful could hate a timeless classic like *Romeo and Juliet*.

"It's called *The Tragedy of Romeo and Juliet* for a reason," he pointed out.

She scowled at him. "Don't tell me you're one of those people."

Dark eyebrows rose on his forehead. "What people?"

"The kind who hate love and happily-ever-afters."

He frowned, letting out a contemplative sigh. "I don't hate love. I just don't think it exists for everyone. And *Romeo and Juliet* did not end in a happily-ever-after. Therefore, not a romance."

A slight sting of irritation wriggled in her gut.

"Let me guess," he said with a knowing grin. "You're a stars-in-the-eyes hopeless romantic who believes everyone has a perfect soulmate out there just waiting for them."

She sniffed, taking umbrage with his accurate assessment of her. "Maybe. Is that such a bad thing?"

He shook his head, his smile turning soft. "No. I think it's great actually. But unfortunately, that's not the way the world works. Not everyone gets their happily-ever-after. In fact, some people are stepping stones for everyone else's happy ending."

What did he mean by that?

Before she could ask, he continued.

"But *Romeo and Juliet* still isn't a romantic story. It's one of Shakespeare's tragedies. 'For never was a story of more woe than this of Juliet and her Romeo.'"

"Fixes lights and memorizes Shakespeare." She arched one eyebrow at him. "The man has layers."

He chuckled, shaking his head. "Not really. My mother was on the board for the Denver Performing Arts Center for years. We went to all the shows as kids. Saw a lot of Shakespeare. Guess it kind of stuck."

A board member of an arts community? Who were his parents? Didn't seem like the kind of position the parent of a contractor would have. Once again, she was reminded how little she knew about Kell.

"You don't believe in love?" she asked. "Like, at all?"

He leaned back against the hard brick wall. His brow furrowed as he stared past her, not focusing on anything in particular. If she had to guess, she would say he wasn't staring at anything in the room at all. He looked the way she felt when she was going over memories in her mind. Pensive and...sad.

"I believe in the love you have for your family, your friends, pets—if you have them—and I do think some people out there find a forever kind of love." He paused, furrow turning into a hopeless frown. "But I know that kind of stuff isn't for me. True love...isn't my style."

"That's a pretty pessimistic way to think." She slapped a hand over her mouth, knowing blurting that out had been rude. She hadn't meant to. It just slipped out. Sometimes her mouth was faster than her brain and she said the wrong thing.

Kell stared at her for a moment then burst out laughing. Her face flamed, not sure why her comment was so funny or if he was laughing at her. She didn't think it was the latter. Kell might not believe in love like she did, but the man wasn't cruel.

"I think that's the first time someone has called me pessimistic," he said, his laughter dying down. "Normally that's my brother Mal's nickname. He's gonna get a chuckle out of this when I tell him."

Grateful he was laughing at the scenario and not her, she pressed on. "Not a single one of your significant others called you pessimistic when learning about your 'no true love' belief?"

She would have called him out for sure.

He winced. "Eh, I'm not really into labels. I'm more of a 'let's have fun until we're done' type guy."

The way he said that felt like something more. She heard an undertone of pain in his carefree words.

"Not into labels. Very original," she teased. "No guy in the history of the universe has ever said that to cover for his commitment phobia."

He took a step forward and bopped her on the nose with

his finger. "And a true romantic who believes in happily-ever-after—not cliché for an art lover at all."

She ducked her head to hide the flush she felt rising on her cheeks at his touch.

Down, body. He doesn't believe in love. He might turn me in to Donald. He's not for us. No matter how sexy and sweet we find him. Stop falling so fast—remember what happened with Larry. Don't play the fool again.

"Might be cliché, but it does sell tickets. Which is why we are billing our *Romeo and Juliet* aerial show with the tagline *Romance in the Skies*."

He nodded. "Sounds like I better get my ticket before they sell out."

She snorted out a strangled laugh. "No worries there. We've barely sold any tickets, and the show is in less than four weeks. We'll be lucky if we get half a house."

A heavy sigh left her. It was always a struggle to pack the theater for a show, but lately it seemed like no one wanted to venture out to see live theater. She could really use a sold-out show.

"Low ticket sales?" His lips turned down, brow wrinkling. "But it sounds so cool. I would think everyone would want to see an aerial performance."

She shrugged, thinking the same thing, but the truth was in the lack of ticket sales. "People love consuming art, but they don't like supporting it with their money. I don't know, maybe I'll run a half-off ticket sale closer to the show date."

She'd lose money, but at least there'd be people in the audience to cheer for her students. They deserved it.

"Hmm." Kell brought a hand up to stroke his chin. "Don't discount tickets just yet. I may have some ideas to pack the house."

"You have ideas to sell tickets to an aerial show?"

Dropping his hand, he grinned at her. "My mom was on

an arts board, remember? Plus, my family has…experience in getting people to support certain causes."

Okay, that didn't sound cryptic and suspicious at all. Suspicious or not, she was grateful. She needed all the help she could get. The way her finances were, she wasn't above selling her soul to fill the house.

A loud grumbling sound filled the room. Her face flamed as she realized the sound came from her stomach. Kell, bless his heart, pretended not to hear a thing. It did remind her of the initial reason she came down here. To ask him to lunch. And check to make sure he wasn't spying for Donald, but he didn't need to know that last part.

"Are you taking a lunch break or moving on to the next task?" She didn't want to interrupt his work if he was in a flow. She hated when people did that to her.

He reached down to his bag and pulled out his clipboard, looking over the papers on it.

"I could break for lunch. I was planning on starting in on the bathrooms after fixing the lights. Figured that was the next highest priority."

Yes please, especially with the show coming up. Those back bathrooms would be in full use by the cast. Having them up and running with no leaks or plugs would be wonderful.

"I was just heading out to grab a bite if you want to tag along," she said. There. That sounded like something a friend would say.

He leaned down to tuck the clipboard back into his bag, smiling as he rose again. "Sounds great. What do you have in mind?"

So many things when it came to this man. Things she should absolutely not have in mind considering the odds of them ever happening. Zero. Swallowing down what she really wanted to say, she smiled and asked, "How do you feel about tacos?"

CHAPTER SEVEN

Kell loved tacos. They were the perfect food in his opinion. Spicy meat and delicious veggies all wrapped up in a corn tortilla you could pop into your mouth. He would never say no to getting tacos. Which is how he found himself leaving the theater with Piper to grab a friendly lunch.

He said *friendly* because he noticed a very clear shift in her attitude toward him when he said he didn't believe in true love. Her body had gone rigid, the flirty spark in her eyes snuffed out. He'd ruined any chance of them exploring their chemistry the moment he doom-and-gloomed all over her fairy-tale beliefs.

Which was for the best, considering he was betraying her trust by keeping the sale a secret. The stinging burn of guilt and anger scorched his chest. Damn Donald to eternity.

On the one hand he regretted his decision. He felt a magnetic pull toward this woman. One he desperately wanted to explore. But on the other hand, he believed in being honest when it came to relationships. Point one, the fact that he didn't do them. It would be cruel to lead Piper on, knowing he could never give her the commitment she desired.

Which led him here, walking by her side on a sunny summer day toward Civic Park where a line of food trucks sat. Delicious smells filled the air the closer they got. Each one held the unique scent of their trade-food style. His stomach growled, wishing it was bigger so he could sample each and every delicacy. He'd have to make a point to come here for lunch every day he worked this job so he could try all the options offered.

"Are these trucks here every day?" he asked, pointing to the row of vehicles.

"Yup." Piper smiled at him. "Every day, rain or shine. Except in the winter, I guess. Once the snow starts, the season kind of shuts down for a lot of them."

Made sense. He wondered what the business owners did in the winter months. Selling property was a year-round gig. Though the spring through fall seasons were the most profitable, he and his brothers still made deals during the winter months.

"Wait until you try these tacos." Piper clasped her hands together, rubbing them as her gaze filled with hungry anticipation. "They're the best in the world!"

He seriously doubted that. He'd been all over the world. Sampled cuisine from top chefs and family-run restaurants that had been in operation for generations. No way could a small taco truck in Colorado be the best in the world.

"That's an awfully high bar you set there," he said, glancing over at her as they took their spot in the back of the very long line for the taco truck.

"It's true." She nodded. "In fact, let's bet on it."

"Bet?"

"If you agree that these are the best tacos you've ever eaten, which they will be, you have to let me give you an aerial lesson."

He blinked, a ball of anxiety crawling up his throat at her words. "Excuse me?"

She laughed. "You heard me. If you agree these are the best tacos in the world then you have to get up in the apparatus of my choice and I'll teach you some aerial moves."

Why in the world would he ever need to learn aerial moves?

They were cool and fun to look at, but the thought of doing that spinny drop thing she did the other day horrified him.

"Come on, Kell," she said, when he continued to stare at her, not speaking. "You can't tell me you're scared of being a few feet off the ground on a stage. You work on roofs, right? That's way higher than a sling."

He shook his head, taking a small step forward with her as the line moved. "It's not the height, it's the falling and breaking my neck."

"People fall off roofs all the time and break stuff."

He frowned, having had a few close calls with that himself over the years. Very unpleasant memories. "Thank you for that reminder, but I'm not actively throwing myself to the ground when I'm working. You, however, with the spinning and dropping, seem to be tempting fate every day."

She lifted one shoulder in a small shrug. "It's fun."

He snorted. "You have an odd definition of fun."

A heavy sigh left her. "So I've been told."

Shoot! He hadn't meant it like that. He'd just been teasing her, but he could see how his words could come across as insensitive. His brother Mal misinterpreted his intentions when he wasn't clear enough at times too.

"I'm sorry, I didn't mean—"

Piper waved a hand in the air, a soft smile tilting her lips. "It's okay, I understood what you meant. But there are some people who think what I do is…silly."

What? Who? He thought her aerial stuff was amazing. Stunning and beautiful. A dance form and an athletic achievement. Not necessarily something he wanted to try for himself, but he enjoyed watching her do it. When he wasn't terrified she'd fall and break her neck that is.

"My parents never understood my love of aerials, and those who aren't in the community tend to get annoyed when I go on a tangent talking about all the different apparatuses, or the history of aerial arts. I know it can be boring for people who aren't into it. I just love it so much."

He shook his head. "Boring is the last thing I'd call it, and anyone who dismisses your passion is the one who's boring. Special interests are great. One time in high school I saw a video about deck building. Something in me clicked and I spent the next month hyperfocused on learning every step of the deck-building process from ground prep, to post holing, to framing and sealant."

She grinned up at him, a teasing light entering those dark brown eyes. "Does that mean you accept the bet?"

Didn't seem like she was going to let this go. He chuckled softly, admiring her determination to get him to try aerials. Yeah, not going to happen. But since he had extreme confidence that while this truck's tacos smelled amazing, they certainly weren't going to be the best he'd ever had, there was no risk in saying yes. But…

"What do I get if I win?" He tilted his head and stared down at her, way down because the petite woman was at least a foot shorter than his six-one.

Her face scrunched up as he posed the question.

"It doesn't matter because I'm going to win."

"So confident," he laughed softly. "But that's not a very fair bet. There have to be stakes. You could lose."

She waved a hand in the air as if the very idea was preposterous. "Not going to happen, but I suppose you are right. The bet needs to be even."

The line moved ahead again. Piper scooted forward, leaving a larger-than-usual amount of space between her and the customer in front of her. The guy behind him was so close he could smell the dude's breath. It wasn't pleasant. But it didn't bother him too much to be packed tightly in line. Piper seemed to be bothered by it very much, judging from the way she intentionally left space and the way her fingers kept tapping against her thighs. He wished the line would move faster so they could grab their food and move somewhere with less people.

An idea popped into his head. The words were out of his mouth before he thought about it. "I can grab the tacos if you want to find a place for us to sit and eat."

Piper's thoughtful expression fell into one of confusion. "What?"

Clearing his throat, he lowered his voice and leaned down so the people around them wouldn't hear. "You seem...uncomfortable. I don't mean to assume, but my brother Mal hates crowds too. Gets kind of tense and fidgety in them."

His gaze moved down to her fingers, which stopped tapping immediately and closed into a fist. Damn, he'd made it worse. Now he'd implied she should hide herself. Not his intentions at all.

"I didn't mean to upset you," he said. "I simply wanted to give you an option if waiting in line was overwhelming you."

A million emotions passed over her face. They flew by in a rush, too fast for him to identify them. Finally, she graced him with a soft, somewhat sad smile.

"It's too bad you don't believe in love because you'd make great boyfriend material."

He snorted out a laugh. Yeah, that was that problem. He'd been a great boyfriend before, but each time, no matter how caring and attentive he'd been, every relationship had been missing that spark. Considering each of his exes found the spark with their very next partner, Kell had come to the conclusion he was the flint to start the fire...

For everyone else but him.

Terrible but true.

"Thank you for the offer," Piper continued. "But I'm okay. Do I hate crowds? Yes, but the tacos are worth it. And don't think you're getting out of the bet by being sweet, mister."

She pointed a finger at him, the teasing light entering her eyes again.

Grateful that he hadn't offended her, he teased back. "Technically I haven't agreed to the bet yet. You're still avoiding the stakes if I win."

"Never gonna happen, but okay. What do you want if you win?"

A date with you.

No. He couldn't say that. Piper had made her stance on dating versus hookups very clear. As much as he'd love to take her on a date that ended with making her breakfast at his place the following morning, he knew it would only end badly. Considering he'd be seeing her every day for the next six weeks, a situation like that could get uncomfortable fast. Plus, there was the pesky little detail of the huge secret he was keeping from her.

The second she found out he not only knew about the theater sale but was the realtor in charge of selling it…she'd hate him for sure.

His gut cramped. Bitter anger and resentment at Donald rose again. Damn the man for being a coward and not telling his tenant he was selling. And damn himself for signing that stupid contract with the NDA.

Nothing to do about it now but move forward.

"Hmm, let's see." He stroked his chin, thinking about something appropriate he could use as betting stakes. "Oh, I know. If I win you have to let me help you fill the seats for your show."

She blinked. "I don't think you know how betting works. It sounds like I win in both outcomes."

True. But he couldn't tell her he was feeling guilty. This was penance for his upcoming offence. Perhaps if he helped her sell out the show, she'd have enough funds to find a new theater and wouldn't hate him. He had no idea why he cared so much if this woman he barely knew hated him or not, but he did.

He shrugged, not wanting to reveal anything. "If you don't want to bet then—"

"Nope," she quickly interrupted. "Bet's on, sucker."

She stuck out her hand. He grinned, grasping it with his own. His large hand engulfed hers as they shook. He could feel the coarse calluses on her palm, no doubt from her aerial training. Despite the roughness, her hand was warm and delicate. The feel of her skin against his heated his entire being. A bolt of desire shot straight down to his core. Damn. Why did he have to be attracted to the one woman he couldn't have?

She sucked in a harsh breath, her eyes filling with need as her hand pressed against his. He pulled her closer, his body refusing to listen to his brain. Thinking only of the woman it wanted in front of him. Piper went willingly. Stepping closer to him until their bodies were a hairbreadth apart. Her lips parted, catching his attention with their plump, pink temptation. His head started to lean down of its own accord. Her eyes went hazy, lids dropping as she rose on her toes and—

"Next in line!"

The shout broke the spell.

Piper's eyes opened wide as her cheeks flushed a pretty pink. She dropped his hand and stepped forward toward the order window, avoiding eye contact. Damn, that was a close one. They'd almost forgotten they were all wrong for each other.

"A number three, please and—" She paused, turning to him. "What do you want?"

You.

"Dealers choice," he said to her, unable to think of anything but the huge mistake they almost made.

She nodded, turning back to the man in the truck. "Two number threes, please."

He reached for his wallet, but Piper paid before he could get it out.

"I got it." She waved him away when he tried to give her cash. "I invited you so it's my treat. Unless you hate the tacos. Then that's blasphemy and you can pay me back."

He chuckled, grateful the awkwardness had passed, and she was back to teasing again.

Their order was up in record time. He grabbed the two paper containers each holding three delicious-looking corn tortillas filled with ground meat, chopped onions and peppers, slices of avocado and some green on top that looked like cilantro. He brought one container to his face and sniffed.

"Yup, cilantro," he confirmed.

"Oh, shoot!" Piper stared at him in horror as he placed the dishes down on the picnic table she'd picked out for them to enjoy their lunch. "I forgot to ask if you're a cilantro-tastes-like-soap person before ordering."

"Worried you'll lose the bet?" He grinned, taking a seat on the bench.

She sat across from him, grabbing her food and pulling it to her. "Ha! Not a chance. Even cilantro haters love these tacos. But I might suggest you pick it off if you hate it."

He grabbed one of the tacos in his hand and shook his head. "No soapy taste for me. I love cilantro."

"Oh good, me too." Lifting her own taco, she raised it high in the air. "To getting you up in a hoop, or sling, or maybe loops."

He wasn't sure what that last one was, but unfortunately for her he wasn't getting up in any of them because she wasn't going to win. Still, he raised his own taco.

"To me filling your theater on opening night."

She rolled her eyes, bringing the taco to her lips and biting down. A soft, pleasure filled moan left her lips as she took her first bite. He shifted on the bench, reminding himself she was enjoying the food and his body needed to chill. To distract himself he took his own bite.

One second in, he knew he was screwed.

Flavors exploded on his tongue. Rich, meaty, spicy, pure heaven wrapped in a corn tortilla. His eyes closed as a deep moan came from his own throat. Piper had been right. These were the best damn tacos he'd ever had in his life.

Oh no.

He opened his eyes to find her staring at him with triumphant glee all over her face.

"Come on," she prodded. "Say it."

Not wanting to admit defeat yet, he shoved the rest of the taco in his mouth, enjoying the delectable taste of his doom before responding. "Fine. You're right. These are the best tacos I've ever had."

"Yes! I told you. Ooh, I can't wait to get you in the air."

He wondered how long he could hold this off. Something told him the experience was going to be extremely embarrassing. Hoping to distract her from making any solid plans, he came up with an idea.

"I'm still helping you fill seats for the show."

She paused with her taco halfway to her mouth. "You really don't know how betting works, do you? Suit yourself. Honestly, I can use all the help I can get, and you need to get more familiar with aerials anyway."

He ignored the excited little squeak as she added that last bit and focused instead on how he could help her sell out her show to absolve his betrayal.

CHAPTER EIGHT

"Who is the hottie handyman?"

Piper glanced over at the question. Rachel, her best friend and ex-girlfriend, sat on the stage, stretching out her straddle. Rachel's dark green eyes were curious as they stared up into the audience where Kell was fixing some of the broken carpet grippers on the stairs. Not top priority fixes, but Piper had tripped and nearly tumbled down them yesterday. Kell had seen and moved the repair up his list immediately, claiming it needed to be fixed before the show so no one in the audience hurt themselves.

She hadn't argued with that. The last thing she needed on top of all her money troubles was an injury lawsuit.

"Shh!" She scowled at Rachel. "Not so loud! He'll hear you."

"And he is…"

"Kellen. Donald hired him to fix up stuff around here."

Rachel let out a relieved sigh, pointing and flexing her toes as she continued to stretch. "Finally! I swear I didn't think that jerk was ever going to fix anything around here."

"Same," Piper agreed, moving her legs together and bringing her nose to her knees. Her voice came out slightly muffled as she continued to explain Kell's presence. "But I guess all my emails finally got through. He showed up the other day and has been hard at work ever since."

With each passing day her suspicions that Kell was a spy

started to slip away. She was still being vigilant, but a small flicker of trust started to grow. Flaming brighter with every sweet deed he completed.

"Sounds like Donald finally hired a competent contractor."

"And he's sweet too, considering how we met." Oops! She hadn't meant to say that out loud. Too late. Rachel's head whipped her way, eyes wide.

"How did you meet?"

A soft groan left her. She glanced around the stage where the cast was warming up for the afternoon's rehearsal. Knowing her best friend wasn't going to let this go, she lowered her voice and spoke.

"I kind of thought he was a robber and hit him with a Wiffle Ball bat."

"What?"

"Shh!"

A few curious eyes, including Kell's, glanced their way. Piper ducked her head, deepening her stretch and hiding her embarrassment.

"You have to tell me everything," Rachel said gleefully. "Right now."

With a heavy sigh, she launched into the explanation of the morning she'd heard noises on the stage and thought Kell was there to steal things...or worse.

"He was very sweet about it when I explained," she said after getting the whole story out. "He even apologized for scaring me and asked me to show him every fix needed, including the ones Donald didn't mention."

"Wow, talk about a white knight."

"That's what I said." She shared a grin with her bestie as they moved on to cat-cow stretches. "Kell's been great, going above and beyond to fix whatever needs to be done even if it's not on Donald's list."

"Kell?" Rachel arched one dark eyebrow.

She shrugged, arching her back to stretch the muscles. "His friends call him Kell."

"Ooh, so you two are friends then?"

Glancing at Rachel under her arm, she took in her best friend's cheeky grin. She knew that look. Sadly, Rachel was about to be very disappointed.

"Get that thought right out of your head. He's a true-love hater."

Rachel frowned, moving into frog pose. "What does that mean?"

She shrugged, following into the position to stretch her hip flexors. "We were talking about the show the other day and he said *Romeo and Juliet* is a tragedy, not a romance."

Rachel lifted one shoulder. "Technically he's right."

She glared. "Not you too."

"Face it, babe. You've always been a romantic."

One of the reasons they worked as friends, but not lovers. Rachel was a realist. While she could handle Piper's romantic notions as a friend, she hadn't been able to deal with them as a girlfriend. A few weeks into their relationship they decided to call it off and be friends instead.

"But the play is one of Shakespeare's tragedies," Rachel went on.

"Whatever." Piper waved away the very logical point. "It doesn't matter. He said he doesn't date. He's not into labels."

"Ah, commitment phobia?"

Piper shrugged. Possibly, but she sensed it went deeper than that. Not like she'd ever find out. No sense in getting closer to someone who laid out their feelings on dating and relationships so clearly. She might be an optimist, but she was not going to jump into anything that was doomed from the start.

"Then he's not your Prince Charming," Rachel continued. "Maybe he could be a Prince Just for a Night or Two?"

Piper shook away the tempting thought. "You know I can't do that."

She'd tried casual hookups. It never worked. She was a heart-on-her-sleeve type of gal. Feelings always got involved, whether she wanted them to or not. She couldn't help it. Not once had she been with someone where it didn't turn into a relationship of at least nine months. Rachel was the only exception, and they turned into besties, which was another kind of loving relationship anyway.

"I'm sorry, babe. He sounded good for you."

She thought so too, which is why it sucked so much to have to see him every day. Temptation in a tool belt.

"And it's about time for you to move on from Larry the Loser." Rachel growled out the name, bitter and harsh.

Her best friend knew all about how her ex took all the money and ran. She didn't know Piper was living in the theater. It was too embarrassing to admit. Besides, she knew if she told, Rachel would insist she come stay with her and her girlfriend in their place. A five-hundred-square-foot studio apartment. No thank you. She was fine where she was as long as no one found out.

"I'll find someone, eventually." Just not Kell. A sad sigh left her.

"Well," Rachel said, moving up on her knees to stretch her arms. "I think that—"

The rest of her statement was interrupted by a very loud curse and the sounds of tools being dropped. Piper sprang to her feet, jumped off the stage and rushed into the audience, up the stairs to where Kell was gripping one hand tightly to his chest.

"Kell! What happened?"

She knelt by his side, heart stopping in her chest as she spied dark red liquid seeping out from his clenched fist through his work glove.

"Damn carpet runner slipped and got me. Sliced clean through my glove." He shook his head. "Sorry about cursing. I'm fine."

"You're bleeding," she pointed out.

Kell released his fist, unclenching and pulling off his glove. She gasped at what he revealed. A four-inch slice ran from the bottom of his palm up to nearly his pinkie. Blood oozed from the cut, terrifying her with the sight.

"We need to get you to a hospital."

He huffed out a small laugh. "For a little cut? It's fine."

"You might need stitches," she insisted.

He shook his head. "The glove took the worst of it. I'll need some butterfly bandages at most."

Stubborn man! She glanced down at the carpet runner. Half of it was raised in the air. It looked like a snake, poised for another attack. There wasn't much blood on it, but the silver metal was speckled with dark brown rust spots.

"What about tetanus? That thing looks rusty. When was your last tetanus shot?"

Kell frowned, eyes narrowing in thought. "I guess it has been a while."

"That settles it. Hospital." Tetanus was no joke. "Let's go."

He blinked up at her as she stood, holding out her hand. "You don't have to take me. I can drive myself."

"With that hand? No. Safety first. I'm driving."

A small grin tugged at the corner of his lips. He nodded toward the stage where every single cast member was watching them with rapt attention.

"What about your class?"

She shrugged. "This isn't a class. It's rehearsal for the show and Rachel can take over." She turned, using her stage voice to loudly call out. "Rachel, can you take over rehearsal? We have an emergency."

"Not an emergency," Kell grumbled. "Barely a scratch."

She rolled her eyes. Save her from stubborn men.

"Can do, Piper," Rachel answered, then told everyone on stage to follow her in warm-ups.

"There," she said, turning back to Kell and holding out her hand again. "That's settled, now I'm taking you to the hospital. Let's go, mister."

Kell grinned, the sight making her stomach flip-flop. She told her body to cool it. She was just helping. Like she would for anyone who got hurt in her proximity.

But when Kell slipped his uninjured hand into hers, allowing her to help him up, a sharp zing of heat and desire engulfed her. She quickly dropped his hand once he stood. Dang it. She really wished she could do casual hookups, but she knew herself better. One night in Kell's bed and she'd fall hard. Since the man didn't do forever, she'd be left with nothing but a broken heart and she wasn't sure how many more of those she could take.

CHAPTER NINE

This was ridiculous.

Kell sat on the firm hospital bed. The paper stuff they used over the bed crinkled underneath him with any slight movement. It was sweet that Piper was worried about him, but this rush to the hospital had been entirely unnecessary. He could have wrapped the wound up, finished the workday and headed over to get a tetanus shot after.

"I don't think it needs any stitches," Dr. Walker said, examining his hand. "Surgical glue should be sufficient. You say you cut it on a piece of metal?"

"That's right." He nodded to the middle-aged Black man, who noted something on the computer next to the bed. "I was repairing a carpet runner. The edging trim slipped and got me clean through my glove."

Dr. Walker nodded. "And when was your last tetanus shot?"

"I'm afraid I can't remember, but I believe it was more than ten years ago."

The sound of clacking filled the room as the doctor typed something into the system. "I see. Then you'll need a booster shot. Better to be safe when dealing with things like this."

He nodded his agreement, swearing he heard a soft "I told you so" from the side. He glanced over to where Piper was sitting in a chair against the wall. Her face held a smug look of vindication, but her eyes were filled with worry.

For him?

He wasn't sure how to feel about that. Usually, he was the one worrying about everyone else. It was a strange feeling having someone fret over him. He didn't know what to do with it.

"I've put it in the system. A nurse should be in soon to administer the shot and we'll get you all fixed up."

"Thank you, Doctor Walker."

Dr. Walker smiled at them both before heading out of the room. Silence filled the air. He could feel the energy thicken, heard the tapping of Piper's foot against the hard floor.

"It's okay," he said with a soft chuckle. "You can say it."

There was a beat of silence. Then.

"I told you so."

A squeak sounded as she rose from the chair and came over to stand in front of him. Concern marred her brow as she frowned.

"I told you this would need to be fixed."

Hoping to tease the worry from her eyes, he lifted one finger, pointing to his injured hand. "Technically you said I would need stitches, but I don't."

Her eyes narrowed. "But you do need a tetanus shot. I was right about that."

He shrugged. "You got me there."

"Ha!" Now it was her turn to point. "Admit I was right about going to the hospital, just like I was right about the tacos."

He waved his uninjured hand in the air. "Eh, I still say I could have waited until I was done."

"And bleed all over everything?" Her eyes widened. "You can't be serious."

He wasn't. She had been right to stop work and head to the hospital right away, but the more he argued with her, the more the worry in her eyes turned to exasperation. He'd much rather she be annoyed with him than fear for him. He didn't want Piper to be stressed, especially over him. There was no need for anyone to worry over him. He could take care of himself.

"Why are men the most stubborn creatures on the planet?" She threw her hands up in exasperation. "I swear you could be drowning in a pool of quicksand a woman warned you about and you'd all insist it was nothing more than a child's sandbox. I can't believe…"

Her words trailed off as she stared at him, light dawning in her eyes.

"Wait a minute. Are you disagreeing with me as a distraction?"

Busted.

"You seemed worried," he said with a small shrug. "There's no need, I'm fine. And I noticed since we got here you looked…tense."

She grabbed a lock of hair, twisting the dark brown strands highlighted with streaks of blue around her finger as her eyes cast downward.

"I don't like hospitals. They can be…overwhelming. The lights are always too bright and there's harsh chemical smells. Plus, the beeping of the machines and loud announcements over the speaker. It's quite the sensory overload."

"Then why did you insist on coming with me?" If she hated hospitals that much, why was she here?

She shrugged, refusing to look at him. "You couldn't drive yourself with that hand, and it happened at my theater so it's my responsibility."

Not even close. Donald owned the theater so any issue with his injury would fall on him. Irrelevant in this case anyway. This had been entirely his fault. A moment of carelessness. Besides, he was fine. A little glue, a small shot and he'd be right as rain.

"Thank you for coming," he said softly, realizing how hard this had been for her to do. "If you want to take off, I'm good now."

Her head snapped up, fingers dropping from her hair. "But how will you get back to your car? It's at the theater still."

They'd taken her car here. The thing was so old and worn down he was surprised it still worked.

"I can call a rideshare."

She shook her head. "No. I'm fine. You're almost done anyway. We're just waiting for the—"

Before she could finish her statement there was a knock on the door. It opened and the doctor came in, followed by a tall white man in nurse scrubs who looked so young Kell wondered if the guy graduated last week.

"Okay," Dr. Walker said, sitting on the round stool and wheeling it over to where Kell sat. "Let's get you fixed up and on your way."

The nurse held a tray with a variety of items on it. After the doctor washed his hands and put gloves on, he cleaned Kell's wound again. Next, he pressed the skin together as he moved the tube of surgical glue along the cut. Kell still maintained that he could have done this himself with a few butterfly bandages. The glue seemed like overkill. But the relieved smile on Piper's face as the doctor finished up was worth the fuss he decided.

"And now Brandon here will give you your shot," Dr. Walker said, standing. "I want you to keep the wound dry for the next forty-eight hours. After that you can shower, but no soaking the area. Pat dry and don't pick at the glue. It will dissolve on its own in a week or two. Keep an eye out for any sign of infection. If it appears red or starts oozing or you contract a fever, come back in right away, understand?"

He nodded. "Yes, sir."

"I'll leave you to it. You both have a better night."

Dr. Walker left and Brandon took his spot on the stool. The young man opened another alcohol wipe and cleaned a small spot on Kell's upper arm. Next, he reached for the small syringe on the silver tray. Kell heard Piper suck in a sharp breath. He glanced over at her to see her face go pale.

"Hey," he said, holding out his hand. "You okay?"

She grasped his hand tightly, nearly cutting off the circulation with her grip.

"I don't like needles."

He laughed in surprise. "Really? You have like a dozen tattoos."

She glanced down at the flowers cascading down her arm. "That's different."

"How?" He tugged her to the side, positioning his body so she had to focus on his face and couldn't see the nurse, needle poised above his arm.

"Tattoo needles are in that gun thing. You can't really see them. And after I get cool art forever."

"Fair point, but after a shot you get protection from diseases."

"I didn't say I didn't get them," she argued. "I said I don't like them and—"

"All done," Brandon announced, putting a bandage over the injection site. "I have a printout here with all the instructions the doctor told you. Feel free to give us a call if you have any questions and remember to look out for signs of infection. Y'all are free to go."

"Thank you, I will."

The nurse gathered the tray of supplies and left the room. Once they were alone again, Piper narrowed her eyes at him.

"You did it again, didn't you? With the tattoo needle stuff. You were trying to distract me?"

"Maybe." He squeezed her hand. "It worked, didn't it?"

A soft smile graced her face. "Thank you."

She squeezed back before releasing his hand and stepping back. "Should we get you back to your car?"

He nodded. "And you back to rehearsal."

Piper glanced at the clock on the wall. "It'll be over by now."

Damn. Now he felt terrible. He knew how important this show was to her. "I'm sorry for causing you to miss it."

She waved away his apology. "It's fine. Rachel can handle things for the night."

"Is she your assistant?"

"Assistant, best friend, best ex, and all-around angel."

"Best ex?" He tilted his head at the phrase. "Do you have a worst ex?"

She barked out a laugh that was in no way humor filled. "Only about a dozen of them. I don't have the best track record when it comes to dating."

Why on earth not? She was funny, smart, beautiful and talented. If he believed in love, he was sure he'd fall right at her feet. He must have looked confused, because Piper swallowed, cheeks pinkening as she explained.

"People find me charming at first, but then as time goes on, I guess the charm turns to annoyance. They think I'm putting on an act and then seem to get disappointed when it's like, no that's my real personality. The Manic Pixie Dream Girl problem."

"I'm sorry, what?"

She grabbed a lock of hair and twirled it again. "It's this theory I have. You know how the Manic Pixie Dream Girl character is always this quirky girl who does random things and has weird interests?"

He nodded. He wasn't a huge movie guy, but he'd seen enough to understand the concept.

"I think Manic Pixie Dream Girls are just autistically coded women. But in real life, the reality of our 'quirks' don't go away after a ninety minute movie run time. The allure quickly fades for a lot of people, and I turn from 'charming' to 'annoying' real quick."

He frowned, hating that she had to deal with that. Hating that people were so shallow and uninformed. Her theory made sense. It also made him angry. For her and every other person who had to deal with people treating them that way.

"I take it Rachel didn't find you annoying?" If she didn't, he couldn't imagine her being labeled the best ex.

"No, sadly we just realized we worked better as friends than girlfriends. To be honest, it's usually the guys I date who get annoyed with me when it turns out I'm not their quirky muse or whatever."

"Their loss," he grunted, angry at every single one of those idiots who had Piper in their arms and let her go. If he wasn't cursed by love, he'd snatch Piper up and never let her go.

She shrugged, clearly unable to see her worth thanks to the jerks of her past. He wished he could find every one of them and give them a lesson in manners.

"Should we head out?" he asked, desperate to change the topic and get that doleful look out of Piper's eyes.

"Yes, please. I am so ready to leave."

He rose from the hospital bed. His stomach cramped, a soft rumble sounding. Glancing at the clock, he frowned.

"It's past dinner." No wonder his stomach was pitching a fit. "Should we grab a bite before heading back? My treat."

Piper waved away his offer. "Oh, that's not necessary."

"I know, but I want to. Think of it as a thank-you for taking me to hospital."

She chuckled. "You mean *insisting* you go to the hospital."

"Hey, you were right."

"Naturally." She smiled.

He laughed, loving her charm. How could anyone find her annoying? Idiots.

"Plus, I owe you for the tacos," he added.

"Well, when you put it that way," she said, tapping her finger on her chin. "I supposed we could grab a bite."

A huge grin split his lips as they made their way to the door and out of the room. Spending more time alone with this woman was the very last thing he should do. They'd already agreed they were too different in the relationship department. They wanted different things, so starting anything was a recipe for disaster. And yet he couldn't stop this driving pull tugging at him whenever he so much as thought about her.

This was bad, he knew that.

Then why did it feel so right?

CHAPTER TEN

PIPER FOLLOWED KELL'S directions down the city streets. When he asked her where she wanted to go, she told him to pick. Decisions were a bit beyond her brain capacity right now. Hospitals were always unpleasant for her. Not only was she overwhelmed and her senses frazzled, but they also brought back memories of her emergency appendectomy in the sixth grade. Everything had turned out fine, but the experience had been far from pleasant and left a lasting bad memory for hospitals in general.

"The restaurant is on the right, just here," Kell said, pointing with his uninjured hand. "There's a lot you can park in after the building."

Thank goodness. Parking in Denver was a nightmare. Any place that had a lot downtown was prime real estate. Even the theater lacked in that area. Their tiny lot only held about a dozen cars. Thankfully the grocery store next door didn't mind if patrons parked in their lot for shows. She wished Donald would put a parking structure on their lot to hold more cars, but considering he'd only just agreed to the fixes she'd been asking for for years, she doubted that would ever happen.

"Yup, just turn in here," Kell said as they arrived.

Piper parked her car, glancing up at the side of the brick building adorned with a stunning mural of a large humpback whale swimming gracefully in the ocean. The letters of the restaurant's name swirled around in the water.

"The Blue Pearl. I've been wanting to try this place."

The seafood restaurant had recently opened, garnering great press. She'd been meaning to try it as she loved seafood but was unfortunate to live in a landlocked state where it wasn't a go-to delicacy.

"Glad I picked it then." Kell smiled at her. "Shall we?"

They got out of the car and headed toward the front doors. It was midweek, past the dinnertime rush, but the new restaurant was still packed. Her stomach rumbled, nerves rising again as they had to push through a crowded entryway to make it up to the host stand in order to put their names on the list.

"Kellen Thorson, two," Kell said, smiling pleasantly at the white woman with dark hair slicked back in a low ponytail standing at the podium.

The hostess's smile was tight as she tapped away on the tablet in her hand. Clearly it was a stressful and busy night. Piper could relate. She'd done her time in the serving trenches years ago. It had been awful. People were the worst when it came to eating out. In her opinion, everyone should be required to work a customer service job for at least two years so they knew what it was like. Then maybe there wouldn't be so many rude customers making people cry just for doing their job.

"I'm sorry, we have a forty-five-minute wait time, but—oh." The woman blinked as she stared at the screen in front of her. "Mr. Thorson. Yes, right this way."

"Thank you."

Thank you? What? What about the forty-five-minute wait?

Piper frowned, confusion pushing out the frazzled energy as Kell grabbed her hand and followed the hostess. The woman weaved around the tables in the large main room. Piper caught bits of conversation from the tables they passed, but what she really wanted to know was what the heck just happened. How did they skip the line?

They finally stopped near the very back of the large room. A small booth table sat in a corner, slightly secluded from the rest of the dining area. The high walls of the booth surrounding three-quarters of the table provided a barrier from the sights and sounds from the rest of the room.

"Here you are," the hostess said, motioning to the table. "Your server will be right with you."

"Thank you." Kell nodded, motioning for Piper to sit first.

Still confused over what was going on, she slid into the booth, breathing a sigh of relief when the noisy clatter of conversation and eating dimmed. Kell slid in on the other side of the booth, picking up the menu the hostess had left on the table for them and perusing it.

She waited exactly three seconds before getting to the point. "What was that?"

Kell tilted his menu down, blinking at her with confusion. "Huh?"

"That." She waved a hand to where the hostess had just been.

"I'm not following."

Really? Or was he acting bewildered on purpose?

"This is a brand-new restaurant," she started. "It's been featured in Westword, on the news, even on that fancy cuisine blog Rachel follows. You saw the crowd up front and the hostess said there was a forty-five-minute wait time. But you give your name, and *poof*, suddenly we have a table right away."

"I always have a table right away here."

He said it like it was the most normal thing in the world. Like it wasn't weird that he had "a table" at one of the hottest restaurants in the city.

"And how did you manage that? Did you sell your soul or something?"

He chuckled, putting the menu down and placing his forearms on the table. He leaned across the tabletop. She mimicked his movement until their faces were inches apart.

"I'd tell you," he whispered in a low, seductive voice. "But then I'd have to kill you."

The corner of his lips ticked up in a playful smile. She grabbed her menu and lightly smacked him on the shoulder. The black cardstock made a small thunking sound as it struck its mark.

"Hey!" He laughed, sitting back against the booth's back. "I'm injured, you can't hit an injured man."

"I hit your uninjured side and you're being willfully obtuse! Now tell me why you can waltz into the hottest restaurant in the city and have a standing reservation."

He shrugged, picking up his menu again and scanning it as he answered her.

"My brothers and I…helped the owner with this place so he made sure to have this back table ready for us whenever we wanted. The staff also uses it if we're not here."

"You guys did contracting work here?"

He shrugged. "Among other things."

That sounded…odd, but then again, she knew all about tit for tat among business owners. She had her own "I scratch your back, you scratch mine" deals with a few places. Like the yoga supply store that gave her students a discount or the lighting company that got free show tickets in exchange for new gels and bulbs. You had to hustle to stay in business these days.

She picked up her menu again to glance over the selection. Her eyes nearly fell out of her head as she saw the prices. Holy cow! Nothing was under thirty dollars. Not even the salads. What in the world could be in a salad to make it thirty-five dollars?

"My treat, remember?" Kell said, giving her a knowing look.

He must have seen the sticker shock on her face.

She leaned in close again, not wanting to offend any of the

workers should they pass by and hear. "Kell, this place is ridiculously expensive. I can't let you cover my meal."

It was too much, even for friends.

He waved away her protest. "It's fine. You got the tacos, remember?"

"The tacos were six bucks. Just breathing in this place will cost you sixty."

He laughed softly, placing his menu back on the table and staring at her with a soft warmth in his bright blue eyes.

"Piper, I promise you, I can afford it."

"How?" Her eyes roamed over the prices again, hoping she'd misread the totals. Nope, still ridiculously expensive. "I know what it's like to be a small business owner, Kell. I don't know how much contractors make, but I do know what a tightwad Donald is, and I can guarantee you he's not paying you splurge-at-seafood-restaurant prices."

She desperately wanted to eat here, but not if it meant putting Kell's finances in harm's way. Her finances being what they were, she would never do that to another person. A thought occurred to her.

"Does the owner give you a discount on food too?" Seemed like overkill for doing his job, but maybe Kell and his brothers hadn't charged the guy at all for their work and this was how he paid them back.

"No." Kell shook his head. He focused on his menu, refusing to look at her. His brow furrowed. "My family…is comfortable."

She snorted. "That's something rich people say when they don't want to admit they're rich. You're a trust fund baby then?"

He scowled. "No. Not exactly. My family's businesses do very well."

"'Do very well,'" she muttered under her breath. "More rich-person talk. How rich are we talking? Millionaire? Billionaire?"

"Didn't anyone ever tell you it's not polite to discuss finances?"

Checking out the meal options, she lifted one shoulder in a small shrug. "Yes, but no one has ever been able to explain why."

Saying something was a rule meant nothing without the reasoning behind it. She never understood why people thought it was okay to just state something without explaining why. An old therapist told her that was a trait of her autism. She considered it common sense. Something a lot of people lacked, in her opinion.

Kell stared for a moment, tilting his head slightly as the corner of his mouth moved up in a knowing smile. "Do you have a problem with rich people, Piper?"

"Only when they hoard their wealth at the expense of others suffering," she answered truthfully. "In my experience, most rich people are selfish jerks."

He laughed. "Knowing a lot of them, I have to agree. But I hope I'm the exception to the rule. Yes, my family has money, but our parents also insisted we work hard and give back. Which is why my brothers and I run a housing charity. We buy abandoned properties and fix them up, then we donate those houses to unhoused families in need and take care of the property tax as well."

Her heart melted a little at his reveal. "You do?"

He nodded. "We've housed nearly fifty families since we started the charity."

Well, shoot! She'd been a little excited to find out he was rich. It was something she could use to combat her rising desire for this man. If he was a trust fund baby, she could put him in the category of rich snob who didn't care about those around them. But it sounded like Kell and his brothers cared deeply about helping those in need. Dang it! Why did he have to be a love hater? Every new fact she learned about him set him firmly in her Mr. Right box.

Every one except the big one.

He didn't believe in happily-ever-after.

Frustration at her conundrum mounting, she pushed it aside and focused on what Kell had revealed about his charity work.

"That's amazing, Kell. I guess that means you're not a completely horrible rich person. You're more like Ebenezer Scrooge, post ghost haunting."

He laughed, the rich, deep sound vibrating from her chest all the way down to her toes. Warming up all the places in between.

"Thank you. I try to keep Christmas in my heart all year round."

She laughed along with him, glad they could remain friendly even as she started to realize how different they were. When their server came to take their orders, she tried to get away with ordering the cheapest thing on the menu.

"Piper," Kell said, seeming to stare into her very soul. "Please, order what you want."

She sighed, reminding herself this man was apparently loaded—or his parents were anyhow—and he could afford it. Far be it from her to argue with a man who wanted to spoil her. It didn't happen often…or at all really. She might as well take advantage of it while she could.

Taking a breath, she picked up her menu, eyes drawn to the entrée that had been making her mouth water for the past ten minutes. "I'll have the filet minion with the king crab legs. Medium please."

The server nodded. "And for you, sir?"

Kell handed over his menu, smiling at her. "Sounds delicious. I'll have the same."

"Excellent choice. Any wine for the table?"

Kell deferred to her. She shook her head.

"I'm fine with water, thank you."

She had to drive them back to the theater. One glass of wine wouldn't impair her abilities, but she was worried about lowering her defenses around this charming man. She already knew it was a bad idea to start anything. Add alcohol into the mix, and her brain would forget why he was all wrong for her.

CHAPTER ELEVEN

"Holy cow, don't tell the taco truck, but I think this is the most delicious thing I've ever eaten."

Kell chuckled, popping a bite of the tender, juicy meat into his mouth and chewing before swallowing. "Your secret is safe with me."

She laughed when he mimed zipping his lips. She was right. This food was amazing. He knew that because he came to eat here every week since it had opened. Guilt wormed its way into his gut, souring the delicious meal as he recalled his earlier lie. Not a lie really, more of an omission. While it was true he and his brothers did a bit of work on this building when the owner bought it—they put in a top-of-the-line cooktop—that wasn't the only reason the Thorson brothers had their own standing reservation.

He had been the real estate agent responsible for finding and securing the purchase for the owner. He'd been so grateful for the amazing deal he'd promised the brothers a table whenever they wanted.

It wasn't that he wanted to lie to Piper. But he worried if she knew he was also one of the top property agents in the Denver Metro area, she'd get suspicious and start asking about Donald and his plans for the theater. Every fiber of his being wanted to shout out the secret he was keeping from her. It wasn't fair. She deserved to know. She deserved time to make plans. Damn Donald for making him sign that unscrupulous NDA. He never should have taken this job.

But then I wouldn't have met her.

He glanced across the table, watching as Piper dipped a piece of crab into the rich, melty butter. Her eyes lit up with hunger as she brought the bite to her mouth. Eyes closing, she let out a small moan of delight as she bounced up and down in her seat. Pure joy radiating off every inch of her. All from the simple act of eating delicious food. His body tightened with need as his heart swelled.

What was this woman doing to him?

"I can't believe you get to eat here whenever you want." Piper's eyes opened. "I bet this spot gets you a lot of action with the ladies." She waggled her eyebrows but then frowned. "Wait, do you even go on dates? I'm not sure how your deal works."

"My 'deal'?"

"Yeah." She waved a hand in his direction. "Your whole 'love doesn't exist' deal. That must make it hard to date. Do you date or do you just hook up? No judgment, just trying to figure it out."

She had certainly judged him a lot the other day when he said *Romeo and Juliet* was a tragedy, not a romance.

"Yes, I date." He smiled softly at her, grabbing his glass and drinking a sip of water before continuing. "But I make it very clear with the women I go out with that I don't do long-term. And to be completely honest, besides my brothers, you're the only other person who has eaten here with me."

She paused, forkful of roasted carrots halfway to her lips. Her mouth dropped open in surprise. "I am?"

He nodded. Shoving the bite into her mouth, she didn't say anything else. Her brow furrowed as if she was confused by this whole situation. *Join the club.* He had no idea what was going on. His brain knew they were incompatible—they wanted different things in life, they came from different backgrounds, he was withholding a giant secret from her. But the rest of him screamed at him to drop his silly "no dating" rule and take a chance on what he and Piper could be.

I can't.

Even if he wanted to, the curse would ensure it ended in disaster yet again.

"So why don't you date?" Piper popped an elbow on the table and placed her chin in her hand. "If you don't mind me asking."

A heavy sigh left him. Pushing away his plate, he leaned back against the padded booth.

"I'm cursed."

Her eyes widened. "Cursed?"

He didn't like talking about his odd past, but she deserved to know why he was so adamant about no forever.

"My high school girlfriend and I dated for four years. We were perfect together. Got along great, had chemistry. I thought we were headed toward marriage, but then our second year of college she told me the spark died. We were both stressed with classes, and I admit our relationship had veered more toward a close friendship than a relationship. We broke up but remained friends."

"That's nice," Piper noted. "Unless she broke up with you because she'd been cheating on you?"

"No, it wasn't like that. However, she did meet a guy two months after we broke up. They fell madly in love and were married within a year."

Her jaw dropped wide. "Woah! That's fast. Are they still together? Do you know?"

He nodded. Weirdly, he kept in touch with all his exes. That was part of the problem. "They are. Happily married with three rug rats."

"I'm sorry. I don't see how that makes you cursed—"

"She wasn't the only one," he interrupted her. "My next four girlfriends were the same exact thing. We'd date for a while, everything was going great. Chemistry fizzled. We broke up amicably and then *boom*, they'd find the love of their life right after me. I'm like some weird good luck love charm for everyone."

"Everyone except you," Piper said softly, understanding and sympathy filling her eyes.

He nodded. "A charm for them, a curse for me."

"I don't know that I believe in curses, but I can see how that would make someone resistant to relationships. But it's kind of sad you've given up on love. Love is the greatest thing in the world."

"Says the woman who admits she has a lot of bad exes." He raised one eyebrow. "Sounds like we have similar problems in the love department."

She waved away his rebuttal. "I know I've struck out in the relationship department a lot, but that doesn't mean I'm giving up. My grandparents were married for fifty years. When my grandfather looked at my grandmother, it was as if no one else was in the room. You could feel the love radiating off them. They passed within a day of each other because my grandpa couldn't live without Grandma. That's the kind of love I'm looking for."

Wow. That sounded amazing. His parents' marriage was pretty standard. They didn't argue, but they weren't overly expressive with each other. No wonder Piper was such a hopeless romantic with an example like her grandparents.

"Aren't you worried about being lonely forever?" she asked.

He shrugged. "I've got my family, friends, job and my charity work. There's love in all of that enough for me."

She remained silent, finishing off her meal to the sounds of the dinner rush dying down. Their server came back to take their plates and leave the bill. Piper tried to protest him paying, but he insisted, seeing as how she drove him to the hospital, and he'd ruined her rehearsal.

They got into her car and drove back to the theater, chatting about her time in a traveling circus. He loved the way her face lit up when she talked about her aerials. The passion she had for the art was contagious. It almost made him want to agree to their silly bet and get up in an apparatus.

Almost.

"Are you sure you're okay driving home?" Piper asked for the fourth time.

Kell chuckled. They were sitting in her car just outside the theater. Dinner had been amazing. Not only the food but the company too. He hated to go home, but it was the best thing—for both of them.

"I'll be fine. It doesn't even hurt anymore." He raised his bandaged hand and waved it around to prove it. "You get home safe. How far away do you live?"

She bit her lip, head swiveling away as she fiddled with the air vent by the side of the dash. "Oh, I'm super close. Don't worry about me. You take care of that hand and remember what the doctor said about signs of infection."

He chuckled softly. "Yes ma'am."

She rolled her eyes, but her lips curved into a smile. "Thank you for dinner. It was delicious."

"My pleasure."

The air in the car thickened as they stared at each other. He could feel the heat radiating off her body, see the desire darken her eyes. His hand rose of its own accord, fingers gently brushing her cheek. Her lips parted and a small whimper of need escaped them. Longing pulled at him to lean in closer and cover those lips with his own. Taste their sweetness.

But Piper pulled back.

Sadness filled her gaze as she stared back at him. "Good night, Kell."

He blinked, the spell broken as the reality of their situation reared its ugly head. Gracing her with a soft, sad smile of his own, he opened the car door and got out.

"Bye, Piper."

He got into his car and drove to his house. It was an older home he and his brothers had restored a few years ago. He lived in the heart of the city along with Cash while Mal had a place out in the mountains just outside Denver. As he unlocked his door, mind still preoccupied with Piper and how he'd almost kissed her like a fool, he didn't even notice the man sitting on his couch.

"Hey, dude."

Kell let out a shout of surprise that turned into a curse when he recognized the man with similar dark hair and features to his, sitting there, eating his chips.

"Dammit, Cash. What did I say about coming into my home and eating my food when I'm not here?"

"*Mi casa es su casa?*" Cash shrugged.

"Nice try, but you failed high school Spanish. Get your dirty feet off my coffee table."

"Whoa, who shoved a claw hammer up your butt today, big brother?"

He growled, a headache forming, pounding away at his temple. Younger siblings had the worst timing. It was like a curse. Cash rose from the couch and disappeared into the kitchen. He returned a moment later with two beers. Popping off the tops, he offered one to Kell.

"Spill it. Not the beer," Cash hurried to clarify. "Whatever is bothering you."

A heavy sigh filled Kell's chest as he sunk down onto the soft cushions of the couch. After taking a fortifying sip of his beer, he launched into everything from meeting Piper to their time hanging out, tonight's injury and dinner, and their discussion.

"Ah, you told her about your ridiculous 'curse' theory." Cash nodded.

Kell scowled at his brother. "It's not ridiculous. It's true. Once or twice, I'd say it's a coincidence, but five times? It's a pattern."

"Patterns can be broken." Cash shrugged. "If you like this woman, you should go for it. Maybe she's the one to break the curse or whatever fairy-tale nonsense you believe."

He shook his head. Cash didn't get it. Of course the middle Thorson brother, the playboy dreamer who fell in love every five seconds and fell out of love just as easily would think it's that simple. It wasn't. His curse wasn't the only issue here.

"What happens when she finds out Donald is selling the theater?"

Cash paused, beer halfway to his mouth. He winced, lowering the bottle. "Yeah. That does put a kink in things. She's gonna be mad, I bet."

More than mad. Furious, betrayed, scared…the last one worried him the most. Where would she go after she lost the theater? Would her business survive? What about all the people who benefited from her aerial classes?

"Maybe you can help her find a new theater?" Cash suggested.

He shook his head. Denver was a large city, but it wasn't like there were a bunch of vacant theaters just lying around waiting for tenants. Plus… "I doubt she'll want to talk to me after she finds out I'm the one selling the place."

"You could tell her," Cash suggested.

"You know I can't." As it was a family-run business, all the brothers knew every detail of their contracts. "If I tell Piper Donald is planning on selling the place and not renewing her lease, he can fire me and sue us. That puts Helping Homes at risk. I can't do that."

Their charity was too important. It helped so many people.

He couldn't risk all of them for her...no matter how badly he wanted to.

"Damn," Cash swore. "That is a rock and a hard place."

Tell me about it. He was screwed no matter what he did. What he figured would be an easy repair-and-sell job had turned into the biggest mess of his life, and for once he had no answers on how to solve it.

CHAPTER TWELVE

"IF YOU STARE at that man any harder your eyes are going to pop out of your head," Rachel whispered with a small chuckle.

Piper whipped her head around to glare at her supposed best friend. "I wasn't staring."

"You were, babe. Hard. Like mask dropping, unaware-of-your-surroundings staring."

One of the kids let out a shout of glee, diverting Piper's attention. She smiled as she watched the groups of eight-to-eleven-year-old children spin to their hearts' content in the aerial slings she'd hung for sensory class today. They were enjoying free play for the last ten minutes of class.

"I wasn't staring," she insisted again. "I was simply checking to see how he was doing today with work. The man was injured on the job. I don't want to…get sued."

A pathetic excuse for what she'd actually been doing—ogling those forearms out on full display—and one she knew Rachel would in no way buy.

"Yeah, I'm not buying it."

See?

"Besides." Rachel crossed her arms over her chest and arched one eyebrow. "Donald is the one who hired Kell, so he'd be the one to get sued. Not you."

She had a point.

"Ms. Piper, look what I can do!"

The high-pitched call of excitement drew her gaze as

Kelsey, a sweet nine-year-old girl with fire-red hair and a million freckles gracing her pale face flipped upside down in a mermaid-tail position and spin herself so fast Pipe's stomach started to turn. The joyful cries of happiness from the young girl made her heart swell.

This is why she loved her job. Not just to share her love of aerial arts, but for kids like Kelsey. When the young girl came to her first class, she'd been quiet, refusing to talk to anyone, almost fearful. But when she saw the other kids happily playing, receiving grace during a meltdown, and being allowed to be their enthusiastic authentic selves in her class, Kelsey had opened up. Piper understood that all too well. So many times as a child she'd been told to be quieter, calm down, stop acting so weird.

She always found it odd that society considered excitement and joy in something "weird." It took her years to realize the problem had never been her being too much. The problem lay with those who wanted to dim her light. She vowed to never make herself quieter or more palatable for others and she tried to instill that in these kiddos too.

"Great job, Kelsey!"

The young girl let out a shrieking giggle, which two of the kids echoed until the class was a fit of boisterous innocent laughter.

"Oops, now he's staring at you," Rachel said.

Piper's head moved of its own volition to where Kell was finishing up work in the audience. Heat burned her cheeks as she saw he was indeed staring at her with a warm smile on his handsome face. That smile should be illegal. She swore one day it was going to give her a heart attack.

Rachel laughed softly. "You both have it so bad."

"We do not," she protested, averting her gaze to focus on the kids again. "And even if we did, it's hopeless. I told you already."

"Yeah, yeah. He doesn't believe in love or dating." Rachel waved a hand in the air. "And you're not a hookup girl. But people can change."

"Ask permission, Caleb," Piper shouted to one of the boys who tried to grab another's sling and spin him. Giving a portion of her attention to Rachel, she asked, "You think I can change into a hookup queen?"

A sputter of laughter left Rachel's lips. "Queen? No, hun, you're too much of a romantic to ever be a hookup queen, but you might like it if you try it."

Now it was her turn to give an incredulous laugh. "I have tried it, and it resulted in a whirlwind relationship where he left town in the middle of the night." Leaving her homeless, but she hadn't shared that part with Rachel.

"Oh, right." Rachel's eyes darkened. "Loser."

Larry had been a loser. Of the highest degree. She would forever be embarrassed she let her romantic notions tip her over the edge with that man. Her quest to find a love like her grandparents' had caused her to pick some real duds. She needed to be smarter about picking partners, less emotional. Another reason she needed to ignore this incessant pull she felt toward Kell. On paper they were all wrong for each other.

"Then maybe Kell will change," Rachel offered. "You can be the one to open his heart and help him believe in true love."

How Piper wished that were true, but after hearing his reasoning last night she doubted anyone would ever get him to believe he wasn't cursed by love. Such a silly notion, but it was hard to argue with the facts. One partner finding forever love after a breakup was normal. Two was a coincidence. But five? She didn't know how to dispute that.

"I don't think anyone can." A heavy sigh left her as she glanced over at Kell sanding down the area he'd uncovered yesterday in anticipation of the new carpet runner he said was coming.

"That's too bad, because it appears plenty of people want to try."

She glanced at Rachel, who tilted her head to the side of the stage where the group of parents stood, waiting for the kids. Usually, the parents were busy taking pictures of the kids in the apparatuses, but today a number of the moms and a few of the dads were staring at Kell. Interest in their eyes. A dark wave of jealousy soured her gut. Ridiculous. She knew a few of those parents were single, and even the ones who weren't had every right to appreciate the handsome handyman. Being partnered didn't mean you stopped finding people attractive. And boy oh boy was Kell attractive. She didn't blame a single one of them, but she also couldn't stop the red-hot rage burning inside at the thought of Kell taking one of them home.

And that right there was why she couldn't pursue anything with Kell. Casual did not work for her. She didn't like sharing, and the thought of Kell hooking up with someone else while he was seeing her…no, she couldn't handle that.

"Hey, Piper." A rich, deep voice called her name.

She turned to see Kell standing at the base of the stage. He placed his forearms on the stage floor and leaned over, neck craning as he smiled up at her.

"Hi. Done for the day?"

He nodded. "Yeah. The new carpet won't get here until tomorrow and I don't want to start a new project until this one is finished, so I'm headed out."

It was nearly dinnertime anyway. Made sense. She was planning on calling it quits herself as this was her last class of the day.

"You ever thought of being on one of those fix-it-up shows, Kell?" Rachel asked, tilting her head toward the side of the stage where the parents stood. "You seem to have a rapt audience already."

Kell laughed, the sound tinged with discomfort. "Eh, not

for me. Showing off for the camera is more my brother Cash's style."

Seeing his discomfort struck a chord in Piper. She hated when people stared at her. Though usually for her it was because she was acting in a way that wasn't considered "normal." She moved her body, crouching down to block Kell from view and to save his poor neck from staring up so far.

"What time will the carpet be delivered tomorrow?"

"Bright and early. I should be here around eight, if that's okay with you?"

She nodded. There weren't any classes until ten, so his load in would be uninterrupted. She made a mental note to be up and ready for the day as if she'd already gotten here early. Though, with each passing day, her "spy for Donald" notion was seemingly sillier and sillier. She couldn't imagine sweet, honest Kell lying to her about his true intentions here. True, she'd been fooled by people before, but judging by his action, all the work he'd put in, all the times he listened to her and took her suggestions, he was the real deal. A simple contractor here to work on the theater. Whatever reason made Donald finally hire him she might never know, but she was grateful.

"That works. See you tomorrow, Kell."

"Until tomorrow, Piper."

He smiled, the sight nearly knocking her off her crouched feet. A deadly weapon, that smile.

"Bye, Rachel," he added with a small wave.

"See ya round, Kell."

He turned to leave, getting exactly two feet before a few of the kids shouted, "Bye, Mr. Fix It Man!"

Kell laughed, turning and waving at all the kids. "Keep spinning, kids, but no puking."

A chorus of giggles erupted onstage as the kids spun faster, trying to do exactly what Kell warned them not to.

Thankfully no one lost their lunch. Class ended with the kids happily dizzy and handed off to their parents. Rachel asked if Piper wanted to go to dinner, but she declined. All she really wanted was a hot shower and a good night's sleep.

If that night of sleep included naughty dreams about a certain handyman, she wouldn't say no to that either. Seemed like the only way she could have Kell was in her dreams.

Once everyone was gone and the theater was locked up, she went to her room. Tossing her clothes in her hamper, she wrapped a towel around herself, grabbed her shower caddy filled with shampoo, conditioner and bodywash, and headed to the locker room. Kell hadn't addressed the water heater issue yet, but there was always enough hot water for one twenty-minute shower. She longed for a good forty-five-minute steam session, but that would have to wait.

After she soaped up and rinsed, Piper grabbed her towel and ran it over her hair, getting the excess water out. Next, she dried off as best she could then wrapped the towel around her, securing it.

"Oh, shoot." She frowned, realizing she forgot the cotton T-shirt she used to wrap her hair up in after a shower to prevent frizz. "Dang it."

Her head was all over the place lately. She blamed a handsome handyman who thought he was cursed. Such a silly notion, but not unfounded. If only there was some way she could convince him. She grabbed her shower caddy and started toward her room. As she left the locker room and headed toward the small staircase where her secret room sat, she heard a noise.

Pausing, she held her breath, listening. Silence filled the back of the stage. The muted sounds of traffic filtered in through the windows, but nothing from inside. Had she imagined it?

She shook her head. "I must be tired."

Staring down at the floor so as not to step on anything, Piper started to make her way again through the darkness of the backstage. She was about three feet from the stairs when suddenly she saw a looming shadow two feet in front of her. Letting out a bloodcurdling scream, she hurled her shower caddy at it. The bottles went flying from the plastic bin, crashing to the floor with a thud and splat as one opened and soapy contents oozed out. The shadow ducked.

"Piper?" The shadow spoke with an achingly familiar voice.

"K… Kell?"

The shadow took a step forward into a small beam of light from a high window. The full moon illuminated his handsome and confused face.

"What are you doing here?" Kell asked.

Oh no! The jig was up.

CHAPTER THIRTEEN

DAMMIT, HE SCARED her again. He had to stop doing that. It would help if he knew she was going to be at the theater when no one was supposed to be here. Seriously, why was she here?

"What are you doing here?" She echoed his question back at him.

He lifted his tool bag.

"I forgot my tools." Not the first time his ADHD made him forget something important and had him turning around. "I'm sorry I scared you, but I didn't think anyone would be here. What are you doing here?"

Her mouth popped open, but no words came out.

The shock of finding her in the dark abating, he finally noticed what she was wearing…or more accurately, what she wasn't wearing. "And why are you in a towel?"

Heat scorched his body at the sight. Tiny drops of water ran down her bare arms, sliding amongst the colorful flowers inked on her skin like a beautiful garden. Her dark hair, hung in wet, messy tendrils around her bare face. The faded cotton towel wrapped around her came to her mid-thighs, revealing even more brilliant blooms cascading down her legs. She reminded him of one of those flower nymphs in a fairytale book of Greek Mythology his mother read him as a kid. Beautiful and magical.

Piper's cheeks flamed red. Her head ducked down, hand flying to the knot on the towel, gripping it tight.

"I was taking a shower. Obviously."

Obviously. He got that from the dripping water, the shower caddy she threw at him and the lack of clothing. That last one he was struggling with most. His body tightened with need, the desire for this woman he'd been fighting rising to the top, ready to explode. But he pushed it down. Clearly something was wrong if Piper was here taking a shower in the dark. His baser hormones could chill. He wasn't a creep. He was a grown man. He would control himself.

"I can see that, but why? Why are you showering here and not at home?"

Silence filled the air. He watched Piper's lips roll in, eyes darting side to side. He smelled the lie even before she spoke it.

"The hot water in my apartment is on the fritz. My landlord hasn't fixed it yet. Guess scummy landlords are everywhere, right?"

Her laughter fell flat. He didn't join in. One thing Kell had always been able to do was spot when someone was lying. His brothers hated it growing up. None of his exes had liked it either. Wasn't his fault he was a human lie detector. It came in handy a lot. Like now. Something was wrong. He needed her to tell him so he could help. Desperation pulled at him. He had to do something. The waves of anxiety pouring off her alarmed him.

"Piper."

"What?" She scowled at him, refusing to meet his eyes, defiance stiffening her spine. "I needed a shower and prefer them hot to cold, okay? I was just headed home after."

"Like that?"

"Of course not. I was gonna change."

"Why didn't you change in the locker room where the showers are?" Something about this whole setup smelled fishy. "Why are you backstage in nothing but a towel?"

A small hint of humor ticked up the corner of her mouth as she finally looked at him.

"I've been backstage in far less."

What now?

"This is the theater, Kell. Sometimes you have to do a quick change. Finish one piece and you're in the one after the next? Looks like you're stripping offstage and slipping into your next costume and you better do it in less than five minutes because our riggers are fast. We set up a privacy screen for those who want it, but a lot of us just change in the open. It's so quick it's not like anyone notices or cares. Unless you miss your cue."

Huh. He couldn't say he knew what that was like at all. With his realty work he was always dressed in the finest suits, tailored specifically for him. When he did construction work it was jeans, T-shirts and flannels. There's been a time or two in the hot sun where he and the crew had stripped off their shirts to cool down, but in his line of work no one got naked in front of each other.

The theater was an odd place.

Still, her reasoning didn't answer his question. He knew avoidance when he heard it. If she thought she could shock him into dropping this, she was sorely mistaken.

"Piper, what is going on?"

"Nothing," she insisted. "I just…forgot…something out here and was coming to get it and then you came out of the shadows like a freaking vampire and scared the life out of me. Again! Seriously, you need to stop sneaking around the theater at odd hours. I'm gonna have to put a bell around your neck or something."

Her accusatory grumbles were adorable, but he also saw them for what they were. A distraction tactic. She didn't want to tell him why she was here in the middle of the night taking a shower and wandering around backstage naked. He got that, he did, but if she was in some kind of trouble, he wanted—no—he *needed* to help her.

"Never been one for wearing jewelry," he teased, trying to lighten the mood and ease her worry. "Hazard of the job if it gets caught on a tool. Ever heard of degloving?"

A shudder vibrated her bare shoulders. "Unfortunately, yes. Fine, no bell, but you should at least shout or announce your presence or something."

Announce his presence when he was walking into a building that was supposed to be empty? Something inside his mind clicked. Both times he'd surprised Piper, he assumed no one would be here. The first time because Donald told him. Logical to think the landlord wouldn't know the exact schedule of the tenant. He could chalk that one up to a simple mistake. But tonight. He left knowing her last class of the night was ending. He assumed she'd be going home, just like him.

Both times she was supposed to be at home, she was here.

Dread filled the pit of his stomach. He did not like the road his thoughts were traveling. As much as he wanted to blurt out his suspicions, he knew it would be a bad idea. Piper could be stubborn, he'd learned. Better for her to trust him enough to share. Now he just had to figure out a way to make her feel safe enough to do exactly that.

"I'm sorry I scared you," he started, because it was true. The very last thing he ever wanted to do was cause her stress, and it felt like he couldn't stop doing just that. "I should have announced myself, but I assumed you'd gone home. We all know what assuming makes us."

A small smile curved her lips at his joke. "Did you just call me an as—"

"No," he rushed to say. "Just me, you are an Anthousai."

Her face scrunched up. "A what?"

Oops! He hadn't meant to say that out loud. It slipped.

Those flowers had hypnotized him, causing his brain to short-circuit. The words flew from his mouth without thought.

"A flower nymph. It's from Greek mythology. I had this picture book on Greek mythology as a kid. My mom read it to me every night. I was obsessed with the artwork. It was beautiful. Like oil painting but printed on the page and somehow the texture of the art still came through."

She arched one eyebrow, clearly not following him.

"Never mind, not important. Anyway, there were these flower nymphs, minor goddesses called Anthousai or Anthusa sometimes. Protectors of the flowers. They had flowers growing all over them and your tattoos made me think of it." He waved a hand at her arms and legs. "Silly, I know."

Her face softened. A sheen of moisture glossed her deep brown eyes. She blinked it away as a soft pink blush rose on her cheeks. "It's not silly. In fact, I think it's the nicest thing anyone has ever said to me. No one has ever compared me to a goddess before."

Then people were idiots. Piper far surpassed any goddess ever known. She was beautiful, smart, brave, talented and a million other amazing things he couldn't hope to put a name to if he had a hundred years to decipher. Some lucky person was going to get to spend forever with this amazing woman. He'd give every bit of his wealth if that someone could be him.

But the curse.

He knew if he started something with Piper it would end up like every other relationship he had. It hurt seeing his past girlfriends find their one true loves right after being with him, but he'd gotten over it. Mostly. If he had Piper and lost her…it would destroy him.

Better to never have her at all and save himself the heartbreak.

Not to mention he had a part in her losing her business. A fact she still had no idea about.

Damn this entire situation!

"Flowers make me happy." Piper gazed down at the vibrant ink adorning her skin. "They're so beautiful and they contribute so much to the ecosystem. They provide nourishment and homes for so many different insects and animals. Each one has a unique scent and purpose. They live such short lives compared to other plants, but they're tenacious. The winter may drive them underground, but every spring they pop back up, filling the world with beauty and hope."

Her fingers gently traced down her arm, sliding amongst the garden she'd created. He longed to follow that path.

"I started with this daisy here." She pointed to a faded pink daisy just below her right shoulder. "I got it when I got my first contract with a traveling circus. Daisies symbolize new beginnings. After that I just kept adding. You know what they say about tattoos—you can't have just one."

He chuckled. "I think that's potato chips."

She laughed softly along with him. As much as he hated to ruin the lightened mood, he knew it was time to press.

"Piper," he said gently. "What is going on? Why are you here so late? Are you in trouble?"

Silence filled the air around them. She stared at him, eyes focused on his with such intensity. Finally, she blinked, ducking her head.

"Okay." Her voice was the barest of whispers in the darkness that surrounded them. "I'll show you, but you have to swear not to tell anyone."

Cold dread crawled up his spine at her ominous words.

"Promise me, Kell."

He wanted to, but he couldn't promise to stay quiet if she was in danger.

"Kell?"

"I promise."

She nodded, smiling, but her smile fell when he continued. "As long as keeping your secret doesn't put you in danger."

She processed his words, face blank for a beat before her smile returned. "There's that white knight again. I swear I'm not in any danger. Just…in a bit of a low spot right now."

The knot in his chest eased at her words.

"Come on," she said, turning and heading up the small staircase just to the right of them.

He followed her, wondering where she was taking him. During her original tour she showed him this landing. All that was there was a shelf full of stage props and a window. It was an odd bit of design for sure, but not unheard of for tiny nooks like this in older buildings. His curiosity turned to shock as he watched her slide the shelf to the side, revealing a hidden door behind it. Turning the knob, she opened it to reveal a small storage room with a sink, cot, and boxes. It was clear from the messy blanket and open boxes filled with clothes that someone had been living in here.

"I was taking a shower here, because for the past three months I've been living in secret at the theater."

Her softly spoken confession fell in the air around them. Yet another tangle in the web of secrets that had become his life.

Damn.

CHAPTER FOURTEEN

"Explain."

Piper swallowed hard at Kell's soft demand. She understood his confusion. Most days she was still confused on how she got here. Not the how, really, she knew the exact events that led to her current predicament. But a part of her still couldn't understand how she let them happen.

"I will, but I need a few minutes to…" She waved a hand over her towel-covered form. If she was going to bare the most embarrassing moment of her life, she didn't want to do it while physically bare too. Emotional vulnerability was hard enough. She needed the armor of clothing.

Kell's gaze swept down her body, eyes heating. She clutched the knot on her towel tighter. The temptation to flick it undone and drop the towel overwhelmed her. How she wished she could avoid this conversation by finally giving into the temptation they both so desperately craved.

But she couldn't.

The distraction would only work for a night, and then she'd only be stacking problems on top of each other. Standing her ground, she waited. Kell blinked, the heat in his eyes disappearing. He nodded.

"I'll be right outside."

Once he was outside of the room, door firmly shut, she quickly tossed off her towel. Digging through an open box, she grabbed the first pair of pajamas she saw. The thin cotton shorts and sleep tank covered up barely more than her towel. Like she told Kell earlier, nudity wasn't a huge thing for her that often. Some of her past costumes left hardly anything to the imagination. But for this conversation, around this man, she needed to keep her head clear. With that thought in mind, she grabbed her long fluffy robe from the edge of her bed.

She slipped it on, covering her flower tattoos from sight. Her heart still raced remembering what he'd called her. *A goddess.* That was a comparison she didn't mind. Much nicer than Larry, who told her she reminded him of a tweaked-out cartoon character. Her mood soured at the reminder of who put her in this extremely uncomfortable situation.

"Piper? Are you okay in there?"

Kell's concerned voice simmered her rage, embarrassment flooding back. Her emotions were all over the place. She rubbed her belly. It was giving her a stomachache.

"Yes. You can come in now."

The door creaked open. Kell slowly popped his head in. He nodded when he saw her fully covered, but she thought she spied a hint of longing still lingering in his gaze.

"What's going on, Piper?" He frowned, crossing his arms over his chest. "Why are you living at the theater?"

Her gaze snagged on his forearms. When in the world had she become so obsessed with forearms? Seriously, they were just another body part. Not even a sexy one. But they were sexy on him. She couldn't drag her attention away from them. She wondered what they would feel like holding her in the dark of night. Her body temperature rose under her robe, sweat gathering on the back of her neck. Or maybe that was a drop of shower water she'd missed.

"Piper?"

"Huh?" What were they talking about? His sexy forearms? No, her squatting here. "Oh, right. Why am I living here. Um…that's a bit of a story."

Kell sat down on her cot, staring up at her with all the patience in the world filling those beautiful blue eyes. "I got nothing but time."

She highly doubted that, but she also sensed he wasn't leaving without an answer. So be it. Taking a deep breath, she started in on her story.

"About a year ago I started dating this guy. Larry."

His eyebrows rose slightly. "Larry? Really? Was he in his fifties?"

She rolled in her lips to stop the giggle from escaping. This was not a moment for laughter. "No, twenty-nine. It was a family name. He was like the fourth-generation Larry or something."

He waved a hand for her to continue.

"Anyway, we met at a bar after one of my shows. Normally I hate bars. They're too crowded and loud. I can never hear what people are saying and there's way too many smells. But I go to celebrate with the cast. I went outside to get a breather, and Larry was there on the back patio. We started talking, he asked for my number and after a few dates we were a couple."

Kell's expression darkened. "Then what?"

If he was surmising this story didn't have her dream happy ending, he was right.

"After a month he wanted to move in together." Fast, she knew, but she'd been in love. Or so she had thought. "We were so great together. No fights, good chemistry. I thought it was the perfect next step in our relationship. I had six months left on my lease, so he just moved in with me."

Kell's jaw tightened. "Please tell me he didn't take over your lease and kick you out."

Worse. Much worse.

"Why, has that happened to you before? I thought you said all of your relationships ended amicably."

"They did." He narrowed his eyes. "Stop deflecting and finish the story."

"Mr. Bossy," she muttered under her breath. The corner of his mouth twitched in a small smile.

"Please continue, Piper."

"Fine," she sighed, hating the next part. "Before I tell you the rest, I want to remind you that I am a self-proclaimed hopeless romantic who believes in true love, and sometimes that can bite me in the butt."

His smile vanished, concern and wariness filling his gaze.

"Larry kept talking about our future, marriage and stuff, and how we should combine our finances."

"Oh no."

Oh yes. Looking back, she realized how naive she'd been, but at the time her eyes had been filled with stars and everything was rose-colored. Her grandparents had gotten married after three weeks of knowing each other. When Larry started talking about happily-ever-after so soon into their relationship, she'd assumed he was just the one. Like Grandpa had been for Grandma.

What was that Kell said earlier about assuming? She'd definitely fit that description when she realized how Larry had tricked her.

"We opened up a joint account. I kept my business account separate." Thank the universe for that small insight. "But all the money for bills, rent and life stuff went into our account. Everything was great for a few months."

He frowned. "What happened after a few months?"

Bile rose up in the back of her throat. She hated this part. Hated admitting how ignorant she'd been. How easily duped. But Kell deserved to know the truth.

"I came home one day, and all his stuff was gone. A lot of my stuff too."

A low growl escaped Kell's throat, but she pressed on.

"I called his cell, but I'd been blocked. Blocked on all his social media too. His friends said they had no clue where he was, and the worst part of it was when I went to check the bank…" Shame filled her as she admitted this next part. "All the money was gone."

Kell let loose a very colorful four-letter curse. Yeah, she'd used that word and several others when she'd found out.

"The bastard stole your money and ran out on you?"

She nodded, humiliation heating her cheeks. She ducked her head, moisture gathering in her eyes. The anger had faded, but she still felt so silly she'd fallen for his love scam. Was she so desperate for someone to love her that she'd believe anyone with sweet words and a nice smile? She was beginning to fear she might never find the love she craved, or perhaps…she simply wasn't worthy of it.

"I didn't have money for the next month's rent. I was evicted after thirty days."

Kell swore again. "And you couldn't find another place?"

She shook her head. "I had no money. Without a security deposit, first and last month's rent, no place would even let me look."

Renting was difficult in normal circumstances—her problem made it impossible. People always thought they were one lotto ticket away from millions, but the truth was most people were one bad day away from losing everything.

"What about staying with friends or family?"

She let out a strangled laugh. "My friends are in the same predicament as me. The Starving Artist is a cliché for a reason. None of them have room for me and I wouldn't burden them like that. As for family…my parents divorced over a decade ago and neither of them has been interested in a relationship with me for longer than that. They never approved of my life choices in anything. We don't really talk anymore."

"They sound like pretty terrible parents," he muttered, eyes filled with anger.

Anger for her? Sweet, but unnecessary. Life was what it

was. She learned that a long time ago. It was rarely fair. The only thing one could do was make the best of whatever it handed you.

"My only option was staying here while I saved enough to rent a new place."

One dark eyebrow rose. "Donald lets you stay here?"

Her heart jumped into her throat. Sitting on the cot next to him, she grabbed his hand, staring into his eyes, pleading with everything in her. "No. He has no idea. And you can't tell him, please. If he knew I was living here it would break the lease, and he'd kick me out. Please, Kell, you can't tell him. I just need a few more months to get the cash together. Summer camps start next month and they're always full. I promise I can find a place soon, just please don't tell anyone."

Kell stared at her, a thousand thoughts racing across his face, but she couldn't decipher a single one. She held her breath, waiting, hoping. Finally, he nodded. His hand squeezed hers.

"Of course I won't tell anyone." He lifted a hand. "If you stay in my family's condo."

"Kell, I can't—"

"Just until you sort things out," he insisted. "It's a short-term rental and we don't have anyone on the schedule for the next month. We're redoing the kitchen—some appliances are on back order so it's out of commission, not rentable. But the rest of the condo is perfect. It's just sitting empty. You'd be doing me a favor."

"By squatting?" she asked with a small chuckle.

"No. By keeping an eye on the place while it's empty and letting me out of the bet so I don't have to get up in an apparatus."

"Ha!" She shook a finger at him, recognizing his tactic to sooth her frazzled nerves by teasing her. "Not going to happen, mister. You're getting up in that thing."

He sighed, grasping her hand in his, his face turning serious. "Okay, but please stay in the condo. You can't live here, Piper. It's not safe."

He had a point. The ceiling leaked, and she was risking her lease and her safety staying here all alone with no one knowing. As much as she hated to be a burden to anyone, she could see the worry in Kell's eyes. He didn't make her feel like a burden. He made her feel…safe.

"Okay," she softly agreed.

A relieved breath left him as he smiled.

A weight lifted from her shoulders. Her chest expanded as breath returned. She closed her eyes as a few tears of gratitude leaked out, the warm wetness rolling down her cheeks. Her words were barely a whisper in the small room. "Thank you."

She felt the rough pad of his thumb brush away her tears. Opening her eyes, she stared into the handsome face that haunted her dreams.

"I'm sorry that happened to you." His eyes heated with anger. "If I knew where that bastard was, I'd—"

"Okay, Mr. White Knight, I appreciate the sentiment, but I don't need you to beat up my ex. Karma will get him."

He chuckled. "Of course you would believe in karma. I don't know how you do it."

"Do what?"

"Remain a hopeless romantic after all that."

She shrugged. "I'm not going to let Larry take my money, my home and my sense of wonder. That's too much. I was wrong about him, but that doesn't mean my true love isn't out there waiting for me. Might be silly." She nudged his shoulder with her own, giving him a teasing smile. "But so is believing you're cursed by love."

That got a grin out of him, along with an eye roll. "Touché. And now I'm more motivated than ever to help you fill seats for the show. Why don't you pack up what you need, and we can head over to the condo."

Heart filled with gratitude, she wondered how the universe could put such a wonderful man in front of her, one who was perfect for her in nearly every way and give him the silly notion he was cursed. Maybe she was the key. Maybe she was supposed to show him this curse nonsense wasn't real.

Or maybe she was supposed to break it.

"You really are the sweetest, Kellen."

He smiled, cupping her cheek with his hand and stroking gently. She turned her face into his palm, allowing herself a moment of need.

"Thank you for keeping my secret," she continued. "For not telling Donald. I swear in a month, everything will be okay."

The stroking stopped. He dropped his hand, clearing his throat and staring down at the floor. An odd sense of unease washed over her, but she ignored it. Tonight had been a tidal wave of emotions. They were all crashing in on each other, drowning her in confusion.

"No problem. Donald doesn't have to know anything. I promise."

"Thank you," she said softly, relief filling her. Finally she'd found someone she could trust implicitly.

CHAPTER FIFTEEN

GUILT WAS EATING him alive.

Kell pulled up to the theater, Piper's revelation last night playing over and over in his head. What a grade A jerk her ex was. He wanted nothing more than to find the guy and give him a piece of his mind…among other things. His hand clenched on the steering wheel. He didn't get people like that. How could you pretend to care about someone then up and leave them, taking every penny they had? What kind of monster did that?

Glass houses, my man.

He scowled at his inner voice. It wasn't the same. He wasn't lying to Piper. He was…withholding information he legally couldn't reveal. The rumble in his gut called him a liar. Damn! He had to find a way around that ridiculous contract clause.

At least she had agreed to stay in the condo. Her eyes nearly popped out of her head when she stepped in the two-thousand-square-foot two-bedroom, two-bath home. He hadn't been lying when he said she was doing him a favor. Having someone stay there while they waited to finish the repairs was a huge help. He always hated leaving the rental unoccupied. A sneaky leak could cause thousands in damages. This way, she was helping him while he could help her. It assuaged some of his guilt for the terrible secret he was holding on to. The secret made worse now that he knew she wasn't just losing her studio.

She was losing her home.

No.

Not on his watch.

He had no idea how he was going to help, but determination filled his chest, pushing the guilt down. Even if he had to build Piper a house himself, he'd find a way to make sure she had a place when Donald kicked her out. Hopefully she'd take his help. Unease crawled its way up his spine, tiny pricks of worry poking holes in his plan to save her.

He had to help her. Not just because he felt guilty, but also because he cared for Piper. More than he should. He knew what happened when he fell for someone. The promise to never do it again burned in his soul, but somehow, with each second he spent by her side, Piper was snuffing out that flame. Replacing it with hope for a future.

"Will she even want my help when she finds out?" He spoke the question into the silence of the car.

She might think he was her white knight now, but when she found out the truth, would he turn into a toad?

He shook his head. He'd been spending too much time in the theater. This job was getting to him if he was sitting here thinking about knights, frogs and fairy-tale solutions to real-world problems. Good thing he planned on outside work today. He needed the space to think.

Grabbing his tool bag, he left his car and headed into the theater. Piper was onstage leading a class of teenagers through a warm-up. Her brown eyes locked with his, excitement and some other emotion he didn't want to name filling them.

"Okay everyone, time for conditioning on the hoops. Five straddle ups, five pullovers, fifteen shoulder shrugs and pull some taffy."

The kids moaned, some of them voicing their distaste for one or more of the exercises she called out. Despite their complaints, he noticed they all raced to grab a hoop. Teenage defiance filled every aspect of life, he guessed.

"Hey," Piper said as he approached the stage.

"Hi. How is the condo?"

She grinned. "Like a dream come true. I swear that bed is made of pure clouds. I've never slept so well in my life."

Her warm smile was infectious, and he couldn't help but smile back.

"What are you working on today?"

He let his gaze drift high. "I'm assessing the roof today to see what needs to be done. I'm hoping it'll be small fixes I can do on my own, but based on the number of leaks I've found in this place…"

"Ha!" Piper barked out a laugh. "When has any issue here been a small fix?"

"They would have been if Donald would have addressed them earlier." This beautiful historical building was falling apart all because Donald didn't want to spend money making necessary repairs. It made Kell's blood boil.

"Yes, well, as we've determined, Donald is the worst."

He grinned at her wink. On that they could agree.

"Do you need a ladder or anything?" Piper asked, motioning up to the roof.

"No. There's an access point from the attic. Should be good enough to get me up there for an inspection."

A smile curved her beautiful pink lips. "You're willing to climb out a window onto the roof of a building, but you're scared of a little hoop?"

He followed her head as it waved to the stage where the teens were dutifully following her instructions, with a fair bit of complaining and teasing going on too. A shudder racked his body.

"I know how to be safe on a roof. That… I don't know the first thing about that, but it looks painful and dangerous."

A small giggle escaped her. "That's why you learn from a professional, like me. And I wouldn't start you on hoop.

Sling is a much more forgiving apparatus. Plus, you lost the taco-truck bet. You have to get up there someday."

"Let's plan on later rather than sooner." He stared at the hoops, grimacing, swearing his body could already feel the pain of falling out of one of those things.

"Kell—"

"Oh, would you look at the time," he interrupted, holding up his wrist, which was free of any watch. Walking backward, he shrugged. "I have to go see a roof about repairs."

Laughter spilled from her lips. She lifted a finger and pointed it at him. "Nice try, mister, but you can't avoid this forever. I will get you up on stage."

He turned, heading toward backstage where the stairs to the attic were. "Can't hear you, too busy working."

Her laughter followed him. Like a balm to his soul. It was the most beautiful laugh he'd ever heard. He swore in that moment to do everything in his power to make sure the tragedy to come didn't destroy that laugh forever. There had to be a way to fix this conundrum he'd gotten himself into. He swore to find it.

He made it onto the roof without issue. The real issue came an hour and a half later after he'd done a thorough inspection and found the results…less than ideal.

"Dammit," he swore, wiping sweat off his brow.

The early summer sun beat down, enhanced by the dark roof shingles. The ones that were still attached. He'd been expecting some work needed, but this…this warranted a call. He slipped back inside the attic and sat on an old wooden stool left up there from some production of past years, no doubt. He pulled out his phone and called Donald. Fifty-fifty on if the guy answered or let it go to voicemail.

"What's the issue now, Thorson?" Donald's angry voice loudly demanded.

Oh yeah, he picked up. Kell sighed, gathering all his customer-pleasing charm he could muster before answering. "Hello, Mr. Noll. I'm calling because I did a full roof inspection today and I'm afraid the results were not what we were hoping for."

A string of four-letter curses pierced his ear. Kell pulled his cell phone away, putting it on speaker. No sense in bursting his eardrum. With the news he had, he was expecting a lot more swearing and shouting.

"From what I can tell, this roof is about twenty years old. That's the general end of lifespan for most roofs. In addition to that, there's significant hail damage from years of storms. Multiple leaks, weather wear and numerous missing shingles. You're going to need an entire roof replacement."

He waited while Donald went through every foul word in the English language and some creative new ones as well. Not shocking. He expected this anger. He also anticipated the next words to come across the line.

"Can we put it on the market without replacing the roof?"

A heavy sigh left him. "We can, but we'll need to take about ten thousand or more off the listing price."

"Ten thousand!" Donald shouted. "What the hell am I paying you for, Thorson? You're supposed to be the best in the business. Fixing and selling, a two-in-one package with the highest sell rate in the state, isn't that what you promised me?"

It was, but he and his brothers also promised to sell high-quality properties. This theater, in its current state even with all the repairs he'd done, was mid-quality at best. The prospective buyers he had would not be happy with the quality. They would demand the price be reduced and Donald would pitch a fit. Better to fix it now and save the headache.

"How much is this repair going to cost me?"

He should quote him an astronomical price, but Kell didn't want to risk Donald pulling the contract and going with another real estate agency. Who would look out for Piper then?

"Shouldn't be too much more." He swallowed down the bile rising in his throat as he tried to assuage this monster of a man. "I can call in my brothers to help. That'll cut down on labor costs and I have an in with a guy who can give me a good deal on premium materials."

"Good," Donald huffed. "But don't worry about premium, go for the cheapest stuff that'll do the job."

"Cheaper material will wear out faster."

"The hell do I care? Leave that problem for the sucker who buys this place."

His grip tightened on the phone as he stared at the screen with Donald's name and the timer of their call ticking away. Five minutes. And every single second felt like an eternity.

"You're the boss," he said through gritted teeth, when what he really wanted to do was reach through the phone and punch the guy. Kell had never been a violent man before, but this slimy jerk was testing his limits.

"Damn right I am, so get on this fast. We only have a few more weeks until the lease is up and I can kick that annoying shrew out and list this place."

Fire burned his chest at Donald's words. A growl rumbled low in his throat. He was two seconds away from telling Donald exactly what he thought when he spoke again.

"She doesn't suspect anything, does she?"

"Pardon?" he asked, clearing his throat when the word came out too rough.

"Pitts. With you there doing all this work, does she see through it? Know I'm gonna sell the place?" There was a slight pause. "You haven't said anything to her, have you?"

"No." The word tore from his throat. "She's just…happy repairs are getting done."

"Good. Keep her in the dark."

He should agree and hang up, but his conscience was so far stretched it felt like one more word could snap it in two.

"Don't you think you should inform your tenant of your decision to sell?"

"Why the hell would I do that?"

Because it was what decent people did. "So she can start looking for a new place. She has to move an entire business. Surely you can see how difficult this will be on her. On her business."

Dark, cruel laughter filled the attic. "I don't give a damn about her business. It's a dog-eat-dog world out there, if she can't handle it, so be it. And don't you dare go spilling the beans to her. We have a contract, Thorson, and if she finds out, I will sue you for every penny you have and destroy your precious little charity along with it."

The man truly was a monster.

"Of course, Mr. Noll. I understand how an NDA works."

"Good. Then get to work on the roof ASAP. Time's wasting."

He was a waste.

Kell stared at his phone as the screen went blank. Taking a few, calming breaths, he fired off an email to his roof-tile guy before texting his brothers the new hitch in this job. Replacing the roof wasn't the problem. They'd done it before. Donald was the real issue. He couldn't wait until they were rid of this client.

But then I'll be rid of Piper too.

The thought struck his chest like a blow. He rubbed at the pain. A throb started behind his left eye. How the hell was he going to fix this situation so nobody got hurt in the end? Was that even possible? He felt like his love curse had spilled over into his work life, determined to doom every aspect of his existence. Nothing he could do about it but press on and hope he found a way to make sure everyone came out on top.

CHAPTER SIXTEEN

Piper had just finished rigging the slings for the next class when she spied Kell from the corner of her eye. The teens had all left and sling instruction didn't start for another twenty minutes. Her heart skipped a beat, and she wondered if she could convince Kell to take a small break to chat. She loved talking with him. Odd, since small talk really wasn't her thing. It was uncomfortable and disingenuous. She never understood how neurotypicals navigated such banal chitchat that had no point.

But conversing with Kell was never boring small talk. They talked about real things. He let her gush about her passions, he shared his painful past with her. She still thought the notion of a dating curse was silly, but she was honored he felt comfortable enough with her to be vulnerable and share. They had a real connection, one she cherished and enjoyed.

She was about to open her mouth and suggest a friendly chat when she saw his face. Her mouth hung open, words halted on her tongue. He looked…angry. She'd never seen Kell angry before. True, she'd barely seen the man outside of the theater, but he'd been frustrated by a few of the repairs over the past three weeks. This, however, didn't look like frustrated anger. His face was pinched, jaw tight, but his eyes were…worried.

She had no idea what put that look on his face, but she

made a silent vow to address it right this very minute. Hurrying over to him, she placed a hand on his arm.

"Hey, you okay?"

Kell glanced at her, blinking as his head swiveled, taking in his surroundings. He seemed surprised he was in the theater. What could have him so upset he wandered down from the roof without even realizing it? Now she was really worried.

"Huh? Oh, yeah, yeah. Just…" He scrubbed a hand over his face, letting out a deep sigh. "Work stuff. Nothing you need to worry about."

Normally she'd let that go—she might miss a lot of social cues, but she knew when someone didn't want to talk—but his work stuff currently involved *her* work. "Um, did, uh, you tell Donald about…"

She lifted a hand in the air and waved it toward the small staircase with the prop shelf and her secret room. Her heart pounded in her chest as fear seized her.

She'd been wrong. He was a spy. She let her guard down and he'd told Donald everything. Now she was about to be kicked out and—

Kell snatched her hand out of the air, gripping it between his and holding tightly. His thumbs stroked her skin, warm and rough, but comforting at the same time.

"No. Never. I promised you I wouldn't tell Donald, and I never break a promise, Piper. Never."

She stared into his bright blue eyes. Eyes the color of a summer day. The kind that was filled with hope and promise of good things to come. Closing her eyes, she took a deep breath, her nerves calming at his reassurance. See? She had been right to trust him. Her spy notion was as silly as his curse fears.

"Thank you," she whispered.

One of his hands left hers to cup her cheek. The touch held

warmth and reassurance and…something more. Something they both agreed not to explore, but it was getting harder and harder to ignore. Especially when he was being so wonderful. Keeping her secret, providing her with a safe space to live. Not only safe, but fancy too. He cared for her in a way no one else in her life ever had. Giving without expecting anything in return. Tired from fighting this attraction, from hiding her secrets, from the struggles of life in general, she gave in. Piper pressed her face into his palm, seeking the safeguard she felt there. He truly was her knight in shining armor. Or dark flannel technically.

"It's just Donald complaining about the roof and being a giant tool, per usual."

Her eyes popped open, and she grimaced. "Is it that bad?"

He dropped his hands then ran them through his short, dark hair, frustration clear. She missed the contact immediately.

"Yeah. The whole thing needs to be replaced, which he was not happy to hear."

She snorted. "I bet he wasn't."

That got a small smile out of him.

"I managed to convince him a new roof was needed, and my brothers and I can do it at a decent price."

"Your brothers are coming to work on it with you?"

He nodded. "As soon as the materials come in. Should only take us a few days. Week, tops. We'll start the repairs after your show so if any issues occur it won't impact your performances."

She waved a hand in the air. "I'm not worried about that."

He raised one eyebrow. Okay, she'd been a little worried about that. Aerial performances and construction-work sounds did not mesh well.

"I'm sorry Donald was being such a jerk," she said.

"It is what it is. At least he agreed to the repair or…things might get dicey during hail season."

He paused before he said the last part, as if it wasn't what he originally intended to say. She noticed he did that sometimes. Like he was going to say one thing, thought better of it and said something else. She had no idea what that was about, but considering she wasn't the most skilled at conversation either, she let it go.

His shoulders were still tight, body tense. A call with Donald would do that to anyone. An idea sparked in her mind. Good thing she knew exactly how to ease the tension a rage-inducing conversation with her scummy landlord caused.

"Come with me." She grabbed his hand and tugged him onto the stage.

"Wait, Piper, what are—"

"Just come," she insisted, pulling him to center stage where she'd hung her favorite purple sling.

"Oh no. Hell no." Kell shook his head, dropping her hand and crossing his arm over his chest. "You are not getting me up in that death trap."

She couldn't contain the eye roll. "You spent all morning up on a roof that's falling apart. If anything is a death trap, I wouldn't say it's my job."

He frowned, shaking his head. "No."

Sticking out her bottom lip, she gave him her best sad eyes. "Please? I swear there's nothing better to relieve tension than spinning in a sling."

His frown turned into a devilish grin, gaze sweeping over her with heat as he cocked one eyebrow. "Nothing? Cause I can think of something much more…horizontal."

She swallowed, her throat drier than it had ever been before. Other parts of her were so hot and damp she felt as though she'd just done an hour-long spin tolerance class. How could this man turn her on with nothing but a look and a bit of innuendo?

"Mind out of the gutter, mister. I have a class in twenty minutes."

He chuckled, and a rush of butterflies took flight in her stomach.

"Besides, you have to get in the sling. You lost the bet, remember?"

He groaned. "Okay, you win. What do I do?"

Yes! She loved winning. Loved teaching aerials even more. And she especially loved introducing the art to people who would never think to try it in a million years. Kell fit that description to a T.

"It would be better if you were wearing different clothes." She frowned as she took in his appearance.

Kell glanced down at his jeans and dark blue flannel. "We should probably wait until I can find some spandex or something, right?"

"Nice try, buddy." Now all she could think about was Kell in spandex. "But you're not weaseling out of this. I did an entire routine in jeans and a leather corset once. It sucked, but I made it work and so can you. Though you should take the flannel and your shoes off."

His fingers worked the buttons, deftly flicking them open one by one. He shrugged the overshirt off his shoulders, revealing a tight-fitting black T-shirt underneath. He placed his flannel on the stage floor, his biceps flexing with the movement. A wave of heat scorched her skin as sweat gathered on the back of her neck. She wished she could blame it on the broken AC, but that had been one of the first things Kell had repaired. No, this heat wave was all due to the man in front of her. Ridiculous. She'd seen dozens of fit people in her years as an aerialist. Kell's arms were no different than anyone else's.

Except they were.

Because they were his.

"Now what?" he asked after he'd taken his shoes off.

She shook off the naughty thoughts playing in her mind and focused on the task at hand.

"First I'm going to have you stand with the sling around your back and in your armpits."

He frowned. "I don't follow."

She guided him to the fabric, positioning him where she wanted him. "Now grab the fabric with your hands and we're going to try an invert."

"A what?"

"Invert. Put the fabric on your lower back and bring your knees up to the outside of the fabric and lean back."

He raised one eyebrow in disbelief.

"Trust me, you can do this."

Shaking his head he followed her instruction. The sling was low enough that with some help from her he managed to invert without too much trouble.

"Good. Now I'm going to give you a little spin." She pushed on one of his knees, giving him a slow spin.

"I feel ridiculous," he said.

She held back a snort of laughter. He did look a bit silly. "You look great. Like Spider-Man."

He chuckled. "Liar."

"No, really. I call this pose Spider-Man for my kids' class. Upside down with your knees bent, you totally look like the friendly neighborhood superhero."

Kell let go of the fabric with his right hand, moving it in front of him to do the classic Spider-Man web-shooting pose. Unfortunately, as a newbie with no sense of balance yet, releasing the fabric caused his body weight to shift in the sling. He started to pitch to one side. Thankfully his knees were still on the outside of the fabric, keeping him in the sling even as he slid to one side, landing in a front balance.

"Oof, damn!" Kell dropped his other hand, losing all connection with the sling and sliding out onto the mat, landing on his backside.

"Kell! Are you okay?" She rushed to his side, sitting on the mat beside him, grateful to see a smile on his face as he looked up at her.

"That was…something. Glad I tried it. Bet fulfilled." He winked.

Playfully smacking his shoulder, she pointed a finger at him. "Oh, come on, that was barely one move and you were doing great until you let go."

"You never seem to hold on when you're practicing."

He watched her practice? Of course he saw her practice, the man was here every day working. Logically he would catch a glimpse or two of her during that time. It didn't mean anything that he watched her. Only…it did. It meant a lot to her.

"I have years of study and practice," she responded. "You are a novice, so hands on the fabric until you're comfortable enough to let go."

"Honestly, I'd rather watch you. You're beautiful in the air, Piper. Like a fairy, soaring through the sky. Your face lights up, radiating joy. Anyone who watches you can tell this is your calling."

All the air left her lungs—no, left her entire body. Stunned, she stared. What response could she give to that? How did this man render her speechless with such beautiful words? Words that burrowed their way into her soul and lit up every inch of her being.

"Thank you," she finally mumbled. Because that's what you were supposed to do when someone complimented you, right? Thank them. What he said was so far beyond a compliment her gratitude felt paltry.

"It's the truth." He nodded, lifting a hand to brush a strand of hair behind her ear.

Her body trembled at his touch. She was so tired of holding

back, so tired of denying herself the one thing she wanted. Maybe that's why she opened her mouth, and words fell out without thought or reason.

"Kell, do you ever think it's not a curse, but you just keep meeting the wrong people?"

His fingers lingered on her cheek, eyes gazing deeply into hers. "I don't know. You're the one who believes in happily-ever-after and fairy tales. By your logic, maybe it is a curse and the only thing that can break it is true love's kiss."

Normally a line like that would have her groaning and running for the hills, but she heard the yearning behind his words. Kell wanted to believe, even if he professed the opposite. She could do that for him. She could prove to him that love, real love, was out there for everyone, including him.

Leaning forward, she placed her palms on his shoulders, then slid her hand around the back of his neck as she tilted her head. His palm cupped her cheek as he drew her to him, dipping his head. He hesitated, allowing her to have the final say in what was clearly a line they were about to cross.

She'd been doing aerials for over a decade. Dropped from heights of over twenty feet, even done a silks photo shoot hanging off the bottom of a hot-air balloon. None of those experiences were as terrifying as this moment. Because she knew, deep in her soul, the second their lips touched, her life would never be the same.

Eyelids drifting shut, she closed the distance between them. The second her lips brushed his, fireworks exploded behind her closed eyes. A rush, unlike anything she got from doing a drop, plunged her heart down to her toes and back up again. Her skin prickled with electricity. His hand moved to the back of her neck, gripping tighter, pressing her closer as he swept his tongue out, seeking entrance. She gladly complied, reveling in the taste of this man who had tempted her for far too long.

Her heart cheered in triumph even as her brain shouted out a small protest. Whatever. She'd deal with the consequences of her rash actions later. Right now, she was drowning in a sea of blissful sensation. Good heavens, Kell could kiss! Her body demanded more. Just as she was about to debate breaking her rule of no hookups, the sound of laughter pierced the air.

Kell pulled away just as the theater doors slammed open, revealing a group of students here for the sling class. Breathing heavily, Piper touched her fingers to her lips, the feel of Kell still there. She feared it always would be. A brand on her soul.

His bright blue eyes, filled with heat, stared at her with longing. "I'm sorry."

"I'm not." The words were out before she could stop them. Not that she intended to. She wasn't sorry for what happened, and she didn't want him to be either. "I enjoyed kissing you."

A slow grin spread across his face. "Me too."

Relief filled her at his words.

"I should get back to work." He nodded to the students coming in. "You too, it seems."

He stood, helping her up which was nice since her legs had turned to jelly the moment their mouths met. Squeezing her hand, he turned, grabbed his discarded things and headed backstage. She watched him go, doing her best to hold on to the warm feeling in her chest and ignore the sharp warning in her gut that everything was about to change.

CHAPTER SEVENTEEN

FIVE DAYS.

It had been five very long days since he'd lost his head and kissed Piper. Technically she kissed him, but he kissed her back. Even though he knew it had been a bad idea, he couldn't find it in himself to regret it. Even now, nearly a week later, he could still taste her sweetness on his lips. Still feel the warmth of her body heating his. Every fiber of his being wanted a repeat performance.

But work had gotten hectic the past few days with prepping everything for the roof repair, and Piper had been consumed with tech and dress rehearsal for her show. Other than a few friendly waves, rushed hellos and adorable pink blushes as she spied him across the theater, they hadn't had a chance to speak.

All that ended tonight.

He had to talk to her. Make sure she was okay and see what she wanted to do about this line they stepped over. Forget it happened? He hoped not. He knew what he wanted to do, but he also knew if they started anything it would be temporary. That's all he could offer her. Since she'd made her stance on casual very clear, he didn't see how they could pursue anything without one of them getting hurt in the end.

He was usually the man with the plan, but right now he was lost. Logic told him to forget it. Move on. They were too different, wanted the complete opposite things, not to mention the curse still looming over his head. But he'd be damned if he made a decision without asking Piper first. One lesson his mother drilled into his head growing up was to respect people's decisions and not make choices for them. He'd talk to Piper. After the show, of course. No need to add more nerves to her night.

Gripping the bouquet of roses, he adjusted his tie and slipped backstage. The theater was already half full and people were still pouring in. He blinked, eyes adjusting to the dim light backstage as performers hurried around him frantically.

"Kell? What are you doing back here?"

He turned at the voice that made his heart skip a beat. The air left his lungs as he saw Piper. She wore all black, her hair pulled back into a ponytail, a clipboard in hand. She was beautiful, even as she blended into the shadows.

Lifting the bouquet, he started to answer her. "I came to wish you good lu—"

Her eyes widened, and she squashed her hand over his mouth, halting his words. "Don't say it!"

"Say what?" he tried to ask, but the words came out muffled behind her hand.

"The G L phrase. It's bad luck to say that in the theater. I thought your mom was some fancy cultural arts person."

His eyes shifted down to her hand, eyebrows rising. Huffing, she dropped her hand, glare still directed at him. He ducked his head to hide his smile.

"You're right. I should have known better, but 'break a leg' sounds wrong to say to an aerialist before a performance."

"We don't say that either."

"Then what do you say for lu—well wishes," he corrected himself at her warning glare.

"We're dancers, we say merde. It's French for…" She glanced behind her to where couple of kids stood a few feet away, hopping up and down with preshow excitement. "Well, it's just what we say."

He knew a little French, which was why he understood her hesitation to translate the swear in earshot of kids. What he didn't know was why that word was considered good luck for dancers.

"Of course, well then." Lifting the flowers, he bowed slightly. "Merde."

Her scowl eased into a smile as she took the bouquet from his hands, bringing them to her face and inhaling. "Thank you. These are beautiful. You didn't have to."

"I know." He gazed into those beautiful brown eyes, so dark and warm he wanted to sink into them. "I wanted to."

A pink blush rose on her cheeks. "You look very handsome tonight."

He felt his own cheeks warm at her praise. "Thank you, and you look beautiful as always, but I'm confused on the costume. Isn't this *Romeo and Juliet*?"

He knew they couldn't perform in traditional Shakespearean costumes while doing aerials, but why was she wearing all black?

"Oh, I'm not performing. I'm the director and one of the riggers. Gotta stay out of sight." She waved a hand at her dark clothing.

"Ah, that makes sense." A small part of him lamented the fact that he wouldn't get to see her perform tonight. The few times he'd seen her in the air had been entrancing. While he was sure her students would be amazing, Piper's entire soul lit up with joy when she was in the air. It was awe-inspiring to see. "Well, I should find my seat. It's filling up out there."

"I wanted to ask you about that." She stared up at him with wonder. "We sold out both performances. We've never done that before. How did you do that?"

"You assume it was me? Maybe word got out about how amazing you and your students are."

She arched one dark eyebrow. A chuckle left him.

"Okay," he admitted. "I did tell you I was going to do my best to help, but I can't take all the credit. I contacted my mother. She put out the word to her friends. Patrons of the arts, if you will. They jumped at the chance to see such a unique performance of a classic. She sends her regrets on being unable to attend. She's in London right now."

Piper clutched the roses to her chest. "Please give her my sincere thanks."

He nodded. "I will."

As he started to turn to head to his seat, the soft feel of her hand on his arm stopped him.

"Kell?"

"Yeah?"

A hint of worry filled her eyes. He hated it. Wanted to erase the emotion from her entire world.

"Could, um, could we talk after the show?"

Since that was his plan exactly, he nodded. "Of course."

"Good, good." She shifted on her feet, something else clearly on her mind. "There's another ritual in the theater for a good show that some people participate in."

"Really?" While his mother was on the cultural arts board and he attended many plays, he rarely saw the inner workings of the theater. "What is it?"

She looked up at him through her lashes, a faint blush on her cheeks as she whispered, "A kiss for luck."

He roared inside, holding his body very still when what he really wanted to do was take her in his arms and devour her. It had to be a good sign that she wanted another kiss, right? Clearly she wasn't angry with him for the previous one if she wanted a repeat performance. Perhaps their talk later would go the way he hoped.

Cupping her face, he leaned down and softly brushed his lips across hers once. Twice. The barest of tastes, tormenting them both, but he didn't want to push. This was her choice.

Her decision. A moment later, Piper rose on her toes, pressing her mouth firmly against his, opening slightly. He took her hint, deepening the kiss. She tasted like sunshine and hope.

Far too soon for his liking, Piper pulled back. They were both breathing heavily, but the smile on her face made his chest swell.

"I'll see you after the show," he whispered.

She nodded. Someone called her name, and she turned, running off to put out whatever preshow emergency had come up. Slipping out from backstage, he moved to the audience, glancing at the room, now nearly full, for an empty seat. His eyes spotted an empty chair in the middle of the front row with a sign on it. A small chuckle left him as he realized it said Reserved For and his name on it.

He sat, recognizing several people in the audience from his family's circles. Mom had called in all the bigwigs. He'd have to give her something extra special this Mother's Day. The lights overhead dimmed as the preshow music started. The din of the audience hushed, the curtain opened. Showtime.

Kell sat, watching the show in amazement. The performers on stage did a fantastic job of depicting *Romeo and Juliet* with no dialogue. Even if he didn't know the play by heart, he would still be able to follow the story. Their movements were infused with emotion and the music matched the energy.

He was so proud of Piper. What she created here was amazing. Not just the show, but everything with this theater. The grim reminder of what was about to happen to it, to her, stabbed him in the gut. He had to find a way to save the theater, for her. He could not let the end of this job be a tale of woe.

CHAPTER EIGHTEEN

Nothing sounded better than the cheers of a wowed audience. Nothing except Kell in his rich, deep voice telling her she was beautiful. Her heart fluttered as the performers took their final bow. What a night it had been. Opening night was always stressful, but the cast rocked it. No one fell from an apparatus, a cue wasn't missed and they had a full house giving a standing ovation. All thanks to her students' hard work and the promise of a sweet, sexy contractor who stood front-row center, cheering louder than anyone.

"Damn you, Kell," she whispered, hiding in the shadows backstage. Why was he so wonderful? It was impossible to resist him. She knew starting anything with him would be a bad idea. As long as he held fast to his silly curse notion it would only end in heartbreak. Her heartbreak.

But what if I can be the one to break the curse?

She didn't actually believe he was cursed. She might be a hopeless romantic, but she was still grounded in reality. All he needed was someone to prove to him that he wasn't a stepping stone to a better partner. That was easy. She doubted there was a better man in all the world.

The only reason it hadn't worked with any of his exes was because they weren't the one for him. Was she? Who could say, but she knew one thing deep in her soul. If she let Kell get away without even trying to see if there was something real there, she'd regret it for the rest of her life. This wasn't like her previous relationships. She wasn't letting her romantic notions sweep her away. She'd been fighting this thing for Kell since the beginning. It was different this time. Maybe that meant it was right. Maybe Kell was the one she'd been waiting for all along. Which was why she asked to talk to him after the show, and why the butterflies in her stomach were currently fluttering into a tornado of nerves.

The houselights came back up as the performers hurried backstage. She called out "Good show" to them as they rushed past her.

"Remember, we have another show tomorrow night so get lots of rest."

They normally had weeklong runs, but since this was a student performance there were only two shows. Two sold-out shows. She still couldn't believe Kell had managed to do that. No way could a man that sweet be cursed. The universe would never.

The audience filed out. All except one person.

Rachel's voice sounded from behind her. "Hottie handyman sure looks good in a suit."

Piper let out a startled squeak, dropping the curtain she'd been hiding behind as she stared at Kell. He did look unfairly handsome in his dark charcoal three-piece suit. She'd never been one for suits on men—they always looked better on women, in her opinion—but Kell in a suit made her forget there were still people in the building. Scratch that, the world.

"Don't sneak up on me like that," she scolded.

Rachel snorted. "I wasn't sneaking. You were too busy drooling at the guy you like to notice the fact that everyone has left except him and me."

She blinked, glancing around the dimly lit backstage. Silence filled the air. Rachel was right. Everyone was gone. Not surprising. They had another show, so it wasn't like anyone needed to stay to help derig, but normally she noticed as people left and called goodbye.

"Oh no." Worry crept up her neck. "I hope I wasn't rude by not saying goodbye to anyone."

She was usually very diligent about her goodbyes after a show, reminding her cast what an amazing job they did.

"Don't worry about it." Rachel waved a hand in the air. "Everyone was riding the high of a full house. It's understandable that your attention would be focused on the man who made that happen. Seriously, how did he do that?"

When she found out they'd sold every seat in the house, she'd admitted to Rachel that Kell had helped with ticket sales. Her bestie had suggested hiring him on as their marketing manager. Ha! Like she would ever have the funds to hire a marketing person.

"His mother is on an art council," she answered. "I guess she made some calls to patrons of the arts."

"Wow. Sweet, handy and has a good relationship with his mother." Rachel arched her neck, a smile curling her dark red lips. "And he cleans too."

Whipping her head around she stared out in the audience where Kell was going row by row, picking up discarded programs. Her heart flipped. That did it. She couldn't resist this man any longer. No matter what he thought about love and curses, she had to try.

"Piper." Rachel's voice held a hint of caution. "I know that look."

"What look?" she asked, focus still zeroed in on Kell.

"The one where your eyes turn into hearts like some kids' cartoon."

"That's not physically possible."

"You know what I mean," Rachel insisted. "I know I've been singing Kell's praise here, but remember the guy is antilove."

She blinked, turning her gaze back to her friend. "I know, but that's only because he thinks he's cursed. Don't people who believe in curses also believe they can be broken?"

"Oh, babe."

"No, I'm serious. Besides, you were the one who said I should loosen up. Go with the flow more."

Rachel's teeth came out to worry her bottom lip as concern filled her face. "I know, but I mean have a one-night stand with a stranger. Not hook up with a guy who is antidating. I know you, Piper. I don't want you getting your heart broken. Again."

"I won't." She whispered the words, feeling the truth of them fill her. She knew starting anything with Kell would be a risk, but she had to take it. She'd hate herself forever if she missed out on what could be the love of her life.

"If he hurts you, I'm gonna kill him."

She laughed softly. "No, you won't. Naya would be so mad if you went to jail for murder."

"Ha! She'd help me cover it up."

Rachel's girlfriend, Naya, was a sweetheart who Piper adored. She doubted the kind woman would hurt a fly, although she was extremely protective of her girlfriend, so who knew.

"We haven't even started anything yet." They might not start anything. As of now, this was all speculation. "Save the threats for possible future times. And get out of here. I'm sure Naya is out front with the car waiting for you."

Rachel sighed, pulling her in for a fierce hug. "Fine. But please, just remember to take care of your heart first. Make that man show you a good time, but don't fall unless he's falling too."

"You worry too much."

"I'm your best friend. It's my job."

She squeezed Rachel tight, grateful to have someone in her

life she knew she could always count on. They might not have worked out as a couple, but she was so glad life kept them connected. As she pulled away, her gaze went back to Kell. What she felt for him was decidedly not friendly. It was… more, and even if it blew up in her face and ripped her heart out, she knew she had to give it a go or she'd never be able to sleep at night for the what ifs.

Rachel left, waving goodbye to Kell on her way. Then the theater was empty, except for them.

"You don't have to do that," she said, coming out to center stage and sitting on the edge.

Kell glanced over at her with a smile. He made his way to where she sat, stack of paper programs in hand. Placing them on the stage next to her, he stood in front of her with a smile. The edge she sat on made her the perfect height to stare into his beautiful blue eyes.

"I know, but I feel a little bad that so many people left their programs in their seats. Whatever happened to theater decorum?"

She laughed. "Aerial shows tend to be a little rowdier than stage plays."

"I did notice a lot of cheering and wooing during the performance. Can't say I blame anyone. It was amazing. A few of those drops had me gripping my seat in terror, I'll admit. How do you all do that without screaming?"

"The terror is half the fun." She winked.

Kell threw back his head and laughed. The sound wrapped around her like a warm blanket, filling her with the courage to open her mouth and say what was on her mind.

"About the other day…" Her heart started to race as nerves set in.

His laughter died, gaze coming back to hers, a pensive expression filling his face.

"You know the day we…" She waved a hand to the spot

on the stage where they'd shared a kiss. Kell arched one eyebrow, remaining silent. "When *I* kissed you."

The corner of his lips quirked up. "I believe I remember that."

She swatted at him playfully. With a chuckle, he grabbed her hand, then stroked her palm with his thumb, eyes going serious.

"I also remember kissing you back and enjoying it immensely."

The racing eased at his confession. She'd assumed from his enthusiastic participation—and their preshow kiss earlier—he'd been as into it as her, but decoding people's feelings had never been her strong suit. Her autistic need for directness had been a problem in past relationship. She appreciated Kell not expecting her to infer.

"Me too." She smiled. "Enjoyed it, I mean."

He took a step closer, fitting himself between her legs as she sat on the edge of the stage floor, legs dangling off the end. He placed his hands on either side of her hips, leaning down until she could feel the warmth of his breath blow across her cheek as he whispered in her ear.

"Can I confess that I want to do it again?"

She rolled her lips in to keep from squealing like a schoolgirl. Instead, she lifted her hands, placing them on his shoulders.

"I'd like that."

His lips kissed her jaw, just below her ear. The barest of touches that sent a shock wave of heat straight to all her good parts. A small moan escaped her lips as his mouth traveled down her cheek with slow, torturous movements. Unable to fight it any longer, she turned her head, capturing his lips with her own. A growl left his throat, vibrating against her mouth. She let out a surprised squeak as his hand gripped her hips, pulling her closer to the edge of the stage until she was flush against his body.

Colors exploded behind her closed eyelids. All thought left her brain as pure rapture filled her every waking thought. She couldn't speak, couldn't think. All she could do was feel. And all she could feel was the fire this man was stoking inside her. She nearly lost her head and pulled him on stage to have her wicked way with him, but a tiny voice inside reminded her that they needed to talk first.

"Wait," she panted, pushing on his shoulder lightly as she pulled her lips from his.

Kell moved back, breathing heavily. Concern marred his brow. "What's wrong?"

"We need to talk first."

Realization dawned on his face. He blinked, as if only now seeing where he was and what they were doing. A flicker of something flashed in his eyes… Was that shame? Why was he ashamed?

"I'm sorry," he said, stepping back. "I didn't mean to—"

"Stop." She held up a hand. "Before you say anything else I might misinterpret, I need to say something."

He nodded, mouth shut tight.

"I like you, Kell." There, she said it. As scary as it was to think it, saying it out loud had been surprisingly easy. She felt lighter now, freer. "I enjoy spending time with you, and I'd like to do it more. Outside of, you know, here and emergency room visits."

He chuckled, smiling. "Don't forget delicious taco trucks and seafood restaurants."

"Those too," she said with a smile. "I was thinking we could hang out, maybe catch a movie or something? As more than…friends."

His smile slipped. "You mean…like dates?"

Fear started to claw its way up her throat. She nodded, rushing to explain. "I know how you feel about dating and you know how I feel."

"Completely opposite, you mean?" he said with a sad smile.

"Exactly, but maybe we can meet in the middle somewhere."

He frowned. "How do you mean?"

"I know you think you're cursed," she said, reaching out and grabbing his hand in hers. "But curses can be broken. You said it yourself—true love's kiss. Why not give this thing between us a shot? If it works out, amazing."

"And if it doesn't?" he said softly.

A heavy pain filled her, but she knew if she didn't at least give this a try, she'd regret it forever.

"Then we go our separate ways."

He stared at their joined hands, squeezing gently as his gaze found hers again. A wealth of pain, fear and hope burned from their blue depths. She held on to that last emotion with everything inside her.

"I don't want to hurt you," he confessed softly.

"Then don't." She tugged gently and he stepped closer. "Just be honest with me, no matter what you're feeling. Tell me if you're scared or angry or bored. Maybe we try this thing and it's not a fit, I'm not the one to break your curse."

He looked up at her with an indulgent smile. "Really going all in on the fairy-tale stuff, huh?"

"Shh."

He mimed zipping his lips and she had to hold in a laugh.

"All I'm saying is there's something here between us, we both know that. If we don't try to see what it is, where it could lead, we could regret it for the rest of our lives. I know I would."

He nodded. "Me too."

The weight of anxiety on her chest lifted, joy filling her as he released her hand and cupped her face in his warm palms.

"Okay," he said softly. "Let's give this thing a try."

Joy erupted inside her. Piper couldn't believe this was happening. She knew this could be a colossal mistake. Kell still thought he was cursed, but he was giving this a shot. Giving *them* a shot. One wrong move and he'd put that wall up around his heart again.

I won't let that happen. I'll show him just how loveable he is.

Because the truth was, she cared for him. Deeper than even she ever thought she could care for another person. Kell was sweet, kind and deserved all the love and happiness in the world. She was determined to show him that tonight. Now that they'd agreed to see each other, she couldn't wait another second to have him.

"Come here," she said with a beckoning finger. "I want you to see something."

She stood, moving across the stage to where a lone mat was set up from the ending act. The soft sound of Kell's footsteps followed her as he climbed onto the stage, stopping right beside her.

"What is it?"

"Down here."

She lay down on the mat and patted the space beside her. He followed, their shoulders pressing together, her heart racing at the contact.

"Look," she said, pointing up.

"Wow." Kell's soft exclamation sounded in the air.

The stage lights were off, but the houselights from the audience cast a glow on the slings and hoops hung high in the rafters. The reflections off the metal rigging bits caused sparkles of light to shoot through the air like twinkling stars in the night sky.

"It's magical," he said, voice filled with awe. His gaze turned to her, heat burning in those bright blue eyes. "Just like you."

She couldn't stop the smile from curling her lips. Sliding a hand around the back of his neck, she tugged, pulling him to her. He went willingly, latching his mouth on to hers in a soul-consuming kiss. He pressed the full length of his body against hers, but it still wasn't enough to quell the fire burning her from the inside out. She arched up, fusing their bodies together through the fabric they both wore. It wasn't close enough.

Dropping her hands, she quickly started to tug at his clothing. Kell chuckled above her.

"Eager?"

"You have no idea. Lose the clothes, mister," she demanded.

He stood. She lamented the loss of his warmth for two seconds before he quickly stripped his clothing off and her jaw dropped wide. Hello, Hottie Handyman! It was clear Kell's job in construction paid off. His body was a work of art that would make a sculptor weep. She wanted to touch every inch of skin she could see…and she could see all of it.

"Your turn," his deep voice commanded.

A command she was only happy to oblige. Sitting up, Piper made quick work of her shirt and pants. Tossing them off to who-cared-where and leaving her in nothing but her new black bra and panty set. Had she specifically bought it with Kell in mind? Yes. Had it been smart to spend money on frivolous lingerie when she had other bills to worry about? No. Was the hungry look in Kell's eyes worth it? Absolutely yes!

"You are the most beautiful goddess I have ever seen," he growled, climbing back on the mat and coming over to her.

She giggled, the sound turning into a moan when he latched his mouth onto that sweet spot on her neck just below her ear. His hands caressed her bare skin, fingers making quick work of divesting her of her undergarments.

"Shoot, hold on," he said, moving to his discarded clothing and pulling his wallet from his pants pocket. He pulled out a foil packet, quickly tearing it open and protecting them both. Good thing he'd been prepared because she was so far gone, she could barely remember her name, let alone being safe. She hadn't exactly planned for this to happen.

But she was so glad it was happening.

He placed himself at her entrance, pausing as he stared into her eyes. She gasped at the emotions she saw swimming in their clear blue depths.

"Piper," he said softly. "I want you to know how much you mean to me. This is… You are special."

Tears blurring her vision, she blinked them away, swallowing past the emotion clogging her throat she replied. "You're special too, Kell."

His mouth fused to hers as he joined them together. Universes exploded and formed behind her eyes at the feel of their connection. A rush, bigger than any aerial drop she'd ever performed, sent her heart racing through the stratosphere. They moved in unison, as if they'd done this dance for lifetimes. As she felt the wave of completion wash over her, Kell quickened his pace, joining her in the bliss that was their souls and bodies becoming one.

Piper melted inside. Hope filled her even as that tiny voice warned this could all end in disaster. She ignored the voice, staring at the twinkling lights above, seeing only their beauty and the beauty of this moment. Gloom and doom had no place in the start of what she hoped would be her very own happily-ever-after.

CHAPTER NINETEEN

"When was the last time this roof was repaired, Kell?" Cash grabbed a roof shingle, which proceeded to crumble like a dried leaf in his hand.

Kell let out a heavy sigh, anger rising in his gut again at Donald's shoddy landlord duties. "As far as I can tell, Mr. Noll hasn't done any significant repairs to the place since he purchased it fifteen years ago."

"What the hell?" Cash tossed the remaining chunk of shingle off the roof. It sailed through the air, landing in the large dumpster they'd rented below. "No wonder this roof is a mess. I'm surprised the whole theater isn't flooded."

"There are a lotta leaks due to the roof, but thankfully no major damage. Took a lot to convince Donald to even address the roof."

"Sounds like a real jerk," Mal grunted, ripping up shingles and tossing them down.

His brother didn't know the half of it. Donald was a real piece of work. He'd be glad when this job was done.

"Hello up there," a melodic voice called from the attic window.

Kell glanced up to see Piper sticking her head out, a bright smile on her face. His heart skipped a beat, reminding him a part of him very much wasn't looking forward to the end of this project. What was he going to do about Piper? Things had gotten doubly complicated since their magical night after her first show.

He'd gone out with the cast after their final show and enjoyed seeing Piper receive the praise of the cast. The bar had been noisy and crowded, not an issue for him, but she'd clearly felt overwhelmed after a bit. He offered to leave with her, but she didn't want to disappoint everyone, so they wandered out to the back patio, which was quieter and less congested. They spent the night chatting about favorite movies and books. She, of course, loved everything romance while he preferred documentaries and mysteries. It had been a wonderful night that ended with him taking her back to the condo and making out in his car for hours before moving their activities to his back seat, which was not as spacious as he'd like, but they'd been so far gone they couldn't wait.

He hadn't done that since he was a teenager.

But now he had significant heartburn eating away at him. The guilt of the secret he held was manifesting into physical ailments. He had to find a way to tell her Donald was selling the place without violating his contract and risking his charity. But how?

"I got y'all some ice-cold root beer." Piper climbed out onto the roof, three bottles in hand, the necks between her fingers.

His heart jumped into his throat. As carefully as possible, he hurried over to her.

"Hey, don't come out here. It's dangerous."

She gazed up at him with an indulgent smile. "Seriously? You know what I do for a living. Standing on a perfectly solid roof is much safer than doing an ankle hang fifteen feet in the air."

He wasn't entirely sure what an ankle hang was, but based on the name, he bet he didn't want to know. Especially if she was the one demonstrating it. He knew she was trained, but one of these days she was going to give him a heart attack with those tricks.

"Different kind of danger," he insisted. "Besides, there's

rules about who can be on a roof when we're fixing it, safety and legal stuff."

"Shoot, I'm sorry." She quickly scrambled back inside the attic window, popping her head out again and holding the bottles aloft. "I just didn't want you guys getting dehydrated up here."

Her kindness warmed his heart, easing the racing panic that started the second he saw her climb onto the roof. Reaching out, he took the bottles from her grasp with one hand and cupped her cheek with the other. Placing a soft kiss to her lips, he rubbed his nose against hers.

"And that is why you are the sweetest person to ever exist."

She giggled. "If bringing you cold drinks while you work on a hot day makes me the sweetest, you, sir, have a very low bar."

She had no idea. The people in his world operated on a "you scratch my back, and I'll scratch yours" policy. No one did anything simply because they were trying to help others. It was all about how you could benefit, get richer, look better. Even Donald was trying to spend as little as possible to fix this place just to turn it around and sell it at the highest profit he could weasel.

And I'm helping him do it.

Bile rose in his gut at the reminder.

"You must be the famous Piper," Cash said, carefully making his way toward them.

"I'm famous?" She gave Kell a cheeky look.

"Kell says you dance like an 'angel in the sky,' and that's a direct quote."

"Oh, really?"

Cash nodded. "Yup, you've got Old Kell here starstruck. I swear you're all he talks about these days. 'Piper is amazing. She's so sweet and beautiful and you should see her drop from the ceiling. It takes ten years off my life, but it's amazing.' He can't stop talking about you. Like a lovesick schoolgirl."

"Enough, Cash." Kell sighed. *Someone save him from annoying little brothers.* "And what's with the 'old' stuff? You're only two years younger than me, punk. Piper, I'm sorry for him. This is my brother Cash, who doesn't know when to shut up."

"That's me," Cash said with a grin.

"And that's Mal." He pointed to Mal who was focused on the task of ripping up the old shingles but offered a small wave in their direction.

"Nice to meet you both," Piper said, her smile warm and inviting. "I don't mean to interrupt your work, I just wanted to make sure you don't melt out here."

It was a warm summer day, but thankfully they had some cloud cover blocking the sun from blazing down on them. He passed two of the cold drinks to Cash, bending down to place another quick kiss to her addictive lips.

"See that right there? The sweetest."

She blushed, the pink hue flushing across her cheeks in stark contrast to the dark blue streaks in her hair.

"I have a class in a few minutes, but don't hesitate to reach out if you need anything. Nice to meet you, Cash. Mal."

Cash popped the top of his root beer, lifting it in a toast to her. "Likewise, angel."

He glowered at his brother. The man couldn't stop flirting to save his life. Cash just grinned, giving him a wink as he took a deep sip of his drink. Mal grunted, offering a half wave as Piper ducked back into the attic and disappeared into the building.

Once she was gone, he turned to find both of his brothers frowning at him. With Mal that was par for the course. He didn't think he'd ever seen his grumpy baby brother smile. But Cash? Cash was never without a grin, smart-alecky or genuine.

"What?" he asked, twisting the top off his own drink and tossing it down to the dumpster.

"She's nice. I like her."

"I do too." What was Cash so upset about?

"Have you told her about Donald's plans to sell yet?"

He glanced back to the window, worried she might have overhead. Or hopeful she had? If she overheard about Donald's plans to sell, it wouldn't be his fault, right? That wasn't breaking the contract. Damn, he was grasping at straws trying to solve this problem. And it wouldn't work anyhow. If she discovered the sale from him in any way, he could be held liable, and Donald could sue. Even if it was an accident.

"No. You know I can't tell her."

Cash glared. "This is messed up."

"I know but what the hell am I supposed to do about it?"

Cash swore. "There's got to be some way to let her know she's gonna be out of a space for her business in a few weeks."

Not only her business, but her home too. But his brothers didn't know that part. No one did. Save for him. Secretly he was already looking for new theaters and apartments for her. The latter was a lot easier to find than the former. But even if he did find her a new space, that didn't negate the fact that he was keeping information from her now.

"He can't say anything," Mal spoke up, grabbing the last bottle from Cash and opening it. "None of us can. Mr. Noll would sue us for everything we have, including Helping Homes. We can't allow that to happen."

Mal was more involved with their charity than he or Cash. His baby brother had a driving need to provide safety for those who needed it. He wasn't sure why. Mal had never shared what possessed him to fight so hard for others, but he was damn proud of his little brother.

"I know that, Mal, but we can't just leave Piper in the dark," Cash argued. "She's about to lose her business, and her landlord won't even give her a warning she's gonna be kicked out."

Mal's scowl increased, his grip tightening on his bottle. He muttered a dark curse, calling Donald a creative name Kell wholeheartedly agreed with.

"She's not losing her business," he reminded his brothers. "Just the building. And don't worry. I'm on the hunt for a new space."

Cash snorted. "Yeah, cause the metro area is filled with vacant theater spaces that can accommodate aerialists."

"I said I'm on it, Cashel. If you really want to help Piper, then put some feelers out to your contacts." With Cash's charm, he tended to have the best client relationships. All the bigwigs with deep pockets loved his flattery and flirtatious ways.

Cash nodded, his anger deflating as he was presented with a task to help. "I can do that."

"Good." He nodded. "Let me worry about when Piper finds out and, in the meantime, we can do what we do best and find a space for someone who needs one."

Mal glanced at him, a question clear on his face even as his mouth remained closed.

"What is it, Malachy?" Because he knew his baby brother wanted to say something.

Mal worked his jaw, finally opening his mouth to ask. "Are you guys dating?"

The question shouldn't have surprised him. He did kiss her, twice, in his brothers' presence. To most people it would be obvious, but he knew Mal liked to have correct information on things directly told to him.

"Yes," he answered truthfully.

Mal's scowl deepened. "Makes things a bit more complicated, don't you think?"

"What do you think is going to happen when she finds out you're the agent selling this place and you knew all along?" Cash added.

Nothing good.

"Dammit, I know!" He ran a hand through his hair, sweat greasing his palm. He chugged the rest of his drink and tossed the bottle with more force than necessary into the dumpster. It clanged against the pile of broken shingles, thankfully not breaking.

"I know she'll be angry, and she'll have every right to be, but what the hell am I supposed to do? If I tell her, we could lose the charity, and if I don't…" He stared at his brothers, pleading with them to find a solution. "What do I do?"

Cash's gaze turned sympathetic. "I don't know, Kell."

Mal's scowl softened into a sad frown. He shrugged. His brothers were as adrift as he was. He had three weeks to find a solution to this problem, or he risked losing Piper forever.

She's going to leave anyway. Why delay the inevitable?

A dark cloud of impending doom washed over him. If his past was any indication, it was only a matter of time before Piper dropped him and found her real forever partner. What the hell was he doing? He knew this was going to end badly, but for some reason he couldn't stop what was happening. The thought of not spending this precious time he had left with Piper hurt worse than the inevitable heartbreak he knew was coming.

Not having Piper, having Piper and losing her, both were torture. He might as well enjoy the bliss before the downfall. Or maybe he was just fooling himself into thinking this time would be different, even though, deep down, he knew it never would be. Guilt and fear collided in his gut. A deep wrenching pain no amount of antacid could fix. He had to face the facts. Piper was going to leave him one way or another. What he did with their time until then was up to him. He could run from it or…try and make enough warm memories to last through the dark lonely nights without her.

CHAPTER TWENTY

THIS CAN'T BE REAL.

Piper stared at herself in the full-length mirror in the condo bedroom. She didn't look like herself. Well, she did, but a fancy version of herself. Earlier today, a box had arrived with a message from Kell.

I'd be honored if you would join me for an evening of entertainment. I hope everything fits (I checked your sizes with Rachel). See you at six.
Kell

What possible entertainment could they enjoy while dressed like this? She stroked her hand down the dark blue gown, the tiny sparkling crystals bumping against her palm. The smooth silk was covered in them. The dress fell past her ankles, landing just above the floor and leaving her toes exposed in the sliver strappy heels that had also been in the box. It clung to her body perfectly, fitting like a glove. The bodice had some kind of boning structure, allowing her to wear it without a bra, which was nice. One arm was left bare while the other was covered in a flowy sheer lace with bits of crystals sparkling amongst the intricately woven threads.

She'd never worn anything so beautiful.

Or expensive.

She'd seen the designer's name, Vivienne Westwood. A

fashionista she was not—Piper preferred comfort over brand names—but she knew enough to realize this dress must have cost Kell a fortune. Not to mention the beautiful earrings and necklaces that had also been included. The dark blue sapphires glistened against her skin, making the streaks of blue in her hair pop.

She'd done her best with her makeup and hair to match the elegance of the dress. A soft smoky eye paired with a deep rose lip. With her hair, she kept it simple. She had slicked it back and fashioned it into a soft low bun and added a bit of the fresh baby's breath that had come in the gorgeous bouquet of roses Kell sent along with the package.

"We're definitely not going to the movies." Not dressed like this.

A knock on the door interrupted her musings. She glanced at the clock on the wall. Six o'clock on the dot. Grabbing her small black clutch, she hurried to the front door and opened it. The air was knocked clean from her body at the sight she saw. Kell in a suit had been intoxicating. Kell in a tux was about to take her out.

"Wow!" she whispered.

That devilishly handsome grin curled his lips. "Hey, that's my line. You look absolutely beautiful, Piper. Does everything fit?"

She nodded, unable to form a single thought when he looked like he had literally just stepped out of her dreams.

"Excellent. Then are you ready to go?"

She blinked. Words finally coming back into her head. "Go where? Your note said a night of entertainment, but I gotta tell you, most of my experiences with entertainment don't require me to wear a dress that cost more than my rent." Or what her rent used to cost anyway.

"It's a surprise," Kell said, offering her his arm.

Slipping her arm thought his, she allowed him to escort

her out of the building where her stomach took flight once again at what she saw waiting for them.

"Is that limo for us?"

"It is."

She glanced at him from the corner of her eye. "Really pulling out all the stops here. I thought men stopped trying to impress women once they gave it up."

She chuckled, but he didn't join in.

"Only immature little boys use devious tactics to manipulate others into getting what they want." He opened the limo door and offered her his hand. "I'm not trying to impress you, Piper. I'm giving you the things you deserve. And you, sweetheart, deserve the world."

She caught a hint of something in his eyes she couldn't decipher. What she could have done to deserve such expensive clothes and a limo ride, she had no idea, but if Kell wanted to spoil her, far be it from her to stop him. Tonight, she was living out her real-life fairy-tale dream.

Then why did she have a tingling of worry in her gut that something was wrong?

Pushing the thought away, she placed her hand in his and slid into the limo. The ride was smooth, despite the pothole-ridden city streets. She had no idea how the driver managed to miss every bump—maybe the limo was equipped with the world's best suspension system. Before she truly had time to enjoy the luxury of riding in a limo, the car pulled to a gentle stop.

"We're here," Kell said smiling.

"And where is here exactly?" He still hadn't told her what tonight's entertainment was.

Grinning like a kid on Christmas, Kell opened the door, stepped out and offered his hand. She allowed him to help her from the car, her breath leaving her lungs for a second time that night. Before her stood the brand-new Denver Opera

House. Construction had been going on for over a year on the beautiful building.

"What are we doing here?" She frowned in confusion. "It's not supposed to be open for another month."

"To the public," Kell confirmed with a nod. "But tonight is a special preview performance for the angel investors."

She blinked, his words swirling around in her brain. "Angel investors? You're one of the angel investors for the Denver Opera House?"

"My family is. I told you my mother is a patron of the arts. Since she's out of the country and Cash and Mal aren't big on opera, I decided to take someone who I knew would appreciate the skill of the performers."

He led her toward the front doors, her mind still reeling from the shock. She loved opera, but she'd never been able to afford a live performance. The fact that she was going to be able to see a special preview… What was her life right now?!

They headed up the sleek stone stairs flanked by large Corinthian marble pillars. The tall double doors were open, doormen on either side, checking people in. The small crowd of people, all dressed in the most elegant dresses and tuxes Piper had ever seen, slowly made their way inside.

Kell handed a gold-foiled invitation to the doorman, who nodded before handing it back and motioning to a short white woman in a dark usher uniform.

"Your private box seats are ready for you, Mr. Thorson. Should you need anything, Samantha will be at your service."

"Curtain is in ten minutes," Samantha said with a smile. "I can take you to your seats now if you would like?"

Kell nodded. "Thank you, Samantha, we would appreciate that."

"Box seats?" she whispered as they followed the usher. "You have private box seats?"

Kell just smiled with a small shrug.

Samantha led them up a set of stairs and down a short hall. The usher pulled back a large red velvet curtain to reveal a small balcony-sitting area with two very fancy and plush-looking chairs.

"There's a button on the wall just here," Samantha said, pointing. "Please don't hesitate to push it if you need anything. I'll come right away. Enjoy the show."

"Thank you," Kell said.

"Yes, thank you." Piper smiled at the young woman. For a split second, time suspended. She looked at Samantha in her pressed slacks and vest, white button-up underneath, and she was transported to a time not so long ago when she was the usher, picking up shifts to make ends meet between performance gigs. Now here she was in private box seats.

But I'm not really here.

Physically she was, but she had to remember the only reason she was getting this special treatment was because of the man beside her. She wasn't the rich fancy one. How long before someone here saw her for the fraud she was? An interloper, a pretender. At the theater, when he was in his jeans and flannel, she could pretend he was just a handyman. In the same economic class as her. But tonight was shattering her illusion. The man had money to burn. She wasn't sure how she felt about that. At least a sizeable portion of his wealth was going to fund the arts and help house those in need, according to him.

Maybe I should research him.

"Piper?"

She blinked, pulled out of her thoughts by the concern in Kell's voice.

"Are you okay?"

The genuine worry on his face calmed her racing thoughts. No. No surreptitiously online searching into his life. Kell had been nothing but honest with her. She was simply letting her past get the better of her. Kell wasn't Larry. She'd been careful this time. Tonight, she needed to let the past go and enjoy the present.

"I'm fine, just a little shocked at all…this."

"In a good way I hope."

He guided her to one of the chairs, waiting until she sat before taking his own.

"In a fantastic way. I love opera. I've never been able to see a performance live, but I've always dreamed of it."

"Then I am happy to make your dream come true."

The houselights dimmed, and a hush fell over the audience. Kell leaned forward to place a soft kiss on her lips. Her heart skipped several beats. As the curtain rose, she focused her attention on the stage, his words echoing in her mind. She couldn't help but wonder if this beautiful dream they were sharing would last, or if their differences were too vast an obstacle to overcome.

CHAPTER TWENTY-ONE

Last night had been amazing. So amazing in fact that Piper had forgotten half the warm-up and gotten stuck trying to teach the most basic moves to her beginners' class. Her focus was shot. Hard to concentrate when her mind kept wandering back to the way Kell made her body sing last night after the opera. Which had been equally amazing. She'd never felt more like a princess in her life. A small giggle tried to claw its way up her throat, but she swallowed it back down. Time to keep it together. Class was nearly over.

As she walked the class through the cooldown stretches, she smiled. "Don't forget to drink lots of water. You all did great today."

The students thanked her as they packed up and headed out of the theater. Her gaze traveled up to the ceiling. Kell and his brothers were up there working on the roof today. She'd spent the night at his place, and he drove them back this morning. Spending the night in a comfy king-size bed had been a welcome change from her rickety old cot. She hoped to do it again soon. Not just for the bed—the company was the best part.

She let her smile grow, allowing the giggle to escape this time as she started to take down the slings. The teaching day was over. A good thing too, since she was starving. She wondered how Kell was doing. Would he finish soon, want to grab dinner?

Her phone beeped with a calendar alert. Picking it up from the spot on the floor where she'd placed it during class, she glanced at the notification. A heavy sigh left her. There were two weeks left on her lease and Donald hadn't sent her any paperwork on the renewal. She'd been hoping he'd send something soon, so she didn't have to actually talk to the man, but it was getting too close for comfort. She had to call him and get the ball rolling.

Bringing up her contacts, she pressed Donald's number and took a deep steadying breath.

"Yeah, what is it?"

What a delightful greeting. She shoved down her irritation. "Hello, Mr. Noll. This is Piper Pitts."

"I know who the hell it is. Your name comes up on the damn screen."

Someone was in a cheery mood. This did not bode well for her, but time was of the essence, so she pushed on.

"I'm calling about my lease renewal. As you know, the lease is up in two weeks. I was wondering when you would be sending the new lease paperwork for me to sign?"

Silence filled the line.

"Mr. Noll?"

"I'm not," his gruff voice finally answered.

"Pardon?"

"I'm not sending the paperwork over to you."

Confused, she pressed her phone tighter to her ear. "Oh, um, did you want me to come to you and get it or—"

"No," he abruptly interrupted. "I'm not drawing up a new lease with you."

Now she was really confused. A prickle of apprehension tickled the back of her neck. Heart rate rising, she sought clarification. "I'm sorry, I don't understand."

Donald let loose a cruel bark of laughter. "Let me spell it out for you, sweetheart."

Gross. She nearly gagged at the endearment. It sounded beautiful coming from Kell, loving and precious. But Donald spat the word with a condescending sneer that felt slimy and mean.

"I'm not sending any new paperwork over because I'm not renewing your lease."

Her world slammed to a stop. Sweat gathered on her palms. The loud thump of her heart sounded like the drums of doom, leading her into a battle she had no hope of surviving.

"You're not renewing my—"

"I'm getting rid of the headache, once and for all," he interrupted again, as if he hadn't just destroyed her with five simple words.

"Getting rid of…but I don't…all the fixes? You finally put work into…" Realization dawned on her. "Oh, you're fixing it up to sell, aren't you?"

His cruel laughter filled her ear. "You finally used the two brain cells you possess. Yeah, I'm selling the place."

Did Kell know? Did he know all his hard work making this place perfect for her would be going to someone else? Her anger at Donald grew twofold for lying to them both like this. Kell was going to be so upset. Why would a cheap man like Donald even waste his time with fixes? Why not sell the place "as is" and be done with it if he hated it so much?

"I don't understand why you're putting money into the fixes if you're just going to sell it?" Especially when she'd been asking for these fixes for years.

"My agent said it would fetch a higher price if we spruced it up a little. Since he's a licensed contractor, we worked all the repairs into his commission fee. I got a great deal, and I stand to make a mountain of money, so pack your bags, Ms. Pitts."

Wait…his real estate agent was also the contractor? As in… Kell? No, it couldn't be. He wouldn't. Kell was a good man, a kind soul. No way would he have been lying to her this whole time. She refused to believe he could do something so heartless.

"Your agent," she asked with a shaky voice, needing to know the truth. "What's his name?"

Donald barked out another cruel laugh. "You know the guy. He's been working around the place for the past six weeks. Kellen Thorson of Thorson Realty."

Her world turned dark. Piper sunk to the hard stage floor as her heart broke into a million piercing shards in her chest. She couldn't get enough air into her lungs as the panic clawed its way up her throat. She'd been wrong. So very, very wrong. The ridiculous notion she'd dismissed of Kell being a spy had been silly... He was so much worse.

Damn her for not googling him.

"You have two weeks to get all your junk out, Pitts."

Donald's harsh command raked along her spine, but it couldn't touch the pain tearing her soul apart.

"Two weeks isn't enough time," she said, managing to push the words past her dry throat.

"Yeah well, that's your problem not mine. We had a set end date for the lease. Legally I am under no obligation to renew it. Hell, I didn't even have to tell you I wasn't renewing it. Consider this a favor."

A favor? If she hadn't called and inquired, she knew 100 percent he would have shown up on the last day of the lease with eviction papers. Here he was trying to act like he was being generous? The man was a monster.

"Two weeks," he demanded again before the line went dead.

She sat on the stage, body overheating even as her soul felt frozen. How could he do this to her? Not Donald. That underhanded move she expected from the creep. But Kell? She thought they had something special. He understood her, cared for her...or so she thought. Maybe she was as naive as people said. Her initial instincts had been right. He'd been playing her from the beginning. Keeping her from seeing the obvious so she wouldn't do anything to hamper the sale. Not that she could anyway. She had no legal ground to stop Donald. It was his building.

What a fool she'd been.

It was the Larry situation all over again. When would she learn? What her grandparents had was an anomaly. The fairytale love she'd been chasing her whole life had done nothing but rip her heart into shreds. It was time to grow up and face the facts of the cold, cruel world.

Love was an illusion.

She sat on the cold stage floor, wondering what she was going to do, where she was going to go, when Kell's voice filled the air.

"There you are. We just finished up. Wanna grab some dinner? I promise these knuckleheads won't be joining us."

"Hey, that's hurtful, bro." Cash teased cheerfully.

She glanced up at the brothers. Normally the sight of Kell made her heart skip a beat. Not anymore. The cruel spike of betrayal twisted in her chest. She closed her eyes as tears leaked down her cheeks.

"Piper?"

She felt his presence by her side in seconds.

"What's wrong?"

His hand reached out, landing on her shoulder. The warm palm she normally took great comfort in burned her skin. A venomous touch, she now understood. Scooting back, she opened her eyes and glared at the face she once considered to be the most handsome she'd ever laid eyes on.

"Two weeks," she managed to growl out.

He shook his head, confusion pulling his brow down. "I don't understand."

"Two weeks," she repeated, the fire of betrayal burning away the sadness. "I just had a little chat with Donald about my lease renewal. The one that isn't happening because he's selling this place in two weeks."

His face went pale. She thought she heard Cash mutter something in the background, but she ignored it. All of her focus, all her ire, was reserved for the man before her who had broken her heart.

"How could you, Kell?" she whispered, unable to keep the pain from her voice. "How could you not tell me?"

"I wanted to, Piper, I swear." He held up his hands, distress lining his face. "But Donald made me sign an NDA. If I told you anything about the sale, he could sue us into the ground. We'd lose everything, including Helping Homes. I couldn't risk the foundation. I had to…"

"Betray me," she finished for him.

He reared back as if she'd slapped him. "No…no. It wasn't like that."

"Then what was it like? Because from where I'm sitting, it looks exactly like that."

"Sweetheart, I—"

"Don't." She stood, glaring at him, allowing all the pain he'd caused her to seep into her eyes. "Don't ever call me that again. I was wrong about you, Kell. I thought we had something special, but in the end I'm the one to suffer. Maybe you are cursed after all."

She watched as something flicked in his eyes. The joyful spirit she'd always come to associate with this man splintered, resignation creeping into those once-happy eyes. A tiny ping of guilt wormed its way inside, but she shoved it down. She couldn't feel sorry for him when he was the one who knew all along and said nothing.

"Piper… I'm sorry… I…"

Cash came up behind his brother, gently grasping his arm and helping him stand. "Come on, man. Let's give her some space."

Cash gave her a sympathetic glance. She wondered how much his brothers knew. Probably everything. Did they laugh about her naivete behind her back? She felt so stupid!

Kell still stared at her as his brother tugged him away, a sheen of moisture filling those eyes that gazed at her with pain and regret. At least he felt bad. It meant he wasn't a complete monster. Mal glanced down as he passed by her. She followed his gaze to see her hand, fingers furiously fidgeting against her thigh. The anxiety filling her was about to burst into full-blown overwhelm.

"Do you need anything?" the usually silent brother asked.

She nodded over to the one sling still hanging on the stage. "I've got it."

He nodded, moving over to help Cash lead Kell out of the theater. Once they were gone, she walked over to the sling and slipped into the fabric. Placing the sling under her armpits, across her back, she started to spin. One toe on the ground, she used her other leg to gain momentum, spinning faster and faster. She let the tears fall, her movements flinging them against her body as she spun. A deep aching cry ripped from her throat as she lifted her legs, falling back.

The fabric caught on her hips as she spun upside down, but it still wasn't fast enough to calm her nerves. Tucking her knees in close on either side of the fabric, she made her body as small as possible to increase the spin. Finally, the panic started to ease. She stayed like that until the spin slowed, all the blood rushing to her head, tears sliding down into her hair.

"I am fortune's fool." She whispered the very apt Shakespeare quote into the empty theater.

Tilting back up, she placed her feet on the floor, slipped out of the sling and stood on the stage. The place she'd built her business on. The place that held countless performances over the years, helped hundreds of people discover a love of aerials. Not just a theater, but somewhere lifelong friendships were formed. A safe space for sensory seekers. This place wasn't just a building and a business. It was her heart.

And he'd destroyed it.

He'd destroyed all of it.

She thought he was her knight in shining armor, come to save the day, but she was wrong. Kell wasn't her prince. He was the frog, and she was a fool to believe they'd have a fairy-tale ending.

CHAPTER TWENTY-TWO

"This 'woe is me' act is getting old, man."

Kell growled at Cash, pushing past his little brother to grab another beer from the fridge. They were all at his home after a long day of finishing up the roof at Star-Crossed Theater.

"You've been a real bummer on the job. Even Mal thinks so," Cash continued.

Mal grunted, grabbing the beer Kell handed him and shrugging noncommittedly. He thought about not handing a beer to Cash—his annoying little brother didn't deserve one—but they'd had a long workday and Cash was right. His mood the past week had been lower than the Mariana Trench.

"Sorry I'm not Sally Sunshine," he muttered, taking a deep swig of his beer. "But it's kind of hard to put on a happy face when I'm sweating my soul out working on that damned roof."

He was exceedingly glad that job was done. Not only because it had been hot as hell up there, but the roof repair had been the last part of the job. The repair job, that is. He still had to sell the place at the price Donald wanted for it.

"Oh, so the mopey mood has to do with heat intolerance and not the fact that you betrayed Piper?"

His hand tightened around the glass bottle. He hated that word. It was ugly and cruel and…true. He had betrayed Piper. But what choice did he have? He'd spent the past week doing his best to avoid her while he finished work on the roof. As much as he ached to see her, to try and explain again, he knew it was coming from a selfish place. The sight of him only caused her pain. Reminded her of his part in taking her business and home away. He'd already hurt her so much. It would be cruel of him to press the matter just to make himself feel better.

He knew things would eventually end. Story of his life. What he hadn't expected was how deep his feelings for Piper had become. He'd planned to have some fun and get out before he got hurt again. But he'd made a grave error. Now, not only was he hurting, but Piper was too. All because he thought he could have what he wanted for once.

What a fool he was.

"You know you're an idiot, right?" Cash said, flopping down on the couch.

Kell let out a heavy sigh, sinking into the armchair across from his brother. "Takes one to know one, baby brother."

"We're resorting to childish name-calling now?"

He shrugged. Glancing over to Mal, who sat in an identical chair to his right, he lifted a hand. "You want to get in on this brother bashing?"

"I'm not bashing you," Cash insisted. "I'm trying to help you."

"I don't need help," he grumbled, picking at the label on his beer bottle. "I did my job and, in the process, hurt the woman I lo—hurt Piper. I'm a jerk. End of story."

The room fell silent. The weight of his actions pressed down on him.

"You're not a jerk," Cash said softly. "A jerk would imply that you did what you did out of malicious intent. You were stuck between a rock and a hard place. Should you have told Piper what was going on? Yes, but—"

"How?" he shouted, cutting Cash off. "How could I have told her about Donald's plans to sell without violating the NDA and opening us up to a lawsuit? Did you want me to risk Helping Homes? What would have happened then? What about all those people, those families that count on us to provide them with a place to live? A home? How can I put one person over hundreds in need?"

His heart pounded in his chest at the unfairness of it all. He'd tried. He'd tried so damn hard to find a solution where everyone won. But there hadn't been one.

"I couldn't do that to Helping Homes or you guys."

Because it wasn't just his charity. It was Cash's and Mal's too. Damn Donald for telling her! All he'd needed was a few more days. He would have come up with a solution…probably. Now, it was too late. Piper was losing her theater, and he'd lost her.

The curse held strong.

Only if she meets the love of her life now.

He scowled, downing the rest of his beer. The thought of Piper with anyone else made his blood boil. He wanted her to be happy. She deserved happiness more than anyone in the entire world. But for the first time in a long time, he wanted to be that someone. He wanted to be the one to make her happy, to hear her laughter, to hold her in the dark of the night.

I lost that right.

And he had no clue how to earn it back.

"We could have helped you find a way to tell her," Cash said. "You don't always have to take on every problem yourself, Kellen."

"I don't do that—"

"You do," Cash insisted.

He glanced over to Mal for confirmation.

"You always have." Mal nodded.

His inner voice agreed with his brothers and was just as annoying. Sinking back into his chair, he scowled at the two. "Yeah, well, I'm the oldest. It's my job to take care of you two knuckleheads."

"Maybe when we were kids and Mom and Dad left you

in charge, but we're adults, Kell. We can make our own decisions. Help out. You don't have to protect us anymore. We could have helped you find a solution."

"I don't see how," he grumbled. "The clause in the contract was airtight."

"It was a ridiculous clause," Mal muttered, finishing off his beer.

He agreed, but they'd all read it and signed it. It hadn't seemed so bad. Until he met Piper and realized the gravity of what he'd just done. He'd signed his soul away to the devil. A bit dramatic, but it was how he felt right now.

"But," Mal continued. "I understand why you stayed silent. You were following the rules and protecting the people who need us. You did the right thing by them."

The youngest of the Thorson brothers was a strict rule follower. Kell knew rules made Mal feel safe, in control. Still, knowing he did the right thing did nothing to ease the raw, tearing pain ripping his soul to shreds. If it had been right, why did he feel so wrong?

"Sometimes the right thing is the wrong thing," Cash said.

Mal frowned. "That doesn't make any sense."

None of this made sense. It was all one giant mess with no discernible solution. Like the trolley problem. Do you save the one person or the five? Either way, someone is going to be hurt so can there really be any solution that is "right" or is the question, in itself, always wrong?

Dammit. He needed another beer.

He made his way to the fridge, calling over his shoulder. "You guys want another beer?"

"Are we wallowing?" Cash asked. "'Cause beer isn't the drink of a pity party. That's a job for tequila. Of course, last time we did tequila shots you were praising the porcelain gods the next day, so maybe you should stick to something milder for your delicate system."

His little brother was riding his last nerve. Cash turned everything into a joke. Nothing about this situation was funny.

"I'm not wallowing." He grabbed three beers, slamming the fridge door shut with more force than necessary as he glared at Cash. "I'm just…upset. This whole situation is messed up and I thought…"

Making his way back to the living room, he passed his brothers their drinks and sunk back into his chair.

"I don't know why I thought I could break the stupid curse," he muttered, twisting off the cap and drinking deeply.

"Curse?" Mal frowned.

"You gotta be freaking kidding me." Cash pointed the neck of his beer bottle at Kell. "Do you still believe that ridiculous 'curse' notion?"

"What curse?" Mal said, scooting forward on his chair.

Cash pointed to Kell "Fool over here got it into his head that he's cursed by love. That every woman he dates breaks up with him then immediately finds her one true love. It's why he stopped serious relationships a few years back."

He snorted, lifting his beer bottle as he spoke. "You're one to talk, Mr. New Girlfriend Every Two Weeks."

"Hey." Cash held up a hand. "That's different and we're talking about you, not me. You're not cursed."

"I am," he insisted.

"Curses aren't real," Mal replied.

Sure as hell felt real. He'd opened his heart again only for the universe to crush it.

"Let's look at the facts," Cash said, sitting forward and placing his beer on the coffee table. He held up a hand and started counting off on his fingers. "You got hired for a job to fix up and sell the theater, but you couldn't tell the current owner about the sale for risk of losing Helping Homes."

"Yeah, we know all this, Cash."

"But," Cash continued, holding up another finger. "Once

you met the tenant, Piper, you started falling for her and felt guilty so you tried to come up with a way to tell her, but Donald did it before you could. Now she's rightfully mad at you and you guys broke up, leading you to think the curse worked its magic again."

His jaw clenched at the cavalier way Cash pointed it out. "Yeah, your point?"

"If the curse is real, as you so often like to say, then the next person Piper is with will be her one true love."

And he would like to knock whoever the person would be into the stratosphere. Whoever they were, they better treat her like the goddess she was, or they'd have to answer to him.

"So be that guy," Cash finished, sitting back with a smug smile.

"Huh?"

"Be the next person Piper is with. Go to her, Apologize, find a way to earn back her trust and live happily ever after or whatever."

He barked out a laugh of disbelief. Of course Cash would think it would be that easy.

"Are you kidding? You heard what she said. I doubt she ever wants to talk to me again. I ruined her life. Her studio might go under, thanks to me."

"Technically it's Donald's fault," Mal pointed out. "Not yours."

"I don't think she sees it that way." He sure as hell felt responsible for it.

"She's had some time to think." Cash shrugged. "Maybe now she'll be able to realize what a hard position you were in. She's a good person, she'll understand. Go apologize again."

"And what about the theater? Her business? She's going to be kicked out in a week. What am I supposed to do about that?"

Mal shared a look with Cash. "Help her find a new one? Isn't that our job?"

It was, but she loved that theater. He saw it every day. The way her face lit up when she stepped onto the stage. It wasn't just a building to her. It was her heart and soul. Her home. Literally at times. He couldn't allow Donald to sell it off to some random person. No one would love that place like Piper because no one loved like Piper. She loved with her entire being. He knew that because—

"I love her," he whispered into the room. And she loved him. Or she had before he screwed everything up. His only hope was that their love still burned, an ember he could fan back into flames if he apologized and made amends.

"Yeah, man, we know." Cash grinned. "What are you going to do about it?"

He was going to show this damned curse it didn't rule his life anymore. He was going to show Donald he couldn't push people around. He was going to win back the love of his life and give her everything she deserves and more.

He stood, determination set as he stared at his brothers. "I'm going to see a man about a theater."

CHAPTER TWENTY-THREE

As if her life couldn't get any worse, the food delivery guy forgot her crab wontons. Piper grumbled as she dug through the bag, but sadly her wontons did not appear.

"Perfect. Just the perfect end to a disastrous week."

"What's that, babe?" Rachel asked from her seat on the couch.

"They forgot my wontons," she muttered as she reclaimed her seat next to Rachel.

Her best friend had come into the theater that fateful night to grab her yoga mat she'd forgotten, and found Piper sobbing in the sling. After a good fifteen minutes crying in her arms, Piper finally found the words to tell Rachel everything that had happened. She told her about Donald selling the place and how Kell knew since he was the real estate agent. She hadn't even known he *was* a real estate agent.

You think you know a person.

After talking Rachel down from sending Donald a glitter bomb, Piper confessed she had no idea what to do next. Every night this week she'd come over to Rachel's place after classes so they could brainstorm next plans.

It wasn't going well.

Much like her life lately.

"What did I do to anger the universe? Why is it taking a big dump all over my life?" She flopped back against the couch, misery weighing her down.

"Hun, you know I love you, but this 'woe is me' shtick has got to go soon. This isn't like you."

Jaw dropping wide, she stared at her supposed best friend. "Well, excuse me. I'm not sure who I'm supposed to be in times like this."

Rachel grabbed her cashew chicken, opened the carton and plucked a piece of meat with her chopsticks. "Times like these?"

"Yeah, I've never had my livelihood ripped right out from under me while also being betrayed by the man I lo—" She cut herself off.

"The man you…" Rachel raised an eyebrow.

"Nothing," she muttered into her lo mein, digging in.

She would not say the L word. Not about Kell. She didn't love him. She couldn't, or this pain she was feeling would destroy her. It was already ripping her apart regardless, but saying it out loud after what he did… She feared that would be her end.

"Look," Rachel said, putting down her food and swiveling on the couch so she was facing Piper. "Donald is the jerkiest jerk in jerk town."

"He's the mayor of jerk town," she growled.

"The president of jerk town." Rachel smiled.

They looked at each other and at the same time said, "The king of jerk town!"

A fit of laughter followed. It felt nice to laugh again. She hated this sick feeling of dread and sadness lodged in her chest the past week. Donald's actions—those she should have seen coming. She was angry, but not surprised her scummy landlord pulled a stunt like this. If it was just losing the theater, she'd still be distraught, but she could manage. But Kell's betrayal…

That was a wound she feared she may never recover from.

"Okay, so we've determined Donald is a jerk," Rachel said with a nod. "And this past week searching through the rental listings has gotten us zero results for a new place for the studio."

"Don't remind me," she groaned, shoveling another chopstick full of noodles into her mouth.

She had wished on a shooting star the night before she found the listing for Star-Crossed Theater. Fate had been in her favor then. Now, not so much. There weren't many theaters equipped to handle aerial rigging. A dance studio wouldn't work because the ceilings weren't high enough and she'd have to pay for structural support of the aerial equipment. She couldn't afford that.

"There's still time to send him a glitter bomb." Rachel gave her a look. "An innocent looking package sent to his doorstep and when he opens it up...*bam*, face full of glitter!"

Piper still couldn't believe that there were companies who offered that service. As much as she loved the idea of Donald's grumpy face being covered in glitter for all eternity—because that's how long glitter stayed on you, she should know, she was a performer—she shook her head.

"No. At least not yet. I still have one more week to figure things out. Who knows, maybe a miracle will happen, and he'll change his mind about selling." She had a better chance of winning the lottery and she didn't even play. "Besides, he would know it's me and kick me out even sooner. Half of my stuff is still in the storage room."

That night Rachel found her sobbing, she'd also confessed about her living arrangements, staying at the theater after Larry screwed her over, Kell offering his family condo. Rachel had wanted to trash the place—in furious defense of her—but Piper just wanted to get her stuff and never set eyes on the place again. What she first assumed was kindness, she now wondered if his "generosity" had simply been a way to assuage his guilt. She'd been crashing at a cheap motel the past week. Not smart for her budget, but she couldn't be in that condo without thinking about Kell. Wondering how she'd been so foolish, missed all the signs. The pain and embarrassment swirled inside her. A hurricane threatening to destroy what little hope she had left.

Rachel's eyes narrowed. "Yeah, about that. I'm still mad you didn't tell me about Larry leaving you homeless."

She searched very intently for a snow pea in her food, avoiding her best friend's glare.

"I can't believe you decided living at the theater was better than living with me. You know Naya would be cool with it."

"I know." Naya, who was currently at her bartending job, truly was the sweetest woman ever. She'd even spent her one night off last night helping Piper scour the internet for building rentals. "But come on, Rachel, where would I fit in here, huh? There's barely enough room for you two."

"We could make it work."

"You're both very sweet, but no. Thankfully I have a few leads on some room rentals so at least that part of my life seems to be falling into place."

She didn't particularly like living with roommates, but beggars couldn't be choosers. She'd just have to deal with the overstimulation and discomfort of living with others until she got her life sorted out.

"I'm glad to hear that. One problem down, one to go."

Too bad this one looked insurmountable. Piper hadn't even told her students yet. What could she tell them? She had nowhere to teach classes next week. No studio, no theater. She'd have to temporarily close her business. How was she supposed to come up with the funds for a new lease if she wasn't making money teaching classes?

"We've looked everywhere," she moaned into her take-out box. "There's nothing out there that can handle the needs of an aerial studio."

"Maybe you should see if you can ask someone to help?"

Rachel suggested. "Someone who has more experience with this stuff than me and Naya. Someone…in real estate?"

She must have passed out due to the stress because Rachel did not just suggest she ask Kell, the man who betrayed her and broke her heart, for help.

"Are you serious right now?" She stared at Rachel, heart racing. "After what he did to me?"

Putting down her food, Rachel held up a hand. "Hear me out. I know what Kell did was crappy and I plan to make him suffer for it. Don't worry, a glitter bomb is already heading his way—"

"Rachel, no!" She was furious at Kell, but the last thing his handsome face needed was glitter. It would only bring more attention to it.

"Already done, hun. I know he hurt you, but you have to admit the guy was stuck in a very awful position. Didn't he say Donald made him sign an NDA and if he told you about the sale Donald could sue him for everything, including that charity he runs with his brothers?"

She'd told her best friend too much. Rachel wasn't supposed to point out the logic in this situation. She was supposed to be on Piper's side and contemplate posting bogus bad reviews on his business site. Not that she ever would, but she thought about it.

"I bet it killed him not to tell you, Piper, but would you really want him to be the type of person who risked a charity that helps house people in need?"

No. She wouldn't feel the same way about him if he tossed aside others for his own desires. One of the reasons she cared for Kell so much was his generous heart. He was always helping people, herself included. It was Kell who helped sell out their show. Kell who fixed every broken item in the theater even if it wasn't on Donald's list. He would never abandon others for selfish reasons.

"Okay," she admitted. "Maybe he was in a tough spot, but I'm not ready to forgive him."

"Good. Don't." Rachel nodded. "Make the man grovel a little, but don't cut him off completely."

"Not sure that's up to me anymore."

She'd said some awful things to him the night she found out about the sale. Cruel, hurtful things. Her anger had overtaken common sense, mouth running, spewing all the pain she felt back at him. The agonized look in his eyes when she told him he was cursed haunted her in the dark of the night. That hadn't been fair. She'd been lashing out, hoping to wound him, make him feel an ounce of the betrayal she felt. Sadly, it looked as though it worked. The past week he'd been very careful not to cross her path while working at the theater.

"What? 'Cause you had a fight? Ha!" Rachel shrugged off her worries. "The man is head over heels in love with you. Guarantee you send one text, and he'll come running."

She blinked in surprise. "He's not in love with me. He doesn't believe in love. He thinks he's cursed. I was trying to prove otherwise but then…" Everything had blown up in their faces. Much like Rachel's glitter bombs.

"Babe, that man looks at you like you hung the moon and the stars. He is so far gone for you he doesn't know what to do. If he wasn't, would he have been so torn about telling you? Would he be as careful as he is not to upset you by coming into your space while you're angry at him? Would he be texting your best friend all week asking if you're okay?"

"He's doing what?" She pounced for Rachel's phone sitting on the coffee table. "Let me see."

"Ah ah, no." Rachel scooped up her phone before Piper could reach it. "He didn't want to upset you anymore, but he was worried about you. He's been checking in. Nothing creepy or invasive, just—"

Rachel's phone pinged. She glanced at it, a smile curling her lips as she chuckled.

"Speak of the devil. Looks like he got my present."

"Rachel, no!"

Lunging across the couch, she snatched the phone from her best friend's hand. Her heart skipped a beat at what she saw. Kell's face, covered in glitter, a resigned sparkly expression with text underneath saying *I deserve this*. A sob of laughter left her. Her finger scrolled up through the conversation. Kell apologizing, Rachel calling him some very creative names. Kell checking to make sure she was okay. Every day. Every day since that night he'd checked on her. Every day he'd lamented his inaction.

She clutched the phone to her chest, the truth of their horrible situation sinking in.

"Damn you, Donald."

Rachel was right. Kell's hands had been tied. She wouldn't have respected him anymore if he threw away Helping Hands for her. He did the right thing, even if it bit her on the butt in the end.

"I love him," she whispered.

"I know, babe." Rachel pulled her into a warm hug. "And I know this situation sucks, but maybe you could talk to him? Find a way to work all this out? But still, make him grovel. I want you to be happy, but the man needs to suffer a little more."

She laughed through her tears, clutching her best friend tight. "You're the best and he's never going to get all that glitter off."

"I know." Rachel let out an evil snicker. "Serves him right."

She let out a wobbly breath. "Okay, I'll text him. Later. I'm not ready tonight."

"Totally get it. Now what do you say we pop this food in the fridge and head to the bar so my beautiful girlfriend can get us some celebratory drinks."

"What are we celebrating?"

"The possibilities of the future. You know what they say, always look on the bright side of life."

Her future was still too hazy for Piper to look on the bright side, but tonight had brought out some revelations and she had nothing but possibilities ahead of her. The dread of the past week started to melt away as she realized she had more help on her side than she first thought. Kell hadn't lied and abandoned her. He still cared. She clung on to that knowledge with the last bit of hope she had left in her heart. As for what the future held…time would tell.

CHAPTER TWENTY-FOUR

Hey, can we talk?

Piper stared at the unsent text on her phone. It had been there for two days. She kept typing and deleting, but had yet to drum up the courage to hit Send. Logically she knew Kell cared for her, and he hadn't kept silent about the sale of Star-Crossed Theater out of ill intent. His hands had been legally tied. She got that. But the scared little part of her deep inside, that part that had been hurt by others before, tricked and lied to, was still wary.

At least the other parts of her life seemed to be heading down a better path. She'd met her future roommates yesterday and signed a six-month lease. She would be sharing a house with two go-go dancers and a drag queen whose entire wardrobe she wanted to borrow. She still hadn't found a new studio, but it was the middle of summer. Colorado had a few more good weather months, and she'd looked into having the rest of the summer classes outside at Wash Park with her portable rigs.

Not the ideal situation, but it meant that she wouldn't have to close her aerial studio right away. It gave her a few more months to find a place. She would make it work. Now if only she could make this thing with Kell work. But that would require actually talking to the man.

She slipped her phone back into her pocket, message unsent.

"Coffee for Piper." The barista's voice rang out in the small coffee shop.

"That's me, thank you."

She rushed to the counter to grab the sweet elixir of life. The worst part about living in a tiny motel room was not having space for her coffee setup. Thankfully the locally owned shop just a block away had delicious, affordable coffee. She might be on a tight budget, but she could not live without her coffee. At least she'd be able to make it at home again when she moved into the house next week.

Sipping her sweet caffeine fix, she headed out of the shop, back to the theater. The bright summer sun shone down on her, heating her body, making her second-guess not getting her coffee iced. As she walked up to the theater her heart stopped. The large red-and-white for-sale sign had been taken down.

Donald just put it up a few days ago. Had the theater already sold? She wasn't surprised. It was a beautiful building with so much potential. Anyone would be lucky to own this place. She knew he was kicking her out at the end of this week when her lease was up, but secretly she'd hoped he wouldn't be able to sell it right away. Or at all. Selfishly she'd dreamt of Donald coming back to her on his knees, begging to renew her lease. She'd agree, at a discounted rate of course.

But it appeared her dreams were just that. Based on the lack of sign, someone had bought the Star-Crossed Theater. Quickly too. Could someone buy a building that fast? Weren't inspections needed? Loan approvals?

Unless someone paid cash.

Her heart broke thinking of some rich jerk buying this place to turn it into a trendy nightclub or flip it for a profit. It wasn't fair. She loved this theater, spent years putting soul and art into its bones. And now some rich punk was going to do who-knew-what with it.

Swiping away an angry tear, she marched up the front steps into the building. She pulled out her keys and inserted them into the lock, discovering it was already unlocked. Uh oh. She'd locked up before she left, she knew it. Had Donald already given keys to the new owner? That scumbag! She still had five days left on her lease. This was still her place for one hundred and twenty more hours.

Flinging the door open, she stormed inside. The place was empty. As far as she could tell, no one was in the foyer. The slight sound of movement from beyond sounded in the air. Something being moved on stage. Her mood darkened. Someone was in the theater. She started forward, wishing she had the Wiffle Ball bat. Not that she would attack the new owner—if that was who was in here—but this was still her building, dammit, and she had the right to be angry that someone invaded her space.

With a soft tread, she made her way to the doors that led to audience seating. As quietly as possible, she opened the door and peeked her head through. A quick scan of the audience revealed nothing. No one in the seats. As she glanced to the stage, she saw a spotlight on center stage illuminating the dark brown wooden podium they used when people booked the theater for presentations or graduation ceremonies.

"What in the world?" she whispered.

Cautiously making her way inside, she puzzled at what could be going on. She certainly hadn't put the podium on the stage or messed with the lights. No one had keys to the light room except for her. And Donald—as the owner he had the master keys to everything. Why in the world would Donald come in here and set up a podium with a spotlight?

Her heart raced as horrible scenarios crept up in her mind. It would be just like Donald to set up some sick display letting her know the place had been sold. She couldn't see what was on the podium, but she wouldn't put it past him to leave a taunting letter informing her that someone bought the theater. The man was cruel like that.

Carefully making her way up to the stage, she put her coffee down and hopped onstage. Her nerves raced the closer she got to the podium, fingers frantically tapping on her thighs as overwhelm threatened to consume her. Taking a deep, steadying breath, she moved around the podium so she could see if there was anything on it.

There was.

Her heart cracked as she spied the paper lying on the dark wood surface with bold letters declaring it the deed for the Star-Crossed Theater. Her eyes closed as pain filled her chest. One warm tear leaked out, sliding down her cheek. She knew it was coming. Knew someone would buy the theater, but it still broke her heart to lose this place she loved so much. The place that had been a part of her life for the last six years. The place she built her business, taught students, made friends. It was more than just a building. It was a piece of her heart. And now it belonged to someone else.

Opening her eyes, she glanced over the paperwork, a name jumping out at her. Confused, she picked up the deed and read it again. The name didn't change. Disbelief filled her as she tried to understand what it meant. But it didn't make sense. How could it?

"What in the world?" she muttered, reading over the paper again. "This can't be real."

"It's real," a voice from backstage called.

Letting out a small shriek, Piper whirled around, heart in her throat at the unexpected sound. A man stepped out from the shadows. A man who made her heart race and break all at the same time.

"Dammit, Kell! What did I tell you about sneaking up on me like that?"

A small grin tugged at the corner of his lips. "Sorry, didn't meant to scare you. At least you didn't have a bat with you this time."

He chuckled. She didn't join in, but the edge of her lips quivered as she fought a smile. The sight of him, after so many days of not seeing him, made her heart ache and yearn. She wanted to run to him, throw her arms around him and kiss him until neither of them could breathe again. But first she needed answers. And as Rachel pointed out, the man should grovel a little.

"What's going on?" she asked, holding up the deed. The deed that had her name on the owner's line.

How?

Kell sighed, his smile slipping. "I know what I did was wrong. I am so sorry I kept news about the sale from you, Piper. I wanted to tell you so much, but I couldn't. The NDA was unbreakable. I swear if I could have told you without risking Helping Homes I would have. I am so damn sorry, you have to believe me."

She did. As angry and betrayed as she felt, she understood the position Kell had been in.

"I know," she said softly. "It was an awful clause that I should have expected from Donald, and it wasn't fair of him to put you in that situation. I was just collateral damage."

"No, sweetheart, no." He rushed to her side, his hands reaching out to hold her, but he paused. "This is all on me. I'm just as much to blame as Donald. I should have found a way to tell you without breaking the contract. There's always a way, and it's my fault for not discovering it. I hurt you and it's the very last thing in this world I ever wanted to do. I'm sorry, Piper."

She nodded, tears streaming down her cheeks. His apology didn't take away the pain of his betrayal, but it did soothe the lingering anger in her chest, melting it away.

Kell reached up and wiped away her tears with his thumbs,

cupping her face in his hands. "I'm so sorry. I was so focused on trying to find a way to tell you Donald was selling the place I completely missed the solution to the problem."

"Solution?"

He grinned, nodding to the deed in her hand. "The sale."

She shook her head, still cradled in his palms. "But I don't understand. I didn't buy the theater. I can't buy the theater."

She knew Donald, and the guy was probably asking way over what this building was worth. Not that she wouldn't pay it if she had the money. She'd pay anything to own this theater, if only she could.

"But I can," Kell said. "And I did. For you."

Her eyes widened at his confession. "You bought a theater for me?"

Wait until she told Rachel. This went way beyond groveling.

He nodded. "I can't believe I didn't see it before. It was right there. Donald was selling the place, you deserved to have it, I have the money and I didn't even have to pay my own commission. It's a win all around."

She pulled away, shaking her head. "No, no. You can't buy me a theater. It's too much!"

"It's not enough," he insisted. "It will never be enough to make up for my actions. If it makes it easier to accept, we can work out a deal. My family always needs spaces for our charity galas. Take the theater and let us host our fundraising events here."

That sounded doable. Plus, if she let the Thorson family have events here, all their rich friends would see her aerial company information and maybe some of them would become donors or whatever rich people did. Still, she couldn't wrap her head around the fact that he actually bought the place for her. "Who buys someone a theater? This is ridiculous, it's too much, it's…it's…"

"It's true love," Kell said.

Her sputtering stopped. She stared, jaw wide as the L word dropped from his lips.

"You...don't believe in true love."

"I didn't," he agreed. "Until you came along, insisting you'd be the one to break the curse. The curse we both know is silly, but I clung to it so hard. I was afraid of getting my heart broken again. I couldn't understand what was wrong with me. Why I wasn't enough for someone to stay forever. And then I realized. It wasn't me. It was that I hadn't found you yet."

A sob caught in her throat. He gently grasped her hands in his, pulling her close.

"Piper. All my life I thought I wasn't enough, but it turns out none of my past relationships worked out because they weren't with you. You are the one I'm supposed to be with. Call it fate or fairy-tale magic or whatever. All I know is I love you, with every ounce of breath I have inside me. I want to spend the rest of my life making sure you get every moment of happiness and joy you deserve and, sweetheart, you deserve it all."

More tears streamed down her face. At this point she'd be dehydrated if she didn't get some water soon.

"Kell," she whispered between shuddering breaths. "I love you too. You deserve all the happiness and joy too, even when you think you don't. I should refuse a gift as lavish as an entire building, but Rachel did say to make you grovel and I think as far as grand gestures go, this one takes the cake."

He laughed. "I can see her saying that. I'll be picking glitter out of my hair for years, thanks to her."

She laughed along with him, spying a hint of glittery gold in his dark eyebrows.

"I love you, Kell."

"I love you too, Piper."

He pulled her into his arms, staring down at her with a wolfish smile. "You know, someone once told me that a curse can be broken by true love's kiss. Wanna give it a shot?"

She grinned. "Sounds like that person is pretty smart."

"She is, and talented, beautiful, charming, and now, a theater owner."

She closed her eyes, lifting on her toes as he pressed their lips together. Her heart sang at the taste of him. A taste she had feared she might never get to experience again.

Life had a funny way of giving you exactly what you wanted in a way you didn't know you needed. She finally had the theater, and in her name. Her aerial studio was secure and, best of all, her heart would be forever loved.

This first act of life had been a wild ride for sure. She couldn't wait for act two.

EPILOGUE

Three months later

"Piper, darling, that was the most successful benefit we have ever had. You're amazing."

Piper smiled at Mrs. Thorson. They had just finished the first fundraising gala held at the Star-Crossed Theater, benefiting a new charity scholarship the Thorson family was starting for neurodivergent youth and adults interested in aerial arts. It had been Kell's idea, but she'd helped plan the event.

"Thank you, Mrs. Thorson, but Kell did most of the work."

"I've told you a thousand times to call me Jeanie, dear. And I know it was my son's idea, but the magic of the night was thanks to you and your students. My heart was racing with every drop and spin. Now I must go, but I'll see you this weekend at dinner?"

She still couldn't believe she now had monthly dinners at the Thorson mansion.

Her life had changed so much in the past few months. Classes were full to the brim, the theater was running smoothly for the first time ever, she no longer had to deal with Donald the scumbag because she finally owned this place.

But best of all was Kell. After they'd made up, he'd begged her to come live with him. Thankfully her soon-to-be new roommates let her out of her lease since one of them had a sibling in need of a room to rent ASAP.

The Thorson Foundation had three more fundraising galas on the schedule for the year. It worked out nicely as Piper could work the galas in between aerial shows. And displaying flyers for upcoming shows in the lobby, in full view of the gala attendees, was destined to work wonders for ticket sales if tonight was any indication. They'd nearly sold out next month's performance already.

Piper waved as Jeanie left the building. Then, with a happy sigh, she turned around and headed back into the theater to shut the lights off. As she glanced at the stage, a smile curved her lips. There, in the middle of the stage, sitting in a low sling was the man who made all her dreams come true. Kell.

"Does this mean you're ready for another lesson?" she asked, making her way up the stairs onto the stage.

"Not a chance," Kell chuckled. "I just needed to get you on stage so I could do this."

"Do what—"

A gasp left her as Kell slid from the sling onto one knee. He reached into his tux pocket and pulled out a small black box.

"Piper Pitts, you are the most amazing person I have ever had the privilege of knowing. You have the kindest heart, the most optimistic outlook, and I'm still not convinced you aren't actually a goddess."

She laughed out a sob as tears of happiness started to leak from her eyes.

"I once thought I was cursed by love, but you showed me it wasn't a curse at all. I was just waiting for you. My one true love. You've turned me into a sappy romantic and I wouldn't have it any other way. I want to spend the rest of my life falling in love with you each and every day. Will you do me the honor of taking me as your husband?"

"Yes!"

Joy and excitement overwhelmed her. She knelt, throwing her arms around him. The move caught him off-balance and they both fell into the sling. Kell chuckled as he settled them into the fabric. They swayed, embracing as the stage lights filtered through the pink material, casting them in a rosy glow.

"We're the real deal, Piper." Kell kissed her softly, slipping the silver ring with a sparking sapphire on to her finger.

"See?" She grinned. "I told you I was right about happily-ever-afters. And I'm also right about you trying aerials again. See how fun this is?" She pushed off with her foot, spinning them slightly.

He laughed. "Yes to the fairy-tale ending. No to breaking my neck falling out of this thing." A wicked spark of heat entered his eyes. "But I can think of other things we could try in it."

She giggled in delight as his hands went to her zipper. Life had a funny way of giving you the thing you wanted in the most unexpected way. She thought Kell had been all wrong for her, but in the end, he was exactly who she needed. No one knew what the future would hold. All she knew was as long as they were together, things would work out because true love conquers all.

* * * * *

Look out for the next story in the
Love Under Construction trilogy
Coming soon!

And if you enjoyed this story, check out these other great reads from Mariah Ankenman

Cinderella's Bargain with the Billionaire
Accidently Dating the Enemy

All available now!

SERVING UP OFF-LIMITS LOVE

JENNIFER SNOW

MILLS & BOON

To Reagan—
I'll always cherish the memories of our travel adventures.

CHAPTER ONE

Domenico Kasa had drawn the shortest straw and was now ducking for his life.

The stainless-steel spatula whipped past his right ear and landed with a deafening clatter on the tiled kitchen floor. While the utensil would have dented Domenico's forehead if he hadn't reacted so quickly, the knife in the chef's other hand was more concerning.

But the recently *fired* head chef of the Kasa de Paradise Resort wasn't crazy enough to throw that. Was he?

"Christian, settle down." Domenico selected the biggest, heaviest frying pan hanging above the center island in the pristine thousand-square-foot kitchen. Holding it as a shield, he moved closer to the door. "We both knew this was coming."

A string of curse words muttered in French was the only response as the chef resumed slicing the onion on the cutting board in front of him. The knife moved with speed and precision. Then the thin slices of onion sizzled as they hit the pan of melted butter on the stove.

Domenico's stomach growled and his mouth watered as the smell of caramelized onions filled the kitchen. Chef Dubois's French onion soup was the best he'd ever tasted in his twenty-seven years. If only their world-famous chef wasn't also a world-famous womanizer.

Firing the best cook they'd had working at the resort since they opened three years ago on the private island off the coast of Naples, Italy, went against all common sense...but several sexual harassment complaints from wealthy, married, *influential* guests within a few days made this decision an easy one.

"The women here are not like the women in my country," Chef Dubois said, the knife swinging.

Domenico was fairly certain women didn't appreciate being groped in *any* country, but he remained silent until everything sharp was out of Christian's reach. "Regardless, we're letting you go."

"We?"

Right. *He.* He was letting the chef go. His older brothers were hiding under their respective beds. "We will obviously pay your travel costs back to Paris and a month's severance, which should help until you find another job."

Christian laughed. "I turned down four offers d'emploi to come here to this...this...this..." He gestured wildly with the knife, his look of disgust not exactly the expression most people wore when they spoke about Kasa de Paradise.

The luxury resort located on the island owned by the Kasa brothers consisted of twenty-five private villas, various dining options from a formal restaurant to a beachside barbecue, two spa and fitness facilities with tennis courts and golf courses, an infinity pool overlooking the sea, and acres of lush flora and fauna. Daily excursions—relaxing boat rides to zip-lining for the more adventurous traveler—took guests to the remote areas of the island to explore the unspoiled landscape. Nothing was off-limits or unattainable.

With guests transported by boat from Naples to the island, the resort was reserved by the week. Only the most elite could afford the thirty-thousand-euro price tag for the all-inclusive vacation experience.

Movie stars, musicians, politicians and high-end executives were the clientele at Kasa de Paradise, and not one in three years had ever worn the *who farted?* expression the chef wore right now.

"Then you won't have any trouble landing on your feet," Domenico said while the man continued to search for the right insult.

Christian stared at him. "You want to fire me two days before the reviewer from *Travel Island* magazine arrives?"

Not particularly, but the chef had left them little choice. Among a million other ethical reasons, if Linda Frank, the American reviewer for the influential international travel publication, heard about the chef's inappropriate behavior with the guests, they could kiss their hopes for a flattering review goodbye. Unfortunately, they might have to anyway. Nightly four-course meals, tasting menus and event catering weren't going to be easy to execute without a head chef.

"We hope to have a replacement by then," Domenico said.

"In two days? Ha!" More chopping, more muttering, more cussing.

Time to grow a set of balls the size of coconuts. "Christian, I need you to pack your things immediately. We have a boat waiting to take you back to the mainland."

The chef stopped and dropped the knife, glancing at him as though only now realizing he was serious. "You're firing *moi*?"

For the last twenty minutes now.

The anarchy that followed resulted in a bandaged hand for Domenico and resort security—all four of the two-hundred-fifty-pound ex-military—"escorting" Christian Dubois to his living quarters and then to the boat waiting to take him back to Naples.

"Damn," Domenico muttered, joining his brothers where the other two *uninjured* Kasas had been watching the fiasco on the dock from the safety and comfort of the resort's main office. "That went well," he said, collapsing into a plush leather chair near the floor-to-ceiling window overlooking the property. Sixty-five acres that they'd purchased when they'd sold their family's hotel chain, after their father's death. The resort they'd designed, built, and turned into one of the hottest high-end destinations in the Mediterranean in less than four years would have made their father proud. Leonardo Kasa Sr. had always said he was building the hotel chain for their future, but when the man had gotten sick, he'd told the boys to sell the properties and use the money to do whatever made them happy.

Failing their father's legacy with an unsuccessful venture wasn't an option.

"At least it wasn't your tennis hand," his oldest brother, Leo, said, nodding to the bandage the resort's medic had wrapped around Domenico's left hand.

Thank God the chef's aim wasn't as fantastic as his French onion soup. Otherwise Domenico might have required stitches.

"Yeah, don't you have an evening lesson scheduled with Mrs. Conway?" his other brother, Mario, asked. The deep grin spreading across his face told Domenico that he did *now*.

"When do the Conways check out? Tell me it's tomorrow." Guests ran from Sunday to Saturday, and the

Conways—two real estate tycoons, a husband-and-wife team—had originally booked one week...which they kept extending. Due to a lull in reservations during the fall months, the brothers weren't turning away their money.

A former professional tennis player, Domenico offered lessons as an added benefit to the resort, and Mrs. Conway was booking every available time slot in his schedule...but somehow her skills continued to get worse.

"They rebooked for another week," Leo said, checking the reservation files on his desk.

Fantastic. While Linda Frank was there, Domenico would have additional stress he did not need. "You have to start telling them we're full," he said. Mrs. Conway, a five-foot-ten forty-five-year-old redhead with surgically enhanced...everything...might not have appreciated Chef Dubois's advances, but she seemed to be encouraging any attention Domenico was willing to bestow.

"We're *not* full," Leo said.

Domenico turned to look at Mario, who was reviewing the new resort brochures. "Why not?" When they'd first opened the resort, they were full all the time. Lately reservations had been down at least thirty percent. They'd expected a dip after the initial opening, but thirty percent would put them in operational danger zone if it continued.

"Hey, I just got back from Spain, remember?" Mario was immediately on the defensive. "Sourcing that expensive wine the reviewer raved about last month in her article about Spanish vineyards."

Mario was in charge of marketing and promotions of the resort, but he was off on sourcing expeditions more than he was on the island. And Spain seemed to be a favorite port of call. Domenico couldn't help but wonder if something other than vineyards was occupying his brother's time on these trips. The expense reports seemed to suggest so.

"Besides, I keep telling you both that we need to offer open reservations during the slower months. You two refuse to listen."

"Exclusivity is what Kasa Island is about. Guests book a full week or nothing." Limiting reservations to clientele who could afford the cost of a full week's stay gave the resort their high-end, luxury status. Allowing guests to check in for a few nights increased costs and lowered the public perception of the resort. "I'm with Dom on this one," Leo said to Mario. "You need to find other ways to bring in guests."

"Hey, who convinced Travel Island to come here?" Mario said, setting the brochures on the desk and stretching his long legs out in front of him.

"You can't ride that stroke of good fortune forever," Leo said.

"I can and I will," Mario retorted.

"Speaking of…handsy chef did point out *one* minor issue. Who is going to look after the kitchen?" Domenico asked. He hoped his brothers had been working out a new plan while he was being attacked.

The sous-chef was fantastic and they could certainly help in the interim, but the reviewer wouldn't be impressed. They'd have to go through their stack of applicants to see if there was anyone qualified who hadn't yet accepted another position and could be there on a moment's notice… They had no time to put out a job posting and conduct interviews. But getting someone to accept a position at Kasa Island shouldn't be difficult. They paid a generous salary, and the living quarters for the staff were located in a private, secluded section of the island, near the beach. The sound of the waves at night crashing along the shore was Domenico's favorite part of island living.

Mario and Leo exchanged looks. "We have someone."

Oh no.

Fine hairs on Domenico's arms stood up, and his gut tightened. "Don't say it."

"I had to, man," Leo said with a shrug. "Adriana is the only person I trust, and she agreed to help us out to get us through the reviewer's stay."

Adriana Bellarini. His brother's ex-girlfriend.

The Bellarini family had been long-time friends with the Kasas. The brothers had grown up with Adriana and her brother, Alex, which played a huge part in why Leo insisted on remaining friends with Adriana, despite the fact she'd broken his heart.

How much of this decision was based on needing a chef, and how much was Leo's own desire to have Adriana on the island? Domenico knew his brother had offered her the executive chef position numerous times. Luckily she kept turning him down. "Doesn't she have her own restaurant to take care of?"

"She's willing to do us this favor. Alex is looking after the kitchen at Bellarini's for a week," Leo said, with a look that suggested Domenico should be relieved.

He wasn't. And it annoyed him that his brothers had made this executive decision without him. He and Adriana had once been the best of friends, until his tennis training had taken him all over the world. In his absence, she'd fallen for his older brother.

"I suppose she's on her way?"

Leo nodded. "Arriving later today. And you'll have to meet her at the dock and get her settled—I have a Zoom call with potential guests."

Domenico's jaw clenched as he stood. "And I can't change your mind?" He already knew the answer.

"Sorry. We need her," Leo said.

He glanced at Mario, but this time it was the older Kasa brothers who were sticking together.

"Fine," Domenico said, walking toward the office door. "I'll be overseeing every move she makes, but if—*when*—things go sideways, remember I had nothing to do with this decision."

There was no one else Adriana would abandon her family restaurant for. But when Leo Kasa needed her, she was there, especially when a reviewer from *Travel Island* magazine would be at Kasa de Paradise that week. A fantastic review from Linda Frank would do wonders for the resort, but also, her own struggling restaurant could use the boost from the praise of an influential reviewer.

Linda was in high demand, and her reviews were coveted. She was selective about the resorts she chose to visit, and her opinion was gospel all over the world. A rave review from Linda could have a resort at full capacity within the week. A bad review...

Well, she wouldn't entertain that possibility.

This possible added benefit that could come from helping Leo only increased her anxiety as she boarded the *Passage to Paradise* that evening.

"Miss Bellarini, welcome aboard," said the shuttle boat captain, Jon, extending a hand and taking her small suitcase as he helped her aboard. He was a short, stocky man with marine-themed tattoos—a former captain of a cruise ship who'd opted for the peace and serenity of small excursions working for the Kasa brothers.

"Thank you," she said, taking a seat along the bench

at the front, looking out toward the sea. Kasa de Paradise wasn't visible from the mainland, but once they cleared the narrows in the harbor, the resort would come into view.

She'd been on the private island a few times to help Leo design the magnificent kitchen, but then she'd handed the golden oven mitts to the first of six different chefs in four years. He'd offered her the position, but she'd easily turned it down. As beautiful as Kasa Island was, her heart was in her family restaurant. She was desperate to prove to herself that her late father hadn't made the wrong decision leaving it in her hands and not her brother's. Which meant full-time commitment and dedication.

She also feared Leo's offer came from a secret hope that the two of them might rekindle the flame they'd once had. Adriana refused to give him that unfair hope. They were great friends, despite their breakup, and she cherished that enough not to ruin things with another attempt at a relationship when she didn't feel the right spark for Leo anymore.

They'd grown up together. Their love was young love fueled heavily by their family's desire to see a Bellarini-Kasa union—an official combining of their families. At one time, Adriana had thought maybe that union would have occurred with a different Kasa brother, but once Domenico started his tennis career, he'd never looked back. He'd seemed to forget all about her, as evidenced by the photos of him dating other female competitors in the tabloids, which had hurt. Leo had been there, feeling a similar disappointment that his brother seemed laser-focused on just one thing—tennis—and not the family or the family business anymore. The two had bonded over it, and later, fear of disappointing their families had kept her from ending things sooner.

Luckily their friendship and childhood bond had helped ease the heartache of a breakup enough to stay great friends.

Domenico's betrayal had caused a different kind of heartache, one that hadn't completely eased.

The boat pulled away from the dock, and she bit her lip. "How's the water?" Choppy waves reflected the low setting sun, and the mild ocean breeze blew her long, dark hair away from her face as she surveyed them with a nervous look.

"Smooth sailing," the captain said. "The *Passage to Paradise* was designed to glide over the roughest waves. You won't feel but a slight sway, Miss Bellarini."

Everything on Kasa de Paradise was designed with executive-level guests' comfort in mind. Suddenly Adriana was nervous about more than the waves. The resort boasted the best of everything—accommodations, amenities, entertainment and…food.

Would Leo have immediately thought of her if he knew Bellarini's wasn't doing so great?

Maybe that was why he had. She'd never told him that the restaurant was struggling. She knew he must have suspected it when the place was practically empty whenever he stopped by for dinner on the mainland. He believed in her and her talent, and she valued his friendship and support.

Her brother, Alex, on the other hand, thought Bellarini's menu was the problem. He claimed that the decades-old patron favorites needed to be replaced with fresh new dishes, including some healthier choices. Over the last year and a half, they'd head-butted on the issue over and over.

While she knew Alex was right…to some degree…she refused to change Bellarini's into something it wasn't.

Food from the Campania region was all about familiar family recipes passed along from generation to generation. People ate there when they wanted an authentically prepared Italian meal. Her parents had ultimately trusted her with the restaurant. She was determined to make Bellarini's successful again without sacrificing what made it a cherished family destination in the beginning.

She cleared her throat. "So, what happened to Chef Dubois?" she asked Jon.

"Complaints from guests."

Chef Dubois was one of the top chefs in Paris. He'd worked at Michelin-starred restaurants and had secured world acclaim as an inventor of flavor. If his cooking didn't measure up... Her stomach knotted.

"Complaints? About his food?"

"About his wandering hands," Jon said, turning to her with a smile.

She relaxed and laughed. "Well, they don't have to worry about that with me."

Running the restaurant and working long hours doing meal prep, ordering supplies, trying the new recipes Alex insisted she at least consider, Adriana hadn't been on a real date in...three years? She wouldn't even try to remember the last time she'd had sex. At twenty-six, she was practically a virgin again.

Three years single? Could it really be that long?

"The Kasa brothers are very excited that you agreed to come," the captain said.

She knew Leo was pleased, and Mario wouldn't care either way, but she had her doubts that Domenico had readily agreed to this week-long situation. Since they'd drifted apart years before, he barely acknowledged her presence when they were forced to share the same air, and she'd never fully understood what had happened to make him dislike her. He'd been the one to forget about her and their connection while he was off chasing his dream—and gorgeous athletes.

But she had no time to think about that this week. She needed to secure a great review for the resort and her skills in the kitchen.

To help her own struggling restaurant.

"Are Domenico and Mario on the island?" Maybe they were away and she'd only have to deal with Leo.

"Mr. Mario is leaving for Greece tonight, but Mr. Domenico never leaves the island. I can't remember the last time he stepped onto the *Passage to Paradise*."

Right.

Lush greenery bordered by acres of soft golden sand was a welcoming sight moments later as Kasa Island graced the horizon. She could see the resort's main building standing high on the tallest peak of the island, its rustic stone structure and terra-cotta rooftop echoing the style of an Apulian trullo—prioritizing a simplicity that complemented the natural surroundings. Its large courtyard extending along the back provided space for relaxation and tranquility. Even the white-capped waves crashing against the shore below looked peaceful. As Adriana breathed in the sweet, salty air, she felt some of the tension release from her shoulders.

If she had to be away from her restaurant, there was nowhere more appealing.

Kasa Island catered to all kinds of wealthy clientele, but they seemed to have one thing in common—a desire for peace and calmness they sometimes didn't even realize they needed.

Shading her eyes from the setting sun, she saw Domenico on the dock.

He was gorgeous. Tall, dark and traditionally handsome, but he always wore a scowl—at least when he saw her.

The exact one he was wearing now, she observed as the boat drew closer.

She'd been right about one thing—Domenico Kasa wasn't thrilled that she was there to save the day.

No pressure at all.

If he told her where one more thing was in this kitchen, she'd lose it.

"Over here are the…"

"Domenico! Stop, please." Adriana struggled to keep her tone calm and polite. Damn Leo for handing her off to Domenico, but he'd had Zoom calls with potential guests. Now she found herself alone with the brother she'd been hoping to avoid. She and Domenico had once been the closest of friends among the Kasa and Bellarini kids… when they were like, ten, before his ego developed and his face was splashed all over the tabloids. *The playboy of tennis* was her "favorite" of all the taglines.

Domenico turned toward her. She took a steadying breath before saying, "I'm sure you have a million things to do other than show me around, and I *did* design this kitchen, remember?"

She saw his jaw clench as he nodded. His face had yet to display anything other than irritation, and his welcoming grunt on the dock had made it clear having her there was not his idea.

Why was *he* so annoyed?

She was the one leaving her family restaurant in the hands of her brother, who might turn the place completely vegan by the time she got back. "Is there a problem, Domenico?" They could be adults about whatever was bothering him.

Not that she cared, but things would be less stressful that week if he wasn't scowling like a petulant child whenever she had the misfortune of seeing him.

"I don't think you're qualified to run the kitchen."

The bluntness of the words was a little shocking. She hadn't thought he'd actually come out with the truth. And the gut-punch effect had everything to do with the fact that the same words had come from her father on his deathbed. The man had been suffering from dementia, and she had desperately chosen to believe he hadn't meant them.

Domenico Kasa, however, a hundred percent did. Good thing his opinion of her was something she hadn't cared about in a long time.

"Well, lucky for you, you're wrong. So if you could get out, I can start making you eat your words." Which was all he'd be eating if she had her way. That mouth didn't deserve to enjoy anything she made. Her eyes dropped to said mouth, and her own went slightly dry. Unlike Leo's thin lips, Domenico's were full, soft-looking... Tom Hardy lips...

In fact, the brothers didn't share any common traits. Whereas Leo was just over five-foot-eleven, Domenico towered over her at six-foot-three. Leo was athletic but slim compared to Domenico's wider frame. While both brothers had brown hair and blue eyes, Domenico's short, messy waves were darker, and the blue of his eyes matched the color of the Mediterranean Sea.

A mesmerizing sea a woman could get lost in...and ultimately get seasick. She was sure his string of flings over the years could attest to that.

He coughed, covering his mouth, and her gaze flew back to his. "This review is important."

That they could agree on.

She needed a good review as well, not that she was sharing that information with him. As soon as he left, she was getting to work on the menu. Dinner service had been taken care of by the sous-chef and the rest of the kitchen staff. Now the kitchen was all hers for the evening. "I'm going to familiarize myself with the menu right away…as soon as you leave," she said.

Hint hint.

"Just so we're clear, I'm going to be around…a lot."

"Fantastic. But just so we're clear, you need to stay out of my way so I can do my job. As you said, this review is important."

Domenico nodded, folding his arms across his chest.

Seeing the bandages wrapped around his hand, she asked, "What happened?"

"Chef Dubois."

The laugh that escaped her was louder than she'd intended.

Domenico raised his left eyebrow. "You think it's funny?"

Adriana shook her head, composing herself. Barely. "No… I just think there are circumstances where I'd be tempted to stab you myself."

He opened his mouth to say something, then paused and shook his head. "Nope. I'm not doing this with you."

"Doing what?"

"This verbal sparring you somehow drag me into."

"*I* drag *you*…"

"I'm late for a tennis lesson," he said, checking his watch.

One he didn't sound thrilled about. "People still want you to teach them?"

His eyes narrowed slightly as he paused near the kitchen door.

Why had she egged him on? She should have let him leave.

"I once competed internationally."

"Once." What was wrong with her? Irritating him was far too much fun. She didn't know why, but she enjoyed watching his cool, calm demeanor unravel, giving her a glimpse at a different guy underneath. A slightly frazzled, easily ruffled guy. One who wasn't always so in control of his emotions. A glimpse of the sweet, insecure boy she once knew.

She envisioned steam escaping through his ears as he said, "If you don't need anything else…"

"I didn't need anything in the first place," she said, returning her attention to the menu.

"I meant what I said. Expect to be seeing a lot of me in here," he said, storming out of the kitchen.

Alone, Adriana breathed a sigh of relief. Then, as she scanned the kitchen, a slight apprehension filled her chest.

Was Domenico right to be questioning her abilities to pull this off? She'd certainly had her doubts in the last eight hours…

No. She would not let him do that to her. Who was he to question her skills? She was at least still pursuing a career she loved. He'd walked away from his.

Adriana sighed, the rationale not doing much to calm her mind.

This week would be challenging, and it had very little to do with the menu.

CHAPTER TWO

HE SHOULD HAVE put up more of a fight with his brothers. Adriana being here wasn't a good idea. She might be a great Italian chef, but the resort needed someone more well-rounded...

An image of her curvy figure, hugged by her chef jacket, which did absolutely nothing to downplay her appeal, flashed in his mind.

More well-rounded with their *culinary skills*...less so everywhere else.

He ran a hand over his hair as he headed toward the tennis courts. His lack of confidence in her abilities wasn't the only thing weighing heavy on him.

The Kasa kids and the Bellarini kids had grown up together, their families generational friends. His father had grown up with Alberto Bellarini, too. And out of all the kids, he and Adriana had been the closest. Inseparable every summer, actually—up until he started going away to tennis training camps every available moment of his young life. They'd drifted apart then...and somehow over one of those teenage summers, she'd drifted straight into Leo's arms. Family events had definitely been different seeing her with his brother. Not that he cared or was jealous or anything—it was just...weird. She'd been his friend first for all those years.

Did she even remember that? She didn't seem to. Not a "hey, remember when we…" or "wanna hang out like old times?" Nope. She'd been completely wrapped up in Leo all of a sudden and barely acknowledged his existence. Which was totally fine.

But how could she have forgotten the letters? They'd written actual letters to one another whenever he was away—deep, vulnerable, emotion-filled, sometimes funny letters. Hundreds of them over the years, and they'd shared dreams, secrets, doubts… He'd thought they were connecting—falling in love—through those letters.

He still had every single one of them.

How could they not have meant anything to her?

Clearly his ability to read signals was completely off. Perhaps that was why every relationship he'd ever had was surface-level and short-lived.

Adriana's betrayal had really messed him up in the romance department.

He hadn't seen her since she'd ended things romantically with Leo, and he'd been okay with that. They'd both grown into different people over the years.

Her loud, overly expressive personality and sharp tongue were not his style. Her open, transparent nature only made him more suspicious of her intentions with his brother. No one was *that* genuinely sincere and easygoing. He liked the women he dated to be more reserved, more polished and serious…more like him.

And absolutely the opposite of the woman wearing a tennis outfit that barely covered her body, waving to him now as he approached the floodlit Astroturf courts.

"Hey you, I was starting to think I'd been stood up," Pricilla Conway said, a playful pout on her lips, but a scolding look in her eyes that suggested he'd better not be late again.

Reminding her that he owned the resort and wasn't a hired tennis instructor would be rude, so he smiled politely. Making each guest feel treasured was the aim of Kasa de Paradise. No matter how irritating the guest.

"Sorry… I was introducing our *temporary* chef to the kitchen."

This week couldn't go by fast enough. The reviewer's visit was stressing him out. She was evaluating everything—not just the food. In the last few days, he'd barely slept, taking on extra responsibility to make sure the resort was at its finest—checking all the guest room amenities and ensuring the air-conditioning was working as they'd gotten a heads-up from another resort that Linda often insisted on changing rooms multiple times during her stay. He'd personally replaced all the lights along the resort trails as they'd heard she enjoyed late-night strolls. He'd even re-tested all the emergency evacuation equipment and ensured *Passage to Paradise* met all operation codes and standards, even though Jon was always on top of that. There wasn't a thing out of place, and all staff knew to expect to be on their A game—more than ever.

The Kasa brothers needed a sparkling review.

"Yes, I noticed Chef Dubois leaving on the boat this afternoon. I apologize for causing a stir."

He doubted there was a day that went by that Mrs. Conway *didn't* cause a stir. He unzipped a tennis racket and handed it to her. The woman wore a different tight and revealing tennis outfit each time she played, yet she didn't own a racket.

Or seem to get any better at using one.

"No, you were right to file your complaint. We hope

Chef Dubois's actions didn't negatively impact your stay too much."

She waved a hand. "I'm used to the attention, darling. You like my hair?" she asked, tossing her red curls. "Talia at the salon is a miracle worker. I've threatened to take her with me when we leave."

It looked the same as it did every day. Blazing, fiery red—a warning light she was attempting to use as a beacon.

"It looks great," he said, thinking about the way Adriana's dark hair had shone in the light as she'd stepped off the *Passage de Paradise* earlier that evening. Her natural copper highlights had reflected the sun's warmth.

"You seem distracted tonight," Pricilla said, touching his shoulder. He tensed as she moved closer, her breasts against his chest, the view of the ample cleavage distracting. And not in a good way. She was far too forward and obvious in her interest to appeal to him in the slightest, and she was a married woman. Not to mention a very vocal guest that liked getting her way.

So far, he'd mastered the art of turning down her not-so-subtle advances without damaging her ego. Leo and Mario had both reassured him that he didn't need to teach the woman if he was uncomfortable, but he wasn't intimidated by her—annoyed mostly.

"Just an eventful day," he said with a forced breezy air despite the tightening anxiety in his chest.

"Yes, you are under a lot of pressure," she said in a babying tone that sounded like she was speaking to a three-year-old. "Why don't we cancel the lesson for tonight."

Best idea he'd heard all day.

"And head down to the beach..." Her breath was close to his ear, and her voice was more like a purr.

He forced a breath, removing her hands from his shoulders. "Nope," he said with a forced laugh. "I promised you we'd improve your game so you can show off at the country club back in California…next week," he added for good measure. He really hoped she would be leaving next week. How much more of her inappropriate advances could he take without snapping? "So, let's get to work." He stepped away to unzip his own racket.

"Are you sure your hand is well enough? I still can't believe you got stabbed defending my honor." The silky, smooth, flirtatious tone had the opposite of its intended effect on him.

Obviously the wedding band Mrs. Conway wore and the fact that her husband was in a chalet a block away meant nothing to her. "My hand is fine, and the resort has a one strike policy regarding complaints from guests."

How many strikes would Leo afford Adriana?

They couldn't afford even one. Linda Frank's opinion could either skyrocket the resort's success or cause it to plummet with a few typed words. Allowing the reviewer here without a permanent chef might be a mistake… Was it too late to postpone the visit?

"You're sure?" Mrs. Conway said.

"Absolutely." Man, he couldn't wait to get this lesson over with so he could take the stress of his day out on some serves from the automatic machine—the only "partner" on the island who could keep up with him.

Pricilla released an *okay, your loss* sigh as she moved to the other side of the net, her hips swaying back and forth, each step giving him the intended glimpse of her butt. "I think you just like seeing me sweat."

He was pretty sure that was *her* guilty pleasure, not his. "Alright, I'll serve first," he said, placing an extra tennis ball in his shorts pocket and tossing the other up in the air.

He swung, and as it sailed over the net, he forced his thoughts away from Adriana. Focusing his full attention on the other woman at Kasa de Paradise who made him completely uncomfortable, who he'd *also* have to put up with during one of the most stressful weeks of his life.

Adriana yawned as she reviewed Chef Dubois's menus for the week and verified that they had enough stock and produce for the variations she intended to make. It was too bad that the chef couldn't keep his hands to himself, because he was really on top of things in the kitchen.

She flipped the pages to the next morning's breakfast prep. Her eyes bulged as she flipped and flipped again. Three full pages of breakfast items?

Was it too late to sneak back onto a boat to the mainland?

The resort promised guests anything and everything they could possibly want, but fourteen variations of eggs? Whatever happened to menu rotation? Cycling the offerings? Surely this was a little overkill.

Unfortunately, *overkill* could be used to describe a lot of things on Kasa Island. Now Adriana was expected to deliver with the same attention to detail and elite-level hospitality.

It was after eleven p.m., and the prep work alone would take hours. She normally would have had the sous-chef and the team do it, but that evening after briefly meeting with the kitchen staff, she'd given them all the rest of the night off, wanting time to refamiliarize herself with the setup and get ready to take charge in the busy kitchen the next day. No wonder she'd seen a few snickers and giggles as they'd readily—and quickly—escaped the kitchen.

The resort might only have a maximum of fifty guests at a time and fifty staff members, but a hundred people were a lot to impress.

Linda Frank would take a lot to impress.

Maybe Domenico was right. Maybe she wasn't the right chef to help them that week. His unconcealed disdain had been a source of fuel for her all evening, an overwhelming desire to prove Domenico Kasa wrong. But now, exhausted and feeling the pressure mount, her confidence waned.

She sighed. Better get to prepping…

Two hours later, removing her chef's jacket, she hung it on the hook near the walk-in freezer. Feeling the late-night heat on her skin, she opened the door and stepped inside.

Immediate relief.

Releasing her hair from the messy bun at the top of her head, she took several deep breaths. Goose bumps collected on her bare arms in her tank top, but she relished the cold, knowing the moment she stepped back out, the intense heat would suffocate her again.

At Bellarini's, she kept her kitchen AC on full blast. Here it didn't seem to matter. Even the sun long ago disappearing over the sea had done nothing to cool the island. Even the slight breeze was warm and wet, coating her entire body with a light gleam of moisture.

She yawned again and blinked the exhaustion from her eyes. Making the decision to come to the island had been easy, and she hadn't felt the burden of the responsibility until now.

She checked her watch. Almost midnight and the next

day would start before five a.m. Leo had assigned her a guest suite instead of a room in the staff quarters as the resort wasn't at full capacity. She longed to crawl into the king-size four-poster bed with the heavenly soft down-filled pillows she knew were awaiting her.

She'd made a good start that evening, and she still had the following full day to finalize the new evening menu and get the kitchen staff up to speed on her changes.

Thank God Domenico had stayed away that evening. He was an annoyance she couldn't afford. And she didn't want him to see the changes to the menu.

A slight pang of guilt hit her. Taking a gamble like this—possibly at the resort's expense—was wrong, but she needed this reviewer to taste her food. The dishes Bellarini's specialized in. It was her restaurant's only hope. It had spent too many years in the red, and if they didn't start making profits again soon, she'd be forced to shut the doors.

She picked up her cell phone and opened the message thread with Alex. Her last message, Just checking in, had been read and answered.

Of course.

He hadn't even tried to conceal his excitement at having control over Bellarini's for the week.

Any torment she felt about using this opportunity to her advantage dissipated. She needed to generate new appreciation for Bellarini's. Restaurant reviewers had given up visiting a long time ago. The restaurant was no longer new and impressive. They were simply a nostalgic landmark in the small Naples neighborhood without enough regulars to keep the doors open, but still paying for the prime real estate spot along the high-traffic touristy street.

Besides, why should she feel guilty about replacing menu items with dishes she excelled at making? The Kasa brothers wanted a shining review, right?

She was rationalizing to ease the guilt, and it was working until…

The memory of Domenico's piercing, untrusting gaze made her shiver. When had he developed a stare that seemed to look straight through her as though they hadn't spent their formative years together? They'd been best friends. They'd shared everything.

Through the letters.

Letters she cherished while he was away. Letters she'd read over and over, hearing his voice in her mind as she'd read. Letters she'd written revealing all her own stories, passions, doubts… Those letters back then had been everything.

But since he'd started going to tennis camps, he always came back more distant, more reserved. The year he'd turned sixteen, the tabloids said he was rumored to be dating a tennis pro from the US. Her heart had shattered, and the letters had stopped. Her sadness and that feeling of loss had her accepting Leo's affection. When Domenico had returned that year to find her dating Leo, he'd practically turned into a stranger… Someone she didn't recognize. Someone who acted as though she didn't exist.

Well, his loss, because she was a great friend. She didn't miss him or their connection one little bit.

She took one last cooling breath. Then, opening the door, she jumped, seeing Domenico standing a foot away. Her hand flew to her accelerated heart.

Hearing the freezer door close behind him, Domenico jumped even higher as he swung around toward her. "Adriana! What were you doing in there?"

"Cooling off," she said, fighting to calm her frantic pulse. "What are you doing in *here*?"

He didn't answer.

His gaze had dropped lower, to her chest. As she glanced down, her cheeks grew hot. The cold from the fridge had turned her nipples into two hard buds poking through the fabric of her tank top.

A flicker of interest registered in Domenico's eyes, and Adriana's embarrassment quickly turned to annoyance.

Oh sure, *those* he liked.

She snapped her fingers in front of her chest, and his gaze whipped up to meet hers. "What are you doing here?" she asked again.

"I was hungry," he mumbled, turning his attention to the smaller fridge.

Adriana moved across the kitchen and shut the door. "Go to the twenty-four-hour snack shop. The kitchen's closed."

"It's my kitchen."

"The kitchen belongs to the chef, and this one is closed. Everything has already been sanitized, and it's getting late. I'm not staying to clean it up again." She didn't want him lingering. He was sure to notice the extra ingredients she'd taken out and prepared for some of her popular Italian dishes. Seeing her own recipes on the counter, she quickly closed the notebook.

"I'll clean up when I'm done," he said.

"Or you could get out. You shouldn't be eating this late anyway." She raised an eyebrow and jerked her head toward his stomach.

A perfect six-pack was visible through the sweaty shirt clinging to his rock-hard body. Of the Kasa brothers, Domenico had the most muscular build. His broad shoulders and tapered waist gave him the illusion of being bigger than he actually was. Unfortunately, his arguable status as the hottest Kasa brother did nothing to move him to the top of the list as her favorite. Not anymore, at least. He was far too serious and arrogant and closed off. When had that transition happened?

No doubt his early success and the fact that he had women dropping at his feet had played huge roles.

And she refused to make the mistake of wondering what might happen if she pulled back those layers to uncover the guy she once knew. She had no interest in finding out what was beneath Domenico's suddenly cool exterior.

None at all.

"Are you implying that I'm fat?" he asked, eyes wide.

Adriana shrugged, loving the increasing annoyance in his tone. Why did she derive so much pleasure from irritating him? It was like a drug. Once she started, she couldn't stop herself.

Unfortunately, he accepted her teasing as a challenge. He whipped the shirt off over his head and flexed his stomach.

Keeping her mouth closed proved impossible.

The outline of the muscles beneath the fabric had lied. They weren't just perfectly sculpted with tanned obliques dipping below the waistband of his shorts. They were drool-worthy. She licked her lips as she scanned the muscular chest and shoulders, drinking in the sight of him as though he were a drop of fresh water in a salty ocean. Her pulse raced, and she prayed he couldn't hear her heart pounding or read the effect he was having on her.

He grinned. "Care to take back your insult?"

She turned away, her need for air at a pivotal point.

"All I'm saying is that eventually the late-night eating will catch up to you."

"I'll take my chances," he said, reopening the fridge door. "What can I eat that won't make a mess?"

She could think of something.

Where had that thought come from?

Probably the sight of his big biceps braced against the fridge. Since when did tennis players have big, sexy-looking arms? During his career, he'd been slightly leaner, or at least he'd appeared that way on television and in the press. Did cameras work in reverse for athletes? Make them look smaller than in real life? Or had he added bulk since retiring?

Why did she care? That was the real question.

She must be exhausted if she was eyeballing Domenico Kasa.

"Is that turkey meat reserved for something in particular?" he asked.

Only her *own* sandwich the next day. "No, go ahead," she said with a sigh, reaching into the large double-wide pantry for a loaf of thick-sliced homemade bread. The faster she could help him reach his undesirable carb belly, the better for her overactive, misbehaving hormones.

Domenico Kasa.

Why was she having to remind herself of that?

Even if he hadn't grown into an arrogant jerk, he was her ex-boyfriend's brother. Yuck!

Only so not yuck, she thought as he bent to retrieve the mustard from one of the lower shelves. Nope, nothing yucky about that butt.

She needed to get out of there before lack of sleep combined with lack of sex in recent years made her do something stupid. Like…offer to make his sandwich.

She gathered her things. "Try not to make too much of a mess."

"Heading to bed?" he asked, his tone implying she was a slacker.

She bit back a sarcastic reply about the hour and nodded. "Yes. Good night."

Just leave.

"Hey, Adriana."

Pretend you didn't hear him.

She paused near the door. "Yeah?"

"Sure you don't want to cool down again in the freezer before you head out? You're looking kinda flushed," he said, an implied smirk in his voice.

Unfortunately, she didn't think the freezer would help. "Good night, Domenico."

His cell phone and hers chimed in unison, and she turned toward him. Reaching into her back pocket she retrieved her phone and opened the text message from Leo at the same moment the smirk died on Domenico's face.

"Oh no," he said.

Reading quickly, Adriana's thoughts echoed his sentiments exactly.

Change of plans. Linda Frank is arriving tomorrow.

CHAPTER THREE

NOTE TO SELF—no more late-night snacking.
 Or at least make sure the kitchen is Adriana-free.

The only thing erasing the image of her body in her thin, tight-fitting tank top from his mind was the news that Linda Frank was arriving early.

He'd been dreading it before. Now his senses were on high alert as he left the kitchen and scanned the dark resort grounds for anything they may have overlooked—a burnt-out lightbulb since he'd last checked or a loose cobblestone along the paths between the villas. Stilettos and slippery stones did not mix but try telling that to women who insisted on ignoring their warning against skinny, sky-high heels posted multiple times in the guest guide to Kasa de Paradise.

Leo had gone to the mainland the night before and wouldn't rush back, knowing the resort was left in Domenico's capable hands. Irritation about his brother's laid-back attitude surfaced. Leo was the one who said they needed this opportunity, yet all the heavy lifting was left to Domenico.

As usual.

Growing up, Domenico always shouldered the brunt of the responsibilities, despite being the youngest of the brothers. The other two showed eager interest in the day-to-day operations of the family resort business, and their willingness to accept their birthright future without question had appeased their father. Domenico's lack of interest had resulted in his father putting more pressure on him to learn the business, conform, focus…at least until he'd found tennis. Then Leonardo Sr. had redirected the stern all-or-nothing approach towards Domenico's tennis career.

Mario rarely spent time within the hotel walls. He was always off on sourcing trips, attending resort and hotel chain conferences to learn about the latest technologies and promotions. He was a genius when it came to marketing and sourcing expensive wines and delicacies, but he wanted nothing to do with the general running of the resort. He'd already left the island again that day and wouldn't be back until after the reviewer's stay.

When their father got sick, Domenico had quit his tennis career to move home and care for him in his final days. A choice he'd never regretted. His days as a pro athlete had been numbered, and this venture with his brothers was the future—a continuation of the Kasa legacy.

If only his brothers could take things a little more seriously.

Thank God Adriana had caught the new sense of urgency, grabbing her chef's jacket and getting straight back to work on pre-prepping for the following evening's masquerade event. Another of Leo's great ideas he wasn't here to execute, having gone to the mainland to meet with investors.

At least Adriana was here, a thought that he refused to read too much into. Thrown into the trenches together, they'd reached an unspoken truce that evening. He'd sensed it before leaving her alone in the kitchen, and he was grateful for it.

Maybe it would help him ignore the intense attraction he felt for her. She was gorgeous—always had been. But now she was also sexy as hell. That wild, unruly hair cascading over her shoulders before she'd pulled it back into a tight bun to get to work had been mesmerizing. Adriana's presence could definitely be felt in a room, and normally he had no trouble removing himself from any room she occupied, but that evening, he'd almost hesitated to leave the kitchen.

Remembering the look in her eyes as she'd taken in his bare upper body…the interest reflected there…was unsettling.

How quickly the mood and tension around them had shifted into a sexually charged vibe.

One that couldn't continue.

They had enough to worry about with Linda Frank's arrival. They didn't need to get friendly again. What they'd had as children was in the past, and too much time had passed to rekindle it. They certainly didn't need any stress-fueled attraction developing between them. *That* would be a recipe for disaster.

Domenico had to make sure they weren't alone together often.

Or at all.

Ever.

Reaching his private villa on a secluded end of the resort, Domenico climbed the steps to the door and stepped inside.

The combination of rustic Italian construction with the traditional decor and modern appliances gave the villa a cozy, welcoming vibe. It lacked the pretentiousness of the rest of the resort buildings and held a charm that reminded Domenico of home back in Marina di Corricella, where his mother's family lived and where she insisted their family stay and grow up, even after their family resort chain made them billionaires. She loved their colorful, quaint family home surrounded by lemon groves near Marina Grande, and she rarely left the charming town. Pictures of the town and family photos framed and hung on the walls were the only real decor. He liked things simple.

A breeze from his open patio doors drifted inside, and he could hear the sound of the waves lapping against the private section of beach.

Knowing he'd find it difficult to sleep, he went into the kitchen, poured a glass of scotch over ice, then carried it out onto the deck.

Outside, he sat in his wicker chair and propped his feet up on the railing. He took a swig of the drink as he watched the waves crash along the shore, but despite the breathtaking scenery all around him, he couldn't erase the image of Adriana's flushed cheeks when she'd caught him staring at her breasts.

Nor could he erase the memory of said breasts.

He sighed, ran his uninjured hand over his exhausted, stressed features, then drained the contents of the glass.

He was in for one hell of a week.

Despite going to bed after midnight, Adriana hadn't needed her alarm sounding that morning to wake her. After the best—albeit short—sleep she'd had in probably forever, the sound of the waves crashing on the beach and the birds chirping outside on her private balcony had lured her awake. She stretched in the heavenly bed, enjoying the feel of the cooling bedsheets against her skin and the way the sheer white curtains blew in the breeze coming in through the open ceiling-to-floor windows.

The room was magnificent with its dark wood accents and white adornments. A chaise lounge sat near the open patio doors, with large white pillows making it almost as inviting as the bed. The open-air bathroom had surprised her at first, but taking a shower outside on the secluded deck with the view of the sea and neighboring islands before she'd climbed into bed hours before had been therapeutic. The day's stress had washed away.

Almost completely.

While the reviewer's early arrival had surprised her, she was ready for it. This way, she had little time to overthink what she was doing. Therefore, images of Domenico's gorgeous body had been the only lingering aggravation she'd had to fight as she'd drifted off to sleep.

Avoiding him and keeping him out of her kitchen would be for the best. She didn't like this unfamiliar attraction that had snuck in out of nowhere the night before. She'd known Domenico since they were two years old, and she'd never once thought of him that way. Their bond as children had been friendship. The one they'd nurtured over their teen years through letters had been…a form of adolescent love. But she'd never experienced this deep desire for him. Certainly not in recent years when their only exchanges had contained under-his-breath grunts or looks of obvious disproval.

It was just his body, all sexy and sweaty, combined with her exhaustion that had sent her common sense on a brief hiatus.

But it wouldn't happen again.

Domenico might have retired from tennis, but she suspected his playboy ways were still in practice.

Her cell phone on the night stand rang with an incoming FaceTime call from Isabella, and Adriana smiled as she answered the call. "Hi! How are you?" She sat up in bed and propped up the pillows behind her.

On the screen behind her friend, her three children ran around the kitchen island, screaming and laughing. Isabella winced at the noise. "Counting the days until school starts again."

Adriana laughed. "Hang in there." Her friend certainly had her hands full with her two sons, Berto, six, and Franco, eight, and daughter Marisella, four. Adriana often envied her friend for her beautiful family but was happy to be Auntie Ada—the nickname affectionately bestowed on her by Marisella, who couldn't say *Adriana*. She wasn't sure yet if she wanted kids of her own. Some days she thought she definitely did, but a babysitting session at Isabella's house always made her realize she wasn't quite ready yet.

On-screen, Isabella disappeared into her kitchen pantry, shut the door and sat on the floor. "Ah, better. How's the island?" She reached for a bag of potato chips and started munching.

"Well, the reviewer is arriving early, and the first event is tonight, so…"

Isabella waved a chip at the screen. "I know you'll crush the review. I'm talking about Leo. Any new sparks flying between you two?"

Adriana shook her head. "Nothing interesting to report. Leo and I are just friends." Which she had repeatedly told her best friend, but Isabella was firmly on Team

Reconnect. She thought Adriana was insane for not entertaining the option.

"Fine. Any hot single guests, at least?"

"I've been too busy to notice." Most guests came to Kasa de Paradise in couples, though. Rarely did people drop the extreme amount on a solo trip. And the luxury resort didn't give off bachelor party vibes.

"Come on, Adriana! I'm trying to live vicariously through you!"

"Sorry, guess my life isn't that exciting," she said with a laugh.

"Well, I'm taking the kids to Bellarini's tonight for dinner because if I have to cook one more meal, I'm going to lose it. I'll check in on Alex for you."

"Thank you. I texted him a few times, and he's definitely avoiding me."

Behind Isabella on the screen, the pantry door swung open, and the three kids stared at her.

"Why didn't you tell us we were playing hide-and-seek?" Berto asked.

"You're counting next!" Marisella said with a happy squeal.

Isabella sighed as she closed the bag of potato chips and stood. "And…my vacation is over. Talk soon, bestie."

Adriana blew her friend a kiss as the call disconnected.

Tossing the sheets aside, she climbed out of the bed and walked out onto the deck. The salty breeze in the early morning mist lifting over the island and the quiet tranquility made her sigh. Her day would be crazy preparing the menu for that evening's event, but for a moment, she would enjoy this.

Unfortunately, her appreciation of her luxurious surroundings brought with it the realization of how alone she was in this Mediterranean paradise. On the deck was a table set for two…and a dark wood-trimmed nest chair meant for two…and a private hot tub for two.

She was one.

All alone on a couples' dream vacation.

Not that she'd ever be able to afford luxury like this. Even when the restaurant was doing well, she'd taken a modest salary, living a low-key lifestyle in a one-bedroom condo near the beach. As she was growing up, her parents worked hard at the restaurant to provide a comfortable life and ensure they always had what they needed. Her father was so different from his best friend, Leonardo Kasa Sr., who strived for success and a healthy bank account, but the two men had gone to the same school as kids and had always been thick as thieves. They respected the other's way of life. Both ambitious and hardworking, the two men had always championed the other's successes. And at their core, family was everything to them both, even if they acted on that priority in different ways. Both wanted to leave a lasting legacy to their families and ensure future generational success…

And at least one of the two men would be proud.

Adriana took in a deep breath of sea air and stared out across the sandy beach below.

A small lizard skirted past her on the deck. Adriana jumped back, then smiled when she saw it scale the wall of the guest suite.

At least she had company.

An hour later, she left her room and walked slowly along the paths through the resort to the main building. The smell of the colorful flowers combined with a faint aroma of citrus was the island's signature scent. It was everywhere, as though spritzed perfectly on the breeze.

The Kasa Island brochure did not boast false promises. This island in the Mediterranean was truly a piece of paradise with its lush natural vegetation, traditional Italian architecture and modern conveniences—it was luxury second to none. And while the serene setting catered to relaxation and rejuvenation of the spirit, the island didn't shy away from extreme pleasure excursions. She could see the zip-line above the trees as she walked and the surfing line in the distant water. There was something for every vacationer.

Beads of sweat gathered on the back of her neck, and she removed her light sweater as she walked. The temperature was already in the eighties, even at that early hour in the morning. Sweating in the hot, humid kitchen that day was going to be her biggest challenge.

That, and *him*.

Tension crept into her shoulders as she saw Domenico on the tennis courts ahead. What was he doing up so early? He'd been up as late as she was. She'd expected—*hoped*—to get a few hours' reprieve from having him lurk around the kitchen and micro-manage her that morning.

A reprieve from drooling over his muscles.

She glanced around the trails. Was there another way to get to the main building without walking past the tennis courts? The signage on the trail pointed in one direction only. The resort's dedication to preserving the native flora and fauna left her no options other than the walking trail she was on.

Maybe Domenico wouldn't notice her. He had his side to her, and he looked focused on the tennis balls coming at him at a crazy speed.

Still, she picked up her pace as she drew closer to the fence around the courts.

Unfortunately, she couldn't help but notice *him*...or rather the chest, arms and stomach that had been etched in her mind all evening. Alone on the court, shirtless in a pair of navy tennis shorts, he battled against a Spinfire Pro, returning lightning-fast balls quicker than she even had time to register them coming. His feet moved with precision back and forth as though anticipating the location of the next one. His broad, muscular shoulders contracted and flexed as he swung and hit each one with an almost violent aggression.

Adriana's mouth went dry. He was hot. Even hotter with the look of determination on his chiseled features, the sweat beading on his forehead and his damp hair pushed back from his face.

She hadn't seen him play in a long time...and never this close.

Shirtless.

Leo had bragged about Domenico's international success over the years, but she'd never been able to get away from the restaurant long enough to attend a match with him. Watching the pro athlete now, there was no question of his skills. Those championships and titles were obviously well-earned. He'd retired from his tennis career at the top of his game to help care for his father when he was sick, but she wondered if he'd really been ready to hang up the racket professionally for good. He was still in top form...

Her gaze settled on his abs flexing and contracting with each breath.

Yep, that form was definitely top-notch.

"You're going to be late for work," Domenico called out, not even glancing her way, never losing focus for the briefest of seconds on the balls whizzing toward him.

Adriana's jaw dropped as she quickly continued along the trail past the tennis courts and out of sight. How did he see her?

Better question—What was she thinking, stopping to watch him play?

Staring at Domenico Kasa shirtless or otherwise was proving to be a pastime that she couldn't afford. Her former childhood friend had somehow gotten to her in the last twenty-four hours in ways she hadn't expected. She'd expected him to be grumpy about her being there, because a scowl was all he ever wore in her presence in recent years. She'd expected him to doubt her abilities in the kitchen, as he'd never once eaten at Bellarini's since she took over as head chef. And she'd expected eventually to be butting heads with him over her menu alterations. But this intense physical attraction to her childhood friend and ex-boyfriend's brother—nope, never, not in a million years.

Therefore, her mission was clear: keep him out of the kitchen and stay away from the tennis courts.

He'd felt Adriana's eyes on him—lingering, drinking him in. Focusing on the ball while being aware of his peripheral surroundings was a situational awareness skill he'd learned as a professional athlete to reduce risk of injury out on the court. Now nothing escaped his notice—whether he wanted it to or not.

Seeing Adriana just now had only given a physical presence to the image he couldn't erase from his mind. He'd even dreamed of her the night before—a delicious dream set in the resort's kitchen that didn't include food. He'd never be able to look at that island countertop the same way again. He felt the front of his shorts grow tight at the mere memory, and he sighed as he stepped out of the line of fire and approached the Spinfire Pro to shut it off.

His cell phone rang as he picked up his towel. He answered the call from Leo, wiping sweat away from his neck and face.

"Hey, bro, when you getting back here?"

The faster he could assign babysitting duties to Leo, the better. Domenico had thought he wanted to supervise Adriana himself that week, but that might not be the best idea. She was turning out to be a distraction he didn't need.

"I'll be back before Linda arrives—just."

"What are you doing over there, anyway?"

"Told you—meeting with a few investors who might be interested in the franchising concept."

Domenico sighed. "Thought we were going to discuss that more." Leo was eager to turn their luxury island concept into a franchise with similar resorts all over the Mediterranean. While Domenico shared his brother's ambition, he wasn't sure he agreed on this particular vision. Kasa de Paradise appealed to guests because of its luxury, but also its uniqueness. If they started duplicating the concept all over Europe, over time not only would it lose its quality, but the lack of rarity would diminish its value.

Mario was still neutral on the idea, so it would basically come down to whichever brother was more persuasive to sway Mario's deciding vote in their favor.

"We are going to discuss it more," Leo said, "but I need to be properly armed for that discussion."

Great.

Domenico sighed as he checked the time on the phone.

He needed to shower, dress and head over to the main building for a meeting with the housekeeping staff. "Well, just hurry up, okay? There's still a lot to do."

"I trust you have it covered. How's Adriana doing?"

Domenico's throat constricted at the mention of her, and his "fine" came out as a growl. He cleared his throat and repeated, "Fine."

"You two playing nice?"

Oh, in his dream the night before they were playing *very* nice indeed.

"Everything's cool. Gotta go," he said, disconnecting the call.

He forced a breath as he tucked the phone away and grabbed his things. He needed to get his head on straight and deal with the long to-do list. No more inappropriate thoughts about Adriana or recalling images from his vivid dream the night before.

His cell phone chimed as he left the courts. Retrieving it, he opened a photo message from Leo with the caption, Found this at the old house while looking for some financial paperwork.

Domenico's heart skipped as he saw a photo of the five of them as kids—Leo, Mario, Alex, Adriana and himself—on the beach. He and Adriana were in the middle, arms around one another. She was smiling at the camera, her dark hair blowing in the breeze behind her, but his gaze was directed on her. He sighed as he caught the look on his preteen face.

So maybe this attraction to her wasn't coming a hundred percent out of nowhere.

Wonderful. Just wonderful.

CHAPTER FOUR

She remembered that summer day on the beach near the Kasa family home, but Adriana didn't recall posing for the group photo she was staring at on her phone in the text message from Leo—nor did she remember ever seeing Domenico look at her the way he was in the image.

Her chest was tight as she zoomed in on the picture so that it was only the two of them in the frame. She was smiling at the camera—almost as though she'd been laughing at something right before the flash went off. No doubt it was something Domenico had said. Years ago he used to make her laugh until she peed. He used to be funny. Odd how that memory struck her now—she'd forgotten that about him.

But it was his expression that had her heart racing. It was, dare she say it, lovestruck? As lovestruck as a preteen boy could be...

A timer chimed on the counter behind her. She sighed as she tucked the cell phone into her apron pocket and got back to work.

Linda Frank was scheduled to arrive in three hours, and Leo had planned a resort tour for her that afternoon, so she only had another hour to prep for the evening before she'd have to clean up.

She slid a multislicer through stacked sheets of pasta,

then carefully dropped the pasta strands into the deep fryer. They sizzled for a minute before she removed them and dipped them in a mixture of sugar, cinnamon and cocoa, savoring the sweet aroma as she worked. After setting them on a tray, she repeated the process.

Galani were one of her guilty pleasures, and they were the perfect bite-sized dessert to complement the sweet tasting menu for that evening's masquerade-themed party.

She shook her head. If anyone could pull off such an elaborate event, it was the resort's entertainment staff. She'd caught a glimpse of the decor and setup in the lower section of the main building that was curtained off in preparation for the event. It already looked magnificent. Dark, rich colors like emerald green and deep red for the velvety textured fabrics of the curtains and furniture coverings added a layer of mystery while in contrast, candlesticks and mirrors in metallics like silver and gold created a striking, regal presence in the room. Pearl beads, long dark feathers and masks of various dark metallics completed the design with an impressive flair.

The five-course sit-down dinner menu that Chef Dubois had planned, however, was less impressive, so Adriana was making adjustments.

She picked up one of the pasta strips, bit into it and closed her eyes as the flavors of cinnamon and chocolate danced on her tongue. "Mmm."

"Are you preparing the food or eating it?"

Only Domenico could ruin this near-sensual experience for her.

He might have had a crush on her when they were kids, if the photo could be believed, but that wasn't the expression he wore on his face now as she opened her eyes.

Licking the powdered sugar from her lip, she said,

"Chefs need to sample their creations before serving them to guests." Reluctantly she held out the tray. "Care to try one?"

"Galani?"

She nodded, avoiding looking at him too long. He'd obviously showered since his morning workout on the tennis court. Dressed in a white collared shirt and tan khaki pants, he looked cool and refreshed—not at all bothered by the intense humidity that had the few tendrils of her hair that escaped her bun curling at the base of her neck.

He looked tempted, but shook his head as he patted his flat stomach. "Someone told me I needed to watch my weight," he said, glancing around the kitchen and surveying the various trays of hors d'oeuvres and sweet bite-sized delicacies. "Is this everything for tonight's event?" He frowned.

She hadn't cleared her new adjustments with anyone, and there'd be no more avoiding the conversation. "Yes. I made some changes to the menu," she said confidently. She refused to let him shake her on this decision.

"Some?"

She scanned the rows of appetizers on the counters. "Okay, a lot of changes. I changed the whole thing." She may have gone a tad too far. "Chef Dubois had a full sit-down five-course dinner planned, but given the nature of the event, I thought a wide selection of finger foods would be more appropriate."

"Our guests like to eat," Domenico said, looking mildly panicked. He fingered his open collar at his neck.

So maybe not so unaffected by the heat. Or was it her and her decision-making causing him to break out into a sweat?

"Yes, but they will be wearing masks and evening

gowns," she muttered, standing her ground. "Bite-sized pieces and things that are consumed best at room temperature is a more appropriate way to go. Not to mention the waitstaff will have a much easier time serving."

A stress line appeared on Domenico's forehead, and she could see a slight throbbing in a darkening vein at his temple. The man was seriously stressed over this.

"Chef Dubois didn't think so," he said.

"You fired Chef Dubois."

He checked his watch, then massaged his forehead as though hoping to ease his frustration. "It's after noon. I guess we're stuck with this."

Stuck?

Adriana's teeth clenched so tightly together, her jaws hurt. "Just because the portion sizes are small doesn't mean they're not delicious." She scanned the trays. Selecting a garlic stuffed mushroom, she approached and extended it to him. "Try this."

Domenico shook his head, his nose wrinkled in disgust. "I'm not a fan of mushrooms. It's the text..."

Adriana reached up and stuffed it into his open mouth.

Domenico's eyes widened in shock at first at the gesture. Then his expression changed as he slowly chewed. Changed from surprise to consideration to an obvious look of approval...and dare she hope...enjoyment?

She smiled. "What were you saying about texture?"

He swallowed the appetizer and nodded at the row of them on the tray with a suspicious look. "Those are mushrooms? They didn't taste slimy at all."

"Not all mushrooms are the same. Some are soft and meaty..."

His gaze locked with hers. "But most are slimy...even the ones that don't appear so at first glance."

"I think you are wrongly accusing all mushrooms of the same crime without trying the full spectrum. Choose the right one and you could be pleasantly surprised," she said, feeling her pulse race in her veins.

He was too close, they were too alone, and she couldn't remember what they were talking about anymore. When he stepped toward her, she couldn't be sure whose hands reached out first, but in a confusing instant, his were on her waist and hers were pressed against his chest. His head bent to the side and his gaze locked with hers as his lips moved closer.

"Is that the case only with mushrooms, or are there more surprises in your kitchen?" he muttered, his lips grazing hers.

She swallowed hard as her fingers gripped the light, soft fabric of his shirt. "You tell me," she said, pressing her body into him.

His mouth crushed hers then, and her breath caught at the intense passion and desire she'd never have guessed he could possess. Gone was the rigid, reserved exterior. Right now, he was open and inviting…and dangerous. Her arms went higher to encircle his neck as she moved even closer, deepening the kiss, her tongue exploring his mouth as his desperately searched hers.

He smelled so good, like the salty breeze combined with the sweet scent of the island, mixed with a hint of expensive cologne. She could breathe that delicious scent in all day. He turned his head to the other side, his hands gripping tighter on her waist as he ran his tongue along her bottom lip, then grabbed it between his teeth to bite gently, before pulling away.

Her eyes flew open in time to see his look of remorse as he released her.

Her hand flew to her mouth, and neither of them spoke.

They didn't have to. The kiss had said far too much already.

Still, he stood there, staring at her...expecting what? An apology? An explanation? He'd be waiting a long time for either.

"That can't happen again," he finally said.

"*You* kissed *me*," she said, fighting to control her thundering heartbeat echoing loudly in her ears.

He guffawed. "As if you weren't begging me to."

Adriana mouth gaped. "You can't be serious. Why on earth would I want to kiss you? You're arrogant and rude and judgmental...and..." She searched for more insults. "You're prejudiced against all fungi."

Domenico took a step toward her, his gaze burning into hers with the same intensity she'd felt in his kiss. "Why would *I* want to kiss *you*? You're loud and uncompromising. You've been here less than twenty-four hours, and you've destroyed a perfectly good menu..."

"*Fixed* an inappropriate menu," she corrected him, taking a step closer, her hands on her hips.

"That's a matter of opinion," he muttered, moving even closer until they were toe to toe—inches apart.

The heat sizzling between them rivaled any coming from the kitchen appliances. Their gazes locked in a tension-filled standoff. She raised her chin an inch more.

"So, you're saying you didn't like the mushroom?"

He hesitated for a long time. Then the heavy exhale that escaped him blew her hair away from her face. "The mushroom was an unexpected pleasure..." he said carefully as one does when they fear their words could somehow be used against them in court. "But one that I don't plan on indulging in recklessly again."

A hint of a smile played on her lips at the tiny victory. "But you liked it?"

Domenico shook his head in slight annoyance that he was giving her the win, turned and headed toward the door. "It might be the best thing I've ever had in my mouth."

Adriana's smile was wide as she watched him walk out. Then her hand flew to her lips, where his had just been, and her smile faded.

What the hell was that?

Without a doubt, the best kiss of her life.

Domenico paced the dock an hour later, waiting for the *Passage to Paradise*.

He had to convince Leo that Adriana was a mistake. Having her at the resort this week had already been a gamble. Now it was a personal liability. That kiss in the kitchen had been an impulsive, stupid move, and he should never have let it happen, but the woman got under his skin in ways no one ever had. The kiss had been almost about teaching her a lesson.

What lesson, he didn't know. And unfortunately, it had backfired.

Instead of showing her who was boss, it told him he wasn't it.

She had to go.

His lack of self-control around her would make this week even more tension-filled and stressful. Added complications were the last thing they needed with so much on the line. A good review from Linda Frank could turn Kasa de Paradise into one of the world's top travel destinations. A negative one could sink them.

This woman was brutal. And she could afford to be.

She was sought-after, and resorts asked her to review them—they essentially gave her the power she wielded.

The Kasa brothers were giving her that power.

Because…they believed in what they'd achieved here through dedication, hard work, commitment…and focus.

Now, after that kiss, Domenico's focus was destroyed.

The sous-chef and the rest of the kitchen team would have to step up and prove themselves. Now was their time to shine. Maybe they'd discover a new head chef.

Seeing the boat approach, he watched as it sailed into the harbor and carefully docked next to the pier.

"Good afternoon, Mr. Domenico," Jon said, hopping off and securing the line.

"Hey, Jon," he said distractedly, turning his attention to his brother as Leo disembarked. "We need to rethink this whole Adriana thing."

Leo shook his head and shot Domenico a silent warning before reaching behind him to extend a hand to a tiny dark-haired woman in a tan skirt and white blouse.

It was too late.

Domenico's palms were instantly covered in sweat, and his stomach did somersaults.

"Domenico, this is Linda Frank from *Travel Island* magazine. Linda, I'd like you to meet my brother and business partner, Domenico."

"Hi, welcome…" This wasn't the way he'd wanted to meet the woman, all frazzled and with the taste of Adriana still on his lips, but here they were. He extended a hand toward her, and she eyed him carefully as she shook it. Her hand was as cool as an ice cube.

They were in trouble.

Why was she staring at him like that? Could she somehow sense that he'd just been kissing their temporary chef in the resort kitchen? Was her reviewer spidey sense picking up on a potential sexual harassment claim?

His heart was pounding so loud he didn't hear Leo until he repeated himself. "Dom, you can let go now."

Right. He was holding her hand hostage in his. He released her. "Sorry about that."

"You're the tennis pro—Domenico Kasa, right?"

That depends. Did she like tennis? He hesitated.

"He is. The one and only. And he usually can speak for himself, but he's obviously starstruck," Leo said smoothly, shooting him a look that said *pull it together*.

Domenico cleared his throat. "Yes, I can. Apologies, Ms. Frank. I was expecting you on a later boat."

She nodded. "Guilty. I like to spring unexpected surprises on my hosts. Speaking of which, I have to say, that boat ride was unexpectedly smooth, and the view coming in through the narrows was breathtaking," she told him with a smile.

So far so good. But Domenico wasn't fooled. Beneath the smile and compliment was a woman with piercing, perceptive eyes just looking for one wrong move, one slipup. Her job was to find the issues, the problems, the reasons guests might spend their money elsewhere. Her readers expected the very best if she recommended a resort, and she took that position of service to the tourism industry very seriously.

"Thank you. We pride ourselves on giving guests the best of luxury from the moment they book with us," he said, taking her bag as they walked along the dock toward the main building.

She nodded. "I did take the liberty of trying out the online registration system under a false name. I have to say again that the process was as smooth and easy as promised. The online concierge was very helpful and knowledgeable," she said.

Each member of the staff from the gardeners to the bartenders completed their three-month intensive training course on every aspect of the resort before they stepped onto the island. It was a process their father had always insisted on for every hotel they opened within the family's former chain. All staff needed to have a basic working knowledge of everyone else's position—not to step in to do it, but to encourage mutual respect among the staff. No job was insignificant in running a resort, and Leonardo Sr. treated everyone with the utmost courtesy and consideration. They hired only the best, and they treated them as the VIP staff they were.

"We take our staff selection process seriously," he said.

"I reviewed your staffing policies, and they are quite inclusive and unique."

"Unique in a good way?" Leo was cheeky enough to ask.

Linda just winked at him.

"So, this is the main building," Leo said a moment later when they reached it and entered. "As you can see, check in is fully automated with the kiosks." He gestured to a row of four check-in machines in the large, open-air foyer where they hosted nightly entertainment with a bar, a grand piano and comfortable lounge chairs and tables. A laid-back yet classy area for guests to relax and unwind at the end of the evening.

Linda moved closer to a kiosk. "In my experience, this can sometimes slow the process. Guests aren't all tech-savvy. Losing the personal touch of guest attendants in favor of technology isn't always progress in the tourism industry."

Right there. He knew not to let his guard down at that smile and wink of hers. Luckily the Kasa brothers were prepared for that particular criticism.

"We totally agree. Our father always said that guests will forgive just about anything as long as they are greeted with professionalism and courtesy," Leo said.

"Your father was a smart man," Linda said. "I had the pleasure of reviewing one of his hotels. Unfortunately it was later in the chain's lifespan, and some things had deteriorated."

Like their father's health. Without Leonardo Kasa Sr. at the helm, the hotel board had started to make decisions around him—decisions that cut costs, but also weakened the Kasa hotel chain. By the time the brothers sold it, it was no longer up to the standard of family pride they'd grown up in.

And they'd seen Linda's review—one that would have been detrimental had they not already closed the deal to sell the hotel chain. Their previous experience with Linda had been one of the reasons Domenico had been wary of this idea, but Mario and Leo insisted this was a great way for the Kasa hotel brand to redeem themselves.

"I commend your decision to sell the chain and open Kasa de Paradise. Smart move, though I understand it might not have been an easy one," she said.

Leo nodded. "Thank you. Our father gave his blessing before he passed, and I think we've done him proud."

"Back to the system," Domenico said, the conversation getting a tad too personal for his liking. "When we put it in, we designed it with guest ease of use in mind. Therefore it's a simple swipe of the armband provided to our guests on the boat. Give it a try," Domenico said, nodding to the armband Linda wore.

Linda extended her arm over the scanner. Immediately the screen lit up with her personal reservation info.

"Welcome to Kasa de Paradise," a smiling guest attendant greeted her on-screen. "Get ready to smile in 3...2...1..."

Linda smiled, and the camera took her picture.

"Thank you," the on-screen host said. "Now you may remove your armband. Enjoy your stay with us."

Linda grinned as she removed the armband. "That was clever. I was going to dock you points for this annoying thing."

Leo took the armband from her. "We know," he said with a wink.

Linda eyed him. "Okay, but from an environmental standpoint, aren't the armbands just a waste of time and useless now?"

Domenico shook his head. "Nope. They are recycled and recalibrated at the front desk."

Linda nodded slowly. "Okay, I like it...but there's still the element of the personal touch..."

"Your drink, Ms. Frank," a voice said right on cue behind them.

He loved their staff.

Even Linda's unpredictable early arrival hadn't shaken them. The moment the three of them had entered, the staff had been discreetly on alert. And the best part was, this wasn't for show. Any and all guests received the same treatment.

Linda laughed as she turned toward the young server with the pressed Kasa de Paradise uniform and sincere smile. "Thank you," she said as she accepted the sweet-and-sour martini with olives from the tray and took a sip.

Domenico and Leo waited for her reaction.

"This is...good. Real good."

Domenico's shoulders relaxed slightly, and Leo's confident smile was back in place.

"You guys have impressed me so far, but don't rest easy. This is only the beginning of my stay," Linda said, taking another sip of the drink.

Domenico nodded. "We wouldn't think of it."

Behind Linda's back, Leo was giving a thumbs-up. While Domenico was just as relieved that the initial meeting had gone well, he knew Linda meant what she said.

She'd only been there ten minutes. There was still plenty of time for something to go wrong.

His chest tightened as he remembered the steamy kiss in the kitchen. Adriana's lips on his had felt like sinful indulgence. The taste of her had rivaled the sweetness of the galani and the delicacy of the mushroom. Her hands gripping his shirt and the way she'd pressed her body into him. It had nearly knocked him on his butt. Had definitely thrown him off his game.

Still plenty of time for something *else* to go wrong.

"See. Told you things would be fine. You need to relax," Leo said an hour later in their office as he collapsed into the chair behind the desk and stifled a yawn.

"Relax? There's a high-profile reviewer touring the facility and interviewing our staff as we speak." Domenico stood at the window, where he could see Linda moving throughout the resort grounds with her tablet. After he'd toured her through the facilities, she'd insisted on a solo tour. Every time she paused too long or jotted something down, his heart raced.

What was she making notes about?

He took his phone out of his pocket and snapped a photo, then zoomed in on the tablet.

Too blurry. He couldn't read anything.

"You've made sure that everything was perfect, so quit stressing. Besides, there's nothing we can do now." Leo stood and picked up his golf putter. He approached the mini-putt green in the corner of the office, rotated his shoulders, lined up the shot, then sent the golf ball sliding into the hole. "By the way, what were you going to say about Adriana earlier on the dock?"

She's both a fantastic chef and kisser.

Heat crept up Domenico's neck as guilt washed over him. It was too late to replace her without Linda noticing the switch, so now he just had to deal with it. Deal with her and having that temptress of a body around the resort all week. And deal with this sudden attraction that, according to the nostalgic photo, might not actually be so sudden. It still baffled him. Had he completely blocked out any feelings he'd once had for Adriana? Was it some kind of trauma self-preservation thing? They'd been great friends. Then that connection had grown over the years through their correspondence…but then BAM! He'd come home from a tennis tour, excited to see her, explore what their young emotions could be for one another, and she was dating his brother!

Talk about a punch to the nuts.

There was no denying he'd liked her back then and was attracted to her now…and it was problematic.

"Nothing," he said. "We're stuck with her." He ran a hand through his hair and checked his watch. "I need to shower and change."

"I had guest services deliver your masquerade outfit to your villa."

Right. These events weren't only for the guests. Leonardo Sr. always said that guests had more fun and embraced the theme nights more when the hotel staff and management teams also participated. He always treated guests as family at his hotels, and families ate, drank and laughed together.

Domenico wasn't totally opposed, but this event in particular seemed a little challenging. At least it did now after Adriana had raised some good points. "You sure we should be trying a new event this week?"

"It's already on the calendar. Guests are looking forward to it," Leo said, realigning his shot. He swung and hit the ball. It went a fraction of an inch right of the hole.

Domenico sighed. "Are you going to play all day, or are you actually going to do some work?"

Leo grinned. "Haven't decided yet."

Domenico shook his head as he left the office. His brother was one of the best business minds he knew, and he was the success behind Kasa de Paradise, but if he didn't get serious about his responsibilities soon, he could also be their downfall. Leo believed that fate played a large part in life and that things always worked out as they should. A belief he'd inherited from their mother. Domenico was more of a take-charge-of-one's-fate kind of guy. Point your destiny where you wanted it to go, rather than following with blind faith.

At his villa, he headed around to the outside shower. Removing his khakis and shirt, he turned on the gentle waterfall stream and surveyed the view around him as he stepped under the water.

This place was magical. Guests arrived here stressed, overworked, exhausted and left feeling rejuvenated, refreshed and reinvigorated. He was proud of what they'd built—a true paradise in a chaotic, unsettled world.

After the reviewer's visit, he'd take a week off, give himself the opportunity to unwind a little and enjoy the perks of the island himself.

He closed his eyes as the cool water ran down his back. An image of Adriana immediately came to mind. Out of all the challenges that week posed, being around her was the toughest.

Why had he kissed her?

And why was he desperate to do it again? It was a mistake, one he couldn't repeat. She was currently an employee, a long-time family friend, and she'd always be Leo's ex.

Off-limits for so many reasons, but unfortunately, whenever someone told him he couldn't have something, it only made him want it more.

Maybe that's all it was. The fact that Adriana was the last woman on earth he could have was making him want her.

Staying away from her wasn't an option, since he was determined to make sure she didn't do anything to jeopardize their review. He was just going to have to learn to control the intense, irrational attraction he had to her.

It was just for a week.

He could keep his hands and lips off his brother's ex-girlfriend—a woman he might have been harboring unacknowledged, buried feelings for since he was a kid—for that long, couldn't he?

Absolutely.

CHAPTER FIVE

ADRIANA COLLAPSED ONTO her bed several hours later. All of the food was prepped for that evening's event, and she had an hour before she had to get back there to oversee the kitchen.

She'd heard the buzz around the resort. Linda Frank was there. The entire staff was vibrating on a higher intensity, and the general mood of Kasa de Paradise had shifted into another level of professionalism and hospitality. The reviewer hadn't been into the kitchen yet, but Adriana was on high alert. This review meant everything. Not only to the Kasa resort's success, but to her own. The food would be highly critiqued as part of the review, and the chance to have her culinary skills praised in such a high-profile magazine by a well-respected reviewer had her functioning on adrenaline alone.

She couldn't mess this up.

She was a skilled and proficient chef. Professional and commanding in the kitchen. She demanded excellence and delivered the same. And as long as she could keep from kissing Domenico Kasa again, everything would be fine.

She rolled over and muffled a loud groan into her heavenly pillow.

The kiss should have been horrible. It should have

made her want to gag. It was Domenico freaking Kasa, the most arrogant, annoying man on earth and a childhood friend. Not to mention her ex-boyfriend's brother. That alone should have made Domenico a nonsexual inanimate object in her mind—like one of the tiki torches illuminating the island trails. She should not have enjoyed it, and it certainly shouldn't have played on repeat in her mind while she'd worked.

She'd kept expecting him to come back into the kitchen for either another round or to explain his actions away. Which she'd been anticipating—or hoping for? She wasn't sure.

He was technically her boss for that week, but it had been clear by the look on his face when he'd pulled away that he hadn't felt one bit in control. That kiss had been as unexpected to him as it had been to her.

Therefore, it didn't have to mean anything, right? Just a little glitch. A little slipup in the heat of an argument. Two attractive, hot-blooded, passionate people who let a moment in time sweep them away.

That was it. No more. No less.

She wasn't sure she bought all that she was telling herself, but it calmed her for the moment.

She rolled onto her back and stared at the ceiling. The breeze blowing in through her open patio doors held the same sweet floral island fragrance. The soft bedsheets and pillows beneath her were comfy and soothing to her tired body. She closed her eyes.

For just a second… She would not fall asleep.

Loud knocking made her jump what felt like seconds later. Her eyes flew open, and her heart raced as she sat up. The room was darker, and a glance outside the patio doors revealed dusk had settled over the island.

Where had the sun gone?

Panic gripped her as she glanced at the clock. Seven thirty?

She'd fallen asleep. An hour nap had felt like six seconds. She jumped up off the bed and peeked through the hole in the door.

Dom.

Oh no. What was he doing here? Another make-out sesh?

No, that would be stupid. Sexy, fun and hot, but definitely stupid.

She fixed her hair as she opened the door. "Hey, I was just going to start heading back." She caught a glimpse of her reflection in the mirror across the hall. After a quick sponge bath and makeup application. She was a frizzy, sweaty mess after all day in the kitchen.

"Good I caught you then," he said, entering the room. "I was bringing you this." He took a big white box from behind his back and extended it toward her.

"What is it?"

"It's for the event tonight," he said as she carried it to the bed.

She removed the lid, and her stomach twisted. A deep red satin dress and matching mask were inside along with a pair of red velvet ballet flats. "Nope. I'm staff. I'm not here on vacation." She needed to get to the event to make sure everything went well—food-wise. She wasn't dressing up and participating.

He shook his head. "You're part of the executive staff. We all participate in the theme nights," he said with a sigh as though he wasn't thrilled about that job requirement either. "It's part of our promise to our guests, so technically it's part of your job."

She swallowed hard as she stared at the outfit he expected her to wear. "Overseeing everything will be challenging in this…"

"The food is already done, and we have waitstaff who will be doing all the work. This is where you get to enjoy some of the perks of employment with Kasa de Paradise," he said tightly.

Was that what this was about? Was he trying to sell her on the idea of working here? Working for them?

No way. Domenico would never hire her full-time.

Unless that kiss earlier today had meant something…

The look of lust reflected in his dark eyes earlier that day plagued her. What had started as an argument-fueled embrace had quickly turned into a full-fledged passionate kiss. But that would only make him more eager for her to leave, right?

Definitely not a reason to want her to stay.

It wasn't as though they could act on whatever crazy chemistry existed between them. She was Leo's ex, and she would never do that to him. And Domenico was loyal to his family. He had to be making the same no-repeat vow she was.

It was in the past; they couldn't change it.

Would she if she could?

Dom checked his watch. "Just hurry. Event starts in thirty minutes."

Adriana nodded as he turned to leave. Then she frowned. "Hey, where did this come from, anyway?"

"The boutique shop on site. We had these ordered in so that guests wouldn't have to bring themed event clothing along on vacation."

She eyed the dress. "How did you know what size?"

Dom's gaze swept over her seductively from head to

toe. "It will fit," he said huskily, letting his gaze linger on her a moment longer before stalking toward the door and letting himself out.

She sighed, staring at the gown with its low plunging neckline and high side slit. Hardly suitable for being on the job. What was Dom thinking?

She couldn't wear this.

Unfortunately, she didn't think she had much choice. Nothing she'd packed would fit the dress code requirement for that evening...and it was gorgeous. Exactly her taste and style. How did Dom know her so well?

What was he thinking bringing such a revealing dress? Wanting to see her in it, perhaps?

She shook her head, hoping to reactivate common sense. It didn't matter. She was here to do a job. Nothing more.

She certainly wasn't here to get caught up in a problematic situationship with a paradise billionaire.

"Do you like my dress?"

At that moment, Pricilla Conway could be standing there in a full ski suit or stark naked and Domenico wouldn't know. His gaze was locked on another dress entering the main building. Vibrant red with gold trim that dipped in a sharp low V at the bodice, made of satiny, almost transparent fabric that clung to a sexy pair of hips.

He was finally grateful he was wearing this stupid mask. Now if the resort's CCTV cameras caught him in the act, no one would immediately identify him as the one who tried to rip it off her.

"Excuse me for a second, Mrs. Conway," he said, still not looking at her and heading toward Adriana.

Behind the red-and-gold mask, Adriana's emerald eyes were blazing fire when her gaze met his.

She looked like one burning flame from head to toe. One he was safest not to touch. Yet the temptation to run his hand along the thin, silky fabric—down her sides, over her tiny waist—to caress the shapely curves of her hips was so strong he shoved his hands deep into his pants pockets.

He shook his head. *Focus.* "Things are running late. Food should have been out ten minutes ago."

"I just stopped by the kitchen." She nodded across the room. "There are the servers now."

Their waitstaff, dressed in black tuxedos and simple black masks, were rolling out the hot plates of appetizers and finger foods she'd prepared earlier that day.

"Good," he said.

Adriana too sighed in relief, and her chest rose and fell, causing his eyes to immediately drop to her breasts. Earlier that day he'd vowed she wouldn't be a distraction. He'd given himself a firm talking-to, and he'd had no intentions of allowing himself to be caught off guard by another impulsive moment of weakness with her. And yet when he'd seen this dress in the boutique window, he'd known it was made for her. He'd been in an almost trancelike state when he'd bought it and delivered it to her room. And now he was staring at those breasts and contemplating kissing her in front of the room full of people.

"Your friend is giving me the evil eye," Adriana said with a nod behind him, snapping his attention back to her face.

He didn't have to turn around to know who she was talking about. "That would be Mrs. Pricilla Conway. She's a little territorial." And the ultimate antidote to the impeding, inconvenient arousal forming in his pants. Maybe having Pricilla around this week was a good thing after all.

"And terrifying," Adriana whispered, moving to stand to his side, out of Pricilla's daggers.

Domenico couldn't suppress a laugh at the all too accurate description. "Yes, she is. I wouldn't turn my back on her for very long."

"Thanks for the warning."

Their gazes met and held beneath their masks. The look in her eyes was puzzling and he longed for the ability to read her mind. What was she thinking? Had she thought about their kiss that day as much as he had? Would she address it? Should he? He was technically her boss, so he should say something.

"Adriana..."

But what exactly?

That what had happened in the kitchen had been a reckless, impulsive act that couldn't happen again and meant absolutely nothing? Not exactly the truth. That he was sorry that he'd taken advantage? Again, not entirely true. She'd been just as into that kiss as he'd been. Arrogance would hazard to say even more so. Again—a lie. He was really into it.

"Adriana," he started again.

She stared at him expectantly.

Those emerald eyes behind that mask were intoxicating. Like, wipe all coherent thoughts from his brain intoxicating.

All he could think about was how much he'd like to take a pair of scissors to that fabric. An image of the satin falling away from her body made him shift uncomfortably, arousal reinitiated.

"I should go check to see if Linda has arrived yet. Don't forget you're here to do a job as well," he told Adriana stiffly before stalking away.

He needed to pull it together. Yes, she was gorgeous. Yes, he was attracted to her. But she was off-limits.

Yeah, that forbidden fruit thing only made the whole thing hotter.

"Hey..." a voice purred to this left as he made his way across the room.

He suppressed a sigh. If the sight of his brother and Adriana talking and laughing didn't kill him, Pricilla was sure to be the death of him. "Hi, Mrs. Conway. You look stunning," he said, taking her extended hand and allowing her to turn slowly, displaying everything she'd put on display that evening in a black, too-tight leather dress. The silver zipper that ran along the front promised easy access, and the black leather mask she wore looked more appropriate for a BDSM session. Domenico scanned the ballroom. "Where is Mr. Conway?"

Her seductive grin faded. "He found his true love already," she said, nodding toward the older man chatting up one of the servers as he sampled the hors d'oeuvres.

"Well, I apologize to have to rush off again, but I need to find the resort reviewer..." He scanned the room. These stupid costumes made it hard to identify her.

"Ms. Frank? She's lovely."

Pricilla's words made him pause. "You've met her?"

She nodded, linking her arm through his and picking an imaginary piece of lint from his suit jacket, where her hand lingered on his chest. "Yes. She was poolside for a little while just before dinner."

He hated using Mrs. Conway as a potential ally, but

he was dying to know. "Did she say how she was enjoying her stay so far?"

Pricilla leaned closer and whispered, "I think you need to be more concerned about how the guests are enjoying their stay… After all, happy guests make for a great review, right?" The sultry smile that curled on her lips didn't reach her eyes. Instead, there was a hint of—a threat?

Domenico swallowed hard. Happy guests he could do. Pimping himself out to this woman was where he drew the line. Not at his resort. Review on the line or not, he refused to be someone's boy toy. "Your husband looks very happy enjoying the food. Perhaps you should join him." He removed her hand from his arm and walked away, feeling her burning gaze on the back of his neck.

Of course the woman with the biggest mouth on the island had to be interested in him. This was not good.

If Pricilla didn't get what she wanted, no one would.

CHAPTER SIX

SWEAT POOLED ON Adriana's lower back beneath the satin fabric as she watched Linda Frank survey the hors d'oeuvres circling the room on the trays later that evening. The event had started to wind down. Maybe all of the full-flavored, decadent options hadn't been the right decision. From her perch near the buffet table, she watched as the reviewer, dressed in a teal-green sequined dress and matching mask, reached for a glass of champagne from a serving tray instead.

Why wasn't she eating anything? She'd passed on the stuffed mushrooms, the mini-quiches... She looked to be contemplating the galani, and Adriana held her breath.

Nope. Linda shook her head and sipped the champagne.

Fantastic. The woman barely ate. Or were the choices not up to her standards?

Adriana bit her lower lip as she watched Linda drain the contents of the glass and check her watch. A moment later, she was waving goodbye to several of the staff.

She was leaving? She hadn't tasted anything.

"She ordered a full sampling plate to go," a voice whispered near her ear. She jumped. Then goose bumps surfaced all over her skin.

Her heart raced and she barely comprehended the

words as she turned to look at Domenico just as he removed his mask.

"What?" she asked, reaching behind her to do the same.

"The servers told me that she ordered a sampling plate of all of the hors d'oeuvres and desserts to be packaged and brought to her room. Something about a fasting diet—she doesn't eat after seven p.m."

Adriana released a sigh of relief but then frowned. "Well, she can't be eating my dinners as breakfast. Dinner service will start at six this week. Guests will have to adjust their schedules accordingly."

She expected pushback or at least an argument, but surprisingly, Domenico nodded. "Already told the activity staff to make the adjustment and send out the revised schedule first thing in the morning. Dinner will still run until ten but start an hour earlier."

She struggled to hide her surprise at his cooperation as she struggled with the tie of the mask. What the…? It seemed to be knotted…

Domenico stepped forward and nodded toward it. "Having trouble?"

She nodded.

He moved closer and reached for her hands, lowering them out of the way. Then he leaned closer, peering over the top of her head and reaching for the mask ties. Her face was inches from his chest, and the scent of his expensive cologne filled her senses.

He smelled good. How? In this heat, he smelled fresh and…like a man who could tear her apart. Like a man she'd readily allow to tear her apart.

Her heart raced. She felt his fingers touch the back of her head as he pulled at the knot in the mask. "It's tangled in your hair. Stay still," he said.

Her knees nearly gave out at the simple command.

Stay still. Yes, sir. Any other positions he'd like her in? What was in that cologne?

Domenico released her hair and moved away from her. "You're free."

"Thank you," she said, her gaze locked with his.

Domenico checked his watch. "I have an early lesson tomorrow…so guess I should call it a night." He hesitated, glancing at Adriana. "I mean, unless you want to…grab a drink?" His gaze searched hers, and she didn't know what answers he was looking for. His close proximity and the tantalizing scent of him moments before had created a whirlwind of turmoil through her. She wanted to get away from him and these unwanted, unexpected emotions…but at the same time, she would rather have a drink with him.

"Never mind. You should probably get some sleep," Domenico said abruptly in her long silence. "Breakfast prep starts at five a.m.," he said, the familiar coolness and note of authority reminding her he was technically her boss this week.

Her expression hardened. So that's what his expression was about—he was waiting for her to do the responsible thing and call it a night? Testing her work ethic?

"You're right—I have an early start tomorrow. Tonight was a good beginning, but we want to make sure we keep impressing Ms. Frank." She needed it just as much as they did.

Domenico nodded, and Adriana hesitated a fraction of a second before leaving the main building and descending the stairs. She glanced behind her and waited. Several guests exited, and she smiled at them as they passed. "Night," she said.

She waited another minute. No sign of Domenico.

Of course not. What was wrong with her?

She headed toward the trail to her guest room. Once she rounded the first bend in the trail, she removed her flats and continued barefoot toward her suite.

The sound of the waves on the beach and the palm trees swaying in the breeze truly made this a paradise. It was easy to forget that they were such a short distance from the mainland, a short boat ride back to all the troubles and worries that awaited her there. She couldn't fault Leo for his laid-back, carefree demeanor. This island life had a way of making her forget that she was there to work.

At one time, all of this had been offered to her.

A lizard scurried past her on the trail, and she laughed as she sidestepped him. "You almost got crushed, little guy," she said as he scurried into the brush.

"Nah, they're pretty fast."

Domenico's voice drifting from the shadows nearby made her heart race. She could barely see him—just his silhouette illuminated by the outdoor trail lights. What was he doing there? And why was she so happy that he was?

"How did you get here so fast?" she asked as she approached him.

"Island cruiser," he said, gesturing to a small vehicle parked on the sand. It looked like a go-cart with off-roading tires.

"I thought you were heading off to bed." Her heart pounded steadily in her chest.

"I had second thoughts about that drink and thought maybe you would too," he said, walking toward her. He was still in his tuxedo, but the tie hung loose around his neck, and the shirt was unbuttoned down his chest. "Join me for one on the beach?" he asked, holding up a bottle of expensive champagne and two plastic champagne glasses.

She swallowed hard. They couldn't be sneaking around the island at night alone for secret champagne rendezvous. Not that this was a rendezvous.

"Do you want to change first...or...?" Domenico asked. His gaze took in her body in the gown, and the lust-filled expression was undeniable.

Staying in the dress it was.

She shook her head. "It's surprisingly comfortable."

Domenico laughed as he nodded toward the path down to the water.

Adriana followed him to the beach, then scanned the sand beneath them. This part of the beach wasn't swimmable, so there were no beach chairs and umbrellas set up. Maybe she should have gone inside for a blanket...

"Hang on a sec," Domenico said, removing his jacket and placing it on the sand.

"Thank you," she said, awkwardness in the air around them. They didn't do nice or gentlemanly. They argued, they teased, they annoyed... Nice was awkward.

Still, she sat on the jacket and tucked her legs to the side as he sat on the sand next to her.

He looked unfazed. Somehow Domenico Kasa—billionaire, former tennis pro playboy—made it seem like sitting on sand in a tuxedo was an everyday occurrence. The tuxedo company should hire him for an ad campaign. The Kasa brothers really did embody the spirit of the island. Part of their success came from the way they integrated into the lifestyle so well. Guests truly felt as though they were staying with family when they visited the resort.

Domenico popped the cork of the champagne with a loud explosion, followed by a stream of liquid spilling down the side of the bottle. He poured a glass for her and handed it to her before filling a glass for himself.

"To a successful first day," he said, clinking his glass to hers.

"One day down, six to go," she said before sipping the champagne. The bubbles danced on her tongue and warmed her. It was the first thing she'd consumed all day besides the taste-testing she'd done in the kitchen during prep. She hadn't even thought about eating an actual meal, but now she kind of wished Domenico had packed a snack for their late-night beach picnic.

"Hungry?" he asked as though reading her mind.

She laughed. "Is it obvious?"

"I can hear your stomach growling," he said, reaching into his pocket.

"Tell me you stuffed galani into your pockets."

Domenico grinned as he shook his head. "I did get the servers to put some away for me, though." He retrieved his cell phone instead and opened an app.

"What are you doing?" she asked, leaning closer to see the Kasa de Paradise guest services app.

"Ordering room service from the twenty-four-hour snack shack," he said, hitting a few items on the list.

Her eyes widened. "To the beach?"

"Yes."

Kasa de Paradise really was a no-wish-went-unserved oasis.

She stared out at the dark ocean waves as he finished placing the order, then tucked his phone back in his pocket.

Silence lingered in the air around them. But for the first time, it wasn't the awkward, strained, tense silence that often enveloped them. She cast a sideways glance at him. He looked so handsome in the light of the moon breaking through a thin cloud layer overhead and the resort lights in the distance behind them.

"So...why the change of heart on the drink?" she asked.

"No change of heart. I just wanted you to say yes, and when you hesitated, I took offence."

His honesty surprised her. "But yet somehow here we are."

"Because ultimately I go after what I want."

Holy hell. He was hot.

All evening at the masquerade, she'd felt his gaze on her, and she'd had similar trouble focusing on overseeing the food service. The way he'd moved about the room, talking to guests, surveying and observing everything. Anticipated guest needs before they did. His presence strongly felt in the room.

"You did good today," he said, changing the subject as he turned to look at her.

"You're surprised?"

"No. Just annoyed to be proven wrong." That sexy grin of his was back. Only she'd just recently—as in the last twelve hours recently—come to see it as sexy. Before, it was irritating and condescending. Odd how one ill-timed kiss could change things.

Or had it started with that old photo bringing back memories of years of friendship followed by a hurtful drifting apart?

"So you're admitting that you were wrong about me?" She eyed him over the rim of the champagne glass as she took another sip.

"About your abilities as a chef... The rest I'm not sure of."

He meant her character, her intentions...and she

wished she could be offended, hand him back his champagne and leave him on the beach alone, but she did have ulterior motives for being there that week and she was gambling with his resort, so she remained silent.

"I'm sure you have some preconceived notions about me too."

She nodded. "I'm not sure how wrong mine are, though."

"Wow. Okay."

"Are you actually able to deny that you are arrogant, moody, self-centered and…"

He held up a hand. "One at a time."

She grinned, feeling a warmth seep across her chest. Must be the champagne. "Okay. Arrogant."

He nodded and took a breath before answering. "It's confidence. Arrogance is talk without action. I put into action every plan I set for myself, and I don't rest until the outcome is the one I expect."

Okay…she could see that rationale. Sort of. He wasn't wrong. He had achieved every goal he'd set for himself. To outside appearances, at least.

"Moody," she said. He couldn't deny that one.

"I prefer brooding—like those men in the Jane Austen era."

She laughed. "That's the vibe you're going for?"

He nodded. "Eighteenth century English nobleman vibes—yeah—the chicks dig it."

"Mr. Darcy you are not, and I'm going to pretend you did not just say *chicks*," she told him, but she couldn't help but smile. This felt…nice. An odd sense of nostalgia was somehow wrapping itself around her—a strange sense of familiarity as though a part of her had never forgotten this connection they'd shared in childhood.

"What else did you call me?"

"Um…" What was the third thing? She thought for a moment. "Self-centered!"

This time he didn't need time to think. "I wouldn't say self-centered. I'd say self-*focused*. I'm consistently striving to be a better version of myself than I was the day before, and I don't allow people to see the work behind that. Therefore they only see the end product, not the struggle, indecision or second-guessing I put myself through. The sacrifices. What I'm giving up—the relationships—I'm giving up to pursue that higher level of fulfillment and awareness."

"Is that why you're a playboy? Too self-*focused* to give attention to a woman."

"Too self-focused to give the *deserved* attention to the *right* woman, yes."

She could hardly criticize that. Wasn't she the same? Hadn't she said countless times that it would take the right man to make her switch her laser focus on building her family business back to what it once was? She was putting herself and her future ahead of all else. "Fair enough."

"And who says I'm a playboy?" he asked with a puzzled look.

Was he serious? "Um…every tabloid…ever."

He scoffed. "I don't read that shit."

Unfortunately, she had! "Maybe not, but the media had a field day with your dating life."

Domenico looked annoyed. "My perceived dating life."

"Oh, those photos looked legit." Did she sound jealous? She hoped not, but truth was, she had been back then. Very much so.

"Those were PR relationships."

She frowned as she looked at him. "What now?"

He sighed. "Publicity driven to help secure attention from the media."

Her eyes widened, and her mouth dropped. "So they weren't real?"

"Nah," Domenico said. "Are you kidding? I was too busy training to actually have a relationship."

Her mind was blown.

All this time thinking he'd been off dating these beautiful athletes with similar drives and passions to his...

This information could have been useful before now.

They sipped their champagne and sat silently together. Then Domenico glanced at her. "What about you? Anyone special in your life?"

Adriana shook her head slowly. "I've dated a few men since Leo." *A few* might be an exaggeration. It had been two. Barely memorable. "But nothing even close to serious. There was always just something missing. A spark."

Domenico laughed and shook his head.

"What's so funny?"

"Just that I didn't believe in all that spark stuff..." He turned to face her and stared deep into her eyes. "Until you nearly electrocuted me with that kiss."

Their gazes locked, and the heat and passion between them were undeniable. His dark eyes reflected the light coming from the moon as they burned into hers. She glanced at his full lips, and the temptation to lean in and get another taste was overwhelming...but they were getting along and keeping their hands and lips to themselves.

Friends. Colleagues. This was good.

At least, that's what she was telling herself.

Slightly flustered, she looked away. "Anyway, the restaurant takes up most of my time."

"How's it doing?" he asked as he reached for the bottle of champagne and topped up her glass.

Adriana stared into her champagne flute. "Not great. There are always so many new places opening up."

"Bellarini's is part of the culture, the landscape, the tradition."

"Tell that to the tourists."

He nodded. "But surely locals are still loyal."

She sighed. "They are, but most are aging, and since the pandemic, a lot of people order in still—as though they'd forgotten that the best part of eating out was that sense of community, the late nights lingering and talking and drinking… Takeout orders result in half the bill."

"That would have an impact."

She was pensive for a moment. Then, "My brother wants to change the menu. He thinks it's old-fashioned and dated, and he's suggesting including healthier options. Low-carb pasta, almond flour garlic cheese toast."

Domenico shivered. "Disgusting."

"Exactly. Thank you."

Adriana and Domenico shared another look.

This connection, the fact that he got it, got her, surprised her.

Their gazes on one another lingered a dangerously long time. He seemed to be drinking her in, looking straight into her soul. Seeing something…what? Whatever it was, he seemed lost in it, intoxicated by it.

She couldn't remember the last time a man had looked at her like this.

They could be friends and colleagues tomorrow. What would one more kiss hurt? They'd already crossed the line anyway.

Domenico seemed to be thinking the same thing as he moved toward her on the sand. She slid her own body closer, her gaze never breaking contact with his.

His eyes left hers briefly to glance at her lips, and her tongue slid along her bottom one. His expression was full of fiery desire when his eyes met hers again. Her entire body tingled with a longing, an anticipation, a desire to crawl into his arms and kiss him until the sun came up the next morning.

He reached for her and…

Headlights illuminated the beach, headed toward them. The light grew brighter quickly.

Domenico pulled away and jumped to his feet. "That would be our food."

An island cruiser approached with a crew member behind the wheel.

Still slightly dazed, Adriana nodded, fighting the disappointment she felt at the interruption. "The service here is amazing." Too amazing. If only the guy had shown up a bit later…a lot later. Suddenly she wasn't hungry anymore. At least not for food.

Domenico winked at her as he walked backward toward the cruiser. "You have no idea."

Adriana felt a rush of heat flow through her. She didn't doubt his words one little bit. Domenico might not give his time to just any woman, but she suspected when he did give his time and attention to someone, he did it with the same intensity and drive he displayed in the rest of his life.

And suddenly—out of absolutely nowhere—she was desperate to be that one woman.

The food was gone. The champagne was finished. Now what?

Obviously the evening was coming to an end. But he didn't want it to.

Domenico threw their garbage into the trash container

on the beach as Adriana dusted the sand off his jacket. She approached and handed it back to him. "Thank you."

"You're welcome."

His gaze locked with hers, and he stared into the depths of her eyes, the moon lighting them up in an intoxicating way. They'd been silent as they'd eaten, but it had been a comfortable, easy silence, not the awkward, tension-filled one they usually endured around one another.

"Guess I should..." she began.

"Want to go for a walk before we call it a night?"

They spoke at the same time, and Domenico nodded. "You're right, it's getting late."

Adriana shook her head. "It's not that late."

It was, in fact—just after midnight, and she would have to be back in the kitchen early again the next morning. But he couldn't seem to let guilt about keeping her out late or the reminder of how important it was for her to do her job right stop him from extending a hand toward her.

Adriana looked at it with a slight expression of surprise, but then slid her hand into his.

Domenico held it tight and kept it in his as they walked along the beach. He glanced toward her, and his breath caught in his chest at the sight of her dark hair blowing in the night breeze. She looked peacefully out at the white caps crashing along the sand in the distance. "You look stunning tonight, by the way."

Adriana's smile was somewhat shy, and she looked caught off guard by the compliment.

"I mean in a non-sexual-harassment kind of way."

She laughed. "Don't worry. I won't report you to HR." She smiled at him, and he swallowed the lump in his throat at the sight.

She was even more beautiful in the moonlight, relaxed and content—with him. That was the most incredible part.

She cleared her throat. "Hey, uh… Leo sent me an old photo today…"

She'd received it too? That meant she'd also probably noticed that lovesick expression he'd had on his face. How did he play this? Admit that he'd seen it too and try to play off the look as nothing…or pretend he had no idea what photo she was talking about?

"Oh yeah…" He wanted to see what she had to say about it first.

"Yeah, it was of the five of us at the beach."

"Those were great times," he said casually.

She turned to look at him. "You remember those summers?"

Only every other memory…since he'd seen that photo again. The sound of her laughter as she'd jumped off the rocks on the cliff into the water below. The way her dark hair always lightened with auburn streaks once the summer sun had gotten to it. The smell of her coconut tanning lotion on her dark skin at the end of the day when she'd hold his waist sitting on the back of his bike as he'd drive them home from the lake. "I mean, vaguely." What was wrong with him?

Her look of mild disappointment had him stopping to turn toward her.

"I remember them very well," he said. "And Leo sent me the photo too."

Adriana nodded. Their gazes met and held for a long breath before they continued walking along the sand.

"Do you visit your mom often?" she asked.

"The last Sunday of every month. We meet for breakfast when I head to the mainland for new tennis inventory."

"How is she? Without your dad?"

"She misses him a lot, obviously, but she's doing okay. She has a new wine and book club, and she's teaching a seniors yoga class—staying busy." He paused. "You should stop by to see her. I know she'd love that."

Adriana nodded. "After the breakup, I wasn't sure…"

"She always said you were the daughter she'd hoped Mario would be," he said with a grin.

Adriana turned and swatted at him. "She never said that!"

He laughed. "No, but she always loved you like her own." His mother had always said she was perfectly content to have three boys, but he knew secretly she'd loved having Adriana around. His mother had been hoping Adriana and Leo would get married and grace her with grandbabies.

The thought made Domenico's stomach flip. "Hey, uh…we should probably get you to bed."

She raised an eyebrow as she glanced at him.

"That wasn't an invitation of any sort. No need to alert HR." Not that he wouldn't mind tucking her into bed that night…

She nodded. Hand in hand, they walked along a trail back towards her suite with Domenico leading the way.

Moments later, Domenico and Adriana lingered outside. Adriana toyed with the room key. "I had fun tonight." She laughed. "I mean, not the masquerade party, but after—with you."

"Me too," he said sincerely.

Adriana hesitated, glancing at the key in her hand. "Well…good night."

"'Night."

Adriana sighed as she turned to go inside.

Say something.

It had been a special night. He'd had an amazing time with her. Holding her hand, walking, talking—she'd enjoyed it all too. He didn't want it to be the end. He didn't want her to go to bed that night without plans to spend time together again.

Despite common sense, he wanted to spend time with her this week on the island.

Did she want that too?

"Hey…" he said, a thought suddenly plaguing him.

"Yeah?" She turned back quickly as though relieved there was more than just a good-night.

"Did you really think I was off jet-setting the world with different female athletes?"

Adriana sighed and nodded. "Your PR person did their job well." She paused, and then her gaze met his. "Well enough that I didn't see any reason not to date your brother."

The realization hit him straight in the chest. Adriana had believed he was dating other people—despite his heartfelt letters and the fact that he'd only ever thought about her when he was away. A deep regret filled him that he'd never even thought about the effect his public persona would have on her.

She turned back toward the building in his moment of silent contemplation. "'Night, Dom."

"Hey…" He couldn't end the night like this, but he wasn't sure what exactly to say.

She turned back…again. "Yeah?"

"I have an opening for an early tennis lesson tomorrow morning…if you're interested." Not exactly smooth, but it was all he could think of in the moment that didn't sound completely desperate. He was offering her a tennis lesson. Made sense, and it was at least a way to gauge if she wanted to spend time with him again.

Adriana sent him a teasing grin. "You sure Mrs. Conway won't be jealous?"

If she caught them, she absolutely would. But it was probably the last reason why it wasn't a good idea. He was choosing not to entertain the other reasons.

"Is that a yes?"

Adriana shrugged casually, but he could tell she was just as happy to have an excuse to spend time with him as he was with her, which had his heart pounding and a warmth flowing through him at the anticipation of it that he hadn't experienced around a woman in a very long time. "Why not?" she said. "I mean, how often does one get an opportunity to be taught by a tennis pro, right?"

"Great! See you at tennis court B at four thirty," Domenico said as he headed toward the island cruiser.

"Four thirty a.m.? What? No, that's like three hours from now," Adriana said.

Domenico grinned as he jumped onto the cruiser. "Better get some sleep, then." He winked and waved as he started the cruiser.

It kicked up a cloud of sand as he tore away from the building, feeling exhilarated. He wouldn't be getting any sleep that evening.

CHAPTER SEVEN

A GENTLE BREEZE blew through the open patio door as the early morning sun rose over the island in the distance. Wide awake, Adriana sat in her bed, coffee cup in one hand, her cell phone in the other—the contact list open to Domenico's name.

She should cancel.

She kept staring at the message thread where the last text from him had been Yep. Confirming his attendance to a surprise birthday dinner for Leo four years ago. She expected to see typing dots appear any second when he too came to the realization that this was not a good idea.

The night before had been magical.

Surreal.

But in the light of day, they couldn't keep spending time together like that. Holding hands? What had they been thinking? Those long, intense, gazes—holy hell! They were asking for trouble.

How had they even gotten to this point?

She mentally recapped the last forty-eight hours.

Arriving on the pier to meet grumpy Dom.

Bickering in the kitchen.

Mild irritation—turned to attraction with the late-night snack incident—aka abs.

Full-on heated exchange in the kitchen that led to the most passionate kiss of her life.

Then, a successful event followed by the most incredible evening with the mind-blowing realization that all those years thinking he was living this playboy lifestyle had been a falsified narrative for promotion?

She wasn't even sure what to do with that information as she stared at the message thread. Domenico may not have been the playboy the media had made him out to be—made her believe him to be—but he'd still developed a massive ego and acted as though she didn't exist for all those years. That had hurt too...

She had to cancel.

This early-morning tennis lesson had nothing to do with tennis, and they both knew it. He'd panicked, wanting to spend more time with her but not knowing how to ask, and she'd agreed for the same reason.

But it had to have been just the island's beauty, the salty air and glow of the moonlight combined with the champagne, that had made them both get swept away in the moment.

That morning, he too had to be realizing this wasn't a good idea.

Typing dots!

Adriana sat straighter abruptly, nearly spilling her coffee.

She waited…

No message. No more typing dots.

Seriously Dom?

What had he been about to say?

She bit her lip. Should she text him?

No, then he'd know she'd been sitting there staring at his name on her phone.

She sighed and waited, but when no more typing dots appeared and the time on her phone revealed four fifteen, she swung her legs over the side of the bed and got up.

She went to the dresser where housekeeping had unpacked her clothing for her with turndown service the night before and opened a drawer. She didn't really have tennis appropriate gear. Just shorts and sports bras for working out, if she had the time.

She reached in and selected a cute pale pink set—tight shorts, bra top and matching half sweater that she'd bought for a yoga class where the instructor had been hot, but he'd only been teaching as a fill-in so he'd never gotten to see her in it.

She got dressed and stared at her reflection in the mirror. She looked sporty sexy. Was that the vibe she wanted to go with?

OMG Adriana! It's just a workout outfit! Quit overthinking it! What else was she supposed to wear working out?

Okay, she could have gone with a frumpy T-shirt...

She was reading way too much into the clothing choice.

Domenico saw women dressed in skimpy tennis outfits all the time. Her outfit probably wouldn't even register on his radar.

Dressed in his tennis gear, Domenico waited on tennis court B for Adriana. He checked his watch and ran a hand through his hair. "What am I doing?" he muttered. This was not a good idea. Why had he suggested it the night before? The chemistry between them had been off the charts, and she'd practically been begging for a goodnight kiss—the lingering outside the room door, the fidgeting with the keys, the teasing. Adriana didn't linger, fidget or tease! At least not with him!

This was bad. Very, very bad.

He couldn't be entertaining these feelings with his brother's ex-girlfriend.

Though last night's revelation that she'd agreed to date Leo because she thought he'd been seeing other people had him spiraling. He couldn't believe all this time, he'd been hurt by a betrayal that he'd essentially caused.

Still, he should cancel this lesson before things got complicated.

He'd tried. He'd opened his phone to their message thread. Typed...deleted. Typed and deleted.

But the truth was, he wanted to see her again this morning. And whether it was nostalgia from that old photo or the heat from the kiss in the kitchen or the romantic island vibes the night before as they'd walked hand in hand along the sand in the moonlight, all he knew was that he'd wanted to see her again.

They'd once been friends, and maybe a part of him just wanted that back—the friendship.

Adriana rounded the corner on the trail headed toward the court, and Domenico saw her approach.

It was so much more than wanting his buddy back.

His gaze swept over her—took in the tight pink curve-hugging yoga shorts, the bra top that barely contained her amazing breasts and the light sweater that hung casually off one shoulder. One beautiful, perfect shoulder with tiny little freckles that he just wanted to connect with his tongue.

So very badly.

"Sorry I'm late," Adriana said, stopping in front of him.

"I'm actually surprised you showed up at all." Honest caution. Obviously, his nervous system believed it was the best way to approach this situation they found themselves in.

Adriana nodded and released a breath as though she had been spiraling with this all morning. "Me too." She hesitated. "Do you think this is a good idea?"

"Teaching you to play tennis? If I remember correctly, you suck at it, so it can't hurt." Jokes. His nerves had moved on to jokes.

Adriana shot him a look. "You know what I mean. What are we doing, Dom?"

How did he know?

Domenico sighed. "Leo told me to play nice, so that's what I'm doing." *Okay, we're lying now.*

"And that's it?"

Was she relieved? Disappointed? Not buying his BS?

He studied her, but her expression was neutral—giving absolutely nothing away. She had to know that wasn't it. The kiss should have told her it was far more than that. The hand-holding on the beach and the long, intense gazes filled with so many unspoken words…hell, that old photo…

Domenico nodded. "That's it." Panic.

"Okay…" Adriana removed the tiny half-sweater thing and placed her hands on her hips as she scanned the courts. "Where do we start?"

By putting that sweater back on. How was he supposed to concentrate on teaching her anything when she was standing there looking like…that? Curves for days, her ample breasts filling out the strappy sports bra, her tight stomach—all on display. The sight of her would throw the best tennis player completely off their game, and he didn't claim to be the best anymore.

With her looking like that, he'd barely be an adequate instructor.

And he wasn't buying that innocent look on her face—not even for a second. She had to know how amazingly hot she looked in that outfit. Those sports store manufacturers shouldn't be allowed to sell sexy workout clothes. They were a major distraction.

But if Adriana knew the effect she was having on him, she was hiding it as she stood there looking at him expectantly. "Well? Let's go, tennis pro."

Right. Teach her how to play tennis.

And try not to get too turned on in the meantime.

Domenico looked away as he took a deep breath. "Okay, let's get you a racket." He approached his gear, selected one for her and extended it.

Adriana took it and of course held it wrong.

Domenico sighed. "Like this," he said. Standing behind her and wrapping his arms around her, he positioned her hands on the racket. "This hand here…this hand here."

His breath was blowing the tendrils of hair that had escaped her ponytail at the nape of her neck, and he could see tiny goose bumps surface on her skin. It was twenty-seven degrees outside already this morning. She certainly wasn't cold.

"Okay, let's try serving the ball," he said, taking a ball out of his pocket. His hands still around her, he tossed the ball up in the air and helped her swing at it. They missed.

"Let's try again," he said, taking another ball from his pocket. He moved in closer to her, his full body connecting to hers. His hands around hers, their grips tight on the racket. He breathed in the sweet scent of her and took in the new view of her cleavage from this vantage point. Could she feel how turned on he was?

The temptation to toss the tennis racket aside, turn her around to face him and kiss her until they were both hot and sweaty for other reasons was overwhelming.

She turned her head to look up at him. "You good?"

Oh, he was great. Just desiring a woman he shouldn't have been.

"Yeah," he said, tossing the ball into the air. They swung, and the racket connected with it. The ball sailed effortlessly over the net to the other, empty side of the court. "Not bad." He slowly released her, despite every inch of him wanting to hold on. "Think you can do that? On your own?" Standing there any longer with his arms around her would only lead to trouble.

A lot of trouble.

She swallowed hard and nodded. "Yeah, I think I got it."

"Great." Twirling his racket in his hand—a long-time nervous energy habit of his—he made his way to the other side of the court, and that's when he noticed…

Pricilla watching them from the balcony of her villa. Even from that distance, he could tell she didn't look happy.

"You know how to play tennis—you taught me," her best friend Isabella said through the cell phone screen later that morning.

Grabbing a set of oven mitts, Adriana opened the oven door and took out a veggie lasagna, then popped a meat one in before answering. "I know, but he offered, and I…"

"Wanted to stroke his ego?"

Wanted to stroke the muscular forearms wrapped around her, mostly. She shook her head as she approached a mixing bowl and poured flour into it. "I'm just trying to keep the peace—for the sake of the review."

"Your plan was to steer clear of him."

"Well, he's making that difficult, observing my every move." And eyeing her like he wanted to eat her for breakfast. The way he'd looked at her in her workout gear this morning had confirmed that hot yoga instructor totally would have asked her out had he seen her in it.

Too bad.

"Isn't that annoying though?"

"It was at first. But I understand he just wants to make sure everything goes well. There's a lot at stake."

Isabella eyed her. "Oh my God. You're falling for him."

Adriana reached for the salt to add to the bowl. "Nope. No. Not even a little. That's ridiculous." She poured the salt in and started to stir.

Isabella raised an eyebrow in amusement. "Then why did you just add sugar instead of salt to that bread?"

Adriana's eyes widened as she glanced at the container. She sighed and shot Isabella a look. "Cause you're distracting me."

"Uh-huh… I'm not the one distracting you." Isabella looked seriously unimpressed.

"What can I say? I don't know why, but all of a sudden, there's…an attraction there." She lowered her voice.

"It's Leo's brother."

"I know!"

"And technically your boss."

"I know! I know." She'd been telling herself the same things over and over. Unfortunately, once she was around Domenico again, common sense went out the window.

"Stay focused. Keep your head in the game," Isabella said.

"I will," she said, dumping the contents of the bowl and starting over.

"It smells delicious in here." Linda entered, sniffing the aroma.

"Gotta go," Adriana told Isabella, disconnecting the FaceTime call and smiling to greet the reviewer. "Good morning, Ms. Frank. How was your breakfast?"

The reviewer was dressed in her usual neutral colors that day with seafoam-green jewelry accents that Adriana recognized as items from the gift shop—a good sign.

"Compliments to the chef. I've never had crispy salt-and-pepper French toast before. I admit I was skeptical, but you made me a believer."

Adriana's smile widened as she nodded. "As kids, my brother hated how maple syrup makes French toast soggy—it's a texture thing. My grandmother came up with the recipe for him. It's definitely a favorite at Bellarini's."

Linda leaned against the counter and nodded. "Your family's restaurant in Naples, right? I remember seeing it from my research of the staff."

The woman was thorough—it didn't surprise her that she knew everything about each of the staff at Kasa de Paradise. In her online search, she'd probably also discovered the previous relationship between Adriana and Leo. There were plenty of photos of the two of them together online with the announcement and grand opening of the resort. Should she address it?

"Yes. I'm only here for the week," she said.

"Ah…" Linda made a note on her clipboard.

Uh-oh, maybe she shouldn't have said that. "But I also helped design this kitchen before the resort opened. Would you like a more complete tour?" she added quickly.

Linda nodded, then said, "Do you happen to have any more of that French toast hidden in here?"

Adriana laughed. "Absolutely." She opened the fridge and retrieved the container of leftover French toast. She opened the lid and handed Linda another slice.

Linda carried it and ate as Adriana toured her around the kitchen.

"When Leo and I first talked about the kitchen design, we were immediately on the same page. We wanted to prioritize functionality and efficiency, featuring professional-grade appliances, ample workspace, and tools to facilitate culinary endeavors, with an emphasis on workflow and ease of movement for multiple cooks."

Linda nodded her approval as she chewed. "I suspect it's a pleasure to cook here, but nothing beats the intimacy of a crammed, busy, chaotic kitchen—like the one I'm sure you have at Bellarini's."

Adriana laughed at the accuracy. "Bellarini's kitchen is a closet compared to this one, and while it has professional appliances, they don't compare to the quality at Kasa de Paradise. But somehow the closeness and chaotic nature seem to add flavor and a sense of home-cooked charm to the meals. As if the food absorbs the love and commitment the kitchen staff have for one another and the pride we put into every dish."

Linda stared at her as she spoke, and Adriana realized she'd taken the focus off this kitchen. "But this kitchen is superb!" she said quickly, gesturing to the appliances. "Professional-grade ovens, a powerful gas range with high BTU burners, and a robust ventilation system to handle intense heat and smoke. Warming drawers to keep food hot and multiple ovens, including convection and steam models." They continued to walk through the area, and Adriana pointed out the other amazing features. "Expansive marble countertops and large islands that provide additional prep space and often serve as a central hub for staff to work together. Multiple deep sinks with high-arc faucets, pot fillers over the range, and large, well-organized pantry storage. Sub-Zero refrigerators and freezers are amazing for their capacity and freshness-preserving features."

Linda nodded and took notes as they continued the tour.

Adriana glanced at the notepad—all positive comments so far. She breathed a sigh of relief as she summed it all up. "The overall design emphasizes workflow and efficiency, with appliances and tools strategically placed for easy access and seamless transitions between tasks."

Linda popped the last of her French toast into her mouth and made a final note. "Thank you for that tour—very thorough." She closed her eyes as she chewed. When she swallowed the bite, she opened them. "But now for the most important question."

Adriana held her breath. *Don't mess this up.*

"You make this French toast at your restaurant, Bellarini's? It's a menu staple?"

Adriana relaxed as she nodded with a proud smile. "Every Sunday for brunch."

Linda licked her fingers. "Then expect me for brunch whenever I'm on this side of the world."

Adriana beamed. "Thank you. We'd love to host you—as my guest."

"You truly are a talented chef—Adriana. My sampling tray was incredible. I assume you learned to cook from your family?"

She nodded. "My father and grandmother taught me. My mother was an amazing chef as well, but she passed away when I was little. My grandmother taught me all the family recipes, and then my father taught me how to make them on a larger scale—a little faster and cost-effectively without losing the quality and taste we've been known for for generations."

Adriana's smile faded at the sound of a throat clearing in the kitchen doorway. She turned to see Domenico standing there—an unreadable expression on his face.

Had he heard her go on about Bellarini's?

He looked amazing—showered and now dressed in khaki shorts and a navy button-down collared shirt, open at the throat.

The temptation to slide her hands inside that open collar...

"Ready for the Jet Ski tour, Ms. Frank?" he said, interrupting Adriana's thoughts.

"Yes!" Linda said excitedly. She turned back to Adriana. "Thank you again. Quite impressive."

Adriana nodded politely, her gaze sliding to Domenico.

His proud and grateful look made her breath catch in her chest.

"Shall we?" he said to Linda, extending an elbow to guide her out of the kitchen.

The reviewer took one look at the exposed forearms below the rolled shirtsleeves and eagerly linked her hand through. "We shall."

Lucky woman.

I need to see you in the office.

That's all the text message said, but Domenico's heart pounded in his ears as he made his way to the office, still dressed in his wetsuit from the Jet Ski tour with Linda Frank—one that would have been a lot of fun had he not been stressing out over Leo's text message the whole time.

Did he know about his and Adriana's late-night rendezvous? Or the early-morning tennis lesson? Had Pricilla said something? Complained about his rudeness the night before or embellished what she'd witnessed between him and Adriana on the tennis court that morning?

Sweat gathered on his lower back under the unforgiving wetsuit material as he entered the office.

Leo finished a call and hung up the phone, then glanced up at him. His expression was unreadable. Then he laughed. "You could have changed first."

"Thought it might be urgent," he said awkwardly, but relaxing slightly. If his brother was upset, he wouldn't be laughing at Domenico's appearance.

"You're dripping all over the floor," Leo said, smile gone, a slight annoyance taking its place.

Domenico sighed. "What did you want?"

"I have to head over to the mainland tonight. There's a problem with the new linens we ordered for the guest villas. They got the sizing wrong, and…"

Leo kept talking, but all Domenico heard was that his brother would be off the island that evening.

Domenico shoved his hands in his pockets and nodded, desperately trying to hide how excited he was at the news. Guilty too, but mostly excited. There was no point denying he wanted to spend more time alone with Adriana, exploring the connection from last night and this morning. And hearing her talk about the kitchen at Bellarini's and hearing her passion for her career and her family restaurant this morning had made him melt a little. Sure, she'd been supposed to talking up the state-of-the-art kitchen at Kasa de Paradise, but he couldn't fault her pride in her family's business and the generations of chefs that had taught her everything she knew. It was endearing.

So, why was he struggling to quiet the nagging thought in the back of his mind that she might still have an ulterior motive for being here. Probably because she did—securing a good review of the food on Kasa Island would help her family restaurant—but was that really so wrong? Win-win... Unless she jeopardized what guests expected from their resort in favor of making food that would get Linda Frank to write highly of her culinary skills. Linda's review was important, but the experience of guests was still first and foremost.

"No problem. I can hold down the fort," he said casually.

Leo eyed him suspiciously. "What's up with you?"

"Nothing." Too quick. Too high-pitched.

Calm down, Dom. She might not even want to see you tonight.

Though the expression on her face in the kitchen earlier that day said otherwise.

Leo continued to study him intently. Sweat collected on Domenico's forehead and dripped into his eyes under his brother's scrutiny. The Kasa brothers were close. Too close. And Domenico was the one with the worst poker face. He could never successfully hide anything from them. As kids, when they got in trouble, he always got them grounded with his inability to lie or pull a fast one on their parents.

"You seem different," Leo said.

"I'm not different."

Leo nodded emphatically. "You totally are. You're

less…on edge. Like, if I didn't know better, I'd think you'd gotten laid for a change."

He wished. His pulse raced, and his mouth went dry. He may not have gotten laid the night before, but Leo's spidey senses weren't completely off the mark. He had to be careful. Maybe he should tell him…but that was a discussion he had to have with Adriana first. Confessing to Leo had to be a joint decision. One they were both on board for and ready for the consequences of. "I assure you I'm still as focused as ever."

Leo laughed, and Domenico's shoulders relaxed.

Interrogation over.

"Okay, well, I'm going to go get changed." He turned and headed toward the door.

"Hey." His brother's voice made him pause. "Late-night craving last night?" Leo asked behind him.

Domenico swung around to see his brother reviewing an invoice on the desk.

New panic gripped his chest. "What do you mean?" he asked slowly.

"Last night. There was a midnight food delivery on the resort app with your signature."

Right. His brothers had access to the app just as well as he did. Wow, he really wasn't good at sneaking around. Which was why he shouldn't be. And if he and Adriana were going to keep…hanging out, they'd need to be honest. Soon. Just not right this second.

"Oh, yeah… Didn't eat much at the event. Nervous stomach."

"Looks like a lot of food for one person." Leo eyed him. "Do I need to remind you of the policy you created? No dating guests?"

Domenico shook his head so fast, his neck cramped. "That's not happening. I was just hungry. Really hungry."

Leo shot him a chastising look. "Adriana's not going to poison you with her food. At least, I don't think so."

Domenico cleared his throat. "About Adriana…"

Leo glanced up at him expectantly.

I like her. I'm insanely attracted to her.

Nope. He couldn't out them without her permission.

"She's turning out to be a great help."

Leo nodded as he stood and gathered his things. "Speaking of…" Leo picked up a stack of résumés and handed them to Domenico as he exited the office. "Find us a new head chef. Adriana's made it clear she's a limited-time offer."

And one that shouldn't be on offer to him.

CHAPTER EIGHT

A TENNIS BALL sailed over the net and was returned with impressive speed and precision, catching Domenico so off guard, he almost missed returning the shot.

What the?

That afternoon, Pricilla was unusually focused for her lesson and not her usual flirty self.

Domenico struggled for breath as he tried to keep up with her unexpected pace. He returned the ball a little harder and faster, and she expertly returned it. He hurried to the opposite side of the court, but he wasn't quick enough.

Match point for Pricilla.

Since when? He slaughtered her most days. He nodded, impressed, as he approached the net. "Wow. You've gotten a lot better," he said knowingly. He could recognize when he'd been played.

"I might not have been completely honest about my skill level," Pricilla said coyly. That day she was dressed more the part with a tennis outfit that covered most of her assets but was still flattering.

Trying a new tactic to get his attention, perhaps?

"Hustling me?" he teased, keeping the mood light. She'd been cool and distant when they'd arrived and clearly still annoyed from the night before's brush-off at the masquerade event, but he hoped this meant she'd gotten the hint. Maybe she'd stop coming on to him.

Instead, Pricilla leaned over the net, giving him ample view of her cleavage. "I think we both know why I requested these lessons," she said in a tone only describable as a fierce feline in heat.

Domenico shifted uncomfortably. So much for retreating. She looked even more determined and on her game now. He almost preferred the flirty, flighty Pricilla. He'd welcome that version back over this driven-to-get-what-she-wanted alpha female standing across from him.

How did he let this woman down gently? Refuse her advances *again* without upsetting her? A high-class guest with friends all over Europe was not the enemy he wanted to have or one the resort could afford. A one-star Yelp review from Pricilla Conway would outweigh a million five-stars. Not to mention a disgruntled guest while Linda was still here was not ideal.

He cleared his throat. "Mrs. Conway…you are an amazing woman, but we have a policy not to get…" he paused and lowered his voice as another couple arrived on the courts and waved at them "…intimately involved with our guests."

Couldn't argue with corporate policy, right?

Pricilla moved closer, grabbed the front of his sweaty shirt, pulled him in and whispered in his ear, "I won't tell."

Domenico guessed influential, powerful seductresses didn't care about corporate policy. Or causing a mild scene in front of the other resort guests.

Aware of the other couple's intrigued expressions and their eyes on them, Domenico reached for her hand and gently untangled her fingers from the fabric of his shirt, then moved away. "You're here with your husband," he said gently. She had to respect him for not wanting to put her in a compromising position in her marriage.

Pricilla's demeanor turned frosty, and her expression was one that would reduce a boardroom full of executives to a weeping puddle of dress shoes and ties. "Do you have a point?" she said in a clipped tone.

Obviously not.

Domenico sighed. "I'm sorry... I didn't mean to offend or to imply..."

"Does the resort also have a policy about owners getting intimately involved with hired staff?" Her voice was a little too high.

Domenico stilled as he glanced quickly at the other couple, who weren't even trying to hide their interest in their conversation. "It does," he said quietly through clenched teeth.

"You have no problem bending one rule but not another?"

"I don't know what you mean."

Pricilla eyed him, long and penetrating, then she shrugged—the frostiness melting away as though she'd been placed in an oven. "Must be my mistake, then," Pricilla said airily, unfazed as she collected her things and left the court.

Which left him slightly fazed.

What was he doing pacing outside the main building, waiting for Adriana to finish up for the evening? He should go to his villa for the rest of the night and quit playing with fire. Especially after his interaction with Pricilla.

Adriana was off-limits.

Sure, they had a connection. Sure, there was more passion in their kiss than he'd felt in ten relationships.

And sure, the sexual tension radiating between them that morning had been fire, but…she was still Leo's ex.

And staff.

He was breaking two rules. So far, he'd been caught breaking one by the feisty, vengeful Pricilla Conway. Which could end up being disastrous enough. He didn't need Leo finding out he'd broken the second one. Otherwise he'd be cleaning up the mess of bad press for the resort and a bloody broken nose.

He should just go. Avoid Adriana as much as possible for the rest of the week, then go back to barely talking for the rest of their lives.

Easy. Done.

Adriana exited the main building, and instead, Domenico approached—his feet on autopilot. "Hey."

Awkward.

"Hey," Adriana said just as awkwardly.

It made him feel a bit better that they both seemed to be alternating between flirting shamelessly obviously and not being able to put a full sentence together.

He cleared his throat. "Dinner service went well."

A neutral compliment. Safe. Couldn't read anything into that.

"I think so…" she said, shuffling her feet and glancing around them.

What now?

The silence grew deafening as a long moment passed with neither of them speaking.

Just say something, moron!

She looked amazing in a pale blue tank and cutoffs—not exactly an executive-staff-appropriate off-duty wardrobe, but he had zero issue with her breaking the rules. Lots of rules. All the rules.

Domenico cleared his throat. "I was wondering if maybe you'd like to take a walk?"

Adriana looked conflicted, and he immediately wished he had let her speak first. "I don't know, Dom. Leo isn't going to be okay with this."

So that was her concern too. It made him feel better that Leo was the stumbling block for her and also frustrated. He shouldn't even be putting her in this position. Brothers couldn't date the same woman—full stop. This moral dilemma should have been his cross to bear alone—in secret—the way he'd apparently been carrying it for years.

There was no doubt in his mind that the disdain he'd always felt for Adriana had been repressed attraction and admiration because she was dating his brother. A self-preservation thing.

Why couldn't those feelings have stayed repressed?

Maybe because the situation had changed when he realized that he might have inadvertently driven Adriana into Leo's arms! And now he was constantly spiraling with thoughts of what if.

Either way, Adriana was right, and she was voicing it, so he should respect her internal conflict and acknowledge that she was correct. They should go their separate ways. Put an end to this before it got even more complicated and out of hand.

"Leo's on the mainland tonight," he blurted out instead.

Adriana looked torn but definitely tempted when her gaze met his.

Why was he pressuring her into this when they both knew it was the wrong thing to do? Seriously, what was wrong with him? Was he trying to sabotage everything the brothers had worked hard to achieve together? This would be an act of betrayal that they might not be able to move past.

Retreat and retract the offer.

Tell her she's right—we should forget what happened and not let anything further transpire.

"Only if you want to," were instead the words that came out of his mouth.

Not exactly retreating and retracting!

Adriana was silent for a torturously long time. Then she said, "I want to."

Oh, thank God.

Only not.

Now that she'd agreed, it felt like they'd taken an unspoken step forward together into deceit and betrayal, which made him uneasy. All those years feeling like Adriana had betrayed him and their friendship in pursuing a relationship with Leo and here he was encouraging actual betrayal…but unfortunately, in that moment, looking into her captivating eyes, all he could think about was the way they'd shone in the moonlight the night before and how her laughter had carried on the breeze and how after leaving her, he'd felt happier, lighter, and more fulfilled than he had in years.

"I'll meet you on the beach in an hour—at sunset?"

She nodded. "At sunset."

The twilight hour known to inspire all kinds of sins.

What was she thinking, pacing the sand, waiting for Domenico to go on another romantic moonlit walk with her?

She was asking for trouble. *They* were asking for trouble. Yet when he'd invited her, her heart had soared, and she'd felt a stirring in her like never before. All day she'd thought of him as she'd worked. While she knew this wasn't a good idea, it was all she longed to do.

As she watched him approach, her palms started to sweat.

Still dressed in the khakis and blue dress shirt from that morning, with his hair slightly windblown, he looked gorgeous. She knew he was just as freaked out and guilty about these growing feelings of attraction as she was, but he too seemed to be pushing them aside in favor of following his own desires.

To be with her.

The thought made her pulse race.

"You showed up," he said as though he'd doubted it.

"So did you."

He nodded and extended a hand to her.

She stared at it for a long moment before sliding hers into it. He held tight as they started to walk along the quiet section of guest-free beach.

"Sorry about this morning—the question tour," she clarified when he looked confused. "I was trying to keep the focus on the resort, but Linda kept bringing her questions back to Bellarini's."

Domenico shook his head. "It was totally fine. Listening to you talk about the family restaurant was really nice. I think it went a long way with her. Your passion as well as your skill." He turned to look at her, and her breath caught in her throat.

The temptation to wrap her arms around his neck and kiss him was insanely strong. But she refused to make that first move. If he wanted to kiss her, he would.

He cleared his throat, and his expression was suddenly serious. "There is one thing we need to be careful of."

"Besides Leo?"

He nodded. "Pricilla Conway."

"Ah, that cougar closet tennis star who's been trying to seduce you."

Domenico's eyes widened. "You knew she was faking it?"

Adriana laughed at his naivety. "You're adorable when you're oblivious."

Domenico shot her a look. "She saw us on the court together this morning."

She nodded, conflict resurfacing. "Maybe we shouldn't be doing this. There's a lot at stake."

Domenico stopped and turned to face her. He reached out and touched her cheek softly. "Believe me, I know. If there was any way I could fight this urge to be with you, I would."

She swallowed hard. His gaze burned into hers and his gentle caress became more of a grip on her as his hand slid to the back of her neck, drawing her closer. She took a step toward him and wrapped her arms around his neck. He peered down at her before slowly lowering his face toward hers.

The kiss was soft, gentle and quick, but it had her entire body on fire.

He pulled back and released a deep breath. "Look, maybe this can't actually go anywhere, but I feel like we should explore this insane and inconvenient attraction—to get it out of our system?"

Adriana nodded. "A short-term fling?"

"Exactly," Dom said. He extended a hand, and Adriana stared at it a beat before accepting it.

They shook. Then quietly, hand in hand, they continued along the beach, a comfortable silence and unspoken understanding between them.

A little while later, a small villa appeared in the distance, and Domenico led the way toward it. "Mi casa," he said.

Adriana looked with admiration at the villa in its simplicity, surrounded by nature. "This is where you live?"

Domenico nodded. "Leo and Mario prefer guest suites in the main building, but I like it out here."

"I can see why. I think you have the best view on the island." Adriana scanned the long, deserted stretch of white sand, the swaying trees and the view of the mainland in the distance, illuminated at night.

Domenico stared at her. He moved closer and touched her cheek. Adriana lifted her chin upwards to stare into his eyes.

"I do right now."

Adriana swallowed hard. "Domenico, I'm enjoying my time with you…"

Domenico caressed the side of her cheek affectionately, moving even closer to her. "But…"

"Leo."

"Yeah. That's a problem, isn't it?" he asked, only moving even closer. He wrapped one arm around her waist and drew her into him.

Adriana didn't resist. "I mean, it is, right? For you too?"

"Of course it is. But I've gotten good at pushing it aside the more time we spend together." Domenico held her tight against him and traced his finger along her jawline.

"We can't do anything to hurt him," Adriana said softly, but the hint of wanting in her tone encouraged him to continue his motions.

"What if he doesn't know?"

"Dom…"

"Look, I love my brother, but things have been over between you two for a long time," he said huskily, rationalizing things for the both of them. He was trying to make them both feel less guilty about their growing, undeniable connection. So far it was working.

Adriana nodded. "Keep talking."

"And Leo loves us both. He'd want us to be happy, right?"

She sighed and cocked her head to the side. "Now you're stretching a little…"

Domenico chuckled softly as he pulled her in even closer, lowered his face toward hers. "Is it working, though? Do you feel at least a little bit better?"

She felt amazing there in his arms, his breath warm against her skin, his lips just inches from hers and his attraction-filled gaze locked on hers. "Yes." The word was no more than a breathy whisper if it existed at all.

Domenico lowered his head further, and his lips met hers. A soft sigh escaped her as Adriana sank into him, giving in to the kiss. Her hands reached up and tangled into the back of his hair, holding his head firmly in place.

He wasn't getting away so quickly this time. She needed this kiss. Longed for it.

His mouth searched hers with a desperation as though he'd never quite be satisfied. She returned the kiss with all the passion in her soul as she clung to him and his arms held her tight.

Both out of breath moments later, they slowly pulled away.

Domenico's gaze was intense, full of attraction as he stared down into her eyes. "Want to come inside?" he asked, his tone gruff.

Adriana didn't hesitate. "More than anything."

Domenico and Adriana entered the villa, kissing and removing one another's clothing as they made their way toward Domenico's bedroom.

Domenico stopped, hesitated as he studied her intently. "You sure about this?"

"About being with you—right here, right now—yes."

Domenico bent at the knees, scooped her up into his arms, carried her inside the room and placed her onto the bed. She scanned the space quickly, taking in the wicker rattan furniture of the room—the four-poster bed and reading chair in the corner—simple island vibes. A curtain blew in the window, and she could hear the waves crashing against the shore outside.

He unbuttoned his shirt and tossed it onto the chair before joining her on the bed.

His body never ceased to impress her. Muscular and sculpted, but also strong and capable—there was a difference. Muscles could be built in a gym but true strength came from years of dedication, hard work, putting his body to the extreme in pursuit of excellence.

Domenico Kasa demanded excellence.

Which made her suddenly very self-conscious as he reached for her and started to remove her shirt.

"Wait," she said. He instantly stopped, let go of the fabric. "Sorry."

"No. Don't be sorry. I—uh—I just—um." Rarely was she ever at a loss for words, but how did she tell him that she was nervous he'd see her flaws when he clearly didn't have one, despite her ribbing? "Um…"

"This is a bad idea? You're not comfortable?" he asked, genuinely, sincerely concerned, which just made her want him even more than the sight of the muscles bulging in his biceps.

"Not in the way you mean," she said slowly.

"Okay…"

She sighed. "Look, it's been a while, and I work long hours. I'm not a gym rat, and I love pasta…all kinds of pastas and desserts…"

He frowned quizzically. "I really don't know what you're trying to say."

"I'm not…" She still struggled for the right words. She gestured his physique. "This."

Domenico looked confused for a second. Then he smiled. "I would hope not. If you were, you wouldn't be in my bedroom right now, turning me on, hotter than I've been in years."

She was doing that to him? She knew he was turned on. That was evident by the bulge in the front of his pants. But was he really feeling her as much as she was aching for him?

He touched her cheek gently. "Adriana, since we were kids, I've always thought you were the most breathtaking pain in the ass I'd ever seen."

She'd take it.

She reached for him and pulled him down on top of her. Her mouth crushed his, and he drew back briefly in surprise. "So, we're doing this?"

"Less talk, more getting naked," she said, sitting up and lifting her arms above her head for him to remove her shirt. He did. Then he continued to remove the bra and her shorts, tossing everything aside.

Exposed in only her thong underwear, under his lust-filled gaze, she shivered on the bed.

"Cold?" he asked with a grin, knowing that the shiver was caused by her every nerve ending quivering at the anticipation of his touch, his hands on her flesh, his lips against her skin. "You won't be soon." He spread her legs and lowered himself between them. His hands trailed over her exposed skin at her neck, her chest, between her breasts. His gaze drank her in, following the path of his fingers along her skin.

Adriana's entire body sprang to life beneath his delicate but deliberate touch as his fingers trailed along her stomach...and farther down.

He slipped his hand beneath the lace waistband of her thong as he lowered his head to her nipple, circling it with his tongue before taking it in his mouth and sucking gently. His fingers brushed over a soft mound of bare flesh, reaching her sweet wetness between her legs.

"Dom," she said, arching her back on the bed beneath him.

"Do you like that?"

She nodded, biting her lip to stop from moaning.

His lifted his gaze from her breasts to her face, and he watched her expression as his fingers stroked her.

"You have too many clothes on," she said, desperate to have him as naked as she was. Feel his skin pressed against hers.

He slowly broke away, stood and tore off his khakis... then his briefs.

Adriana took him in, and her heart raced. Domenico Kasa was definitely...proportional. He reached for the waistband of his briefs as he nodded at her thong. "Take that off."

The commanding tone in his voice normally would have irritated her, but in that moment, in that context, she was more than happy to obey.

She slipped her fingers inside the fabric at her hips and slowly shimmied them down over her hips, thighs, legs and feet, tossing the fabric onto the pile of discarded clothing on the floor.

Domenico removed his briefs and stared at her on the bed—naked, waiting, and more than ready for him. "Open for me," he said. She eagerly complied, spreading her legs apart to allow him to lie between them. The moment his body made contact with hers, he closed his eyes and groaned.

It felt so good. Too good. Dangerously good. She couldn't wait a second longer.

"Condoms?"

Seconds later, covered, he hesitated, his body aligned with hers, his hands on her waist, ready to be one with her.

"Ready?"

Such a loaded question. Was she ready to give herself completely to a man she'd once thought of as a childhood best friend, a man whom she'd spent years bickering with, believing he disliked her, a man she suddenly realized she was so attracted to and connected with that nothing else mattered in that moment except being close to him? Giving all of herself to him?

She nodded, and a cry escaped her as he entered her.

Domenico groaned. "You are so perfect." He slid in and out, slowly at first, then faster, and harder, until she was panting and begging beneath him.

"Dom, Dom, Dom..." She moaned and writhed, holding his hips against hers and rocking with his rhythm as he went deeper and deeper. "Dom, don't stop."

He moved faster, harder, pumping in and out of her with an intense urgency as though he needed to own her, take full control of her body.

He had it. "Oh God, yes." She let her head fall back as her body trembled beneath him.

She was so close already—just from the feel of him moving in and out of her while his hands gripped her hips and his mouth kissed along her neck, her chest and over her breasts.

It had been so long. Her body was telling her just how much she'd deprived herself of this pleasure with its incredible desire for release. But it was also so much more than that.

She stared up at him. At Domenico Kasa.

In that moment, she knew what her heart had always known. He was the spark she was craving and missing. He'd been the source the entire time. Giving in to him, surrendering to these feelings, was the only thing she could do. The only thing she wanted to do with her entire body, mind and heart.

His gaze met hers and held—deep, hard with the passionate intensity of a lover waiting a lifetime for this connection. For this moment in time.

She gripped his arms as she felt him explode inside her and her own ripples of orgasmic pleasure following seconds behind. She arched her back and pressed her hips into his as she felt him plunge deep one last time. His body shook above her, and she held on tight as the intensity of the orgasm brought her release like none she'd ever felt before.

As though this physical release was the manifestation of a lifetime of repressed feelings that were finally free to be communicated, explored…and reciprocated?

Satiated and spent, Domenico slowly slid out of her body and lay next to her on the bed. He immediately pulled her to him, and she cuddled into every curve of him, enjoying the sensation of being so close, so intimate…so safe and secure.

So sure.

That should have been a terrifying feeling, yet it wasn't. Not even a little bit.

He brushed her hair away from her face and kissed her gently on the forehead.

"That was…unexpected," she whispered.

"Unexpected, but also as familiar as if it had been destined to happen."

Surprised that he felt that way too, she pulled back slightly and looked into his eyes.

"I feel it all now—the attraction and connection I've always had for you and with you. I feel it all. I feel you," he said.

And her heart felt it all too.

Adriana rested her head on Domenico's chest and traced her finger along the sculpted muscles. Domenico gently kissed the top of her head, and she cuddled in closer to him. "Did you always know you wanted to be a professional tennis player?" She remembered him playing as a kid and being good at it, but she didn't remember it ever being something they talked about in depth back then.

"My dad always knew. Took me a little longer to get there."

"He encouraged it?"

"*Encouraged* is a mild way to put it." Domenico paused, trailing a finger along her arm. "Our father was a visionary—a very smart businessman who believed your best chance at success in life was to play to your skills. He was both charming in the right situations and cutthroat in the right situations. That's how he got ahead in this competitive tourism industry. And he enforced that same mentality and belief system on Leo, Mario and me."

Adriana gazed at him as he spoke, afraid to say anything or interrupt for fear he'd stop talking. Domenico rarely opened up. He'd always been the most quiet, reserved Kasa brother, even as a kid. It meant something that he was sharing all this with her. Obviously their physical intimacy had meant enough to him to have him opening up on another level.

"Anyway, the summer was not about relaxing or goofing off in our household. It was an opportunity to either learn the business by hanging out with him and our mother at one of the resorts or going away to some kind of camp. Leo and Mario always opted for the resort, but I chose different sports camps. Turned out I was a natural at tennis, so my dad decided we'd go all in on that. He saw that I wasn't as interested in operating the resort chain as the others were, so he said, 'tennis—that's your new passion'…and I didn't have an alternate solution, so…"

"Tennis was your new passion."

He shifted on the bed, pulling her even closer. "Exactly. Look, did I always love it? No. It was grueling training to be the best, because only that option existed for a Kasa. But it gave me a fantastic career. I have no complaints."

Adriana nodded. It had to be tough to be work so hard for a dream that you didn't fully want. But she knew Leonardo Sr.'s intentions were sincere. He saw potential in his son, and Domenico benefited from the intense, strict support from his father.

"What about you?" he asked in her long silence.

"Tennis might not have been my calling," she said teasingly.

Domenico tickled her, and she laughed and wiggled away. He stopped and drew her immediately back into his arms. "I meant, was running the restaurant, becoming a chef at Bellarini's the only dream you had for yourself?"

Adriana nodded. The only one she would share, at least.

Domenico pulled back and studied her. "No, it wasn't. Spill it. What did you want to do?"

"It was silly." He might have opened up, but his childhood dream career had transpired. She hadn't even attempted hers, and she'd never told anyone about it.

"Doubt that," he said gently.

Adriana sighed. "I wanted to be an F1 driver," she said, and waited for him to laugh or make fun.

Domenico's face took on a pensive look for a moment. Then he nodded. "You would have been good at that."

She pursed her lips and swatted at him.

"No, you really would have. You're skilled with your hands. You have sharp reflexes and reaction skills, and I know you like speed. You're fearless…"

She scoffed. "Hardly."

He propped himself up on his elbow and turned to look at her. "You are. I saw how you handled things when your dad got sick. No one else knew what to do or how to handle him. That stubborn old man refused to listen to anyone…and your father was a very intimidating man. You stood up to him and made him realize he needed to get help. That's fearless."

Adriana swallowed hard. That had been one of the toughest, scariest things she'd ever had to do. No one ever went up against their father—not her grandparents, not her mother, not Alex. When he'd gotten sick with dementia, no one had the courage to tell him he needed to take a step back from the restaurant—after nearly accidentally burning down Bellarini's—but she'd done it. And when he'd voiced his concerns about her taking over the restaurant, insisting maybe it should be Alex, she'd fought back then as well. And she refused to let her recent lack of confidence make her question his ultimate choice.

"I didn't think you were really paying attention to all of that."

"You and Leo were a thing. Believe me, I paid attention a lot. More than I should have."

"Trying to protect Leo—from my ill intentions." She knew he always worried that she was latching on to a Kasa for the financial benefits. Maybe it was because he sensed the lack of true connection between her and Leo and that made him hesitant to trust.

"Partly. But not entirely."

Domenico stared into her eyes, and Adriana's chest tightened. The conversation turning to Leo brought the fact that she was in bed with her ex's brother to the forefront of her mind again. "Speaking of Leo…"

Domenico sighed and rolled onto his back. "Speaking of Leo…"

"This would hurt him, wouldn't it?" It wasn't really a question.

Still, Domenico nodded, confirming it. "This would hurt him."

Great.

Domenico pulled her closer, and she rested her head against his chest. "But not exploring this connection between us would hurt us."

She sighed. He was right, but could they selfishly allow themselves the happiness of spending time together—even though it can't last?

CHAPTER NINE

It had to be the hottest day on record so far that year. There wasn't a cloud in the sky, and only the faintest of breezes blew every other minute as the Kasa resort staff set up for the staff-versus-guests beach volleyball tournament. Eight teams—four comprised of executive staff and four made up from guests who'd registered to participate—would play one another with the winning team gaining a point. Leading teams would play off in semifinals and then finals.

Leo stretched a few feet away. As Domenico approached, he fought the guilt of having sex with his brother's ex the night before. This morning it was all he could think about. The image of her was burned in his memory, and their agreement to keep this whole thing casual, just a fling, was torturing him. It was smart. It was the right thing to do. But damn, he couldn't shake the desire for it to be more than that. Yet he wasn't sure he was capable of fully trusting her.

He cleared his throat as he stopped next to his brother and started mimicking his movements, stretching his hamstrings. "How did it go on the mainland? Linen crisis averted?"

"Turned out it wasn't even our order that got messed up. Total waste of a trip."

Not entirely.

Domenico nodded and cleared his throat again. "Hey, Leo…" He wasn't exactly sure what would follow, but he was desperate to get a gauge on his brother's level of attraction to Adriana. Whether he was actually still holding out hope for some kind of future together or if he was really fine with just being friends as he claimed… and maybe how he'd feel if Adriana started a new relationship. "You and Adriana dated for what? Four years?"

"Six."

Domenico turned around to the sound of Adriana's voice answering the question, and immediately his body sprang to life.

Adriana stood there wearing the sexiest sporty bikini he'd ever seen. It was, in fact, the Kasa de Paradise logoed bikini that all of the staff would wear that day to compete in the volleyball tournament, but Leo's "holy hell" was the only way to accurately describe how it looked on Adriana's body. Her curves made the thing look lethal.

Good thing she was on the staff team. Otherwise she'd be a massive distraction to Domenico's game. Not that they'd actually win—corporate rules were that guests always won. But they still liked to make their opponents work for it so they at least didn't feel the game was entirely rigged.

"Hey, Dom—close your mouth," Leo said with a grin.

"Ready to lose?" a female voice said behind him.

He turned to see Pricilla in a modest one-piece and matching sun visor. She smiled politely with a hint of cocky competitiveness.

"Bring it, Mrs. C," he said, embracing the spirit of competition and trying to ease the sting of his rejection the day before. Maybe they'd finally reached an understanding. Maybe she realized her actions had been inappropriate, and he'd simply been setting some boundaries.

She moved closer. "Oh, I intend to, darling," she said, and slapped his butt. "See you in the finals," she called over her shoulder as she sauntered away.

Okay, so maybe not.

Linda appeared on the beach, and he forced all thoughts of both other women—Adriana and Pricilla—out of his mind as he turned toward her. She was wearing flowy pants and a loose-fitting tank top, and he frowned. "Not going to play?"

Linda laughed. "My beach volleyball career ended before it began, honey." She gestured to her thin frame. "Not exactly the sporty type."

"Well, you're in for a fun time regardless. This competition is always a tense one," he said as she took a seat in a lounge chair and prepared to spectate.

"These loungers are the most comfortable beach furniture I've ever sat in. Only thing missing is a…"

Her words were cut short as a resort staff member arrived with a drink for her. She laughed as she gratefully accepted it.

"You were saying?" Domenico asked with a grin.

He loved his staff. The team members not participating in that day's events would be circulating refreshments to the spectating guests, keeping the players hydrated and playing DJ and motivators to keep the energy on the beach high all afternoon.

He nodded toward his team. "Gotta go strategize."

Linda nodded, already enjoying her drink. "Good luck!"

Domenico joined Leo, Adriana and other employees making up the staff team. They huddled up, and he deliberately avoided Adriana's eyes as he gave instructions to the team, naturally taking lead as the professional athlete in the group.

"Marco and Bella, you two are our beach volleyball pros, so naturally you'll team up. Lorenzo and Sofia, you're both completely new to the sport, an easy win for the guests. Leo, you are our top server, so you'll take that position. And let's partner you with Sofia. I'm fast, so I can work both sides of midcourt as needed..." He paused as he finally glanced at Adriana. "You'll be with me near the net..." In front of him, where he could stare at her perfect butt all game.

She nodded.

"I want Adriana to play with me," Leo said, turning to Sofia. "No offense, Sof. Adriana and I just used to play together all the time, so we make a great team."

Yeah, a million years ago. Quit living in the past, Leo!

Sofia shrugged. "All good. Dom, guess it's you and me?"

Guess he didn't have a choice. Making a fuss over it would raise all kinds of flags. Besides, Adriana was avoiding his gaze, too, and it was killing him not knowing what she was thinking—if she was regretting the night before or just playing it cool in front of Leo.

"On three," Leo said, putting his hand in the center. Sofia's went on top of his, then Adriana's. Domenico stared at the pile of hands a moment.

"Come on, Dom," Leo muttered, misreading his hesitation.

He placed his on top of Adriana's, and immediately electricity coursed through his arm.

The others joined in.

"One, two..."

"Go team!" the others said as they broke away.

"Right, go team," Domenico mumbled awkwardly as they made their way onto the sand.

In position at his court, he glanced across the net, where their opponent guests had taken position—Pricilla as midcourt point like himself. Obviously confident in her volleyball skills.

The competitive streak in him peaked, but then, across the beach, Adriana bent her knees slightly and got into position in front of Leo. His brother's look of appreciation made his pulse race for a different reason.

The matches started. To say Domenico looked like he'd never played a sport a day in his life would be an understatement. His concentration was shot as his attention was constantly diverted from his game to the interaction between Leo and Adriana on their court.

Laughing. Fist-bumping. Chest-bumping. Butt-slapping.

Domenico was losing his ever-loving mind.

The sound of Adriana's laughter drifting across the beach, the familiar interaction between her and his brother, the fun they seemed to be having was making him full-on jealous. A rare feeling for him. One he didn't like.

Naturally his team did not advance to the finals.

Leo and Adriana did. Against Pricilla and a stock broker who was clearly a professional volleyball player in a former life.

Domenico collapsed into a lounger next to Linda, and a resort staff member handed him a drink.

Linda peered at him over her sunglasses. "Looked like you'd never seen a volleyball before."

Domenico laughed. "I was definitely off my game. Maybe don't mention it in your review."

Linda grinned. "I report what I observe. Good thing those two are fire!" she said, nodding toward Leo and Adriana.

Domenico's gaze landed on them, and his heart raced. They did work well together as a team. They were great friends and had a history. They had chemistry and love. Was there still something there?

His gut twisted at the thought as the final match began.

The music got louder and more up-tempo, and resort staff and guests watched with intense interest as the game was played. Evenly matched and exciting…up until the last point, when Leo made a deliberate miss and Pricilla and her partner won. The two celebrated like they'd won gold at the Olympics, and Leo and Adriana were gracious in "defeat." He watched as the two of them shook hands with the winners and then shared a secret smile.

He couldn't take any more. All day, Adriana had barely looked at him. She hadn't said a word, and her interaction with Leo had Domenico literally feeling sick in the stomach.

He pushed up from the lounger. "Excuse me, Ms. Frank. Enjoy the medal ceremony. I have a few things I need to attend to." He walked away down the beach toward his hut, the sound of laughter and fun drifting on the breeze behind him.

He didn't look back.

Her silver Kasa de Paradise beach volleyball medal around her neck, Adriana scanned the beach for Domenico.

Where'd he go?

The rest of the staff and the guests were enjoying the music and refreshments, but he was gone. She sighed. During the afternoon, it had been so hard to stay focused on the game and keep things casual around Leo when all that was going through her mind was whether or not Domenico regretted their evening before…and whether he wanted a repeat.

She did. Desperately. But unfortunately, she already knew their pact to keep the attraction to a one-week-only fling was going to be impossible, for her, at least. Their time together—their intimacy—the night before had changed things.

"Close game," Pricilla said, approaching her. Her gold medal proudly on her neck, she'd been strutting around like a peacock. It took all of Adriana's strength not to admit they threw the game.

Guests were the priority.

Even snobby, rich, annoying ones.

She forced a smile. "You're quite the volleyball player. I take it you've played before?"

"I was a division champion in a lot of sports." She glanced across the beach, where her husband was asleep in a hammock. "So was he at one time—can you believe that?"

"That's how you met? Through sports?" she asked.

Pricilla nodded. "We had the same track coach in college. We were quite the couple back then."

The note of wistfulness in her voice gave her the briefest rare moment of sincerity. Adriana almost felt bad for her. Couples often grew apart as life happened. Maybe that's what happened with the Conways.

"Well, I'm sure he'll be happy to see that medal around your neck," she said.

Pricilla removed it, and her frosty demeanor returned. "It was just a silly game, honey."

Pricilla sauntered away, and Adriana sighed. A hint of humanity had been so close.

Leo approached and wrapped an arm around her shoulders. "We totally had them," he whispered.

She laughed. "We will always know the truth."

"Want to grab a drink?" he asked, looking at her expectantly.

Her gut twisted. That day must have felt like old times for him. Laughing, teasing, flirting a bit…but he had to understand that things were really over. Especially now. There was no way they could ever be together again after she'd been with Domenico. "Leo…"

He held up a hand. "It's okay. I get it." He removed his arm from around her and smiled. "Today was just…nice."

She nodded. "It was."

An awkwardness fell between them, and he checked his watch. "Guess I should shower and prepare for dinner too."

"I'll see you there," she said. Then she stood there as he walked away toward the main building.

She hesitated, eyeing the trail toward her guest room. Then her gaze drifted down the beach to a secluded, off-limits area.

Was he hallucinating? Had the heat that day given him heatstroke?

Domenico stepped off the steps of his beach hut and headed toward the water…where Adriana splashed in the surf.

"Water feels like heaven," she called out when she saw him on the sand.

"You're trespassing," he said, watching her. His heart raced, and he couldn't describe the relief he felt seeing her there. For the last hour, he'd fought irrational thoughts and images of her with Leo.

"Shut up and get in," she said.

He rarely swam in the sea, but in this case, he could make an exception.

For her, he was realizing, he'd made a lot of exceptions.

He removed his T-shirt and waded into the surf. "Feels a little cool," he said, taking in a sharp inhale as the water level reached his groin area. He sucked in a breath and plunged, refusing to look like a wimp in front of her.

He resurfaced beside her, instantly wrapped an arm around her waist and drew her into him. The scents of her coconut-flavored skin and floral hair reached his nose, and he breathed her in along with the salty ocean air. If someone could bottle this intoxicating aroma that embodied life on Kasa de Paradise, they could sell it in the gift shop and make a fortune—that smell of forever summer.

But then, it wouldn't be the same on anyone but Adriana. Her aura was what made it special.

His hands gripped her slippery wet waist, and he lifted her up onto his lap. She wrapped her legs around him as they continued to bob on the water. "What are you doing here?"

"You disappeared after the game awfully fast," she said.

"Bit of a sore loser," he said.

"Used to winning, huh?" she teased.

"In sports—yes. Besides, I didn't think you'd notice me leaving."

A slow grin appeared on her face. "Are you still upset that I partnered with Leo? Cause you could have fought for me."

He could have that day, but he didn't. Would he? When

it truly mattered? He stared into her gorgeous eyes, and in that moment he knew he'd risk just about anything. "Choosing my battles, I guess."

She licked the salt-water droplets from her lips, and his body ignited.

She grinned, feeling his arousal. "Wow, doesn't take much."

His grip on her skin tightened, and he drew her even closer. "I wouldn't say that. You are a lot of woman, Adriana."

She shot him a look.

"You're energy. You're exuberant, unyielding energy, and this intoxicating physical prowess that you have—that's what I mean."

"Good save," she said with a laugh.

That laugh.

When had it gone from irritating him to being a sound he cherished, lived for, couldn't hear enough?

She lay back. Keeping her legs wrapped around his waist, she slowly lowered her body into the water, letting her hair float like a halo all around her.

She was no angel. She knew exactly what she was doing. In that position, her stomach was long, toned and lean, and the view of the underboob beneath that tiny bikini top was driving him mad.

He reached out. Placing a hand below her back, he forced her upright, then he stood and headed for shore, her body still wrapped around him.

"Hey, I wasn't done in the water," she teased.

"You're done in *this* water," he said, carrying her across the sand, up the beach and straight toward the outdoor shower on the outside deck. He gently lowered her to the wooden planks and reached for the taps behind her.

Cold water sprayed from the faucet above. Adriana's breath caught sharply as it cascaded down her back.

Domenico adjusted the dial until warm water flowed. He stepped in under the spray along with her and placed a hand on her hip as he drew her into him. He lowered his head to hers and kissed her gently but with intention.

After all the torturous teasing he'd endured that day watching her with his brother, he needed to reclaim her—every inch of her.

A soft moan escaped her lips, making him instantly rock-hard. That simple little sound had him feeling like a god. The idea that his kiss, his touch could generate that vulnerable sound of pleasure from the most beautiful set of lips he'd ever tasted had his ego doing back handsprings and gave him all the confidence in the world to make her feel amazing.

He gently slid the fabric of the bikini straps down over her shoulders, down her arms, exposing her breasts as the fabric fell to the wooden planks at their feet. He swallowed hard, taking in the sight of the perfectly round mounds, the erect nipples aching to be touched, teased, kissed...

Holding her still pressed to him, their lower bodies connected, he cupped one breast and squeezed—gently at first, then more roughly. His thumb rolled over the hardened bud, flicking the nipple, then pinching gently... harder, and then a little harder.

Adriana moaned and wrapped one arm around his neck, forcing his head down toward it.

With pleasure.

He took the nipple into his mouth and sucked and flicked his tongue over it. His teeth grazed it. Her grip on his neck tightened and her back arched as she drove her body even closer to him.

He moved to the other breast and savored the taste of her coconut-flavored, salty flesh.

Adriana's breath was labored, coming in pants as she lowered her other hand down his abs and slipped it inside his wet swim trunks. Her hand wrapped around him. He growled against her nipple, pulling it with his teeth.

Her grip on him tightened as she started stroking the length of him.

Driving him wild.

He pulled away from her breasts and slid his fingers inside the fabric on her hips. He lowered the swimsuit bottoms down over the sexy curves as the water cascaded over her. He bent on his knees in front of her as he lowered the fabric down her legs, placing kisses along the beautiful skin as he went. She stepped out of the bikini bottoms, and he dropped them next to the bikini top on the wooden planks.

Starting at her ankles, he trailed his fingers upwards over her calves, the backs of her thighs…until both hands cupped her butt. He drew her hips forward and buried his head between her legs.

Adriana's head fell back and her hands tangled in his hair as she widened her stance to give him better access.

"Amazing," he murmured against her.

Holding her to him with one hand, he slid the other between her legs, inserting two fingers inside her wet body.

Adriana's fingers in his hair pulled gently. "Domenico… Dom…"

The desperation in her tone made his entire body come to life with desire—an intense need to have her, but more a determination to please her, make her say his name in that way over and over.

Her panting grew louder, and her legs on either side of him trembled slightly.

No way was she coming that quickly.

He gently moved his head away and got to his feet. He kissed her thoroughly, allowing her to taste herself on his lips. He lifted her, and she wrapped her legs around his waist. Then he pressed her up against the wall of the hut. He looked deep into her eyes—seeking permission, searching for hesitation.

"It's okay. I want this. I want to feel you inside me," she said.

That was all the permission he needed to bury himself deep within her. He moved in and out of her. She gripped his shoulders, her nails digging into his flesh. Panting, moaning, desperate to feel him fill her.

He plunged deeper and deeper inside her, his desire for her only increasing as he neared the edge.

"Adriana…"

"Please, Domenico."

The sound of her begging rivaled the sound of her laugh and the sound of her saying his name. He didn't know what made him more crazy for her.

"Adriana…" He moved back slightly and stared into her eyes, teetering on the edge, desperate with need.

She nodded, the lust in her expression nearly killing him.

He moved in and out of her several more times and felt his orgasm bearing down on him. He moaned as he fought to delay his release until he knew that Adriana was with him.

Adriana clung to him. "That's it, Domenico... Yes, more..." she said, a pleading desperation in her voice.

She clenched her muscles around him as she ground her hips into him. He lifted her hips up and down as she clung to him, her breathing and moans growing louder in his ears as they reached their climax together. Her body sagged and he held her tighter as they fought to catch their breaths, spent and satiated.

"Adriana you are so incredible," he murmured against her lips, kissing her.

"You make me feel incredible," she said.

He slid out of her body and gently lowered her to the wooden planks. He reached for the soap and lathered her body. Taking his time over the sensitive areas.

She did the same. Moments later, after rinsing off, he turned off the water, and they went inside the room.

Domenico closed the door, feeling his body already coming to life once again. His need for her was unlike anything he'd ever experienced before.

When he turned to see her on the bed, the look in her eyes told him she was ready for him again too.

This woman was incredible. And there was no question—Leo could have her as a volleyball partner, but Domenico would fight for her when it mattered.

A wineglass in hand, showered and in fresh, clean clothing, Adriana walked around the villa later that evening after spending the afternoon in the kitchen on dinner prep. She looked at Domenico's tennis trophies on display. "You did have a very impressive career."

On the sofa, Domenico, dressed in a pair of shorts and sweatshirt, looking casual, comfortable and relaxed, stretched his arms along the back as he nodded. "I put in the work. It paid off."

"Why did you really quit playing professionally?" Adriana asked, joining him on the sofa. She curled her legs under her as she sipped her wine.

"Well, I could say it was because Dad was sick and Mario and Leo needed my help with the business…but truth is, I was becoming a dinosaur. Every year there were younger, faster, better players arriving on the courts. Can't compete with youth."

Adriana sent him a shocked look. "Humbleness? From the great Domenico Kasa?"

Domenico laughed and pulled her onto his lap so she was straddling him. "I told you, I'm not the arrogant guy you think I am," he said, gripping her hips and staring into her eyes with unconcealed attraction.

"I'm starting to believe it." She toyed with the strings on his sweatshirt. "Teaching here on the island is enough for you?"

Domenico sighed. "Not really, but I have to face facts. And my success did help in bringing in guests in the early days."

Adriana grinned. "Ah, there's the confidence…"

Domenico tickled her, and she wiggled to escape. "Stop, I hate being tickled," she said through her laughter.

"I know. I remember," he said, reluctantly stopping.

She stared at him. Their gazes locked on one another. "Look, I don't want to spoil the mood. I'm having a really great time with you this week…but are we going to tell Leo?"

Domenico hesitated and looked slightly pained.

She was assuming there was a need to. That this would be something they continued doing. But maybe this was just a weeklong fling for him—something he had no intention of pursuing once she returned to the mainland.

"I mean, we probably don't need to as it was just this week…" She desperately hoped she sounded casual as she stared into the red liquid in her wineglass, avoiding his gaze.

"Is that all it is?" he asked.

Was he disappointed? Or relieved?

The unreadable Domenico was back.

"Yeah… I mean, that's what we agreed to, right? You're here full-time on the island. I'm on the mainland full-time, so it's not like we can continue this—whatever this is…"

"Can't we?"

Another question instead of an answer! Infuriating Domenico was back!

"I'd like your thoughts on it," she said calmly, though her mind and heart were racing. They'd gotten close again that week and she'd let her guard down. She'd opened her heart to him—to the possibility of them—again but that may have been a mistake. If he really only saw this as a week-long fling and then went back to the Domenico that barely acknowledged her, it would destroy her.

Domenico put his wineglass down and looked serious as he said, "I think this week has been—enlightening—for us both, and there are some things that make this—whatever this is—complicated."

She nodded and waited, but that seemed to be all he was going to say on the topic. Complicated. He was leaving off there with no suggestions for a resolution to this complicated scenario they found themselves in.

That said it all, really.

She downed the liquid in the glass, climbed off his lap

and stood. "I should call it a night." She reached for her things, and Domenico reached for her. He wrapped an arm around her waist and drew her back down onto his lap.

"Hey," he said.

She refused to look at him. There was no way she was going to let him see she was upset that he wasn't willing to try to figure this out, that it really had just been a week of passion for him… That's really all it might ever be. All it ever could be.

A tightness gripped her chest, and a desperate need to escape before Domenico could see he'd gotten to her sent her into flight mode.

But he refused to loosen his grip on her. "Hey," he said, gently tilting her face to look at him.

She kept her gaze lowered to his chin.

"Hey," he said again.

Adriana slowly lifted her gaze to his.

"Where are you going?"

"To my room. Another early morning."

Domenico sighed, searched her expression. He looked uncertain what to say. "You seem upset."

Way to read the room, Dom!

Adriana shook her head. "Nope. Not at all."

Domenico studied her. "Look, I…" He paused. For a long time.

Oh, this was torture! She needed to get out of there. With as much of her ego and heart intact as possible. She reached for his hands on her waist and slowly lifted them off her. "Dom, it's totally cool. We're good. There's nothing to figure out. As you said, things are complicated, and there's no point trying to complicate them even further." Each word stuck on her tongue as she said it, the way a lie used to when she was a kid.

Guilt glue, her mom had always called it.

"Adriana…just stay the night."

No way. Her pride was far too strong for that. "I'm going to call it a night, but I'll see you tomorrow." She kissed him gently and quickly. The kiss of someone desperate to go all-in but being forced to retreat out of self-preservation.

Domenico stood and reached for the island cruiser keys. "Give me a sec. I'll drive you back."

She shook her head quickly. "No, it's a beautiful night and still early. I'll walk." Adriana opened the villa door and glanced back over her shoulder. "Night, Dom."

"Night," he said as she closed the door.

Outside, she took a deep breath, feeling only more tightness in her chest as she exhaled. She headed down to the beach, and a heavy disappointment settled in her gut when it became clear he wasn't going to follow.

CHAPTER TEN

THE LAST OFFICIAL night on the island for that week's cohort of guests was formal night—a favorite and highly reviewed evening that featured an elegant six-course meal, champagne and the glitz and glamour of Hollywood complete with a red carpet and photo opportunities.

The main building's dining room was elegantly decorated with white-and-black decor throughout featuring pressed, white linens covering the tabletops and chairs. Large crystal chandeliers had been hung, creating a kaleidoscope effect in the room as the crystals caught the light from hundreds of candles positioned throughout the room—the only light adding ambience and a romantic vibe.

Waitstaff dressed in black tails served meals to the beautifully attired guests, who all seemed relaxed and happy, though maybe a little sunburned and having overindulged after their week at Kasa de Paradise.

Adriana sat at the guest of honor table with the Kasa brothers and Linda Frank, and the vibe was slightly tense at the table. Not that Linda or Leo noticed. The two of them had completely hit it off that week and were chatting like old friends across from her. But whenever her gaze drifted to Domenico, he was always staring at her. With this questioning look that she knew was asking if things were okay? If they were okay? If he'd completely messed up? And honestly, Adriana had no idea.

She hadn't slept well the night after leaving him in his villa and had found ways and reasons to avoid seeing him for the remainder of the week—hiding out in her room whenever she wasn't in the kitchen. He'd been putting out fires every day—a staff injury that needed a trip to the mainland hospital, an excursion cancellation due to weather that could have resulted in unhappy guests had he not scheduled an alternate activity, and other resort responsibilities—so he hadn't been around much either. They'd clearly both felt the tension the other night and both opted for space. Not communication.

Today she had been in full dinner prep mode, and he'd been overseeing the main building's dining room transformation. Therefore, they hadn't crossed paths. She'd at least expected to see him in the kitchen once that day as part of his overseeing everything, but he'd never shown up.

Looking at him now was killing her. Dressed in a tuxedo, he looked gorgeous—distinguished, handsome, and to everyone else, in control and composed. Only she could see the wheels turning in his mind. She knew he was thinking about this being their last evening together as much as she was and the way they'd left things unresolved.

All day as she'd worked, she'd been rehearsing what she'd say when they did eventually speak.

Domenico, it was fun, and I'm happy that we reconnected and shared this special week together. One I'll always cherish.

No more. No less.

He didn't need to know she was falling for him. He

didn't need her asking how they could make this work or putting that kind of family pressure on him. And he certainly didn't need to be trying to communicate with her right now in front of the room full of people and at a table with Leo and Linda.

She frowned, seeing him make a motion with his head. *What?* she mouthed.

He nodded toward the serving room where the next course was being prepped.

She hesitated, then set her fork down. She stood slowly and smiled. "Excuse me, I'm just going to check on the next course."

As she made her way across the room, she could feel Pricilla Conway's glare on her. That woman was far too perceptive, and she was not hiding the fact that she suspected something was going on between her and Domenico.

The woman wasn't wrong, and Adriana hoped she could keep it to herself for another twenty-four hours. As she reached the dinner prep room, she could see Domenico stand and excuse himself at the table.

Leo shot him an odd look. Then his gaze drifted across the room toward her.

His expression made her heart pound. A look of realization or at least suspicion registered on his face as his gaze shifted from her to his brother crossing the room toward her.

Uh-oh.

She shook her head at Domenico when he locked eyes with her. Jerked her head toward the restrooms instead.

He looked puzzled, and she jutted her chin toward their table, where Leo was still watching.

Abort, she mouthed as Domenico drew closer.

He frowned, and she sent him an exasperated look.

"Oh my God! Someone help! My husband!" Pricilla's shriek echoed throughout the ballroom.

All heads—including theirs—turned toward the commotion at the Conways' table.

Adriana was briefly glad for the interruption, until she saw Mr. Conway gripping his throat and struggling to breathe. Pricilla jumped up from her seat and continued to panic as Mr. Conway fell off his chair onto the floor.

From opposite ends of the dining room, Leo and Domenico rushed to their sides.

Adriana slowly approached, and the other diners all stopped eating and chatting to watch.

Including Linda Frank.

Leo grabbed his radio on his belt and spoke into it. "Medic required in main dining hall. Stat!"

Domenico knelt next to Mr. Conway. "Are you choking?"

Mr. Conway shook his head.

Dressed in a very short, very tight LBD, Pricilla bent next to Domenico—close. Inappropriately close, especially given the circumstances. "It's an allergic reaction. He's going into anaphylactic shock. Help him, Dom!" She clutched Domenico's arm like she was the one in distress, and he shrugged her off abruptly.

"Pricilla, please," he said, his tone short and sharp.

He was hot when he wasn't putting up with BS.

Leo didn't think so. He sent his brother a murderous look at the insensitivity. "Medic is on the way. Do you have his EpiPen?" he said gently to Pricilla.

Pricilla's red hair shook wildly around her shoulders. "No! We didn't think he'd need it! We filled out our guest profile, so I assumed the kitchen staff were competent enough to follow it." Her voice rose, and Adriana turned to glance at Linda, who looked slightly disappointed.

Other guests seemed uneasy as they eyed their meals and took in the poor man who continued to gasp for air, clutching his throat on the floor.

"Tell the medics to hurry! Please!" Pricilla shrieked.

Domenico turned to Pricilla. "What did he eat?" he said calmly.

Pricilla's expression switched from scared to angry as she glared at the half-eaten bowl of pasta on the table at her husband's spot. "This pasta! It must have had seafood in it."

Adriana glanced toward Linda again, who watched with a careful eye. Then she studied the food on Mr. Conway's plate. She shook her head. "No, there wasn't any seafood in this dish."

Pricilla advanced menacingly toward Adriana. "Then how do you explain this?" She motioned to her husband, who was now turning a very dangerous shade of red.

She didn't want to argue in an emergency, but she wanted the medic to know this might be more than an allergic reaction. "Mrs. Conway, I can assure you…"

"Maybe if you weren't preoccupied all week…"

What? Really, now?

"Pricilla, let's focus on your husband, okay?" Adriana's voice was calm despite her pulse throbbing in her veins. Being outed at this moment would be a disaster. And a man's life was at risk.

On the floor, Domenico looked ready to shut down Pricilla's implications. Leo sent the three of them questioning glances. Pricilla's cold, threatening gaze blazed into Adriana's, and she looked ready to burn the place down.

"Move aside! Make way!" The medic's arrival couldn't

have come at a better time—for all their sakes. He gestured for everyone to move and crouched next to Mr. Conway as Domenico and Leo stood and backed away to give him space.

"Allergy?" The medic asked, opening his bag.

"Yes. Seafood," Leo said. "Presumably."

The medic quickly gave Mr. Conway an EpiPen injection. A second later, the man took a big breath, the panic instantly leaving his expression.

"Thank you," he croaked.

"He'll be okay," the medic told them, zipping his bag. "But we should probably bring him to the mainland hospital just to be sure."

Pricilla dropped to her knees and clutched her husband's hand, brushed his receding hair back off his sweaty forehead—barely hiding how disgusted she was by the act. "Darling, you scared me."

"I'm okay now," Mr. Conway said, looking surprised but eating up his wife's half-hearted all-for-show affection.

Pricilla turned toward Leo, Domenico and Adriana. "You almost killed my husband! We don't pay thirty-two thousand dollars a week to have our dietary restrictions ignored by…this…" She gestured insultingly at Adriana.

Domenico stepped forward. "Adriana says there was no seafood in this dish."

Leo looked at Domenico in surprise for coming to Adriana's defense.

Pricilla looked even more enraged. "Are you calling my husband and me liars?"

Across the room, at her table, Linda was taking it all in. Adriana gestured silently for Domenico to back down, to not make a scene. As heartening as it was that he was coming to her defense, they still had a review to secure.

Leo, also obviously desperate to appease Pricilla while saving the review, stepped in with a cooler hand and gentler approach. "No. Not at all. I'm sure there was a misunderstanding. We will launch an…"

Pricilla gestured to her husband's plate on the table. "Taste it!"

Leo shook his head. "That won't be necessary. As I was saying, we will…"

Pricilla picked up her husband's plate and shoved it toward Leo. Leo's spine tensed, his height growing an extra inch, and Domenico's hands clenched at his sides.

Both brothers now looked done with this over-the-top display from their guest. The Kasa family didn't do disrespect well and could only be pushed so far.

But Linda was watching, and after an immensely positive week, Adriana didn't want to see it all go wrong over this. Despite knowing she was in no way at fault, she stepped in. "I apologize, Mrs. Conway. Sincerely. I'll check with the kitchen staff right away to see if anyone might have added…"

Pricilla walked toward Adriana and dropped the plate of pasta. It shattered at her feet, making a mess all over the floor and Adriana's heels.

Domenico moved between the two women. For a moment, Adriana thought he was going to unload on the guest, but he touched Pricilla's shoulder gently. "It's been a very emotional, trying evening for you and your husband. We apologize for this. Let's call it a night. I'm sure Mr. Conway could use your support as he gets some rest."

"I demand…" she started.

"All demands will be taken into consideration in a more formal setting once your husband has been thoroughly cared for." His tone was resolute—leaving no room for argument.

Pricilla looked enraged, but what more she could say in the moment? She stormed out of the dining room after her husband and the medic.

Leo and Domenico exchanged *that was a close one* looks, but Adriana's gaze was locked on Linda's disappointed expression.

"This is a disaster. We could have killed someone because of an oversight." Leo ran a hand over his face as he stormed into the office.

Domenico followed close on his heels. "Adriana says there was no seafood in that dish."

"And yet one of our guests almost died." Leo loosened his bow tie and undid several buttons on his dress shirt as he paced the office.

"Since when do you doubt Adriana?"

"Since when do you stand up for her?" Leo stopped pacing and eyed Domenico suspiciously.

"I just think we need to investigate this further before blaming her," he said slowly.

"You are the first one to say that guests are always right—even when they are so blatantly wrong."

Domenico sighed. He hated when his brothers threw his own policies back at him. Especially this week when he was bending the rules. Or had been. Until Adriana seemed to vanish off the island whenever she wasn't in the kitchen. Since the night he'd regretted letting her leave his villa with things unresolved, his week had gone crazy with work demanding his time and attention, but he'd been desperate to get some time alone with her. There were things he wanted to say. He hoped the words would come to him in the moment. But she'd clearly been avoiding him, and time was running out. "In most all cases—yes, that's true," he said calmly. "But you know Pricilla Conway is vindictive."

Leo's eyes narrowed, and he looked even more accusingly at Domenico. "What exactly would she have against Adriana?"

Domenico looked away. "I don't know that she has anything against Adriana. I just mean that she's a bit obsessed with *me*, and maybe she assumed there was something going on."

"Why would she assume that?"

Was it hot in here? Felt like someone turned the heat up over the island by a thousand degrees. Sweat collected on his lower back under the tuxedo jacket and shirt, and he loosened the bow tie. "I don't know. I hang around the kitchen a lot… There was one morning I taught Adriana how to play tennis… Mrs. Conway saw…" Man, his mouth felt like a desert. Water. Water would be really great about now.

A look of realization dawned on Leo's face. "You've got a thing for her."

Domenico's awkward-sounding scoff got caught in his throat. "Mrs. Conway?"

"Come on, man, you know who I mean. You like Adriana. Is there something going on between you two?"

No. Nothing. Never.

Leo placed the palms of his hands on the desktop—his brother's tell when he was about to lose it—as he waited.

Just lie.

"Look, I wanted to tell you…"

Okay. Apparently, he was going with the truth.

"You're hooking up with my ex-girlfriend? When the

reviewer is here?" The vein in his brother's forehead was pronounced and pulsing.

Hooking up? Sort of, but not exactly. *Hooking up* made it sound superficial, and despite his totally chickening out a few nights before when faced with the opportunity to tell Adriana that his feelings for her were real and more than just physical, this week had meant something to him, and he wanted to see her again. Often. However that looked or however they could make that work. It definitely wasn't hooking up. But they had in fact hooked up, so he was conflicted about the right answer here.

"It's not like that..."

"You *love* her?"

Uh-oh. Which one would be worse to Leo? A casual fling or real feelings?

"Okay, it's exactly like that—we're hooking up."

"You are unbelievable, Dom," Leo said, advancing toward him, his fists clenched at his sides.

Domenico refused to retreat even an inch. He didn't want to fight Leo, but if he had to, he knew he could kick his brother's butt. He hoped it wouldn't come to blows. They were both rational adults who could communicate like men. "Things have been over between you two for years."

"So that makes it okay? What happened to the bro code? We're actual brothers, so that makes this betrayal even worse." Leo's nose was inches from Domenico's chin.

"Hey, I could accuse you of it first. Adriana was my friend when we were kids."

"As you just said, you two were just *friends*. And we were *kids*. Hardly the same thing."

"I liked her."

"Then you should have made your move! Then *I* never would have, because *I* have this quality called loyalty." Leo's voice rose. He looked genuinely hurt.

Domenico's gut twisted in a knot. He hated arguing with his brothers, and he knew this time he was at fault for going behind Leo's back. He sighed and placed his hands on his hips. "Look, I'm not going to apologize for this connection between Adriana and me, but I do apologize for not talking to you first."

Leo's eyes narrowed. "Connection? So it wasn't just sex?"

Domenico shook his head. Confident Leo would have hit him by now if he was going to, he shoved his hands in his pockets and let his shoulders slump. "Believe me, neither of us expected this to happen."

Leo was silent for a long moment, his angry expression never dissolving as he took in the idea of his brother and ex-girlfriend together. Domenico waited, watching his brother's turmoil. At this point, he'd happily take a shot to the chin—prefer it over the anguish on his brother's face.

Finally, Leo took a step back and shook his head. "I trusted both of you."

That statement hit its mark.

Their partnership, their friendship, their brotherhood was all about trust and respect, and he'd lost both in his brother's eyes right now. Once lost, trust was hard to recover in the Kasa family. They forgave easily, but slights were never forgotten.

"Leo..."

Leo held up a hand as though to say *save it*. He'd clearly heard enough as he stormed out of the office and slammed the door behind him.

***

Alone in the kitchen, Adriana reviewed the recipes in that evening's menu. Not only did the pasta Mr. Conway consumed not contain seafood, none of the dishes did! There had been no seafood prep in the kitchen that day at all, and therefore no way that cross contamination could have occurred or an oversight could have happened.

Leo stormed in, and she glanced up at him. He looked stressed, annoyed and completely on edge, and she was desperate to put his mind at ease. Whatever happened to Mr. Conway was not their fault—not her fault. "Leo, I've been looking over all of these menus, and nothing calls for any kind of seafood."

"Maybe you made a mistake," he said coolly.

Adriana shook her head adamantly. "I didn't. You know me. I'm diligent, especially when it comes to food allergies. I reviewed all of the dietary restrictions the day I arrived. I was careful…"

"Well, maybe you got distracted."

Adriana caught the chilled tone and the implication of the words. She stilled as she set the recipes down on the counter. "What are you talking about?"

"By my brother."

His tone said he knew—he wasn't surmising or guessing.

Domenico told him? Why would he do that without at least giving her a heads-up? If things weren't serious and they weren't going to see one another after that week, why would he risk being honest with Leo over what was just a harmless fling? Why hurt Leo or put their working relationship in jeopardy?

Was there more to this week for him? Was that what he was trying to tell her that evening before the chaos and commotion started? There certainly was for her. Her heart raced, but then she saw Leo's hurt expression, and it plummeted to the depths of her stomach.

"I should have told you. I'm sorry, Leo…"

"I don't want to talk about it," Leo said, annoyance in his tone now. Which broke her heart in two. He cleared his throat and continued, "I just came by to tell you that you can leave in the morning."

He was dismissing her? "But you still haven't hired a permanent chef. I can stay a few extra days…"

"Not necessary."

"It kinda is," she said with a tight laugh.

"We can't afford more mistakes," he said. "Domenico was right. I never should have trusted you with something so important."

Adriana gaped as though he'd slapped her with the echo of her father's lack of faith. Leo had always been the one person she could count on to have her back and yet here he was morphing into a harsh critic she didn't even recognize. And while he might have defended her moments ago with Mrs. Conway, Domenico had been against her being there that week. She hoped she'd proven herself to him…but this fiasco might have just reaffirmed his belief that she wasn't a good enough chef for Kasa de Paradise.

Leo left the kitchen, and a devastated Adriana watched him go. She scanned the kitchen, tears burning the backs of her eyes, then gathered her Bellarini's recipe book and turned off the kitchen light as she exited for the last time.

Tired and defeated, Adriana packed her clothing into a suitcase an hour later. Disappointed in herself for hurting Leo and confused about where she stood with Domenico, she tossed things unfolded into the suitcase. Her gaze fell on the masquerade dress and shoes in the closet, and the memory of that night on the beach with Domenico made her chest tighten.

She had to talk to him before she left. Find out what had happened with him and Leo. Maybe get the courage to ask him what he'd been about to say earlier that evening. What had been so important that he'd wanted to sneak away from the dinner?

She didn't want to get her hopes up too high. Things might be quite different now after Leo's reaction to the news. It might have changed things for Domenico.

Did it change things for her?

A knock on the door made her hesitate before opening.

Domenico stood on the other side. His expression was tired, conflicted, but also held a trace of attraction and affection. Her shoulders relaxed slightly.

Adriana moved away from the door, and Domenico entered the room. He immediately reached for her and took her into his arms. She released a deep sigh as she sank into him. Despite the conflict she felt over Leo and the wrongful accusation by the Conways, being in his arms, breathing in the scent of him, sensing his strength and commitment to whatever was going on between them made her feel a bit better.

"Look, accidents happen. I don't blame you," he said gently, kissing the top of her head.

Adriana stilled and the peace she'd been experiencing vanished. "I didn't make a mistake. This wasn't my fault."

"Well, how did seafood get in the sauce?" He sounded pained that he had to call her out, and her frustration overtook all other emotion.

She freed herself from his embrace and backed away from him. She folded her arms across her chest. "I can't believe you believe her over me." But she could believe that he still doubted her, and that hurt.

Domenico stepped forward and reached out a hand toward her, but she shook her head. He sighed. "I'm sorry... but I asked one of the chefs to test the sauce left on Mr. Conway's broken plate. There was definitely seafood in Mr. Conway's pasta sauce."

"That's impossible! I reviewed all the menu items, went over all the recipes in the kitchen an hour ago—there was no seafood!"

"Adriana, I don't want to argue. It's done now. Mr. Conway will be okay. We will figure out how to recover from it if Linda's review isn't perfect. Let's just move on, okay?" He reached for her again, tried to draw her into him, but she held firm.

"Do you believe me?"

He ran a hand through his hair. "Adriana..."

Adriana trembled with anger and disappointment. Unbelievable. She nodded toward the door. "Get out so I can finish packing."

Domenico touched her arm gently. "Don't be like that. I'd like to stay with you."

"Why?"

"Because I...like you."

Like. Not love. And since when?

"Really? Cause according to Leo, you knew I'd mess this up. You never trusted me to run the kitchen in the first place. You never wanted me here." That all hadn't bothered her before, but it did now. So much.

Domenico sighed. "Look, I admit that at first, I was nervous, okay? But you proved me wrong. About a lot of things."

Was that supposed to make her feel better? Should she

be grateful? "I'm glad I was able to be something unexpected for you. Please leave."

"Adriana… Leo knows about us."

"I know. He came to see me in the kitchen. A heads-up would have been nice, by the way." If they were going to hurt Leo by coming clean, they should have decided that together. Being blindsided like that hadn't been fair.

This was good. Anger was good—better than a broken heart.

"I didn't even tell him. He saw the way I was defending you…"

"Well, I don't need your defense." Adriana turned her back to Domenico and continued packing. She tossed a still-damp swimsuit into the suitcase and sighed. "I apologize about the review." The words were said through gritted teeth because she was sorry that the review would be negatively affected by that evening's drama, but she also knew it wasn't her fault. Not in the way he'd implied. It was their fault for not hiding their connection better in front of a vindictive woman who loved to hurt people because she was unhappy with her own life.

She heard Domenico move toward her and swallowed a lump in her throat when he placed his hands on her shoulders. She stilled, and a silence fell between them for a long, conflicted moment.

"I don't care about the review," he said. "Not anymore."

She knew the words were meant to make her feel better, but she knew they were BS. More importantly, *she* still cared about the review. Linda Frank mentioning this oversight would affect *her* and Bellarini's more than Kasa de Paradise. How could he not even see that? She whipped around to face him. "I do! Don't you get it? The rest of the review will be incredible, but the negative review of the food here this week is going to damage *my* reputation. It's going to hurt my restaurant too."

Domenico's expression hardened, and he let his hands fall away from her. "That's why you came. That's why you changed our menu. To get a glowing review for Bellarini's."

It wasn't a question, and she had no intention of hiding it. "My restaurant needed the boost, and Leo needed help," Adriana said, raising her chin defiantly.

"So you took a gamble on my resort?" Domenico stepped back.

She resisted the urge to move forward and reach for him. To reassure him that it hadn't been a gamble—she was a competent chef. Considering that evening, her argument lost a little footing, perceivably at least, but still, she refused to allow him to make her feel inadequate. "I don't see it that way, but if you do, then yes, I guess I did."

He leaned against the open patio door, lowered his head and took a deep breath.

"And us? What was that about?"

His gaze was downcast, and his body language was guarded. There was no way she was putting herself out there and telling him the truth about how she felt. What she wanted this week to have been about.

"I don't know, Domenico. You tell me."

Domenico finally looked up. His gaze met hers, and he stared at her.

Silent.

Neither of them spoke for a long, painfully awkward moment. Both daring the other to be the first to speak.

She was running out of air, but she refused to give in.

Suddenly, Domenico pushed off the patio doorframe and headed for the door. "Have a safe trip home." He left the room, and the door closed gently behind him.

Adriana watched him leave—her pride and conflicted heart preventing her from stopping him. Alone, she sat on the edge of the bed, sad and disheartened. "Damn it."

She eyed the suitcase and then the time on her cell phone. Her desire to flee overwhelmed her, and she stood and quickly packed the rest of her things. The last *Passage to Paradise* boat sailing for anyone needing to leave the island unexpectedly left in ten minutes. Technically this wasn't an emergency, but she knew Jon would take her back to the mainland tonight if she asked.

Therefore, Adriana boarded the *Passage to Paradise* eight minutes later.

Domenico stood on the sand outside his villa, watching the *Passage to Paradise* sail away. He knew Adriana was on it, and there wasn't anything he could do about it.

Yet this irrational urge to dive into the water and swim after the boat was overwhelming.

And then what? What would he say to her when he did catch the boat?

He'd had every opportunity to tell her how he felt moments ago in her room, and he'd let his pride and fear of being rejected prevent him from being honest about all the things in his heart. They'd agreed it was just a fling, and he'd once believed that she loved him only to watch her fall for his brother. He was terrified of fully opening himself up and committing to her now.

But the truth was, he'd fallen for her this week. Not fallen—fallen deeper—a part of him had always loved her.

As kids, that connection had been there, but through time, distance and separate life paths, they'd both pushed it aside. It had sat unacknowledged for so long.

This week had reopened his eyes to it. To the deep love he had for her.

These feelings had knocked him on his butt, then filled him with a sense of hope for a future he hadn't really thought was in the cards for him. And it might not be. Because he hadn't taken the chance.

As the boat left the narrows and disappeared in the light of the setting sun, Domenico turned and headed back toward his hut, knowing he'd just let the woman he loved sail away with his heart.

Linda, Leo and Domenico stood on the dock the next morning as other guests boarded the *Passage to Paradise*, relaxed, refreshed, sad to see their vacation on the luxury island resort come to an end.

Mr. and Mrs. Conway were already on board. Pricilla, wearing dark sunglasses and an oversized sunhat, refused to look toward Domenico.

She wasn't the only one. Leo had refused to look his way or acknowledge him at all that morning, and the tension between them had to be apparent to the reviewer. It lingered as thick as the heat in the sea air.

But if she knew something was off, she was professional enough to hide it. "Thank you both again for this incredible experience. Kasa de Paradise is really something—a true oasis on this coast."

Domenico handed Linda's suitcase to the boat captain and looked nervous as he said, "About your review…"

"Look, Dom. I can't ignore what happened at dinner last night." She paused, lowering her voice and sending a side-eye glance toward the Conways. "But I will consider the source of the complaint in my overall rating."

"I appreciate that. Thank you," Dom said gratefully.

"We'd hate to have not lived up to our father's standards of guest experience."

"Please tell Chef Adriana that even with the mix-up or whatever it was…her food was the best I've had in years. It's too bad she had to leave early. Though the chefs were fantastic this morning."

Domenico avoided Leo's intense gaze on him as he nodded. "I'll be sure to pass along both compliments."

Linda boarded the boat and put on her sunglasses as she took a seat. "My review will be posted on the *Travel Island* website next week. I look forward to visiting again."

Domenico and Leo waved as the boat pulled away. Once Linda and the *Passage to Paradise* were out of sight, both men silently headed off in opposite directions.

CHAPTER ELEVEN

BELLARINI'S WAS BUSY, bustling, chaotic. All of the tables inside the dining room were full, and there was a lineup of customers waiting for a table in the lobby as Adriana entered her family restaurant the following afternoon. She looked around.

Surprised and more than a little confused.

"Welcome to Bellarini's. Do you have a…" The hostess, Valentina, paused and smiled nervously when she glanced up from the reservation book and saw her. "Adriana! You're back early! We weren't expecting you in until tomorrow."

Adriana continued to look around the dining room—where every table was full. For lunch. On a Friday. "What's going on? Did someone reserve the restaurant for an event?"

Valentina looked slightly sheepish. "No…"

"Did one of the other restaurants close unexpectedly?" Was this divine overflow from someone else's misfortune?

"No."

"Valentina! Say more, please!"

Valentina shrugged and looked reluctant to embellish. "It's been like this the past four days."

"Really? Why?"

"You should talk to Alex," she said before scurrying away.

Adriana smiled at diners—unfamiliar new faces—as she headed further into the restaurant. She waved at several regulars as she made her way to the kitchen, but for the most part, she didn't recognize anyone. Where had all the new customers suddenly come from?

Her stomach knotted with unease.

What did you do, Alex?

Adriana pushed through the swinging door and entered the kitchen. Full staff on deck, scurrying to fulfill orders but in a surprisingly controlled and organized way as though they were used to this level of business. In the center of the commotion, Alex directed the sous-chefs and waitstaff expertly.

She scanned the dishes being prepped. Some she recognized. Others...

Her chest tightened. "Hey, Alex."

Alex turned and looked slightly panicked to see her. "Don't be mad," he said, speaking quickly.

Whenever anyone started any conversation with those words, it was never off to a good start. Adriana folded her arms and raised an eyebrow. *Stay calm.* "What's going on?"

"I tried some of those new menu items I've been asking you to try...and, well, they've been a hit." Her brother looked proud despite knowing he likely annoyed her.

"A few new items have this place at full capacity?"

Not buying it.

"Okay. A lot of new items and a social media post or two..." Alex added a garnish to a plate and sent it out.

Adriana glanced at the familiar-looking entrée leaving the kitchen. Familiar but not quite a Bellarini's menu item. She could tell by the texture of the white cream sauce. "They don't look that different, but they definitely are." The kitchen even smelled different. Not bad. Not worse. Just…different.

And different was making her nauseous.

"That's the point. On the outside, they look like Bellarini's traditional menu, but the ingredients are different, some slightly healthier, some tweaked for a varied flavor or texture…"

Alex picked up a piece of garlic cheese bread from a tray and handed it to Adriana. "Try this."

Adriana stared at it with disdain. "If this is almond flour…"

"Just shut up and try it."

Adriana took a bite. She chewed slowly, waiting for the disgusting taste or at least chalky texture to land on her tongue, but it didn't. The bread was actually moist and soft…

Dared she use the word *delicious*?

What kind of witchcraft was this?

Aware of Alex's scrutiny, she shrugged casually. "It's okay…"

"It's more than okay. It's delicious. And carb-free. I can't make it fast enough." Alex reached for the rest of her bread, but Adriana sighed in annoyance and popped the garlic bread into her mouth.

"What else did you change?" she asked while chewing.

A sous-chef placed a dish on the counter in front of him. "Let's just get through tonight's service. Then we will talk, okay?"

Adriana looked ready to argue, but the extreme pace in the kitchen left no room. "I guess I don't really have a choice."

"Great. Well, in the meantime—grab an apron and get to work," Alex said.

Adriana gaped slightly. This was her kitchen.

Or at least, it was.

That day, her brother was in full command.

Her chest tightened as she scanned the kitchen. It didn't even feel like hers anymore. Gone was the easygoing vibe full of fun banter as everyone was laser-focused on the orders coming in. The dishes might look familiar but they were different and even the regular music had been replaced with a more recognizable Italian melody.

This restaurant was her entire life. She'd made so many sacrifices to keep it the way her parents and grandparents had…and now she wasn't sure she even belonged there.

But then, where did she belong?

The alternative—a life on Kasa Island—wasn't an option anymore. Domenico had made that very clear.

She suddenly felt like maybe everyone was right—that she wasn't good enough anywhere.

"Adriana! Let's go," Alex said, cutting into her thoughts.

Adriana sighed as she grabbed an apron and got to work.

Hours later, once the restaurant was empty and everyone had left for the evening, Adriana—exhausted by the intense pace that hadn't let up all day and into the evening—sat across from Alex in a booth. On the table between them were register receipts from that week and Alex's new menu. Adriana turned the beautifully designed menu over in her hands. "You did all of this in a week?"

"No. I've been working on it for a year." He took a sip of wine and sat back in the booth, looking relaxed, pleased, and more than confident and ready for this conversation.

She was not. After the week on Kasa Island with her

heart and mind in constant turmoil, that unexpected day in the restaurant and this long-overdue discussion with her brother were the last things she'd been expecting to deal with.

"You really were hopeful I'd get on board with this?" To go through the trouble of having menus made? When did he even have time to get these printed? Clearly, a motivated Alex was an unstoppable Alex.

Alex took a deep breath and sat forward. "Actually, Adriana, I was planning on opening my own restaurant."

He was what? She dropped the menu and her bottom lip. She stared at him that way for a long moment, waiting for her brain to catch up.

"I made these menus months ago because I was considering a new place of my own," he said a little more gently, but still with determined confidence.

"Seriously? But this restaurant has been in the family for three generations. You'd just up and leave like that?"

Alex shook his head. "Not just like that. After years of asking you to consider making some changes. Some necessary upgrades and revisions. Asking you to at least consider my ideas. Ideas that I've just proven to work."

"Oh, come on, Alex. You had one great week. These crowds will die off."

"At least the restaurant wouldn't be a ghost town in the meantime."

Ouch.

Alex softened his tone as he continued, "I don't mean to offend, Adriana. You're a fantastic chef, but you have to realize that if we don't adapt, Bellarini's won't be around for a fourth generation."

Adriana sat back, considered her brother's words. She knew the menu was old, but it consisted of recipes that had been in the Bellarini family for decades. Each dish represented memories. Each taste, each smell...all brought back generations of good times together, eating as a family, laughing and talking into all hours of the night. They were more than just recipes.

But she couldn't argue that sometimes traditions didn't pay the bills.

And Alex had a right to forge his own path, start something he fully believed in, something he could be proud of the way she was proud of what they had right here—all around them.

"So, you're leaving? Starting your own place?"

"I don't want to. I want to implement these changes permanently here."

"What about my menu? Grandma's menu? The regular guests who love Bellarini's for what it currently is..." She stared at the new menu in her hands. Pain showed in her expression. "Was."

"I'm not suggesting eliminating the old recipes completely. Just offering both options. It's worked well this week. In fact, take a look..." He reached into a folder and produced a mock-up of a new Bellarini's menu with two sections, Traditions of Taste and Evolution of Flavor.

Guests could choose which they preferred.

It was a great idea. A way to move forward but preserve the past, but...

"Supply costs will double. The workload doubles..."

Alex nodded to the revenue numbers from that week. "We made more this week than we made in three months."

Adriana winced at the truth, and Alex touched her hand. "It's not your fault. New restaurants are adding to our competition all the time. We need to evolve or..."

Close up shop.

Adriana was silent for a long time. This was the right thing to do, but it was just so hard to do it. Not unlike so many other choices she'd faced that week. Leaving the island—escaping—without being honest with Dom had weighed on her all day. She should have at least told him and let things unfold as they would have.

Better to live with the knowledge that she'd gone after what she wanted than live with regret.

Same for the future of Bellarini's?

Finally, she reluctantly nodded. "Okay...we will try it your way for a while."

Alex looked relieved as he squeezed her hand. "Great. Because I'd hate to leave here. This is my home too."

Adriana scanned the restaurant, then studied the new menu in her hands, a look of uncertainty on her face.

She hadn't been brave enough to take a chance on her and Domenico, but she was determined to find the courage to save her family restaurant.

A few days later, Adriana sat on her cozy sofa across from Isabella. They had wineglasses in hand.

"I can't believe those jerks actually think you could be responsible for that guest's allergic reaction," Isabella said in appropriate bestie rage. Her friend was in her pajamas, having responded to Adriana's SOS text in record time.

"There was definitely seafood in the sauce, according to one of the chefs." Though she still had no idea how it could have happened. There had been zero reason to have any ingredients containing seafood anywhere near the food prep that day. She'd replayed the day over and over...

Isabella shook her head. "I'm not buying it. You're the most diligent chef I know."

"Thanks, friend." But Isabella was a ride-or-die. If

Adriana hit someone with her vehicle, Isabella would claim the other person must have been at fault.

However...

Adriana sipped her wine and shot her friend a glance. "You should have told me about Alex making those changes."

Isabella looked slightly sheepish, but the other key quality in their friendship was brutal honesty. They always gave it to one another straight. No sugar-coating or enabling. "I'm sorry, but you saw for yourself how well it worked."

"The crowd the other day was hard to ignore." She stared pensively into her wineglass with a conflicted look. "I've agreed to try it Alex's way for a while."

"That's big of you. It is his family legacy too, and I think you need to trust him."

Adriana nodded. It wasn't that she didn't trust Alex. She was starting to feel like she couldn't trust herself. A new menu meant proving her skills as a chef beyond the Bellarini traditional recipes that she'd known how to prepare since childhood. And that week at Kasa de Paradise had only furthered her doubt in her ability to take risks.

She'd walked away from Domenico because of the uncertainty. The uncertainty of his feelings for her, the uncertainty of their ability to make a relationship work, the uncertainty of a future together. She'd thought that she'd gotten to know Domenico again—the real Domenico. But what if she'd just imagined it? Giving up and walking away instead of being vulnerable had seemed like the safest option.

Unfortunately, playing it safe left her with a struggling restaurant and an aching heart.

Isabella hesitated. "Have you talked to Dom?" she

asked. Another bestie trait was being able to read Adriana's silence.

She shook her head. "Probably for the best. I think I drove a wedge between him and Leo, and for what?"

"The love of a lifetime?"

If she admitted that, her heart might shatter. Therefore, she scoffed. "Before this week, I could barely tolerate him."

"They say there's a fine line between love and hate." Isabella raised a suggestive eyebrow. "And you two did have a history of friendship."

"Well, he hasn't reached out to me." And they said if a man wanted to, he would. I mean, technically she wanted to and she wasn't, but that wasn't the saying. "Neither has Leo." And that made her feel a whole new level of sadness. She and Leo might not be meant to be romantically, but they were such great friends. She hated the thought that she could be losing him. He'd meant a lot to her their entire lives, and the hurt in his expression that night in the kitchen had made her feel terrible.

Though not as much as Domenico's refusal to believe her and fight for her, for them.

"Leo loves you, and even he knows deep down that you two were not right for one another. He'll come around," Isabella said gently, sipping her wine.

She hoped so. In the meantime, "I think the best thing to do is forget all about the Kasa brothers and their fantasy island." After all, she was going to have her hands full with the new Bellarini's menu.

"Can you do that?"

Maybe when she was so consumed with work, she wouldn't have as much time to think about Domenico and how much she missed him. The way he drove her crazy—in all the best ways. They way he'd looked at her as though he'd loved her forever. The way he made her body come to life with the simplest touch...

"What choice do I have?" she said with a sigh.

She'd already made a mess of things. She refused to make things worse.

A *Travel Island* magazine notification chimed on her phone. Adriana opened the app and saw the resort review posted. "The *Travel Island* review is live." Her hand shook slightly as her finger hovered over the link.

"Read it!" Isabella moved closer and peered over her shoulder.

"I can't. What if it is horrible?" Her knees bounced, and she thought she might be sick. She had been uneasy about so much since leaving Kasa de Paradise—the review not least of all. The Conways' incident was a serious one, no matter who was at fault, and she knew it wouldn't reflect well on the resort. It wasn't something Linda Frank could have overlooked.

"Not knowing won't make it better," Isabella said.

"You read it," Adriana said, handing Isabella the phone.

Isabella set her wineglass aside, clicked on the review link and cleared her throat. "A paradise on the coast—a review of Kasa de Paradise by Linda Frank."

Adriana held her breath as Isabella read.

"The experience on Kasa de Paradise begins with an unforgettable voyage on the..."

Adriana waved her hand. "Skip ahead... Look for anything to do with the food." She couldn't sit through five thousand words of Linda's review right now. She'd read the full article later. She needed to know what the woman had said about her part.

Isabella hummed as she scanned. "Okay...here we go. Ready?"

No. She nodded.

"The food at Kasa De Paradise was everything indulgent and satisfactory. The kitchen, led by award-winning chef Adriana Bellarini, was well-run and served a variety of options to suit even the most expensive palate. Despite a mix-up in the kitchen and an allergy scare, Ms. Bellarini is destined for greatness with her abandonment of flavor restrictions, truly catering to those who appreciate luxury indulgences in all aspects of their vacation. With the combined elements of tradition and modern embellishes, Ms. Bellarini is a top chef—a treasure in any luxury resort kitchen."

Adriana released a sigh of relief and sank back against the sofa cushions.

"See. Destined for greatness...a treasure... This woman knows what's up," Isabella said, smiling proudly at her.

Adriana laughed as she nodded toward the phone. "Okay, read the rest of the review now." Her heart felt a little lighter as she settled in to listen, but she was only half paying attention as her mind wandered to Domenico. Had he read this yet? Would he reach out once he had? Once he saw that she hadn't completely sabotaged his resort that week?

And what if he did—what then?

Worse—what if he didn't?

CHAPTER TWELVE

A BEAUTIFUL, SUNDRENCHED DAY settled over the island as new weekly guests enjoyed the resort's activities. Crew members moved about facilitating activities and tending to the grounds as Domenico hit tennis balls shooting out at maximum speeds from the Spinfire Pro on the other side of the court. He sent one ball after another flying across the net. Nothing was as therapeutic as whacking the hell out of the green spheres, but that day even the strenuous activity wasn't working to erase the thoughts and conflict about Adriana from his mind.

Mario appeared on the courts behind him and folded his arms across his chest as he leaned against the fence. "Looking a little sloppy."

Domenico ignored his brother as he kept on whacking the balls.

"Did you see the *Travel Island* magazine review?" Mario asked.

"Yep."

"Four and a half stars. Not bad."

"Not five," Domenico grunted. If that last incident with the Conways hadn't occurred, maybe they'd have received the coveted five stars from Linda Frank. He was holding on to that sense of blame and irritation with Adriana as fuel to keep from reaching out to her. For the last three days, she'd been on his mind constantly. Wherever he went, wherever he looked, there were reminders of her and their time together. She'd spent one week on that island, and yet she seemed to have permeated every inch of it. He saw her everywhere. He swore the scent of her skin had somehow become the island's new signature aroma.

And things here felt different now without her. Not as vibrant. Not as alive.

Mario sighed as he approached and turned off the machine. "You and Leo ever planning on speaking to one another again?"

Probably not.

In three days, they'd barely exchanged three words. What he'd done was wrong—in that he should have told Leo and not hidden it from him. But he didn't regret being with Adriana. And his brother being upset was understandable, but if Leo was being honest with himself, he didn't even really want to be with Adriana. Leo loved the bachelor life, the carefree freedom. He said so all the time.

So why did they both have to suffer? Didn't seem very brotherly.

"You guys are being jerks," Mario said, typing on his cell phone.

Domenico lowered the racket and fought for breath as he shot his brother an annoyed look. "Do you need something?"

"I need my brothers to stop acting like idiots so we can properly run a resort."

That would be ideal, but, "It's complicated."

"That what your Facebook status says?"

Mario's irritating grin was the last thing Domenico needed on his frazzled nerves and conflicted heart. Domenico moved around his brother to grab his towel. He wiped the sweat away from his neck and face.

"Look, man, Leo and Adriana were over a long time ago. They weren't right for one another."

"Tell that to Leo." His brother was the one hung up over Adriana. Had been for years. Not that he was making excuses for his behavior, but whether he and Adriana were together or not, she wasn't in love with Leo anymore.

"I did," Mario said.

"What did he say?"

"He told me to screw off."

Domenico flicked the machine back on and returned to hitting balls.

Mario shrugged as he started to walk away. "Anyway, I thought you should know that Mr. Conway's seafood reaction wasn't Adriana's fault."

What?

A ball flew from the machine and hit Domenico in the head as his attention swung to Mario. He mumbled a cuss word, rubbing his forehead and moving out of the line of fire. He approached Mario. "What are you talking about?"

"Housekeeping found a package of powdered shrimp in the Conways' room after they checked out. Hidden beneath the mattress."

The woman tried to kill her own husband? That was low. Even for her. "Are you serious?"

Mario shook his head. "Looks like Mrs. Conway was trying to eliminate her husband from the love triangle you three had going on."

Domenico shuddered at the thought. "There was no love triangle."

"Maybe not one that included Mr. Conway."

Mario was annoying. "So, you're saying Mrs. Conway put the powder on her husband's food? You're sure?"

"I mean, we can't prove it, so there's no point calling the police about it or anything, but it looks that way. Why else would she have something she knew her husband was severely allergic to in the room?" He paused. "I just thought you'd like to know that Adriana wasn't to blame."

"Did you tell Leo?"

Mario nodded and grinned. "He's groveling pretty good with six dozen roses being delivered to Bellarini's as we speak."

Of course Romeo was.

Domenico quickly packed up his tennis racket and headed off the court.

Mario called after him. "By the way, we still have an opening for a head chef!"

Adriana scanned the six dozen red roses on the counter in the kitchen of Bellarini's. She knew who they were from without having to read the card.

Leo.

Roses were definitely not Domenico's style.

She sighed as she read the card. *I should never have doubted you. Forgive me?*

He must have been happy with Linda Frank's review. It wasn't her coveted five-star, but it was very flattering, and she did highly recommend Kasa de Paradise. It was a relief that Leo had reached out. She'd been worried that their friendship was over. The thought had weighed heavy on her along with so many others.

She tucked the card inside the pocket of her chef's coat and retrieved her cell phone. She opened the text message thread to Leo and typed, Always...forgive me?

Three dots—typing…
She held her breath as she waited.

For falling for the wrong Paradise billionaire? I'll get over it eventually ;)

Adriana smiled sadly as she tucked the phone away and got to work.

Within moments of opening for lunch service, the kitchen was busy, food orders coming in one after another. A lot of orders were from the traditional menu, but quite a few were Alex's new recipe options and those Adriana struggled with.

Alex returned to the kitchen with an entrée barely touched. "Table fourteen is sending back the seafood lasagna. They asked for whole wheat noodles and half-fat cheese."

"Half-fat cheese. What's the point of eating?" Adriana grumbled. She took the plate from her brother and dumped the contents, then started over.

Dish after dish was returned…

"Who eats like this!" Adriana yelled in frustration after the fourth one.

Alex pulled her aside. "Hey… I know this is challenging, but get your head in the game."

"It's these choices! You're giving people far too many."

"It worked fine last week."

"It's not working now."

Sous-chefs and staff turned to look their way, and Alex dragged her into the walk-in freezer. Once the door closed behind them, he said, "You agreed to try this."

"I am trying." It was a lot to expect, especially with the crazy pace they were suddenly working at. As much as the business was good for profit, she missed the slower pace where she could really deliver on quality. She hadn't even had time to leave the kitchen to go greet guests—chitchat with the old regulars and tell the Bellarini's history to new ones. The other parts about working in a restaurant that she enjoyed. The personal touch and dining experience she knew brought guests back time and again.

This pace wasn't allowing her to operate the way she thrived. It was stressful, chaotic and not the career she loved. But it was only the first day, so she took a breath. "Familiarizing myself with the new recipes will just take some time."

Alex nodded. "Then how about letting me take the lead? Just until you're up to speed?"

The stubborn Bellarini streak in her awakened. Absolutely not. She was in charge. She was in control. This was *her* kitchen.

One she wasn't successfully running at the moment.

The realization that she was spiraling mid-lunch rush in the walk-in freezer hit her like a block of ice to the forehead. She had to admit that she simply couldn't do this yet. She did need time. Alex was already familiar with the new recipes, and she had to admit, his way of running the kitchen had been smooth and efficient despite the heavier workload. He was cool and calm under pressure.

She also had to reluctantly admit that her head just wasn't in the game since Kasa Island. Her thoughts were constantly drifting to Dom and their magical nights together on the island. The way he looked at her, kissed her, held her—her head and heart were a mess. They'd both said it was just a weeklong fling, and obviously that been true for him…yet that spark between them told her he felt something deeper too.

But she had no idea what to do about Dom…about them…or her restaurant.

Therefore, for the sake of Bellarini's, she fought her pride as she nodded. "You take the lead."

Leo sat at his desk, résumés for a new head chef in front of him, as Domenico entered the office. "Hey…" he started nervously.

Leo didn't look up. "I guess Mario told you about the Conways?"

"Yeah…"

This was awkward. They needed to start talking again. They couldn't continue to run a high-end luxury island resort without communicating. Besides that, they were brothers. They'd overcome worse than this, and he refused to let their complex feelings about Adriana come between them.

They both loved her. In different ways.

And neither of them should be without her.

One thing had become blatantly clear these past few days—Domenico *couldn't* be without her, so he had to somehow make this okay for Leo.

Domenico sighed. "Look I'm just going to say it. We need a new chef, and Adriana is perfect for the position."

Leo sighed as he looked up from the résumés. "I tried already. Years ago. She turned it down."

"That was before."

Leo looked up, a mix of amusement and annoyance in his expression. "You think you can change her mind? Make her give up her life on the mainland and her family restaurant—for you? *I* wasn't enough after years of dating, but after a week together, *you* are?"

Leo was not going to make this easy. The last thing he wanted was to hurt his brother's ego, but he knew his connection with Adriana was stronger after one week than it had ever been with Leo. She'd felt that way too, but Leo didn't need to hear that.

Besides, it really wasn't about him, or at least not fully. "Not for me. But maybe for the opportunity to cook the way she loves to cook."

Leo frowned. "She has that now."

Domenico moved closer to the desk and lowered himself into a chair across from his brother. "No, she doesn't. Alex has been trying to change things. Implementing a new menu. Bellarini's isn't doing so well anymore. Or at least, it wasn't until last week, when Alex was running the show."

Leo stared at him. "Adriana told you all that?"

"Some of it." The not doing so well part. The rest he'd discovered by scrolling the Bellarini's social media page. The new menu was advertised, and videos of lines outside were posted. Alex's new way of doing things was working—at least for the restaurant's bottom line.

His heart ached for Adriana. It couldn't be easy implementing these changes. He knew she longed to see Bellarini's thrive for many more generations based on the way things always were...but change was inevitable.

He hoped maybe she'd consider a big one for her own future, because in the recent days without her, she was all he could think about. He suddenly didn't want to spend his life making this resort a success without her by his side. The week before had changed things. Had changed him.

Leo dropped the résumé in his hand and sat back in the seat. "You two really got close?"

"I know you don't want to hear it, but yes. And I am sorry, man. I never intended to have feelings for her. You know that. Before last week, I thought I could barely stand being around her." He paced the office and ran a hand through his hair. "Turns out that tension wasn't exactly from hating one another..." He stopped pacing and turned to point a finger at Leo. "And really, this is your fault."

Leo folded his arms across his chest. "You've got three seconds to explain that before I punch you in the face."

Domenico reached for his cell phone and opened the message thread between them. He scrolled to the photo of all of them as kids. "You sent us this."

"It's a cute old photo."

Domenico handed Leo the phone. "Zoom in on my face." He waited while his brother did.

Leo peered at the image. Realization dawned in his expression. Then he handed the phone back. He sat up in resolve. "All I know is that you have it bad for my ex-girlfriend."

"I do." No sense lying about it. He didn't want to. He wanted to shout his feelings for Adriana from the rooftop of the main building and let it echo all the way to her heart on the mainland. Admitting his feelings to his brother and seeing if this was something they could overcome was the first step.

Leo was silent for a moment. "Do you really think she'll consider the position?"

"Only one way to find out."

Leo let out a long, deep breath. "Then go get her, man."

Relieved, Domenico nodded and sat in the chair across from him. He had his brother's blessing to be with the woman he loved. A huge weight was lifted from him.

Leo gestured for him to leave. "Like—now. If you haven't noticed, we're in desperate need of a chef."

"Right," Domenico stood. He hesitated, then extended a fist toward his brother.

Leo stared at it, then grinned. "Not quite at the fist-bumping stage yet, bro."

"Understood," Domenico said with a grin, but knowing all was forgiven, he left the office with a clear head and determined heart.

The restaurant was closed and empty—all guests and staff gone for the night. The lights were dim, and only soft Andrea Bocelli music played as Adriana walked around the restaurant and looked at the pictures of her family on the walls. Memories the restaurant held came flooding back.

This was her history, her legacy, her life... What would she do without Bellarini's? But if she didn't adapt to the new menu and new vision for her family's business, there would be no future generations of families to feed at the restaurant. Her parents and grandparents had always worked so hard to keep the doors open, and Bellarini's was an important part of the culture here. She wouldn't let her own stubbornness and pride stand in the way of its future success.

Handing the reins to Alex that day had felt like failure. Defeat. She shouldn't feel that way. They were a team. But she couldn't shake the unease in the pit of her stomach that they were turning Bellarini's into something she soon wouldn't recognize.

A knock on the door caught her attention, and she turned to see Domenico standing outside the glass window.

Her heart stopped, then immediately started racing. What was he doing here? Leo had sent flowers, but she hadn't heard from Domenico—no apology, no link to the review, no confession of love...

But now he was standing outside.

Her first instincts were to hide. Hope he hadn't seen her inside. She was a mess after all day in the hot kitchen. She probably smelled, and she was far too conflicted right now to deal with whatever reason he was there.

But he was there. And every fiber in her being needed to know why.

She took a deep breath, squared her shoulders, then went to the door and opened it. "We're closed," she said, her voice tight.

"I'm in love with you."

He what?

Adriana's mouth dropped as she stared at Domenico for a long time.

Domenico shifted uncomfortably in the silence that continued to linger. He cleared his throat. "Can I—uh—come in?"

Right, he was still standing outside, and she'd essentially left him on read after his confession of love.

Adriana stepped back to let him enter. When the door closed behind him, she took a deep breath. "What are you doing here, Domenico?"

"I just told you. I'm here because despite my best efforts, I'm in love with you."

Despite his...

"That's romantic." Adriana folded her arms across her chest. After not believing her and accusing her of almost poisoning a guest, going silent for days, then showing up out of the blue with a confession of love, he was going to have to do a lot better than that. The whole Mr. Darcy thing might have worked in Jane Austen's era, but they'd already discussed this. Domenico could not pull that off.

"No, it isn't. Nothing about us is. But you had romance with Leo. You don't want romance," Domenico said, his usual challenge back in his tone.

The slight arrogance that used to annoy her was attractive right now. When had that shift occurred? How had Domenico Kasa's overblown ego gone from the thing that grated on her last nerve to the thing that made her want to fling herself into his arms and make out with him right now?

Maybe because she knew the man and the intentions and the vulnerability beneath it. She knew the heart of the boy she'd always loved beneath it.

Also, because he was right. Romance was for first loves—the ones meant to open one's heart, the ones meant to teach the lessons on how to love and be loved. It was to make the heartache worthwhile. At this stage in her life, she wanted truth and trust and a deep connection that surpassed romance to the level of *being* love for one another, embodying love.

She didn't want romance. She wanted the raw, passionate intensity they'd had that week on the island. Desperately craved it.

Still, he had work to do. And because heated tension defined their entire relationship, she rose to the challenge. "Then what do I want, Domenico?"

"You want a spark." He lowered his gaze and shook his head. "Screw that. You want a blazing flame. Like the one we have burning between us."

Adriana swallowed hard as she stared at him. She did want that. So much.

Domenico moved closer to her. He picked up a strand

of her hair and twirled it around his finger, fighting for the right words. He took a deep breath, opened his mouth, shut it, then sighed.

When he finally spoke, the words came out gruff and sincere. "You drive me absolutely crazy. That sharp tongue of yours and your inability to ever be wrong... You are so stubborn all the damn time."

Really. Wow. "I'm stubborn? What about you? I've been gone almost a week, and you haven't reached out."

"I've wanted to. I've been going crazy without you."

Oh.

"I might have missed you a little bit," she said, the thick emotion in her voice calling her out.

Domenico caressed her cheek gently. "You were right, you know. You didn't make a mistake. Mrs. Conway added powdered shrimp to her husband's pasta."

Adriana's arms fell to her sides. Her expression was one of disbelief. "She tried to kill her husband?"

"We can't prove that, but based on the amount of effort she put into trying to sleep with me, I wouldn't be surprised. And likely she knew how quickly medics could arrive with the EpiPen. I think it was more a jealous rage thing to try to sabotage the resort review."

"Seems extreme. Rich people are crazy."

Domenico grinned. "Not all rich people. Anyway, the point is, I should have believed you."

"Is that an apology? Cause Leo sent six dozen roses..."

Domenico cut off her words, swooping in and pulling her into his arms. He stared into her eyes and brushed her hair away from her face.

Forget flowers.

Her heart raced and her pulse pounded as he held her close to his body and stared down into her eyes. The look of love and sincerity radiating in his expression nearly stole her breath.

"I'm sorry, Adriana. I'm sorry I treated you badly when you were with Leo. Seeing you with my brother killed me. You should have been with me instead. And then your complete disdain for me…"

"Can you blame me?" she whispered.

"No. And I'm sorry I didn't believe you were capable of running the kitchen. You are the perfect chef to run Kasa de Paradise's kitchen."

Adriana stiffened slightly. Was that why he was really there? To convince her to come work on the island permanently? Her stomach flipped…but surprisingly not entirely in a bad way.

Domenico touched her chin. "Not that I'm asking. I know you love your life here. This restaurant is your home. But if you won't consider the position on the island, at least give us a chance. You and me. I'll come back and forth. Maybe you can visit the island every other week—let Alex take the lead here in your absence? What do you say?"

It was nice in theory, but, "You never leave the island."

"I'm here now."

Adriana hesitated for a long moment, emotions evident on her face as she stared up at the man she was desperately falling in love with. "The chef position is still available?"

Domenico's expression lit up with cautious optimism. "For real? You'll come to Kasa de Paradise?"

Adriana surveyed her family restaurant from the corner of her eye. "Alex is right. Bellarini's needs to move into the next generation… He can do that better than I can."

Domenico nodded slowly. "So, you're taking the position because you're giving Alex the restaurant?"

Adriana wrapped her arms around Domenico's neck and rested her forehead against his chest. "I could take another position at a different restaurant if that was the reason."

"Then why?" he asked, his voice gruff and full of intensity.

Adriana kept her head pressed against his chest, unable to look up at him for fear that he'd see just how much she loved him written all over her face. "You really need me to say it?"

"I really do." Domenico placed a finger gently under her chin and lifted her face to look up at him. His gaze burned into hers with all the intensity and passion straight from his soul.

"Because I'm in love with you, Domenico."

Domenico smiled as he lowered his lips to hers. "About time you admitted it."

Adriana opened her mouth to say something, but Domenico silenced her with a kiss. Adriana sank into him and quit fighting the inevitable, returning his kiss with all the desire and love in her heart.

Giving in to the fact that she'd fallen for a paradise billionaire.

The right one this time.

* * * * *

MILLS & BOON®

Coming next month

BODYGUARD'S SAINT-TROPEZ TEMPTATION
Bryony Rosehurst

Her pinkie finger prickled, a zap of energy crawling up her arm, and she opened her eyes to see Dani's hand beside hers on the railing.

She still faced the party, and didn't look at Sasha at all, but she was there. Comforting her.

Something tugged at Sasha: the urge to close the gap between them, bury herself in this new, unexpected safety.

Dani's finger twitched against hers, just once, and then she pulled away, and Sasha remembered that she wasn't a friend, and she certainly wasn't a soft place to land. She was here because Sasha had paid her to be here, and really, that meant she was the same as everyone else.

Except she didn't *feel* like everyone else as Sasha continued to endure that night's socialising. The opposite. If the lines blurred, it was because Sasha needed them to. She needed someone she could trust, and Dani Sharpe was the closest thing to it.

When the silhouette of the Saint-Tropez coastline returned to view, Sasha could finally breathe. She'd made it through the night, and she'd never have to see these people again.

Continue reading

BODYGUARD'S SAINT-TROPEZ TEMPTATION
Bryony Rosehurst

Available next month
millsandboon.co.uk

Copyright © 2026 Bryony Rosehurst

COMING SOON!

We really hope you enjoyed reading this book. If you're looking for more romance be sure to head to the shops when new books are available on

Thursday 21st May

To see which titles are coming soon, please visit
millsandboon.co.uk/nextmonth

MILLS & BOON

TWO BRAND NEW BOOKS FROM
Love Always

Be prepared to be swept away to incredible worldwide destinations along with our strong, relatable heroines and intensely desirable heroes.

OUT NOW

Four Love Always stories published every month, find them all at:

millsandboon.co.uk

FOUR BRAND NEW BOOKS FROM
MILLS & BOON MODERN

Indulge in desire, drama, and breathtaking romance – where passion knows no bounds!

OUT NOW

Eight Modern stories published every month, find them all at:

millsandboon.co.uk

OUT NOW!

Available at millsandboon.co.uk

MILLS & BOON

OUT NOW!

Available at
millsandboon.co.uk

MILLS & BOON

LET'S TALK
Romance

For exclusive extracts, competitions and special offers, find us online:

- **f** MillsandBoon
- **X** @MillsandBoon
- **◉** @MillsandBoonUK
- **♪** @MillsandBoonUK

Get in touch on 01413 063 232

For all the latest titles coming soon, visit
millsandboon.co.uk/nextmonth